# The Lost Canvas

Julie D. Simmons

# The Lost Canvas

*A Novel*

**PALMETTO**
PUBLISHING
Charleston, SC
www.PalmettoPublishing.com

Copyright © 2023 by Julie D. Simmons

All rights reserved

No portion of this book may be reproduced, stored in a retrieval system, or transmitted in any form by any means–electronic, mechanical, photocopy, recording, or other–except for brief quotations in printed reviews, without prior permission of the author.

Hardcover ISBN: 979-8-8229-1487-2
Paperback ISBN: 979-8-8229-1488-9
eBook ISBN: 979-8-8229-1489-6

# *Dedication*

I once worked with a woman named Sandy. For an entire year, we were the best of friends. But then I moved away. Life in a new place took over, and many months passed. I thought of Sandy, each time with guilt because I hadn't reached out. One day, I sat outside on my patio and wrote her a long letter. She sent a shorter one in return. At the end of it, she wrote, *people come in and out of our lives, some for only an encounter, some for days, and others for decades. In any condition, they were put in our path for a reason, but we don't get to question the time they stay.*

Sandy was right. Like choices, each of those people shaped my being, taking a role in who I am. Some I loved, and some I didn't, but either way, considered. Some were there long enough to provide a sense of comfort and contentment, or harmony and hope, while others were the dark and unfortunate antithesis of such.

Some of the places and events in this book are loosely based on real places and events, but none of the people are. Except for Daisy, who gave her full permission. While this work is pure fiction, if you know me, you might recognize yourself in these pages, or the ones that come after them. Or maybe you won't, because you didn't see yourself as I did.

# *Prologue*

Millions of years ago, in the middle of the Mediterranean and deep within the earth's crust, tectonic plates collided. Like a swimmer progressing into ocean waves, the African plate dove far beneath its Eurasian cousin. Ancient sea floors were forced upward, and in separate processes, first formed the Alps, the Dolomites, and the Apennines, a spiny chain running south on a peninsula. The ground buckled, and rocks piled high. Deep below, temperatures rose, and pressures built, turning limestone to marble. Combining forces created an endless cache of supplies, a geological canvas abiding for engineers, artisans, and builders who would come to be in the Birthplace of the Renaissance.

Millennia passed, rains fell, and the winds danced among the mountain peaks and the Adriatic Sea. Erosion moved sediment between the two, forming protected valleys with gentle slopes. A harmonious balance of geology, sunshine, and weather—a combination conducive for making grapes in a most excellent terroir but also superb for figs, olives, and dates. People inhabited the land, raising animals and cultivating plants, creating picturesque landscapes with rows, orchards, vineyards, gardens, and farms that exemplified the most beautiful and astute husbandry practices on the earth.

With generations of effort, from Rome and Florence and out into the countryside, customs accumulated, and like the raising of healthy children, understanding and wisdom grew. Learned techniques became repetitive, and the people passed down their stories and skills, establishing continuity meant for preservation. From the

Ancient to the Renaissance to the Baroque and then the Romantic, creativity evolved and flourished.

The beauty and wonder of the art, architecture, science, and ways of law established by the Italians, a source of utmost pride, gave good reason to hold on to traditions and craftsmanship still revered across the world today. To maintain a certain way of life and family solidarity, villas and farmhouses were all built to endure, ensuring a legacy created by their own hands. And from the art of spoken and written words sprang many a good story, such as the one that follows.

# Part I

# Chapter 1

Katie Bauer took the front steps out of the historic hotel and, like most days, jaywalked across the street to Travis Park. The green space, an oasis in downtown San Antonio, drew local lunch crowds, students, and even occasional tourists. With sweltering Texas temperatures fading, the day bright as the calendar months reached toward another year, live oaks stretched across old grounds of the Alamo mission. Situated on a wooden bench, Katie took an apple from her big tote and searched for other options. *Should I eat the peanut butter crackers or the apple first?* As she pondered that, her phone buzzed. Digging around in the bag again, she located it, glancing at the caller ID before answering.

"Mr. Pickett. I was just wondering about you." Before he answered, Katie collected her things, and rose from the bench, tossing the half-eaten fruit into a nearby trash bin.

Forgoing small talk, Mr. Pickett went straight to business. "I have something for you."

"I'm on my way." Katie exited the park and, glancing up at the St. Anthony, shielded her eyes from the sun. This side of the art nouveau hotel was partially shaded, steel floor-to-ceiling arched windows set into its north wall. Graceful and sinuous, like turn-of-the-century French models, they provided a clear view into the interior of the Peacock Alley lounge. Transparent windowpanes revealed gold and green carpets, velvet furnishings, period chandeliers, and sconces, their fixtures fusing structure with ornament. She focused, however, on the white plastered walls, the space and columns in between, that belonged to her.

As curator for the historic hotel, Katie filled the spaces in the lobby, lounge, and hallways with art. Her roles included marketer, art historian, buyer, researcher, event planner, exhibit designer, and facilitator for interactions between guests, art, and artists. In five years of employment, she had proved her talent at selecting and acquiring works that transformed the common areas into a true gallery, both for long-term and temporary exhibits.

In a space like the St. Anthony, interruptions by doors, windows, and other features presented compositional challenges, but Katie liked irregular dimensions. Putting all the pieces together, researching, acquiring, framing, and placing art, she sculpted the brand of the hotel and sold paintings.

Taking a left on Travis Street, she hurried down the block. Going right at the light to cross onto Jefferson, Katie maneuvered through the city with ease. She passed other historic hotels and churches built just after the Texas Revolution and skipped down a flight of stone steps onto the riverwalk to avoid street traffic. The Paseo Del Rio, a fifteen-mile-long network of landscaped walkways and bridges, framed the banks of the San Antonio River.

A gift of life certainly derived from a generous deity; the river originated from a great underground aquifer. Central to the city's deep cultural origins, indigenous people had thrived along the waterway for thousands of years.

After the Age of Discovery, with water more valuable than gold, explorers established a series of missions, expanding Spanish New World influence. Franciscan priests, backed by the Catholic Church and royal financing and accompanied by master carpenters, masons, and blacksmiths, taught the trades to Pueblo Indians, building five missions along the river, all a few miles apart. Each included a chapel, protective walls, and indoor living quarters.

Native Americans in the area, made weary by vicious Apache and Comanche attacks from the north and weakened by European diseases, traded their idols for saints, accommodating more Spanish conversions to further the colonization of the local peoples. In a symbiotic relationship, the Crown expanded Spanish civilization while the natives welcomed the benefits of shelter and food in exchange for defending the northern frontier for the Spanish empire. Excepting a historical blink with the French, the Spanish flag flew across the land for over three centuries until Mexico took over for more than a decade.

Latin influence made permanent marks that abounded throughout the river city, with red clay rooftops, stucco facades, and archways decorated with intricate painted tiles. Mariachi bands added to the ambience, making local cuisine taste even better. Situated below street level, the pathway provided locals and visitors a scenic route for navigating the city.

At the bottom of the steps, Katie slowed while people, umbrellaed by giant cypresses, ambled along the winding stone walks to consider restaurants or shopping. The water was cool and green, dotted with occasional groups of ducks. They swam across the surface, making upside-down V patterns in their gentle wakes. *Paddlings*, Katie thought. This was a trivia game she liked to play in her head. The correct terms for groups of animals. *A group of birds could be called a flock, but paddlings are more specific and correct to ducks.* Pigeons, scavenging for crumbs beneath café tables, fluttered near her feet. *A band of pigeons.*

Some of the birds here on the riverwalk, ducks in particular, were celebritized local characters with proper names. Tourists often stopped to get photos while children threw small pieces of bread into the water. Katie paused next to two little boys and pointed out into the river. "Look. See the duck with the funny neck? Her name is Georgine."

"That one right there?" The smaller child pointed. Georgine dove under, headfirst, orange feet flapping at the surface.

"Yes! That's her!"

The boy's parents smiled at Katie. "Thank you! Say thank you to the nice lady," they said.

Walking away, Katie waved.

San Antonio was a big, small town. Friendly Texans here, in all shapes, sizes, and colors, was an actual thing. This was Katie's town, for which she possessed a fierce and loyal pride. It mattered to her that visitors went home with good things to say about the city and the locals.

Popping back up on Presa Street, she arrived at La Villita, a shopping village just beyond the riverbank with a three-hundred-year history, a cornerstone to the city's foundation. The "little village" was a cultural hub and home to shops of local artisans and craftsmen. Katie ducked into her favorite gallery. An old-fashioned bell on the big wooden door announced her arrival.

"Mr. Pickett?" As she entered the estate gallery, a sense of reverence enveloped her. As if she were stepping into a cathedral, she spoke a little quieter and walked a little softer. On paneled walls were private, collective sums from the past. Lifetime collections, some eclectic and others homogenous, defined years, interests, and meticulous considerations by their owners. These assemblages, biographies of souls, represented histories of personal evolution. She studied a small oil of sailboats anchored in a bay. Most likely the Mediterranean. She picked it up and turned it over. Nonmitered stretcher bars on the back of the canvas told her the painting was European. Looking closer, she noticed a faded address, *Sorrento, Italy*. Maybe the owner's residence or a frame shop? Or that of a gallery? The hardware was somewhat grimy, and the gilded frame was hand carved. She turned it back around to study the front. *The signature must be on here somewhere.*

"Katie." Mr. Pickett approached the girl, then, "Katie!"

"Oh!" She took a moment and a deep breath. "You startled me."

"I'm sorry." He placed a hand on her shoulder. "Nice, isn't it? When?"

Nodding, she replaced the little seascape where she had found it. "Turn of the century, a little before."

"That's my girl," he said, giving her a slight squeeze. Tall and lanky, Mr. Pickett's hand wrapped fully around the front and back of her shoulder. Huge, generous, and kind, they had loved a wife for half a century, a family, and grandchildren. His wife gone, his children grown professionals in other places, his affection was mostly reserved for Kaiser. These days, Kaiser came to the gallery with Mr. Pickett. Each morning, the two shared a concha, a sweet Mexican bread with white icing, and a short commute from the bedroom neighborhood where they lived off Broadway into downtown. Kaiser at his side, Mr. Pickett rubbed the black Doberman's ears. Stoic and silent, the big dog leaned into him. "Wait until you see what I have for you, Katie."

"You have my attention." She followed him behind the counter and into the back of the gallery.

Supporting each other on the far wall of his office, new stacks of paintings waited, most still wrapped in layers of brown paper. Mr. Pickett took a large piece from the front of the assortment. Slow and steady, he removed the painting from its encasement and set it upright on a large table, giving Katie eye-level perspective.

"This one isn't part of that estate." Mr. Pickett gestured toward the paintings. "It came in by itself. A man from New Braunfels brought it in. Said it belonged to an aunt, and she had hung it in her house as for long as he could remember. No idea where she acquired it."

Katie absorbed the painting with sunset tones in the distance and earth tones, silver to sage, in the foreground. Mr. Pickett stood back, arms folded across his chest, and waited. An apparent signature, in darker paint—she didn't recognize the artist. Spontaneous brushstrokes flowed across the canvas. Their dark vertical emphatic marks created textures, and at the top were blue and gold pigments blending. A fiery half orb in the background drew the eyes to a horizon, and cool colors rendered faraway hills, with twinkles in the sky, some of them falling toward the ground. It reminded her of something smooth by Santo and Johnny. Making her heart beat one tick faster, the internal music grew louder and more distinct. Starting at the corners of her eyes, Katie's entire face broke into a smile.

"Just what I thought," Mr. Pickett said.

"Can we?" Katie asked, gesturing toward the back.

"It's all yours. I haven't touched it."

Katie squeezed her hands into fists, just for a few seconds to stop their jittering. She turned the painting over to begin.

"The frame is European, but I feel like the painting is not. No, it isn't. The art is one hundred percent American. Midcentury?"

Neutral, Mr. Pickett shrugged, allowing her to continue.

"It's figurative, don't you think?" Katie asked. "There is something dreamlike about it. Sad and hopeful at the same time." A dust cover protected the back, deteriorating and not original. Mr. Pickett handed her a utility knife, and she set to work. Chiseling glue and yellowed tape, she worked her way around the edges. The paper crumbled, revealing not a canvas but a hardboard with a handwritten inscription. Katie took a quick breath. "Exordium," she read. "My Dear Benjamin, Plu que' hier, moins que demain. Mary Renata."

"The quote is in French. What does it mean?"

Katie was already searching on her phone.

"Exordium is Latin. It means 'beginning,'" Mr. Pickett said, reading glasses balanced on the bridge of his nose. "See what the translator says for the rest."

"The beginning"—Katie repeated— "more than yesterday, less than tomorrow. A gift from Mary Renata to Benjamin. Look here. There's a commercial stamp on the board. It says Zecchi."

Mr. Pickett concurred. Turning the painting over to the front side, Katie studied the signature. A bold line cut the upper left-hand corner. "It could be a *V*. Maybe an *M*? Does it say Vosta? Mosta?"

Mr. Pickett peered through a magnifying glass. "I'm going to go with M. Costa," he said.

"Mary Costa? Mary Renata Costa?" The painting, done with brush, also had hints of a knife, with certain sections built up. Though dynamic and independent, the piece regarded formal structure with faith in efficacy of action. The meaning in the lines depicted a geometric genius, assuring that composition balanced chaos.

Katie turned to face Mr. Pickett. They looked at each other, her shoulders falling just a little. An unknown. Still, the artist possessed evident training, and Katie knew she would not leave the gallery without it. Without provenance, however, the hotel would not fund the purchase. A strict policy—the history of ownership and transmission of all their in-house art showed authenticity and lack of alteration. This level of risk management protected both patrons and the legitimacy and reputation of the hotel. It would be up to her to run the evidence down with no gaps of any kind.

Mr. Pickett quoted a price, which Katie agreed was fair.

"I can give you some time," Mr. Pickett told her. "You know I'll hold it for you."

"Thank you, but I want to take it today. Give me a second." Katie fumbled with her phone and banking app. To cover the cost, she transferred from her savings to her checking account. Mr. Pickett slid the painting back into its protective sleeve.

"I really appreciate this, Mr. Pickett." Sometimes Katie thought over these types of pieces. But this one…well, she just knew. She would run down its history in her own time. Mr. Pickett's gallery had a following, and Katie knew he could sell the painting regardless.

"It belongs with you." The corners of Mr. Pickett's eyes wrinkled like thin parchment. "I'm excited to see where this goes. You never know."

"You never know," she repeated, resting her hand on the frame.

"I think Kaiser and I are calling it a day," he said. "Can we give you a ride back to the St. Anthony?"

Unless it was raining, Katie walked to and from work. But today was Friday. The painting was cumbersome, if not heavy, and hectic traffic convinced her otherwise. "It would be great if you could drop me home. This," she said, her hand on the encased art, "isn't going back to the hotel. Not just yet."

"You take Kaiser, and I'll carry the painting." Mr. Pickett handed her a thin leash. Symbolic, it neither held nor guided him. The big dog stayed Velcroed to their sides. Even in the busy metro area, Kaiser refused all distractions. Mr. Pickett turned out the lights and locked the door, and out they went to his older-model white Cadillac four-door sedan. Kaiser got into position in the front seat. Always on duty, ears at attention, he surveyed the city from the windshield. Mr. Pickett and Katie guided the painting through the door. "Let's put Mr. Exordium in the back next to you, Katie."

Pedestrians, commuters, and buses mingled, creating typical afternoon congestion. Drivers sped up, taking turns overtaking each other between signals.

"Not going to get there any faster. I'll see you at the next red light." Mr. Pickett, maintaining a slow but steady speed, reached over and patted Kaiser.

On the short trip from La Villita to the Majestic Tower, Katie checked her cell. There she found a series of texts, the final one ending in *Hello?!* Working backward, she read them all, realization dawning. *The charity gala is tonight!* She checked the time; it was only three o'clock. Relief washed over panic, she wasn't late. She still had plenty of time. She would throw her hair up and freshen her makeup. The dress she planned to wear was hanging in her closet, ready to go.

Mr. Pickett pulled up to the front of the Majestic and got out to help Katie unload the painting.

"Thank you so much." Katie gave him a genuine hug.

"You're welcome and tell that young man I said hello."

"I will, and I'll talk to you soon," she said and hurried into the gated entrance and then toward a big set of elevators set in marble and trimmed with lacquered and burled wood. She pushed the button for the smaller, private elevator beside those, and up she went to the apartment where she lived with her fiancé, Tre Haman.

## Chapter 2

Katie and Tre's building housed the Majestic Theatre in its first six levels. Built in 1929, the tower boasted a large and elaborate structure of brick and stone supporting eighteen floors in all. The entrance on Houston Street included its original, expansive cast-iron canopy with masculine sets of Doric columns framed by a classic theater marquee and a decorated theater box office made of marble and matching cast iron. Under the long, protective covering, theater posters behind acrylic advertised upcoming shows and performances along the outer walls. The building's narrowness gave an illusion of grand height sweeping upward toward its big Texas sky. Pointed arches with finials adorned the front facade and roofline. Though more modern and not as intricate as its European cousins, the architecture reflected American-styled gothic elements.

The interior of the atmospheric theater, designed to whisk one away to an exotic Spanish castle's courtyard, intended patron interaction with a surprising, eclectic environment of mission style, baroque, and Mediterranean. An unorthodox mixture, it somehow worked together for its purpose. Its vaulted ceiling featured blue skies, floating clouds, and twinkle lights representing authentic constellations. Stuffed birds in flight, along with those cast in plaster, rested on gables and eaves. Horticultural carvings displayed decor from far-flung places, and flora from a plethora of latitudes from grape vines to cactus to bluebonnets. Furnishings imported from Tuscany and curved hardwood balconies and handrails provided adequate opulence for even the Greatest of Gatsby's. The theater, a created world, a fictional escape, had been forcing suspension of disbelief in even the most skeptical, and enthralled people from across the globe for nearly a century.

The elevator opened to a large foyer flanked by a row of windows fifteen feet high on the east and west sides of the apartment. Her platform wedges clicking on polished oak floors, Katie carried the painting into the living room and leaned it against the back of a large sectional sofa. Velvet and Victorian, not Katie's style, it matched the other antique furnishings inside. All the furniture was Tre's—rather, his parents' furniture.

During Tre's freshman year, his father opened the San Antonio branch of their financial firm and purchased the penthouse on Houston Street. After Tre graduated, he took over the local management and moved Katie into the penthouse with him.

A tuxedo jacket draped over his arm, Tre stood still. His mother, in a long formal gown, was finishing his bow tie with a perfect square knot. They turned to look at Katie. Seconds ticked by until Tre said, "You didn't answer my text messages."

"I'm sorry." Katie looked down at her shoes. "I didn't see them until just a few minutes ago."

"You probably didn't have your phone with you for the past two hours. You said you'd be home sometime after lunch," Tre said. His words too spaced apart, their cadence was even and measured.

"I did have it, and I did say that. And I'm sorry. I…I. Really, I… something came up, and time got away."

"Well. No matter. She's here now, dear," Harriet said, brushing imaginary lint from Tre's lapel. "Go along, Katie. I don't know how you'll ever have time to do something with your hair."

Pressing her lips together, Katie hurried to the master suite. Once in the bathroom, she placed her phone on the vanity. Ten after three. They didn't need to leave until four thirty, but Tre liked her home early for these events. Not that she minded, but Tre also wanted Katie, "involved in the community. In as many community events as possible." So she was. Nudged by Harriet, Katie participated at different levels in various local charities and clubs, the optics good for the Hamans and their associates.

Tre worked for his father at the San Antonio branch of the company, which offered specialized and personalized investment management and niche financial services. Together with his father and other advisors, Tre managed wealth for the wealthy. The main office for their business was in Highland Park, a town within the Dallas area, and Mr. Haman the second's home base.

Harriet told people that they were from Dallas. They lived in Dallas but were not from Dallas. Saying the Hamans were from Texas was like saying the original Bushes were from Texas. It is true that George Herbert and Barbara moved to Midland, Texas, with GW as a two-year-old toddler. His parents too late, the younger George just missed his citizenship. But George's wife, Laura, a full-fledged Texan, and both of their daughters were born in Texas, making them Texans and GW a citizen through marriage to Laura. People could live or grow up in Texas and live there for a long time. But they couldn't be *from* Texas unless they were born in Texas, a distinction with which any Texan would agree. Only guys like Davy Crockett, William Travis, and Jim Bowie, among other firsts, got a pass.

All the Hamans originated from Birmingham, Alabama. They moved to the Lone Star State when Harold Haman the Second decided to break with a large firm and start his own. Five-year-old Tre started kindergarten in Dallas, graduated from a private preparatory school, and stayed in state for college. At the University of the Incarnate Word in San Antonio, he received a degree in finance and met Katie.

Annoyed at Tre for making her feel late, along with the certainty that he had expressed as much to his mother, Katie showered, willing the warm water to wash away prickles on her skin—the ones that popped up on the back of her neck when Harriet used that tone.

"We're from Dallas. Oh yes, Highland Park, such a sweet little bedroom community. Yes, we are from Dallas." Ridiculous, wet, the emphasis on exactly the right words, Katie mocked Tre's mother. One hand on her hip, the other pointing in the air, she forced her voice into a high-pitched trill.

"Katie. What are you doing?" Tre's muffled voice came from the other side of the shower door. "What time did you tell Roberto to pick us up?"

Blinking water from her eyes, Katie wiped the steam from her side of the glass in an oval just big enough to look through. "Just singing a song. Four thirty, Tre. I asked Roberto if he could come at four thirty." Stepping out, she took a white bath sheet from a hook and wrapped it around herself.

Tre, perfect and handsome in his tuxedo, stood holding a structured silk strapless. "This one?" Checking his neutral expression, Katie felt a bit guilty about her theatrical production. Quick and internal, however, she rationalized. Her shower shenanigans were immature yet better than alternative reactions. Tre's mother was not worth the entanglement. *Coping*.

Feeling that it was more difficult than it should be, Katie reached up and touched Tre's cheek. "Sure," she said, most of the animosity evaporating away with the water droplets. Not intending on wearing black, she sighed, laying the knee-length dress across her vanity ottoman. "I won't be long," she called to Tre's retreating silhouette.

Katie finished pinning up her hair. She turned, straining to see the back in the mirror. The simple twist accentuated her blond highlights. Classic. She zipped herself up, slipped on a pair of nude heels, and hurried back into the living area.

Tre turned, looking at all of her. "Good choice," he said.

"Oh. Oh." Harriet's first "oh" conveyed surprise and the second one approval. "You did do something with your hair after all."

A thank-you not warranted, Katie nodded at Harriet.

"And this?" Pointing at the painting that he and Harriet had unwrapped, Tre left the question open ended.

"It's what I got caught up with today. What do you think?"

Tre shrugged. "It's fine. I mean, I don't know."

"It certainly is, Tre," Harriet said. "And would you call it contemporary? But I guess you two prefer modern art more than I do. It's messy. I can tell there are some kinds of trees here." She pointed. "And I suppose the outline of people there at the bottom—it reminds me of finger paint. I can't tell what it is supposed to be. But I guess that doesn't matter. The question is, is it worth anything?"

"That's what I tell Katie, Mother. It's worth exactly the amount that someone is willing to pay for it. And it is Katie's job to convince them. The more the better, right, babe?" Tre kissed the top of Katie's head and checked his watch. "We need to get going." Ushering Katie and his mother out, Tre locked the door behind them. Down the elevator they went to a black Suburban waiting on the street.

Harriet got in first, Katie after her, then Tre. "Where's my husband?" Harriet demanded.

"Mr. Haman will meet you there," Roberto said.

Katie looked over at her future mother-in-law. Sometimes she couldn't believe the comments she made and wondered whether she did so around her own friends. Harriet was an attractive woman, though her features were not feminine. Tre had his mother's Greek nose, perfect and straight. Dark irises and eyelashes matched her hair; olive skin glowed against her amber dress. Harriet appeared at least ten years younger than her sixty-one, although almost no one knew her actual birthdate. Katie's eyes wandered to the top of Harriet's hairdo. All the way to the unusually high top of it. Reminiscent of a 1960s beehive, Katie imagined a little cardinal's nest hidden away up and inside it. She imagined three little yellow beaks wide open, waiting on dinner, as seen from a bird's-eye view.

"What is it, Katie?" Tre asked.

"Oh, nothing," she replied.

"You have the strangest look on your face."

"I'm just excited for tonight," she said, the chirping babies' relentless, red scrawny necks reaching up over the edge of the nest. *A group of cardinals is called a Vatican.* Distracting herself, she addressed the driver. "Thank you for coming to get us, *Tio*." Katie touched the man's shoulder from the back seat.

Pulling away from the curb, Roberto checked the rearview mirror and smiled.

"I don't mind helping you out tonight." His hair silver, his teeth looked white against his brown skin. "*Ciao, ciao, ciao,* everybody," he said, but it sounded more like *ciaociaociaoeverybody*. Roberto talked fast. He also talked a lot. If he wanted, he could speak in five other languages—Dutch, German, French, Italian, or Spanish.

## Chapter 3

Born in Santo Isidoro, Portugal, Roberto migrated to South America when he was just a boy with his mother, a teacher, and his father, an engineer. In the sixties, like many other Europeans, they sought the economic boom in Venezuela. In the beautiful country, a melting pot of natural resources, people, and culture, making a life on its northern coast was easy. When it was time, the Raes sent Roberto to the United States for college. Following in his mother's footsteps, he pursued a degree in education. At university, he met his future wife, Elise, and after graduating, brought her back home with him to Caracas. After Roberto served a mandatory stint in the Bolivarian military, he and Elise—now both history professors—raised another generation of Raes.

But Hugo Chavez took over the country as El Comandante. Using the Robin Hood system, he nationalized nearly everything, expanding welfare programs no nation could afford. Preaching equality but driving equity, Venezuela buckled to her knees. With gasoline cheaper than bottled water, inflation rose, and shortages abounded, forcing Venezuelanos to find as many additional jobs as they could fit into a day. Besides professional teaching, Roberto, a black belt, taught Judo classes to adults and children. Always hustling, he landed contract jobs for foreign businesses requiring translators. From there, he made connections with United States–based oil companies, who recognized Roberto as the perfect security asset.

Americans, even the suave and well-traveled, tend to twitch when they hear phrases like "widespread violent crime such as murder and kidnapping," which unfortunately abounded as Caracas fell into the World's Top Ten Most Dangerous Cities list again and again. Roberto's charm, ability to adapt, and skill set kept him working, leading to introductions, a business relationship, and a friendship with Lewis Bauer, Katie's father.

Lewis began his career working on the Texas High Plains as a roughneck. In a never-ending, flat landscape wrought with tumbleweeds and dust devils, he navigated his way in and around the oil industry, doing everything from surveying to drilling to pipelines to executive offices. By the time Katie was born, Lewis was making his living as a consultant, contracted to supervise activities on location for petroleum companies. From exotic seas to the Burgan oil field in the Middle East and to Kazakhstan and South America, Lewis traveled the world. Katie lived with her grandparents at their family ranch in South Central Texas, but sometimes she went on adventures with her dad.

Katie spent many exciting summers with Lewis and the Raes family on Venezuela's Caribbean seashores, boating to nearby islands, swimming and diving down into the ocean piscinas for giant sea biscuits and starfishes. Drinking *bebida de la vida* on the beaches and eating spicy meat-filled *arepas*, the days long and warm, Roberto and Elise became second parents to Katie, their house in the city her second home. Mariana, the oldest of the Raes children, was Katie's same age.

During the early years, the two girls built sandcastles, catching crabs in tidal pools to add to their moats. Growing taller and braver, they explored small islands and nearby archipelagos. Never minding and hopping over and past green iguanas, they climbed rocky inclines for the perfect jumping-in spot. The giant lizards, heads bobbing and forked tongues flicking, watched until the girls disappeared, then went back to the business of scouring for left-behind picnic scraps. Underwater, Katie and Mariana held their breath, down and down, peeking into crevices and small caves. If they were lucky, they'd find a giant porcupine fish. The funny-looking creature would inflate to a caricature of itself, spawning the girls' hysterical laughter once at the surface.

As the summers passed, the equatorial sunshine painted Katie's hair lighter. Her skin a dark-golden hue, her Spanish improving, she passed for a local. Before anyone was ready, the girls transformed into teenagers. Late into the night, they'd discuss great matters of importance such as nails, boys, and college.

But meanwhile, Venezuelan president Chavez acted with schemes of a crazed man intent on a path to economic destruction. All the while promising to equalize wealth, he waged a war with the private sector and ramped up production at the mint. The faster he produced bolivars, the more they devalued. As inflation soared, the government slapped price ceilings on basic food products such as beef and dairy. At this rate, the few private companies that remained could not profit and were forced to halt production. Free things came at unattainable prices, bringing violence, starvation, and misery.

With inflation rampant, no food on the shelves, and no medical supplies, like the Israelites fleeing Egypt, the Venezuelanos who could left in a mass exodus. With the help of Lewis and good legal advice, Roberto and Elise shuffled their family into the United States. Mariana, now an attorney, immigrated with her parents as professionals and her two younger brothers as students. Welcomed by the Bauers to their family ranch, the Raeses began again.

# Chapter 4

"Ok, everybody. We'll be there in just a few minutes." Blaring the horn at pedestrians and vehicles, Roberto nudged out onto the busy street. "I like this car," he said, accelerating.

Harriet rolled her eyes. Roberto's driving habits South American style, she grabbed on to the seat in front of her to keep from sliding across the leather into Tre or Katie. Ten minutes later, the Suburban halted in front of the San Antonio Museum of Art.

"It's better if you get out here," Roberto told them, avoiding the parking lot across the street.

"Yes," Katie agreed. "Let's go in through the front. I'll find the event coordinator and make sure everything is ready to go."

Before they exited the vehicle, Roberto reached in back for Katie's hand and placed a coin in her palm.

"For good luck tonight," he said, winking at her. It was a thing they shared, she and Roberto.

---

One summer Friday night, when Katie was six or seven years old, after taking a water taxi to the lively town of Puerto La Cruz, the Bauers and Raeses strolled along the Paseo Colon. In the late afternoons, locals came to this place on the huge Bay of Pozuelos to socialize with friends or family or to have a meal. The sun low, Pinero boats lined the water's edge in the calm bay, salty water slapping against their hulls with the rising tide. Shoved into the sand and up onto the beach, the colorful open vessels made a pretty picture. Along the oceanfront strand after dinner, the group paused at this vendor or that, purchasing little tchotchkes. Bags full of shell jewelry, hand-sewn dolls, hands sticky with sweet *pastalitos*, they meandered along the crowded promenade.

Three teenage boys roughhoused nearby, shoving one another this way and that. One of them slammed into Katie. Surprised, she found herself flat on the ground. Closest to her, Roberto picked her up, the other kids collecting her scattered items. Before she reacted, he brushed her off and handed her a coin stamped with the image of Simon Bolivar, South American military and political hero. "For you, no more bad luck tonight. Ok?" Getting her breath back, Katie rubbed her eyes, nodded, and placed it into her pocket. Their secret over the years, the two exchanged the same coin back and forth at unexpected times.

---

"What did he just give you?" Harriet asked on the sidewalk.

"Oh. Just a coin," Katie said, moving just steps in front of the other two.

"He really is odd. Just odd," Harriet said.

There Harriet went again with her ignorant comments. Twice in less than an hour, Katie didn't say anything. With no way for Harriet to comprehend Katie's loyalty to the older man, words were pointless.

Katie's connections in the local art community made it easy for her to organize events at certain venues. The San Antonio Museum of Art was one she and Tre liked to patronize, its ambient feel comfortable yet elegant. Housed in a historic building, originally a brewery, two great towers and crenelated parapets rose above the trio. For tonight, Katie reserved the Luby Courtyard and the Great Hall, where guests could move in and out of doors.

Once inside, they were met by Esme, Katie's friend and event coordinator at the museum, who'd set the space with lounge seating

## Chapter 4

in clusters. Under a large tent outside, caterers piled food tables with charcuterie meats and cheese and other small bites while bartenders readied their tables for guests. "Oh, it looks so good!" Katie exclaimed.

"Hello, my darlings." Flushed and rosy with activity, Esme broke from directing the staff. British, she pronounced *darlings* like *dahlings*. Warm but not too warm, she gave both Katie and Tre an air hug.

"You remember my mother, Harriet Haman?"

"Of course." Esme extended her hand. "You're a bit early," she said, glancing at her watch.

Katie noticed Tre and Harriet locking eyes for a moment.

"As you see, it is all set up for networking," Esme continued. "Your clients can move from the bar to the open spaces or choose seating in these areas for more private conversations, as you suggested, Katie."

Esme's high heels clicked into the vestibule. Overhead, Dale Chihuly's *Persian Ceiling*, a complicated installation of hand-blown glass burst with transparent color. The shapes and forms, organic in origin, spiraled above, creating a canopy between one hall and the next. The group continued out into the courtyard. In the center, a concentric fountain with a stepped pyramid bubbled, its water flowing through cavities that crisscrossed at the structure's center, flanked all around with small groups of comfortable chairs and upholstered love seats with cocktail tables.

Katie nodded. "The setup is great, Esme. Plenty of room for everyone to sit down and relax." Forced standing at an event where all the women wore heels assured early departures. With a live auction planned for the latter part of the evening, they wanted to keep guests there until the end.

"I'm glad you like it. You all please go and get a drink while we finish up."

Tre stared at Esme's back as she retreated.

"Oh look, Mr. Haman is here. I'll get you a scotch," Harriet called out to her husband.

Each year, Katie's employer donated artwork for this gala. "Would you like to see what I brought?" Katie asked Mr. Haman.

"Of course," he said, following her to the front of the hall near a podium.

"First, we have these two that I curated from a local artist. She'll be here tonight. They are part of a series called *River City*." Both oils, the two paintings could be hung side by side or stand alone. One depicted a bright display of a local river boat. Reminiscent of a pontoon retrofitted with rows of seats for interested tourists, the vessel floated by a restaurant decorated with *papel picado*, colorful tissue paper with elaborate cutouts, the background dotted with crowds of people. The other featured a packed jazz bar, the focal point a well-known local trumpeter. Arms crossed, Mr. Haman surveyed both.

Finally, Katie lifted the cover on an easel, revealing a painting framed with an extrawide, intricate gilding with overlapping and intertwining scrolls. Realistic but with loose brush strokes, a dark painting revealed a gritty turn-of-the-century Chicago scene. Depicted in the foreground, five dirty-faced immigrant children stared at the observer, holding treasures retrieved from a nearby landfill—a broken broom handle, a rusty shovel, and a cracked ceramic cream pitcher. One of them stood behind a naked baby riding in an old-fashioned pram. In the background, smokestacks rose about dreary brick factories, billowing their gasses into a gray sky.

"A Taylore," Mr. Haman said. Katie looked at the older man, searching for his opinion. Inscrutable, Mr. Haman was like his southern counterparts. Polished from his cuff links to his Italian oxfords, maintaining a neutral, pleasant facade was key to any setting. Seconds passing, he studied the art, then looked back at her. "It's

## Chapter 4

quite generous, Katie. I will send them my regards on Monday." Then, turning, he said, "Everything is spot on. I appreciate it." he said.

Tre gave Katie's shoulders a little squeeze, and she leaned into him. Using the hand that was around her, he tapped her arm. As she looked up at him, Tre mouthed something.

"What?" she asked.

Just audible, Tre repeated, "What's it worth?"

Katie pulled away a bit, turning her body so that she more faced him rather than stood next to him. Her lips moved to form a silent "Three. Maybe three fifty at the most."

Pressing his lips together, Tre nodded.

Mr. Haman, the only witness to their exchange, interjected, "Tre, can I get you a drink? How about water?" He stared at his son.

Clearing his throat, Tre accepted. "Sure, Dad."

Afternoon light fading, twinkle lights illuminated the patio. People dressed in appropriate clothing filled the hall and outdoor area. Local socialites, sophisticated and perfumed, addressed one another. The venue hummed with the anticipation of a successful event.

"Oh look, Tre. My dad's here!" Katie waved, attracting Lewis Bauer's attention. The man swayed across the hall, his big frame dominating the space around him. His weathered face lean, with features that had set in a long time ago, Lewis was just at home in a pair of worn-out boots as he was in the tuxedo he was wearing tonight. "You look handsome, Daddy. When did you get in?"

"Earlier this afternoon," he said, "after a mighty long airplane ride."

"I'm glad you're back. And glad you came." Katie squeezed his hand.

"You know I wouldn't have missed it." Lewis kissed her cheek. He greeted Mr. Haman and Tre, in that order, his calluses coarse against the hands of the two executives.

"How're y'all?" he asked.

"Why, Lewis. It's been forever," Harriet said. "How long were you away this time?"

"About three months."

"And remind me—from what god-awful place did you just return?"

"Saudi Arabia, ma'am. It wasn't too bad, but I'll for certain spend the next few weeks getting the dust out of my sinuses. And my ears, clothes, and suitcases."

"Hmmm. I can imagine how exotic it is there. Lewis of Arabia!" Harriet laughed at herself.

"Nothing exotic. Just a big desert. I'm glad to be home."

"Katie, show your father the art you brought us." Finished with small talk, Harriet dismissed them, motioning toward the podium.

"What do you think?" Katie asked.

Lewis pulled reading glasses from the inside of his jacket pocket. "The frame's fancy. And what is this? Half-naked forlorn children in Packingtown." Lewis squinted for details and lowered his voice, but only a little. "Well, honey, I wouldn't write home about it."

Katie placed a hand on her chest, feigning hurt feelings.

"It's dark," Lewis went on. "Personally, I go for happier stuff."

Just then, two couples approached midconversation. Tre looked down, shaking his head, his ears turning pink.

"Well, well! It's the Edwards and the Goodwins," Tre said, clapping the two men on their shoulders.

"Hello! Thank y'all for coming out tonight." After exchanging greetings with the two couples, Katie continued her discussion of the painting. "Mr. Taylore focused on social realism, immigrant labor, and the dynamics of city neighborhoods."

"The social realism of those kiddos wasn't exactly the same as Mr. Taylore," Lewis said.

"You're right, Dad," Katie said. "Taylore did make somewhat of a name for himself in his day. Turn-of-the-century elite Chicagoans commissioned him. He socialized with them, painted their portraits, and built a home in Hyde Park with his wife and children. A few of his paintings sold for impressive prices in recent years, and he has originals as well as prints hanging in the Art Institute among other museums."

Listening to Katie, the Edwardses leaned in closer. Ben Edwards, not much older than Tre, bent down and whispered into his wife's ear. Hilary Edwards nodded.

"She's smart and pretty." Lisa Goodwin winked at Harriet. "Katie, this is fascinating. You must tell us more about it later. And by the way, we're in."

"I need to go up soon. What do you think, dear? Harry!"

"Yes, Harriet. Go ahead. Now is fine."

Harriet lifted the edge of her gown to step up on the low platform. In a dramatic gesture, she used her hand to swish her skirt. Directional lighting overhead picked out metallic threads in the fabric, making Harriet sparkle. She took the microphone from its mount and *tap-tap-tapped* it, gathering the attention of most of the party. Reminded of the baby birds, Katie swore she heard chirping. *I've had enough to drink.* She liked champagne, but any more than two glasses gave her a headache. Still, at social gatherings, Tre always placed a glass in her hand.

Harriet addressed the crowd. "Welcome, everyone! *Bienvenidos!*" Her Alabama drawl stretched the vowels out on the Spanish welcome, making it rhyme with *Do you neeeeed toast?* "We are so glad you all could be here tonight! This foundation that educates lower income children in the arts is so worthy, and we thank you all for your support."

"Mother is literally glowing," Tre said.

"She lives for this." Mr. Haman took an extraheavy sip on his scotch.

"We have some beautiful things available on the silent auction, which will be open until nine. But please come take a look at what we have on the live block. I am happy to announce that we have a Taylore original! We hope everyone has a lovely evening, and when it is time for bidding, please be generous with your pocketbooks. Your efforts will benefit children who do not have the same privileges as your children!"

With a soft round of applause from the crowd, Harriet left the podium. Tre, now into his third or fourth drink, leaned into Ben Edwards. "Don't feel like you need to do my fiancée any favors," he said.

Without flinching, Katie craned her neck as if she were looking for something or someone across the hall. Her attempt at aloofness was effortful, and to distract herself she made her hand into a fist and dug her nails in, imagining the little half-moon indentions in her palm.

His eyes wide, Ben took a half of a step back. "Hilary and I started collecting a few years ago, so we're interested. And your fiancée has done an excellent job. I'm convinced these pieces are a real investment."

"Oh, sure, sure. But not as lucrative as your portfolio." Tre winked, slapping Ben on the shoulder. "Let's refill these drinks," he said, but before he went back to the bar, Hilary touched Katie's arm.

"Katie, this is such a beautiful party. You've done all of this, and you work full-time. It's impressive. I can barely keep up with getting the twins to school, much less"—she waved her arm— "organize an event like this."

"I appreciate that." Katie smiled, watching Tre retreat.

"Try not to take what men say too personally."

Katie smiled at the other girl. "I won't, Hilary. And I don't. Unless it's personal." Katie liked Hilary enough. She didn't think she wasn't genuine, but something about her, the Edwardses and the Goodwins, was hard to get to know. *Maybe I'm wrong. Maybe they don't have much to say,* Katie thought. Though never at a loss for filler, actual substance seemed lacking. A pretty girl, Hilary reminded Katie of a frozen soap bubble.

The evening progressed as expected, with talk of art and a bullish market. Harriet took the podium again and announced the close of the silent portion of the auction. A large crowd moved about the tables, placing final bids. Esme picked up the signed sheets with escalating numbers to announce the winners later. Auctioneer introductions made, the live auction began.

In his element, dressed in black tie, the auctioneer stood relaxed at the podium. Shuffling papers, he waited a few moments for everyone's attention. He took the microphone and began.

"Good evening, ladies and gentlemen, and a very warm welcome to the fifteenth annual benefit gala Art for the Children of San Antonio. I am Sebastian Carter, and I will be your auctioneer for what promises to be an exciting evening."

Esme moved the first painting to an easel next to Sebastian.

"The first two paintings we have are by local artist Cynthia Munoz," he continued. "She's right over there. Cynthia, wave so everyone can see you!"

A middle-aged woman with long dark hair and wearing a long fishtail dress did so, and everyone turned and applauded. After a banter amongst the paddles and two final sales, the auctioneer moved on to the main event.

"What we have here is a Taylore, an oil on canvas from 1915, property of the St. Anthony for two decades. Before that it was in a private collection, in the artist's family's possession—his daughter, as a matter of fact. Let's start the bidding at eighty thousand."

Someone Katie didn't know raised her paddle first, and another flew up, and next, Ben Edwards.

"Thank you, sir. We have ninety thousand. Who will give me one hundred?"

Nearby, Tom Goodwin raised his. Paddles flew, potential buyers vying all around the room until Ben and Tom were the last two bidders. Then on they went, back and forth like a tennis match, with the bid nearing a quarter of a million dollars.

Exhilarated, Sebastian leaned over the podium. "Sir, will you give me two thirty?" He pointed at Tom. "Two twenty. We are at two twenty. Two thirty? Fair warning. I'm going to sell." The auctioneer's gavel up, Tre pulled a paddle from behind his back and raised it high in the air.

"Two fifty!" he called out.

Hilary inhaled. Ben looked at Tom, shaking his head, and Tom laughed. Mr. Haman, even and still, glared through his son.

"Thank you, sir! Do I have three hundred?" the auctioneer motioned toward Ben and Tom. "Will you give me two seventy-five? We're at two fifty; I'm going to sell it. Last chance. The hammer is up."

Then with a bang, the gavel came down on the podium. "Sold for two hundred fifty thousand dollars!"

Katie felt her face turning hot. Excusing herself from the group, she went into the ladies' room and splashed cold water on her face from the sink. Not noticing that Hilary followed, Katie took a moment to breathe into a hand towel with her eyes closed. The cool towel and the dark felt good, and she left it there until the racing of her heart diminished.

"Katie."

She removed the towel, placed it into the receptacle, and turned toward Hilary.

"We aren't mad. Really, it's fine that Tre got it."

Katie wanted to say something to Hilary. *Sure, Hilary, it's fine that my fiancé embarrassed me. He behaved in bad form,* or *I bet his dad is going to lose it with him,* or *Tre doesn't have two hundred fifty thousand dollars to spend on a painting.* But she couldn't. If Katie made any words, tears of embarrassment and anger and feeling small all wrapped up together would have dumped all over the basin, spilling onto the counter and then the floor.

"Take a minute and a few breaths and fix your lipstick."

Katie followed the instructions.

"Now, let's go find the boys."

In the hall, the pair found Ben and Tom with a group of investors.

"Manhood measurer."

"He's always got the yardstick out."

"I'd like to buy him for what he's worth and sell him for what he thinks he'd bring," Ben said.

They all laughed and then composed themselves when they saw Katie.

"Thank you for coming. It was good to see all of you," Katie said. She had to leave soon. Now.

"Good to see you too. Can we have lunch one day soon?" Hilary offered.

"Of course," Katie said. "I'm going to find Tre; it's been a long day."

Thankful that most of the attendees had dispersed, she found Lewis right away, conversing with Tre and his parents.

"Looks like it's time to put the chairs in the wagon. Can I give you all a ride home? I'm headed back to the ranch tonight," Lewis said.

"But Roberto?" Harriet asked.

"I sent him on home," Lewis said. "He didn't need to wait around all night for us. Get in with me, and I'll run y'all back to the house."

The city was quieter than when they'd arrived, not unusual this time of year. A light, cold drizzle dampened the streets, and lights from open windows in surrounding high-rises reflected into puddles. High above, miniature people tucked their children into bed. Reappearing in adjacent rooms, some sat together watching the evening news, and others were alone, their silhouettes tipping a glass of wine or patting a dog on their lap.

They quickened their steps to Lewis's truck, avoiding the little golden pools. Katie took off her shoes before stepping up into the front, and Mr. Haman gave Harriet a boost. Tre rode in the back with his parents.

As usual, the Hamans would stay at Tre and Katie's when they were in town, planning to return to Dallas the next day. The ride home was silent except for Harriet chattering nonstop about the newly acquired painting.

"Harry, I didn't know that we decided to bid on the art!"

"I didn't know we did either, Harriet," Mr. Haman said.

Katie rested her head on the glass of the passenger window. Watching specks of rain fall between the rhythmic movement of the intermittent wiper blades, she couldn't wait to crawl into bed, close her eyes, and start over tomorrow. When Lewis dropped the couples curbside, he made a mental note to call his daughter to check on her the following week.

# Chapter 5

Straight to her bedroom, Katie got out of her dress, leaving it rumpled on the floor. She changed into lounge shorts and a T-shirt and climbed right into bed. Looking at her phone, she went through her email and sent a few texts to Esme, Hilary, her dad, and Mr. Pickett. *Mr. Pickett.* She smiled, recalling the best part of her day.

Tre interrupted her thoughts and plan of action with her new painting. "Did you see everyone looking at me when I got the final bid? Did you see the looks on their faces?" Still fully dressed, Tre paced back and forth across the master bedroom with ego-charged adrenaline. "Katie. Katie! Are you listening?"

Katie looked up from her phone. "Yes. I did see their faces, and I am making some appointments for the new painting."

"What? Doing what with it? I'm taking care of that," Tre said.

"No, Tre. The one I brought home today."

"Oh. That thing?" Making a face like something smelled bad, Tre said, "The one without an artist? Katie, I meant to talk to you about that. Look, I don't know what you paid for it or if it's even worth anything. I wish you'd stop wasting your time with all of that. We need to talk about moving forward instead of you spinning your wheels with your job and the time it takes away."

"Takes away from what, Tre?"

"Takes away, Katie, from me. From our life and the one we will have when we're married."

An odd feeling rose in her chest and lodged in her throat. "You know you are the most important thing to me, Tre. I would never do anything to jeopardize that. I think I can be your wife and keep my job."

"But you don't need to keep it. Why would you?"

"Because I like it."

"C'mon, Katie. Is it practical? You need to stop being selfish."

"Maybe I can see about going part-time. A few days a week. Can we talk about this later?"

"I want to talk about it now."

"I'm tired, but I promise I will keep my priorities straight. You are my priority, Tre."

"I'm not tired."

"And because everyone's been drinking tonight. I don't want to argue." Burrowing down into the covers, she closed her eyes, doing her best to not hear any more of Tre's generously imparted wisdom.

"This is exactly what I'm talking about. You're too tired to even resolve this situation. I'm going to get another drink so we can finish this." Tre slammed the door and stomped out and through the hallway.

Sometime in the eighties, a wet bar was retrofitted into the far wall between the living room and the master. Back in fashion, its mirrored glass and gold-tone fixtures contemporary, Tre poured himself a drink.

"Fix me one of those too," Mr. Haman said.

"Oh, hey, Dad. I didn't know you were still up."

"I'm sure everyone is still up. What's going on, son?"

"What do you mean?"

"Let's start with the auction. I don't mind saying that was an asinine move. I suppose you are withdrawing funds from your trust, because I'm not paying for it. Furthermore, Katie said it could go for three fifty. I take it that's what the yelling was about in there."

"In that case, I would think, Dad, that you'd appreciate the investment I just made, and no one was yelling. Katie and I disagree about her job."

Just then, Harriet appeared from the shadows in the corridor. Mr. Haman didn't know whether she'd been standing there all along. *Probably*, he thought.

"Don't play dumb, Tre. You well know you stepped on toes tonight. If I were Katie, I'd be livid," Mr. Haman said.

"Harold!" Harriet cut in. "That's enough. The painting is an investment, and Katie can busy herself with other things that help Tre after they get married," she said, brushing her hand over her son's shoulder.

Mr. Haman took the fresh drink Tre poured. "I'm going to bed. You should too, Tre," he said.

Face down on the mattress, Katie pulled a pillow down over her head. If she held it tight enough, maybe it would drown out the voices. Tre's father sided with her. That wasn't surprising. If she described Mr. Haman in three words, they would be formidable, cautious, and measured. Katie had one thing to discuss with Tre about the painting, which she would do before Monday. Right before she fell asleep, she decided she'd go out to the ranch tomorrow.

The next morning, Katie awoke to sun spilling from the wall of windows in her room onto the comforter. She watched the rays of light, flanked by floor-to-ceiling bookcases, cast shadows over the bindings. When she moved in with Tre, they had spent weeks unpacking boxes of books, mixing hers with his, and organizing them. Starting high on the left-hand side, they arranged them not by genre but in chronological order, with titles acquired from the past, from their childhoods and through college. Katie loved the empty spaces, imagining filling them up with copies chosen by both of them.

In the early days with her fiancé, they wandered through old bookstores in Alamo Heights, searching for specific editions, classics, or anything fun and interesting. One October afternoon they'd skipped classes, culminating in a day forever known as the Most Glorious Book Hunting Adventure Ever. They wore light sweaters as the temperatures plummeted, strong winds and a dark horizon bringing in a blue norther. With no chance to hold on to their branches, leaves fell, skidding after one another in a blur, creating a fall palette on the streets and lawns below. Shrieking with laughter, they ran back to the car, freezing gusts of wind whipping Katie's hair around her face. They lugged the new stacks, safely in their backpacks, up into the apartment. They opened a decent bottle of Bordeaux, and like dealers for a game of cards, together they laid the books on the floor, and she read each title aloud. *Successful Berry Growing*, 1974. *How did we live without this before?* Not original, of course, with bumped corners and browned end papers, but nevertheless a copy of *Art—A Commodity* by Sheridan Ford. And best of all, a first-edition copy of Aldous Huxley's *Crome Yellow*. How she admired the mustard boards and lettering on the pristine spine, long protected thanks to a crumbling original book jacket. Once the books were in their new home on the shelf, delighted by the smell of the old paper, she stepped back once again for maybe the hundredth time, admiring the vertical labels, eclectic in every way that books could take a notion to.

In those years, when they thought life was stressful, the pair lazed around on Tuesdays and Thursdays, since neither of them had class until the afternoon, pulling this copy or that. Lying askew on the bed, propped up against extra pillows, they took turns reading excerpts that might spark a discussion. With a temporary acceptance of implausibility, they became lovers in the mountains of Spain from *For Whom the Bell Tolls* as she read Hemingway. Basking in Michael Ondaatje, poet of fiction, Katie dug for insight and perception, while Tre gravitated toward Kerouac. The Beat Generation a mystery needing solving, he marveled at views of the purposeless in modern society. Their counterculture the antithesis to his own, Tre devoured the pages, searching for vicarious freedom.

---

Squinting, she pulled the covers up over her head. Tre's side empty, she looked at her phone, taking a minute to soak in the quiet apartment and lack of weekday city noise on the street below. It was nearly ten a.m. She groaned, rolling out of bed against her will.

On autopilot, Katie headed into the kitchen. At the counter, she leaned over, reading a note left by Tre. *Work in the office for a few hours. See you later this afternoon.* Last night's sting still resonating, she left it where it was.

"Oh, there you are, Katie. I was wondering whenever you'd get up."

In the middle of pouring her coffee, Katie jumped, splashing a little.

"Tre and Mr. Haman are off to the office. I thought we could make plans today." In front of her, on the dining table, Harriet arranged a giant white three-ring binder, a large leather-bound planner, colored pens, and highlighters, along with a cup of her signature Earl Grey. "We must have at least a year, Katie. It's time to set dates and hire a wedding planner."

Katie squeezed her eyes shut for a few seconds before turning around to look at Harriet across the kitchen island. "Miss Harriet, any planner is fine with me. I'll email you my calendar. The hotel gallery exhibits are scheduled a year out. I only need to work around those."

"You kids tell me some excuse each time I ask." Harriet shut the planner and stacked it on top of the binder. "Can we at least make appointments for dress shopping? Not here. Up in Dallas."

"We can," Katie said. "Give me a date, and I will work it in."

"Priorities. All right," Harriet said, closing the binder with a slap. "I'm going to call Mr. Haman about lunch. You and Tre will join?"

"We can ask Tre, but I'm heading out to the ranch today. I'm sorry I can't go, but I need to go visit with Gran and Grandad," Katie said.

"All right, then." Irritated, Harriet scooted her chair closer to the table. Looking down into the bone china teacup on the table, she swirled the contents, shaking her head.

Back in her room to pack a change of clothes, Katie kicked the black dress from last night under the bed. She'd take it to the cleaners next week. Surveying herself in the bathroom mirror, she tied her hair back. From her closet she pulled out a pair of jeans and a few loose dresses. She chose a patterned cotton boho, slipped it over her head, and picked a pair of sandals to go with it. As an afterthought, she threw toiletries into a large leather tote with the extra clothes. On top, she placed her wallet and keys, with sunglasses on top of her head. She called the valet to retrieve her car and sat on the side of her bed, legs swinging, feet not touching the floor, for a few minutes. *It's quiet out there. I wonder if Harriet went back to the guest room.*

*Your car is ready*, the valet texted.

Katie hopped off the bed and texted Mariana. *Do you have plans today? I'm leaving for the ranch now. Call you on the drive.*

With no sign of Harriet in the common areas, Katie flew out of the apartment, steps ahead of her voice. "Bye, Miss Harriet! Don't forget to get me those dates." Down the elevator, out into the vestibule, and onto the street. Her car was waiting for her.

"Well, get over there on your side, and let's get this thing down like you like it." An ancient little man in an old-fashioned bellhop suit with white hair hobbled around to the back of the 1978 blue MGB on the street side. Positioned on either side of the vehicle, they unclipped, unsnapped, rolled, and folded until the canvas top was down and secured on the little car.

"Thank you, Mr. Al. I'll be back today or maybe tomorrow."

One hand moving his wire-framed glasses up farther on his nose, he waved her on. "Y'all be careful," he said.

## Chapter 6

Katie opened the boot lid and threw her bag in. She liked using British terminology such as *bonnet* or *boot* in reference to her car. Even better were more obscure terms like *wing* instead of *fender* or *cubby box* for *glove compartment*. *I'll put my wallet in the cubby box. I must pay attention to my wing while parking.* She liked doing this with Mariana, who, expressionless, eyes hidden behind trademark giant sunglasses, shook her head at Katie.

In the driver's seat, Katie zipped down the one-way streets toward the freeway, heading north out of the city.

Soon, tall buildings morphed into strip malls and urban sprawl, then into suburbs, where gated subdivisions with elaborate stone entrances and guard shacks lured potential buyers. On either side of the highway, rows of brand-new homes dotted the hillsides. The land was clear cut, the houses in perfect rows, with little variation from one to the next. Gran called it "ticky-tack."

From the time Katie was very young, she and Gran had made this same drive into town and back. Going into town meant leaving the ranch to drive into the city—not unusual, but still a special treat. Her grandmother not young like the other mothers, Katie didn't notice then. From the backseat of the big car, she memorized the patterns on the silk scarves Gran wore. Mostly secured on her hair beneath her neck, sometimes tied at the back or around her shoulders, but never to town without a proper silk square. Singing the entire way, they'd begin favorite tunes at this landmark or that.

## Chapter 6

Billboards with loglines like *Adorning your outer world in a life full of simplicity and luxury views* promised lazy rivers to come, complete with photos of tanned attractive parents holding martinis, sending each child down a faux meandering stream on a colorful blow-up raft. Katie laughed, wondering about oxymorons, uninspired monotony, and terrible albeit effective marketing.

Katie recalled a trip into town for back-to-school clothes shopping when she was big enough to sit up front. They left early in the morning, with a plan to spend the whole day in San Antonio perusing the Boot Mall, as Gran called it.

*Everything's bigger in Texas*, a phrase originating from the sheer geographical size of the state, Texans take the adage literally in just about any sense one can imagine. Towns all over the state lay claim to "The Biggest," from objects to food items to the abstract, such as the size of their hearts.

Outside the center where Gran and Katie planned to shop, the world's largest pair of cowboy boots, created with recycled materials by an Austin artist better known as Daddy-O, was showcased. After their construction, Daddy-O composed the song "Too High, Too Wide, Too Long," guaranteeing the pair could hold three hundred thousand gallons of beer. The boots, assembled in Washington, DC, made their trek to San Antonio in the seventies. Taking as many back roads as possible, still they wedged under at least one overpass, only to be freed with the help of half a dozen trepid men brandishing crowbars.

Though another set of big boots exists in Seattle, some claiming theirs as largest, this is untrue. The Seattle pair measures twenty-four feet tall, whereas the Texas pair measures a full eleven feet higher, hands down making it "The Biggest."

Once in San Antonio, Gran took them first to Los Patios, a large natural area encircled by the city. Under the arms of giant moss-laden oaks on the banks of Salado Creek, seated at tea tables, they lunched on tiny buttery biscuits and crepes. Afterward, down shaded paths, Katie sat on the grass near the water throwing leftover crumbs for the swans. Later, at the shopping center, they browsed through the department stores, bringing armloads of clothing into the dressing rooms, with anything purchased needing approval from Gran.

Katie modeled one outfit after the next, Gran indicating the full turn with one finger in the air in a circular motion. Holding her core tight, Katie executed twirls and double half turns in perfect form, waiting for a nod or a head shake from her grandmother. On this day, Katie crammed herself into a pair of tight low-rise jeans. Getting a shake rather than a nod, Katie protested, "But everyone else…" to which Gran replied, "My granddaughter isn't made of ticky-tack." And that was all that needed saying.

---

Today was Saturday, and stereotypical suburbanites sped around Katie, ushering SUVs full of kids to sports practice on this field or that park. The kids bounced up and down in the seats in ball caps and numbered jerseys, their sticky hands smearing goo from yogurt packets on the windows and one another.

Katie sighed, and the endless traffic lights and intersections spaced out more and more until traffic diminished into distance commuters and travelers. Now in the legitimate hill country, the space opened into rolling hills and promises of mountains in the offing.

In certain sections, the highway cut through hills, revealing stories in the rugged landscape shaped by time and weather. Ages ago, a shallow ocean covered this expanse, along with sea creatures and corals. Plankton expiring, their bodies sank to the bottom. Currents grinding the shells into tiny pieces and waves washing over again and again, like icing a cake, filling in here and there, made the floor smooth. Crystallizing under pressure, they formed limestone beds, a composition of calcium carbonate and other minerals. The surface sturdy yet porous, the terrain's elements vulnerable, and with water creating fissures, a subterranean world formed beneath it. Percolating rainfall through the rock, finding its way down, down, and down, fashioned fanciful dripstones, like underground melting wax creations. Mirrored lakes, streams, and a host of life abounding and unseen, with springs on the surface invited future pioneers to rest awhile, or even stay.

Nearing her exit, Katie breathed in the mountain cedar. Sharp, sweet, and green, it smelled like home. Off the interstate, she slowed to a stop. In typical Southwest Texas fashion, the afternoon promised the chilly morning a thirty-degree temperature differential. Like Lewis always said, if you don't like the weather here, just wait a minute. She dialed Mariana and put her on speaker.

"Don't complain. I waited until after noon to call," Katie said.

"I won't." Mariana yawned. "What are you doing today?"

"Didn't you see my text? I'm headed to the ranch. Come. Don't say no."

"Listen." Katie heard Mariana sitting up, covers rumpling around her. Caribbean Spanish accent heavy, she continued. "Work has been crazy. I was sleeping in today to celebrate finishing a case, but I can go. Did you call up there yet?"

"Yay! And no. I didn't tell them."

Mariana smiled, climbing out of her bed. "They like it when you do that."

"Yes. They do. Text me when you leave, ok?"

Hanging up with Mariana, the road still clear, Katie looked at her text messages, three from Tre. *You're not coming to lunch? Mother says you went to the ranch. What time will you be home?*

Texting back, Katie replied *No, yes, and I'll let you know when I decide what I'm doing.* Erasing the end of the last one, she left it at *I'll let you know,* and then, *I'll text you.*

Katie passed through the lonely intersection and continued northwest, the winding farm-to-market roads just what her little car was made for. She passed a small herd of deer drinking from a clear stream near the road and slowed at a row of post-mounted mailboxes. She turned onto a caliche road and headed down toward the first bump gate.

Common on rural ranches, the step-saving drive-through gates offered a heavy barrier for livestock and kept the driver from having to stop. Get out. Open the gate. Get back inside the car. Drive through the gate. Get back out again. And. Close the gate. Built out of steel pipe, the self-opening and self-closing contraption featured two cables attached to a tall cylinder in the middle. A pro at these, Katie approached, positioning her vehicle in the center of the right side, bumper just touching the wood panels fastened to the gate. The force of her acceleration opening it, the cables twisted around the cylinder at the top. She flew through, the gate swinging like a pendulum behind her with a *Bang! Bump bump*, and finally a tap, until it settled and closed again. Angora goats trotted away, bleating their annoyance, wavy wool cascading across and down their backs. She passed three more gates and a cattle guard, and then she pulled up between a big white farmhouse and a long rectangular ranch-style house, both standing in splendid isolation.

## Chapter 7

Built in the forties, Katie's childhood home, low and rambling, was surrounded by a whitewashed horizontal fence that had held scads of family pets in and livestock out over the years, the rock structure standing stoic. Large stone slabs made a path leading the way to a long, narrow covered porch that ran the length of the structure. Off center in the front was a set of heavy, weathered Spanish Colonial doors. Just inside, a hallway stretched parallel to the outside patio. At one end was a large living area, in the middle of which a giant fireplace with a rock hearth extended eight feet out and around, made of flat stones matching the home's exterior. Next, off the hallway, a kitchen, in conjunction with several bedrooms and baths, pine boards lined the floors and walls throughout. An old-fashioned phone hung on the kitchen wall, back then connected to a party line, a young Katie dragged a dining chair over to reach it. Lifting the receiver, she turned the crank.

"Is anybody there?" she'd ask. Sometimes they were, at which time Miss Helen Campbell might chastise, "Katie. I'm talkin' to Miss Ruth. Now you go on and hang up. It's not good manners to listen in on somebody else's conversations" or "Katie. This is Miss Leona here. Why don't you ride your bike on over and try some of my lemon cookies," to which Katie obliged. Sometimes no one was there, and if that was the case, Katie might check back later if she wasn't too busy.

Katie imagined her mother in that kitchen, face blurry. She saw her floral-printed apron tied around her mother's waist, flour on her cheek, making dewberry pie—cultivated from the sweet berries growing wild on the fence lines, served for dessert or even lunch, but always a summertime favorite. For anyone visiting, just like Elijah's jar of flour, her mother's pie pans and the sweet-tea pitcher never ran out.

One Wednesday morning in early spring, Eileen Bauer dressed her four-year-old daughter in a pair of shorts and a long-sleeve top. Dragonflies here now; the air would not turn cold again.

"I wanna wear my boots with this, Mama."

"Ok. Boots it is. They're on the back porch. I think today is a good day for berry picking," Eileen said, in blue-and-white seersucker shorts and a tank top. Covering herself with her husband's white button-up shirt, she said, "I'll wear boots too."

"Ok, Mama. I'll get the basket."

Hand in hand, the two traipsed out the back door, feet heavy, clunking their heels on the ground. They opened the backyard gate and crossed a meadow. In the distance a lane wound down and back up a hill where at the top, two huge oak trees reached across, their branches entangled overhead. Their personal playground, bushy-tailed fox squirrels ran along the limbs, chasing one another. Airborne, they spiraled from one tree to the next. Bluebonnets blooming, the lupines poked their heads up through the field grass with pride, displaying a heavy new quilt of cobalt. Up and over the hill the flowers spread, all the way back down to the banks of the mighty Pedernales, his waters strong, clear, and green.

But Eileen and her daughter didn't have that far to go. Early in the year, the river was still cold, and there would be plenty of time for floating this summer. Instead, hand in hand, the two headed toward the fence line for the brambles, the little girl swinging a wicker pail, skipping a step in front of her mother. As they approached the prickly vines, broom in hand, Eileen stopped.

"You stay back for just a minute while Mama beats the bushes."

"Why?"

"Because there might be creatures napping there." She pointed under the shady parts.

"You mean li'l critters?" the girl asked.

Her mother nodded.

"What kind?"

"Oh. All kinds. Squirrels or birds. Big fat toads or maybe a snake. We need to let them know we're here," she said, poking the broom around, focusing on the ground they couldn't see. Reaching for her waistband, Eileen secured her radio. A rule on the ranch: *never leave the house without your radio.* The best technology of the day, their range miles and miles, everyone had one. And during daylight hours, everybody left them turned on.

"I hope there's a big fat toad!"

Nothing more than a few honeybees disturbed, the two spent the better part of an hour picking the ripest berries.

"Just the black ones," Eileen reminded.

"Those are the sweet ones," the little girl said, her face and mouth smeared purple.

"You're the sweet one," her mother said, with two taps on her daughter's nose. "Let's get back to the house. Daddy's coming home today, and you're sticky!"

"Can we go back the longer way? Please, Mama?"

"We sure can."

They went back across a different meadow, and Eileen climbed a metal farm gate. "Hand me the basket. Now be a big girl and climb over. Carefully. I'll take your hand when you get up to the top."

"No! I can do it by myself."

"Hold on tight then. Look over your shoulder after you're on this side. That's it. What a big girl you are."

"I don't need your hand. I'm a big girl."

"You sure are," Eileen said.

The little girl ran toward the next pasture, where just on the other side of a fence, the ranch hands worked cattle. All rustled up into a pen, on horseback, they maneuvered them into a squeeze chute for inoculations and new ear tags. Next, they sent them through a swimming bath treated with medicine to keep the cattle tick fever away. Up on the metal pipe fence, holding on to the top rail, she waved.

"*Abuelo! Abuelo,* look at me!"

A Mexican man inside the pen turned and moved toward the little girl on the fence. "*Changuita,* look at you!"

"I can climb just like a monkey," she said.

The old man patted her small hand, then removed one glove and rested his hand on top of hers. Dark and strong, Tacho had worked with his hands his whole life. Born on this land and growing up with Eileen's father-in-law, Tacho was family. He, his wife, sons, and daughters were as integral to the ranch as the ground and the beasts that roamed it. Way beyond the cattle pens were the bunkhouse and the foreman's house, Tacho's permanent residence.

"*Hola Mami,*" Tacho said.

Sunglasses hiding her eyes, Eileen tucked stray hairs falling from a bun behind her ears. Tacho's eyes dropped to the young woman's hand resting on the tiniest bulge on her belly.

"The steers sure do look pretty." She smiled.

"Si si," Tacho agreed, adjusting the straw hat on his head.

There the three stood for several moments watching the other cowboys.

"Ok, sugar plum. Two more minutes. Then time to go back to the house. We have pies to make and maybe some biscuits."

"Yum biscuits," the little girl sang. "Biscuits, biscuits, and more biscuits." The rock house in sight from where they stood, she flew across the field, her four-year-old legs carrying her as fast as they could.

"Wait for me!" her mother yelled, laughing. A sight in their shorts, boots, broom, and basket, Eileen chased her daughter, careful not to spill the fruit.

"I beat you, Mama!"

"You did! Go wash up and meet me back here in the kitchen. We can get these pies going, and then we'll have some lunch."

The little girl ran off to her bathroom where, standing on a stool, she was up high enough to see herself in the mirror. Playing in the sink basin, she washed her face and hands. Using bar soap, she sudsed her cheeks, then arms. Splashing everywhere, more water on the floor than on herself, she remembered the biscuits and ran back down the long hallway to the kitchen.

Humming, covered in flour, Eileen wiped the back of her hand across her cheek. "If you don't wiggle, I'll let you help me roll," she said, lifting the little girl up onto the counter. Together they rolled, cut, and laid lattice dough strips on top of the berries. Into the oven, together with the biscuits, the pastries went.

Minutes ticked by. As they waited for the timer, the phone rang.

"Hello?" Eileen said. Covering the speaker with her hand, she said, "It's Daddy. Go outside and wait for me at your little table. I'll be out there in just a minute with something to eat."

The little girl nodded, first running into the living room to collect a doll left on the sofa. "I'll see you tonight, dear. I love you too," she heard her mother say as she pulled on the heavy door to the outside. Out front, the St. Augustine lush, green, and a little too tall, a child-size picnic table waited. Tomorrow, grass mowing day, the hands would manicure the lawn again. Distracted by her big black and white cat, the little girl dropped the doll onto the cool cement patio.

"Sammie," she said, edging closer. "Sammie, what are you doing? Come here, kitty."

His head perpendicular to hers, the big tom sat motionless on his haunches, a low deep growl coming from his throat.

Almost square in front of Sammie, the little girl knelt, reaching out to pet his head. Sammie exhaled, forcing a puff of audible air, baring his teeth.

"What's wrong, kitty?" Hearing the front door close, the little girl turned her head. "Mama, something's wrong with Sammie."

Midstride, Eileen froze, dropping the plates in her hand. Crashing onto the Saltillo tile patio, warm berries splashed onto her legs and feet and into the grass. Her four-year-old daughter was positioned between the cat and a six-foot western diamondback. Raising his head from its thick coil, slithering into position, the snake unwound his tail. Rattles up, shaking furiously, he gave full good and serious warning—distinctive, like a chorus of deranged cicadas beating their drumlike tymbals. The little girl turned her head in the direction of the snake's horrific spade-shaped head, an earthy brown, a geometric darker shape along its spine. The girl sat close enough to touch the serpent. A twenty-gauge loaded with birdshot just feet behind her in a hall closet, Eileen dared not turn her back to get it.

Quiet and trembling, Eileen spoke. "Katie girl. Do not move. Don't move unless Mama tells you to."

"I'm scared," Katie said.

"You are a big, brave girl. Don't talk, and don't move. It's going to be ok. Remember, now. Do not move."

"I won't, Mama," she whispered. Her mother, taking even and steady steps, crept toward Katie. Just before reaching her, she swooped down, grasping the child under her left arm and turned her away from the rattler. As Eileen spun, the snake's patience worn, it whipped its head forward. Accelerating, he flung his body. Five-inch fangs untucking from its palette, he struck. Deep into Eileen's flesh he hung on, pumping a cocktail of neurotoxins into her upper thigh, nicking her femoral artery.

A high-pitched noise coming from inside her, Eileen focused on the door. The lawn in front of her, she stumbled, picking herself up. Just a few steps to the patio, she fell again, slumping against the door, Katie falling from her arms into the mess of ruined pie. Bleary eyed and blinking hard, she reached out for her daughter's small shoulders.

"Are you hurt? Are you hurt anywhere?"

"No, Mama," Katie said. "I'm ok. You're bleeding. You have a lot of blood on you."

Looking down, Eileen saw. Dizzy, she tried hard to concentrate on the next step. *The radio. Reach for it.* "This is Eileen. Snakebite. Snakebite. Help."

Inside the house next door, Gran heard the call. Still out with the cattle, so did Tacho. Repeating the emergency into the radio, he called, "Snakebite at the rock house. Snakebite!" Changing gears, men all over the ranch stopped and rushed to help. Those in the back pastures ran to their trucks and sped toward the call. Men working near Tacho gathered around him. "Tony! Get the bag!"

"Silas already went, sir!" someone said.

"Let's go!" Tacho led the way, running faster than he had in a long time. *No, no, no.* The words inside his head, he imagined little Katie, crying, an extremity swelling. At the house, they all shouted Eileen's name and found the woman in a heap in the front.

In the years Tacho lived on this ranch, accidents happened. Cowboys got bucked off horses. They got run over by cattle and flipped tractors over. Men slashed limbs, amputated fingers, and got banged up and sliced tangling with calves and barbed wire. There were snakebites, spider bites, and compound fractures. Impaled men lived to talk about it, but never, ever, ever, had Tacho seen so much blood.

A large group surrounded Eileen. Katie knelt, brushing flour from her mother's cheek. Tacho's wife, Maria, brushed past the men. "Tacho, give the baby to me. Hand me the baby now."

"There's no time for an ambulance," Grandad said. "Get an IV going, and let's get her into a vehicle."

At the ranch, they kept antivenom for people and animals in the barn, along with other sorts of medical supplies. Miles out in the country and over half an hour from doctors and veterinarians, it made good sense. Ripping his belt from the loops, Tacho lifted Eileen. He fastened the belt around the top of her thigh and pulled tight, blood spurting onto his shirt.

Now hysterical, Katie screamed, her arms and legs flailing in Maria's grasp. Touching Maria's arm, Gran said, "Ssshhh. Stop crying, Katie. Hug your mother tight and tell her you love her."

Grown men, tougher than old boot leather, looked on helpless, their hands in pockets. Some wiped tears from their faces while others let them fall where they stood. Maria picked Katie up again.

"Tony. Go inside the house and bring me clothes for the baby. *Pobrecita*"—Maria kissed the child's head—"you're coming with me."

From over Maria's shoulder, Katie watched the hands carrying her mother to a truck brought up by one of the men. Gran wrapped her in blankets, towed the IV, and climbed in the back seat, Grandad in front, with Tacho taking the wheel, her daughter-in-law losing consciousness leaning against her shoulder.

"Please take care of Katie. Tell Lewis I love him," Eileen said before falling asleep for the last time. Slipping away, she saw her little girl's smiling face stained with berries and the face of her husband she wouldn't see again. The face of the unknown tiny one, resting inside, she'd keep with her forever.

After it was all over, Gran, Grandad, and Tacho returned to the ranch early afternoon. Today's activities skewed, no one worked their normal duty. They turned the cattle out and left the horses in the corral. The men scrubbed concrete, cleaned up broken dishes, and washed a small blood-soaked doll. They mowed the lawn, and turning on a water hose, sprayed the grass down until Eileen's blood soaked into the soil. Tacho took the truck out to the barn. Gathering buckets, towels, and a scrub brush, he began. Scrub, rinse, soak. Scrub, rinse, soak. Dumping tinted water, he refilled the buckets to start the process over again. There, Tony found his father.

"Papa. Give me the brush. Let me do it."

"No. No, Antonio," the old man said.

"Papa, please. Let me. You should go up to the big house," Tony said, one hand on his father's shoulder, the other taking the brush away. Tacho turned toward his son, shoulders slumped. Like a spring rain coursing through an arroyo, tears flowed along the crevices of the old man's face, meandering across until gravity took over. Alone in the barn, embracing, they let themselves sob, but not for too long.

After cleaning himself up, Tacho walked back up to the white house. He knocked on the screen door, removed his hat, and let himself inside. Looking down at his hands, Grandad sat in his big leather chair. Tacho sat across from him.

"Mr. Lewis?" Tacho asked.

"We wait," said Grandad.

Up in her room, Gran removed her clothing and shoved all of it into a dark-colored trash bag. Her socks still wet and gummy, she peeled them from her feet. She stepped into the shower, water hot as tolerable, and washed. Scrubbing the beds of her fingernails and in between her toes caked with blood, she washed and washed, head back, the spray muffling her cries. Stepping out onto a towel, she used her foot to wipe the prints made before, and putting herself back together, she went downstairs.

"Tacho. Can you please ask Maria to bring Katie up? Ask her if she minds staying up here for a few days."

"Yes ma'am," Tacho said. "Whatever you need."

"And tell cook that I'm taking over for the next week. Breakfast, dinner, and supper," Gran said.

In the kitchen she pulled out two giant pots and filled them with water to boil fryers. Entering the same way as her husband, Maria arrived, little Katie's hand in hers. She set the child down on the floor between the two men in the living room and found Gran in the kitchen. Taking a knife and a seat at the island next to Gran, without a word between them, the two women chopped vegetables for casseroles.

After a delayed flight, leaving a short connection in Atlanta, Lewis hurried to the train in the next terminal. Making it to the jet bridge just before closing, he boarded the regional aircraft and got himself seated. Putting his head back and buckling, he couldn't wait to get home to see his girls. Touching down at San Antonio International, he waited for his bag, and then headed out to his truck to make the drive back home.

Tacho and Grandad, out on the front wraparound porch of the white house, eyes fixed, watched down the road. As soon as caliche dust billowed in the distance, they stood and made their way over to the rock house to wait for Lewis. He pulled up past the last cattle guard and put his truck into park. His senses aware, he saw his father and Tacho leaning against either side of a post in front of his house. The truck back in drive, Lewis rolled up. Grandad stepped out, waiting for his son to come up the path. Across the lawn, onto the stone slabs where Eileen had stumbled, and to the patio where she had fallen.

"What's going on, Dad?" Lewis asked.

## Chapter 7

"I'm sorry, son. I am so, so sorry to have to tell you this," Grandad began. "Eileen—" Grandad, the kind of man who never said anything extra—still, Lewis interrupted halfway through.

"Where is she?" he asked. Lewis went straight back to his truck and drove into town. Straight to Eileen.

At the request of Grandad, the doctors on staff put Eileen in a room. They removed her clothing, bathed her, and dressed her in a hospital gown. Once at her side, Lewis knelt beside her. He found her pale hand under the sheet and placed it against his cheek, holding it there. Brushing her hair back, he kissed her forehead. She looked pretty, like nothing was wrong and she might wake up any minute.

"Mr. Bauer?" A young nurse called from the doorway. "Dr. Graham said to let him know when you got here. Do you want to talk to him?" She carried a plastic bag and handed it to Lewis. "Her things," she said. "And…we didn't get her jewelry. We thought you might want to do that."

Lewis looked inside the bag. One by one, he took out each piece, his white dress shirt, her shorts, her tank top, and laid them on a table in the room. Placing everything back into the bag except for the apron, he said, "Please throw all these away and get me another one for this. I appreciate it. And I don't need to talk to anybody, ma'am."

He turned back to Eileen and took the wedding band from her finger. Then he turned her head with one hand, cradled her face with the other, unfastened her diamond stud earrings, and placed the jewelry in his shirt pocket. Nothing left to do, he pulled a chair up next to the bed. Taking her cool hand again, hiding it between both of his, he sat watching her. He'd been wrong before. This was nothing like sleep. She was still. Too still. The body lying before him looked like Eileen, but it wasn't. Not anymore. Eileen was gone.

Lewis drove back to the ranch. After suppertime now, the white house was quiet, the porch light on. Inside the rock house, he filled one side of the kitchen sink with soapy water and soaked the apron. On the counter sat one and a half dewberry pies and a basket of biscuits. He got a fork from the drawer, took one bite, and then another. Unable to swallow, he spit the pie into the other half of the porcelain basin and left the utensil in the pan. Back to his task, he scrubbed the apron, rubbing the fabric together over and over until the water ran clear. He took it into the laundry room and placed it into the washer. He slid down against the machine and sat on the floor. His head in his hands, he listened to the churning and the spinning until it was done.

After the accident, Katie and Lewis moved into the big white house with her grandparents. She didn't go back into the rock house. But when the Raeses came, they moved in there, and a little at a time, she went back inside. First for holidays or special occasions, then later for a glass of water after playing outside in the heat, until eventually she slept in the big bunk room in the back when it was her turn to spend the night with Mariana. Over time, the old rock house full of good friends and a passel of children prevailed over the unbearable sound of emptiness inside.

## Chapter 8

*Beep! Beep!* Katie blew the horn, gravel crunching under her tires. Lewis stepped out with Gran. Leaving his mother on the porch, he quickened his step to get to Katie, but not before Jack met her first.

"Hey, Jack." Katie knelt and rubbed the black-and-white cow dog's ears. "I've been missing you."

When Katie went to college, she left the dog at the ranch. She had always planned on Jack living with her after graduation. But then she moved in with Tre, and an apartment in the city was no place for Jack.

"Hey! What're you doing here, kiddo?" her dad asked.

"I just felt like coming out today," she said, looking up at him before he embraced her in a big hug. She went to the back of her car and opened the trunk. She grabbed her ropers and handed her bag to Lewis. Wagging his tail, Jack followed them up.

"Are you staying the night?" he asked.

Katie shrugged.

On the porch she hugged Gran, then Grandad, who held the door for everybody. Katie set the boots down outside the door.

"Get on in here, doodlebug," Grandad said. In his eighties, he always looked the same to Katie. Buzz cut white hair and wearing his uniform—a starched button-up shirt, jeans, and cowboy boots. Still in great health, these days Grandad worked fewer hours a day, but as he said, that was because he wanted to.

"We're so glad to see you, dear," Gran said. "Are you hungry?"

"Not yet, Gran. I thought I'd go ride for a little while first. I'll go find *Abuelo* and see if he can get Concho for me."

Lewis exchanged looks with Gran and Grandad. "Sure, honey. I'll call out there and tell them you're headed over."

Katie nodded, kicked off her sandals, and changed into her boots. Lewis and his parents watched the silent girl walk away, Jack following alongside.

"Well. What do you think, Lewis?" Gran asked. "You didn't say much about the gala y'all were at last night."

"Things seemed a bit off," Lewis admitted.

"What things?" Gran wanted to know.

"I can't put my finger on it, but I can tell you this. There's no slack in that girl's rope. She'll get it worked out."

"I'm sure you're right. I'm telling Elise and Maria to come over. We'll be having a party tonight." Gran loved parties.

Concho in his halter, Tacho met Katie out at the horse barn. "*Chiquita*," he said, hugging her. He squeezed her hard, and Katie laughed.

Concho nodded, and blowing air from his nostrils, snorted. "Hello, Concho," Katie said, the animal nuzzling her. "Feel like a ride today?"

The big chestnut gelding snorted again. Patient, he waited while Tacho and Katie saddled him up.

"You be careful out there, *Mija*," Tacho said. "Don't go too fast."

"I will, and I won't," she said.

"Watch your girl, Jack," Tacho said. Concho already in a trot, he watched the three until they were out of sight.

Katie up in the saddle, Concho flew up the lane between the big oaks and back down the other side. A birthday present when she turned thirteen, Concho still worked. A cutting horse, they used him on the ranch to keep him sharp. "Let's go down to the river," Katie said. Concho agreed, walking the rest of the way to the water's rocky edge.

"Whoa," Katie said, patting his neck. She threw one leg over the horse and hopped down onto the ground. She removed her boots and stepped into the frigid water, Jack jumping around beside her. When she'd had enough, she went back to the riverbank and lay flat on her back in the grass under the sun. As she listened to Concho's munching and Jack's panting, her hand on the dog, they stayed still long enough until they both dried. Sitting up, she pulled him closer, almost into her lap. Pressing her face into the side of Jack's neck, she breathed him in.

Border collies are working dogs. High energy and intelligent, they require attention from their owners. Jack worked cattle with the men, and though happy doing his job and getting plenty of exercise, he still missed Katie too. Not in his nature to sit still for long, he did so now. Jack had a soul. Of that Katie was certain.

"All right. Enough lollygagging," she said aloud, laughing at her own verbiage. A little more than an hour back here, and she sounded like Gran. Back in the saddle, its leather creaking, she led Concho into the river. Head down, he took a long drink. They picked their way through the shallow parts, then up the riverbank, riding back toward the house. Weaving around live oaks, mesquite trees, and an occasional prickly pear, she walked Concho through the long grass. With no clouds, the sun was already tanning her legs. Back in the barn, she unsaddled him and put the tack away. Giving Concho a chance to cool—he wasn't too sweaty—she gave him a good brushing.

"Come on, Jack. It looks like Mari is here," Katie said.

A little German crossover was parked next to Katie's up at the white house, Mariana already settled in, the whole place was full of activity. Maria, Tacho, and the Raeses buzzed about. The workday over, the rest of the ranch hands arrived for the barbecue. Out on the lawn the men grilled fajitas on hand-welded pits with fireboxes and smokestacks. Inside the kitchen, in assembly-line fashion, the women created pans of enchiladas. Making enchiladas was an art; there was a right way to do it.

Starting with masa harina for the tortillas, they coated their hands with lard and mixed the dough by hand. Dividing it into small pieces, they made it into flat circles using a wooden rolling pin, then cooked them on a hot griddle. Adding cheese or spicy picadillo meat, they filled, rolled, and placed them in baking dishes. Before putting them into the oven, they ladled gravy on top. Meanwhile, the hands not on grilling duty set up enough tables and chairs for everybody, icing down beer in marine-grade coolers.

"Katie!" Mariana called, coming out to greet her. "Did you go riding in that?"

Katie looked down at her dress. "I guess I did." She laughed.

"I hope you're hungry. You should see all the food."

"I am," Katie said.

Lewis and Gran, standing shoulder to shoulder, watched Katie. Smiling, laughing, joking, hugging all over the place, she greeted everyone.

"She sure does look like her mama," Gran said.

"Mmmhmm." Lewis nodded in a drawn-out agreement.

"It's that boy, isn't it," Gran said.

"Might be," Lewis said.

"I never liked her dating a foreigner."

"Mother," Lewis said, "he's from Alabama."

Speaking to him as if he were seven, Gran said, "If he came from across the state line, then he is technically a foreigner."

Arm in arm with Mariana, Katie skipped up.

"Katie, what's Tre doing today?" Lewis asked.

"He had work stuff this morning," she said.

"You should ask him to come up for supper," Lewis said. "There's plenty of time before we eat."

"His parents are probably still here."

"Well, ask them too," Lewis said.

"I wasn't sure if we had enough plates," Katie said.

Mariana followed her into the house, the two giggling like conspirators.

"I knew it. It is about that boy. He must've done something," Gran said.

"Might have," Lewis said.

In the kitchen, Katie found Maria. Always short in stature, Maria now seemed tiny. Gray and white hair pulled tight into a bun, she jumped, both feet off the floor, when she saw Katie, and kissed her all over her face, Mariana next.

"*Mija, Mija, Mija,*" Maria said, back and forth between both girls.

"*Abuelita.*" Katie bent down, hugging her. "Can I try?"

Maria put a wooden spoon to Katie's mouth to savor the gravy and placed a cheese enchilada on a small plate. Katie cut through the tortilla, lifted the fork to her mouth, and tasted home with a hint of chili. "*Basta, basta.* You'll spoil your appetite," she said, shooing them out of the kitchen.

In a remodel years ago, Gran had moved a few walls, insisting on installing a wine cellar—or, rather, a wine room. The ground too rocky near the surface, nobody in this part of Texas had cellars. The size of a giant walk-in closet, the wine room had floor-to-ceiling mahogany racks for stacking and displaying. Here and there were lattice bins and boxes along the floor for extra storage, and there was a wooden wine table in the center of the room for picking, unpacking, or tasting. Gran organized the wine by region, so the girls started with local selections first.

"I don't want any beer tonight," Katie said.

"Me neither," Mariana said.

"Let's see. What looks good?" Katie asked, laying out the rest of the evening on the table by wine, bottle by bottle in the order they wanted to drink them.

"First, this one," Mariana said, choosing a tempranillo.

"Good choice. Then this. I love this Tuscan wine."

"Ok," the other girl agreed. "Two more?" She laughed.

"At least," Katie said, opening the first one.

Back on the lawn, they socialized, drank, and ate. Seated at a table with Tony and other hands, they caught up with each other. Comfortable and easy, their people, no matter the time spent apart, they always picked up right where they left off.

The sun long down, everyone dispersed, back to the bunkhouse or off to do a final chore. Katie and Mariana retired to the porch, settling in with a new bottle of wine between them. An eclectic mix of wicker and wood, Roberto and Lewis rearranged, pulling furniture closer together. Grandad off to bed, Maria and Tacho said good night. Elise and Gran brought out more wine and extra glasses.

"I'm so glad you girls came up," Elise said.

"Me too." Mariana yawned. "What time is it?"

Katie reached for her phone, realizing the last time she had looked at it. When she'd texted Tre, *I'll let you know. I'll text you.*

The wine in Katie's head, she flinched at a pang of nausea, reading his texts starting three hours ago. *Ok.* Then later, *I haven't heard from you. What am I supposed to do for dinner? I guess I'll go with my parents. Going to assume you aren't coming home.* Sent one at a time, the messages escalated. *Answer your phone. This is really embarrassing. I can't believe you're doing this to me. Answer the phone, Katie. We are going to have a serious talk when you get back here.*

*Great. I'd better deal with this.* Katie sighed, a small knot forming in her stomach as she noted six missed calls in addition to Tre's texting tantrum. Leaning over on the small sofa she shared with Mariana, giving her friend a look, she said, "I'll be back."

Katie went down the hall to her bedroom and closed the door behind her. In the middle of the room stood a white iron bed with a white duvet, flanked by windows with sheers dragging the floor. At the foot of the bed, an antique hope chest held extra linens and blankets. And on top, Katie's bag. She chose the Danish turquoise velvet chair with wooden tapered legs and an ottoman in the corner, dialed Tre, and waited in the dark for his answer.

"Hello."

"Hey," she said. "I saw you tried to call."

"Yes. I did. Glad you could get back to me."

Katie cleared her throat.

"Look. What's going on?" Tre asked, his voice dripping with contempt.

"Nothing is going on, Tre. You left the note that you were working, so I decided to come see Gran and Grandad," Katie said, picking a thread on a throw draped over the armchair. Picking and pulling and picking and pulling, then snapping it off, she rolled it into a little multicolored ball. "Please don't be mad. I'm sorry."

"Nice of you to discuss your plans before you left."

"I just thought—"

"You know, that's the problem with you, Katie. You thought. That's what you do. You think about you and no one else. You just left Mother in the apartment. What was she supposed to do?"

The wine making her head fuzzy, she took another gulp. Rolling her eyes, she left them positioned on the ceiling. *I'm thinking about having another glass of this wine.*

"I'm sorry, Tre. I didn't mean to make you angry." Her voice cracked. "And I didn't leave your mother. She said she wanted to have lunch with you."

"She said. She said. You. Have no interest in planning the wedding or dress shopping or doing all the things you are supposed to be doing," Tre blasted.

"Tre," she pleaded, "I told her I would go to Dallas—"

"Whatever, Katie. I expect you home tomorrow at a decent hour," Tre said, slurring a few words that made it sound like *"I espet you home tomorrow at a thison hour."* A definite emphasis on *thison*.

She looked down at her phone, silence on the other end of the line. *He hung up on me.* Hesitating, she thought about that one thing she planned to say to him about the Taylore, but this wasn't the time. She texted him back, *I love you. I'll be home in time to make a nice dinner.* Something for him to read when he woke up in the morning, it should soften Tre's mood.

Katie threw the colored thread ball out onto the carpet. Back down the hall toward the banter on the patio, she said aloud, "I'll make him a nice dinner. I'll make up with him, and everything will be better." Tipping her wine back, she drank the rest of the glass.

"Pour me another, please, Mari," she said, propping pillows and getting comfortable again. She invited Jack up beside her, and he laid his head in her lap. With grateful eyes, he licked her hand. Back in sync with the reminiscing on the porch, she said, "Remember how mad we made Grandad that time with the go-carts?"

"*Dios mio!*" Mariana said.

Roberto threw his head back in laughter.

"Mari and I were minding our own business. The boys chased us in our go-cart, out into the pasture."

"In the mud," Lewis said. "Making ruts and doing doughnuts. The boys couldn't resist going out there with you."

"I can still see their faces." Laughing so hard now, Katie could barely speak. "The boys sliding under that agarita! Yelling, 'Help us! Help!' Spinning the wheels in the mud, and only more stuck."

"Whose idea was it to get the tractor?" Roberto asked.

"Mateo's!" both girls said at the same time, almost sure it was his doing. The youngest and most mischievous brother was blamed for everything.

"We waited while the boys ran back to get it! Mateo was in his socks while Lucas dragged him. Grandad rode out there just as they were hooking it up with that huge tow chain."

"*Dios mio*," Mariana said again, wiping tears from her eyes. "Grandad says, 'What in the hell are you doing?'"

The group on the porch laughed even harder. Grandad, a solid Southern Baptist, never used profanity. When he said "hell," sheer terror set into the four of them.

"It was like we were playing freeze tag, all of us waiting for Grandad's next move. He got off his horse and walked over to the go-cart. It was deep in the mud and all up in that thorny bush," Katie said.

"Then he told Mateo and Lucas, 'Well, y'all get in there and get on the other side, and let's push this thing out,'" Mariana said, imitating Grandad. "They put it in neutral and pushed it right out." Mariana laughed.

"Grandad got back up on the horse and said, 'Now get on back to the house, and put that tractor up like you found it.' But I swear he was laughing when he turned around," Katie went on. "We were covered head to toe in mud. All of us. I meant to ask about the boys. How are they?"

"Oh, they're great. Studying hard," Roberto said.

"You know they got a house together out at College Station," Elise said.

"That's good," Katie said. "We all need to go and see them one weekend."

"Yes, we should," said Gran, shivering. "We're supposed to get a cold front tonight. I think I'm heading in."

It was long past their usual bedtime. Lewis and Roberto and Elise agreed.

"Should we open another bottle?" Mariana asked, she, Katie, and Jack the only ones left. "And then you can tell me what's going on."

Katie cut the foil and buried the corkscrew. "Oh no, it's crumbling." She poured it into a glass to smell and offered it to Marianna.

"The color doesn't look good." Marianna peered into the glass and took a tiny taste. "I think it's a little sour. You try."

Katie did the same and shook her head. "Definitely not good. Tastes like vinegar." She put the bottle to the side. "Let's go get one more."

Back into the dark house, Katie and Mariana tiptoed into the wine room. As they bumped into furniture, a dish on a small table clattered. "Shhhh!" Katie put a finger to her lips, and Mariana burst out giggling. Their mission complete, the girls made it back out onto the porch. Sipping an agreeable new glass, Katie sighed and told her friend all about the auction, about how Tre snatched up the painting.

"*Ladilla*. So annoying," Mariana said.

"Embarrassing too. I don't understand why he did it. I decided I'm going to tell my boss at the hotel that Tre bought it. I think it looks as if it is in poor taste, so I'm telling him before he finds out on his own."

## Chapter 8

"Why?" The attorney in Mariana kicked into thought. "It is not illegal."

"Not illegal, but it dances around a conflict of interest. My fiancé shouldn't profit from their donation. It's worth more than he paid. He kept saying it's an investment, but I'm going to tell him he can't sell it. At least not anytime soon."

Mariana nodded. "It makes me wonder why he did it. Katie? I wonder, is he hiding something from you?"

"Like what?" Katie asked.

"I don't know. Besides a narcissistic move, something about it screams desperation."

"He doesn't have that kind of money lying around to buy a painting for a quarter of a million dollars," Katie said. "Somehow, the part that bothers me most of all is this. Tre is not impulsive. He's always three steps ahead."

Mariana studied her friend. "I am serious. Take my advice. You need to pay closer attention and dig if you must. It cannot hurt to look."

"How do you mean?" Katie asked.

"His cell phone, his computer, his work. All of it," Mariana said.

"Look for what?" Katie asked.

"You said yourself, the painting was an impulsive buy. Does he need to turn that purchase around because he needs money? It seems more than a bit off."

"I agree with you. Also, his father was not happy about the purchase either," Katie said.

"What did he say?"

"Just negative comments. That Tre better find his own money to pay for it, because Mr. Haman didn't intend to."

"I'm telling you. You'd better keep an eye on him. Besides that, what else is going on? With the phone tonight?"

"He sent so many angry texts. He accused me of leaving his mother alone at the apartment, then indicated I should ask his permission before coming up here."

"Do you think his mother does not like you? Is she causing problems?"

"Oh, she likes me just fine. Mostly because she considers me an orphan. Orphans don't have family members that might interfere with the Hamans' plans. Ever."

"You, an orphan? That is the most ridiculous thing I have ever heard."

"She doesn't know, Mari. She assumes."

"I think I understand. Mrs. Haman thinks an orphan will give her all the holidays, family vacations, and so on without having to share with any in-laws?" Mariana asked.

"Exactly. But there's more. He wants me to quit after we get married."

"Quit what?"

"My job," Katie said.

"I don't even know what to say. You must be joking."

"I'm not."

"Katie, this is crazy. He cannot expect this!"

"I know," said Katie. "I offered to work part-time to appease him."

"Katie!" Marianna said. "Why would you do that?"

"Because. I suppose to make him happy."

"Make him happy or avoid conflict? Are you happy?"

"I guess I'm happy. I think I'm happy enough," Katie answered after a long pause, sitting up straighter. "But I don't know what I'm going to do."

"I know what we are going to do right now," said Mariana. "Drink the rest of this wine. This one is much better than the last."

"Great idea," Katie said.

"Just one boyfriend seems more trouble than many." Mariana laughed.

"You should know. And enough about me. Let's talk about you," Katie said.

In a dramatic gesture, Mariana tossed her dark wavy hair, spilling in cascades. "Nothing new to tell. No interesting new boys."

With Mariana's thin nose and aristocratic features, her mother had entered her in pageants all her young life. Not unusual in their culture, beauty was sought after, attained, and celebrated by contests. Katie, a Texas girl who wore boots and stomped around in pastures with cattle and horses, the opposite of a pageant queen, Mariana showed her by example how to adapt. Going out in public, no shorts unless you were at the beach. And no backpacks—only tourists used those. Never, ever put your purse on the floor. That was for women of questionable moral character. Mariana never went out unless manicured and impeccably made up. Tall and striking, with dark eyelashes shading black eyes, she attracted many options.

They finished the bottle and headed back to Katie's room. They'd spend the night at Gran's. "Mami will not expect me home," Mariana said.

Jack curled up on the floor beside the bed while Katie sank into the familiar cotton tick mattress and pulled the sheets up tight around her and the down comforter up over her head. Her voice muffled, she mused, "Mari, I hate it when wine goes bad."

"I do too, Katie. You are my sister. Whatever makes you happy, I will support you. I trust you to make good decisions," Mariana said. "I will let you know if I ever think your judgment is bad. And right now, with Tre. I need to tell you that I think some things need to change if you plan to move forward with him."

Under the covers, Katie found Mariana's hand and held on to it until they fell asleep. Sometime in the night, Gran came in and spread an extra quilt on top of the duvet.

The next day, just before noon, Katie and Mariana dragged themselves from bed.

"*Raton*," Mariana said. "Huge *raton*."

"Me too," said Katie. "Wine is the worst." Spending time in Venezuela around Venezolanos, Katie got the gist of Mariana's Spanish slang. Literally *raton* means rat, but when someone in Venezuela says they have a rat in their head, it means they have a nasty hangover.

"Maybe not worse than rum, but so bad," Mariana agreed.

"Girls! I hear you getting around in there. Grandad's still making breakfast if you want it." Gran bustled around in the kitchen, pouring orange juice and wiping the counter.

Both stumbled into the kitchen for much-needed coffee and Grandad's biscuit-and-gravy burritos. The caffeine clearing the girls' heads, the four gathered around the kitchen island. Grateful to her grandmother for putting a fun evening together last night, and content, Katie sipped the hot drink. Tre expected her home early, but she put that out of her mind for now.

"I need to be going back to the city soon. I have laundry and things to take care of before work tomorrow," Mariana said.

"Oh, me too," Katie said, her head pounding.

Just then, Lewis came hurrying into the kitchen. "Katie, come on out here for a minute."

She went outside with Lewis. Earlier that morning, he and Jack had gone out with Tacho and the boys to ride fences and move the cattle to the west pasture. New calves in the herd, there were a few nervous first-time heifers. One of them side-kicked Jack, catching the dog square behind the rib cage.

"I don't think it's too bad, but he's real tender. I think I ought to run him to see Doc. I already called to let him know I'm headed that way," Lewis said.

"I'm coming with you," Katie said, flying back into the house for shoes and her cell.

"Go, go," Mariana said. "Call me later."

## Chapter 9

Dr. Lawrence, a country vet, ran a clinic on the property where he lived. The one-man operation functional, the front of the building contained an examination room, a surgical suite in back, and a small office with a desk that doubled as a laboratory. He did not sell organic dog food or shampoos. He did not have a receptionist. He did not employ lab techs or any other kind of tech or have anyone do his accounting. If you had a sick animal, you called Dr. Lawrence. If he didn't answer, you dialed Mrs. Lawrence. The area rural, many of his clients large animals, he still attended to dogs, cats, and just about any menagerie imaginable. Dr. Lawrence's professional and personal life, an agglomerate of animals either acquired or adopted, his montage included cats, a handful of dogs, and even a black bear named Roxy who came to him as a cub after her mother was hit out on the county road. He also possessed alpacas, pet deer, ducks, chickens, geese, and an entire nursery of raccoons.

The origin of Katie's trivia game, each time Dr. Lawrence visited, he gave her the correct term for a new animal group. One day when she was eleven or twelve years old, he was out at the ranch. Taking him to the side, Katie asked him if he knew the term for a group of rattlesnakes. Placing both hands on her shoulders, he said, "A rhumba. A group of rattlesnakes is called a rhumba."

Just about everyone in the county had the code for Dr. Lawrence's place, so when they arrived, Lewis pressed in the digits, activating the gate. As it closed behind them, Roxy bounded toward the truck like a giant puppy. Not a puppy, but a real, live bear. The lane

## Chapter 9

on which they drove wound around groomed mesquite trees leading to the clinic, Roxy lumbering behind them.

Dr. Lawrence came out and met the truck, opening the back door where Katie sat with Jack. "Good to see you, Katie. What's going on here with Jack?" he asked, picking up the dog. He carried him inside and laid him on the exam table. One hand on Jack's head, petting the dog's ears and soothing him, he looked the dog over.

"Let's get some blood and an ultrasound and see what we can find out," Dr. Lawrence said. "Don't you worry, Katie. We're going to fix Jack up good as new."

Her throat tight, hard to swallow, Katie nodded, and she and Lewis waited while the doc went to work. After running tests, he gave Jack an injection and two pills. Opening the door they entered, he whistled and called, "Gracie! Come here, girl!" In seconds a soft, tan greyhound came running inside. Settling down right away, she sat, big black eyes looking up at Dr. Lawrence.

"Say hello to Gracie," he said. "Lewis, come over here and hold her. She's a good girl. Katie, you can stay over there with Jack."

Lewis knelt, one arm around the top of Gracie, the other around her chest. Dr. Lawrence found the dog's jugular and inserted a needle, and Gracie's blood flowed into a bag. In a few minutes, done with that, the doc took the bag over to Jack, inserted a cannula in his leg, started an IV, and administered the contents of the bag to Jack. Gentle and calm, he wrapped the dog's abdomen, behaving as if all of this was a normal, everyday occurrence.

"What's happening?" Katie asked, a few tears mixed with her words.

"Ol' Jack has a little tear in his liver," the doc said. "Yes. Our girl Gracie is what we call a universal donor. Jack's going to be just fine," he promised. "It'll take a little while to finish this." He pointed to the IV bag. "After that, we'll see how he's feeling."

Lethargic, Jack lay still on the table. Looking inside his mouth, Dr. Lawrence noted Jack's gums turning pinker. "I think he's already doing better."

Katie rubbed the greyhound's soft ears. "Thank you for taking care of Jack," she said. She was talking to Dr. Lawrence, but he didn't answer. He thought Katie was talking to Gracie. Gracie wagged her tail. Dr. Lawrence gave Gracie a pound of raw hamburger. She ate all of it, licking his hand after.

"I think you might should leave Jack here tonight, but you can stay if you'd like."

"I'll stay," Katie said.

Lewis figured as much. "And I'll pick you up tomorrow morning," he said.

The doc gave Jack something to help him sleep and settled the dog on some blankets on the floor near Katie. Sitting next to her on an orange midcentury waiting-room couch, the type of furniture expected in the offices of old-school family doctors, with a chrome frame and wooden arms, Dr. Lawrence mused.

"Dogs are something, aren't they? Pure hearted and loyal. You sure can count on them more than you can most people. Isn't that right?" He looked over at Katie, then back to Jack. "They never have a harsh word for you, and they'd follow you through fire if you needed 'em to. The only time they break your heart is when they die." Katie wiped her cheeks, and Dr. Lawrence patted her twice on one knee. "Now, don't you cry another drop. Jack here has plenty of good years left."

Coming up on evening, Dr. Lawrence went into the house and retrieved a plate prepared by Mrs. Lawrence. Checking on Jack one last time before bed, he carried Katie's supper in one hand, a piece of fried chicken, cooked vegetables from the garden, and a sliced and salted tomato. In his other arm he brought a pillow, blanket, and the phone charger she had asked for. The sun going down, she ate the tomato first. After, lying back, she listened to the night approach.

For a long time after Eileen was gone, Katie couldn't sleep. Waking in the night, she'd roam about the house, and in the morning, Gran would find her in various places. On the living room couch, curled up in a chair in the sunroom, or on cooler nights, the front patio. One morning, when Katie was seven or eight, Gran panicked—her granddaughter was not in her bed or in any of the usual places. Sometime in the night, Katie had traipsed out to Tacho and Maria's house. In a tiny spare room, Maria tucked the child into a twin bed laden with homemade quilts and climbed in beside her.

Petting her head, she said, "*Conejito*. What are you doing up so late?"

"I'm scared," Katie said.

"Of what?"

"The nighttime. The noises outside are scary," Katie said.

"There's nothing scary here," Maria said. "Listen to the animals on the ranch. The frogs, the bats, the birds. They're singing to you. Do you hear it?"

Listening, Katie said, "I think so."

Finding consonance with the night, Maria sang Spanish lullabies until Katie slept. "Duermete mi nino, duermete mi amor…"

Tonight, out on Doc's ranch, chirping frogs and Mexican free-tailed bats, articulation practiced for a perfect symphony, harmonized with duetting barred owls. Night-singing mockingbirds, the bachelors in particular, boasted scores from endless repertoires, resounding romantic melodies. High-pitched trilling Cassin sparrows called from down in the thickets while shy coyotes ran *scenderos*, punctuating their howls with a staccato *Yip! Yip! Yip!* Her bare foot just touching Jack, she felt the rise and fall of his breathing. Eyes closing, she startled. Her phone waking up, nocturnal composition was interrupted by text messages populating.

*Bing*, *bing*, and *bing*, they came in one by one. Considering whether to call or text, Katie chose the latter. Tired, she lacked energy for talking and composed a reply instead. *Tre. I'm sorry that I haven't called, and I'm sorry I couldn't come home as planned. Jack was hurt on the ranch today. I've been at the vet this afternoon, and I'm staying with him overnight while he recovers. Maybe we can meet for lunch tomorrow?* She tucked the phone under her pillow and fell asleep. Just before dawn, she awoke to Jack licking her face.

"Hey, Jack," she whispered. Squeezing her eyes closed and rubbing his neck, she sat up and called Lewis.

"How's he doing?" her dad asked.

"Better," she said. "He's up and about on his own."

"That's good news. I can head that way if you think Doc Lawrence will release him."

"The kitchen lights are on over there," Katie said. "I need to call work and tell them I won't be in today. After that I'll walk over and tell him Jack's awake."

Later that morning, Lewis picked up Katie and Jack and headed back to the ranch.

"Dad," she said, her tone resolute.

Lewis's eyes were on the road. "I'm listening," he said.

A perceptive child, Katie thought on things before talking about them. Gran said she got that from her grandad. Patient, Lewis never pried about friends, boys, or school. Not necessary—Kate told in her own time.

"I'm going back to town this afternoon. I might be back tonight."

*Chapter 9*

Katie touched her dad's arm, and Lewis turned his head. Holding his stare for a moment, he said, "Do what you need to do, Katie girl."

Pausing, her eyes fixed onto the rolling hills, it seemed she spotted something in the far distance. "I will," Katie said.

Gran alone in the house, settled on the sofa reading, Katie sat next to her grandmother. She leaned her head on her shoulder and sat like that for a little while.

# Chapter 10

After making a pallet on the floor in the laundry room for Jack, Gran promised to keep him still. Katie got her things together and headed back to San Antonio. Looking at her phone again, she reread Tre's text. *Yeah. I'm free around 1:30.* Katie pulled the rearview mirror down to look at herself. Dark circles under her eyes, her hair disheveled, she needed a shower. Taking the interstate, she exited on Travis. After a quick right on Main and then on to Houston, she pulled up in front of her building.

"Mr. Al. May I leave her here?" She motioned at the curb.

Waving her inside, he acquiesced.

"I won't be long," she promised, hurrying inside to make herself presentable for lunch with Tre. She texted him *Sorrento's*. A family-owned authentic trattoria in Alamo Heights, the Italian restaurant was one of her favorites.

After showering, Katie blew her hair dry with a brush and left it down and smooth. She chose a lightweight fall-colored print dress, a three-quarter-sleeved burnt-orange cardigan, and short camel booties; touched up her sheer lip gloss one last time; and hurried back downstairs. Glancing at herself in the reflective metal of the elevator doors, she fidgeted, hating her elevated pulse and the acid coming up in her throat. She took a breath and held it for a moment before exhaling. Checking the time, she changed her mind, deciding to park her car after all.

"Mr. Al," she called, "I'm sorry, but can you put the car away? I'm going to walk instead."

## Chapter 10

"Sure thing," he said.

"You look sporty behind the wheel," Katie said.

The old man winked and took her little car back into the garage.

With more than enough time to spare, she turned toward the St. Anthony. Not able to stand a thing left undone, she decided right then to sit down with her boss, hoping for a cure to stop the churning inside her stomach. The day bright and warmer than expected, Katie pushed up the sleeves on her sweater and pulled her sunglasses down. Waiting for the traffic light, she paused at the corner of the historic Travis Park Church. The front doors were wide open—lots of activity for a Monday, preparations for a wedding inside. Puffy clouds of hydrangeas framed an arbor around the altar, with ribbons and small bouquets garnishing the end of each dark wooden pew. Looking up at the spire, Katie thought about her promise to Harriet to dress shop. No doubt Harriet favored yards of beaded lace layering heavy satin. Katie imagined the fabric with Chantilly, stiff against her collarbone, neck, and the full length of her arms. A lawn wedding in a sundress suited her better, and the thought made her face flush. Hot and sweaty, she scratched at her shoulder. The walk sign on, she hurried across and up the steps of the hotel and into the lobby. A rush of cold air welcome from the outside heat, she waved at the concierge in passing. Behind the front desk and into a hallway, she knocked on her boss's half-open door.

"Mr. Morrison?" Katie widened the open door a little farther. A distinguished man dressed in an impeccable suit sat on the other side of an antique mahogany desk. "Do you have a few minutes?"

"Hello, Katie. Yes, come sit down." He stood and ushered her in. "How are you? You must tell me all about the gala."

"Actually, that's one of the reasons I came to see you," Katie said. Telling of the auction, she got to the part about Tre and the winning bid for the Taylore.

His hands folded, Mr. Morrison listened, watching her over the top of his reading glasses. "Two fifty is a fine amount for the painting."

"But…" she protested.

"It is not a conflict of interest unless you make it one, Katie. I appreciate your integrity. Now, what else do you have for me?"

Tension on her forehead relaxing, she exhaled. "I found something new last week," she said, relaying the details of the unknown painting. Animated, using her hands to talk, she described the color and lines. "The mood leaps off the board," she finished.

"Well, well," said Mr. Morrison. "Then you must go after it and see what you can find."

"I will, and I will keep you updated," she said.

As she exited the lobby, the bellboy opened the heavy glass door. With purpose, she set out for Tre's office. Just after noon, she'd surprise him rather than meet him at the restaurant.

The Tower Life Building housed office space for the San Antonio branch of the Haman Investment Company. If there was such a thing as an architectural hobbyist, then Mr. Haman was one. He appreciated the tower, built in the 1920s, its form of gothic revival elements combining traditional brick with clay and modern touches of metal and glass. As a boy, he dreamed of designing commercial skyscrapers. Sketching in the margins of his papers at school or on blank paper at home, he visualized the constructions in his imagination rising high in places he visited with his parents. His own father considering such creativity mere folly, Mr. Haman took finance as a route when he entered the University of Alabama.

At the first realtor showing, without hesitation, Mr. Haman signed a lease for an entire floor at the icon of the city's skyline, a thirty-one floor, wedding-cake-shaped building that provided a 360-degree view of the city. The permanent tenants, the gargoyles with whom he shared the space, the fantastical stone beasts protruding from the upper exterior, guarded the structure. Mouths open with overexaggerated fangs, their dragon-like features blurred lines between the sacred and the profane. The grotesques, with stone-carved contorted faces, lined the facade. Defying the laws of symmetry, trapped forever in purgatory, their frozen expressions warded off any evil from entering the tower.

The address of a historic building might attract certain clients, but the interior was just as, if not more, important than the exterior. Not requiring the whole floor for offices, they designed a large, minimalistic lobby with a sleek reception area and a substantial glassed-in conference room. The building octagonal, the floor inside had a circular feel. Private offices lined most of the circle's perimeter, and outside the door of each was a desk in a small area for advisor assistants, with more comfortable lounge settings for teamwork in the center of the space.

Katie waited in the alcove of elevators to go up to Tre's floor. She admired the art deco marble and brass, a complement to the modern space up higher. When she entered the office, the receptionist looked up and waved her back. She was conscious of her footfalls, her boots clicking on the tile and reverberating on the high industrial ceilings, then onto carpet where the bank of offices began. Margaret's chair sat empty at her desk.

Katie went to the door of Tre's office, which was ajar. Hearing voices, she paused before entering. *Is Tre talking on the phone?* No. Now she heard Margaret's voice. Opening the door a little more, clear sight line, both Tre and Margaret, on Tre's side of the desk. Head-to-head, they studied a file in her hands. Long, wavy, and covering her profile, Margaret's honey-colored hair cascaded in front of her shoulder, the ends just reaching the arm of Tre's suit.

"We can move this. And this," Tre said, pointing at the file. "It's fine. I did it last time. You do it now."

Shaking her head in the negative, Margaret's pretty hair moved like a wave, the natural light from the window picking up shiny red undertones.

Katie cleared her throat, announcing her arrival. Margaret jumped a little, standing up straight from her previous position, her seat half resting on the edge of the desk, one foot on the floor. The foot not resting on the floor shoeless, Margaret wiggled it back into her heel, wobbled, and then recovered.

"Hello, Katie. It's good to see you," Margaret said. She closed the folder, smoothed her skirt, and brushed by Katie.

"You too, Mags. How's Nelson?"

"Really good," Margaret said, her face relaxing. "Playing baseball and wearing me out." Now at the door, she held it with one hand, looking back at Tre. Margaret had worked at the San Antonio branch since its inception. Starting out as a receptionist, now licensed, she preferred her job as an advisor's assistant because travel was limited to none. On her own with her young son, it made life easier.

"Before closing, Mags," Tre said. "And send the clients a pair of Spurs tickets."

Biting the corner of her lip, Margaret retreated to her desk.

Something awkward in the space between them, Katie took a step toward Tre.

"Come over here," he said, coming around the desk. His arms open, he closed the expanse. Breathing in his cologne, Katie rested her head on his shoulder.

"I didn't expect you this early," Tre said. "Still want to go for lunch? I planned on it."

"Yes," Katie said. "I stopped by the hotel first and arrived early, so I came straight here." Studying his face, she looked for any signs of animosity. In their last exchange with the texts arranging to meet for lunch, Tre had seemed short, and she didn't know whether he was still angry about her staying over longer than intended at the ranch.

"We can take my car. And speaking of which, I have a surprise for you," he said, unwrapping her from his embrace and nudging her with his elbow, as if she were an old school buddy.

"What is it?" Katie looked up at him.

"You'll see, and you're going to love it! Let's go," he said.

Down the elevator and through the lobby, he hurried her toward the parking area. Pulling a key fob from his pocket, he pointed it in a direction across a few rows of cars. With an excited grin, he continued toward his assigned space. "C'mon, Katie!"

Trying to keep up, Katie quickened her step. "Where's your car?" she asked, looking around.

"Here! It's this one! This is the surprise! I traded my car in for this one! It's a Maserati Quattroporte!"

The new, black Italian car was indeed beautiful. Katie viewed their distorted reflections in the steel.

"Oh," Katie said. "It's nice."

"Go around to the other side and get in!"

No sooner had she slid into the seat, not getting the chance to buckle her seatbelt, before Tre was careening through the lot, tires squealing, the sound exponentially multiplying, bouncing off the concrete walls in the garage.

"You love it, right?" Accelerating into his turn, Tre avoided the freeway, speeding out onto Broadway. At a stop sign, he looked to his right. "Who is that?"

"Who?"

"Right there. In that car. In that new Bentley."

"I wouldn't have any idea, Tre."

"I would think we would." Tre's shoulders slumped. "Hmmm. It's nice. Very nice."

"I guess it is."

"Do you think it's nicer than this car?"

"Maybe. I wouldn't know."

"No. You wouldn't."

Weaving in and out of traffic, he tailgated and used turn lanes to pass. Tre ran through a red light, and Katie let out a small scream.

"You never lift, Katie. Never lift. Otherwise, you won't be first."

Broadway, a major surface street in San Antonio, connected neighborhoods and freeways and linked the downtown corridor to historic and cultural sites, museums, and parks. Referred to by locals as the Broadway Reach, the busy road provided an option to navigate the city.

"But we are on Broadway!" Katie said.

"You need to relax. No one was coming."

Once in Sorrento's lot, Katie sat for a moment, allowing her heart rate to return to normal. Tre already halfway to the door, he looked back at her. "Hurry up, Katie. I didn't call ahead for a table."

She caught up, and they entered together. The host, an Italian man, greeted them. "*Benvenuto!* My favorite couple," he said. "I have a special table just for you today!"

Katie and Tre slid into either side of a black leather booth.

"Enjoy your lunch; your server will be with you in just a moment," he said, lighting a candle on the table and handing them two menus.

Seated, Katie took a deep breath and exhaled. Looking at the menu, Tre began musing over the chicken or veal. Katie didn't need to look. She always ordered the same thing. Homemade meatballs and a Greek salad. "I'm going to go with the chicken," Tre said. He closed the menu and slapped his hand down on it. A bit loud, he attracted the attention of the people at the next table over.

"You can't go wrong with either. Everything is good here," Katie said.

The waiter came and took their orders, and Tre ordered a red table wine. It was Sangiovese-based, dry, light, and fruit forward. Katie sipped hers while Tre texted on his phone. Certain she tasted dark cherries, Katie was learning. She and Tre used to make day trips to hill country wineries, but not lately. "Is everything ok at work?" Katie asked. "Mags seemed distracted today."

Not looking up at her, Tre waved his hand. "I don't know what you mean. Mags is like she always is. Everything's fine. Just usual business," he said, taking a gulp of his wine.

"Tre. We should go out to Fredericksburg one weekend soon. I miss doing that," she said. Intent on his phone, his thumbs clicked the small keyboard. "So, Jack is doing much better." Watching Tre text, she waited for a response. After a minute she went on. "Gran has him confined for now."

"What did you say?" Tre asked, setting his phone on the table.

"I said Jack is doing better."

"You didn't bring him back with you, did you?" Tre's eyes widened.

"No, Tre. He's at the ranch with Gran."

"Oh, ok, good. It's all good then. Remember that time I let you bring him to the apartment. Big mistake." Tre reached across the table for her hand and gave it a squeeze. "I want you to know that I forgive you for not coming home Sunday." He laughed. "You know how much I like your homemade dinners."

Her hand felt clammy and sweated under his. Wanting to escape his grip, she stayed motionless. Afraid she might miss a critical nuance, she did not allow herself to blink.

"Do you like the new car?"

Katie nodded. "I do. It's nice." Lowering her voice, she continued. "Are you sure we can afford it?"

"I would think by now, Katie, that you would understand. We can't afford not to. Things need to look a certain way. People won't invest in a firm that doesn't look successful."

*Is appearing lavish good for business?* Katie almost asked, but instead, "But not over the top, Tre. Would you say a good balance is important?"

"We need to think about getting you a new car as well. You can't be driving that beat-up thing you have."

"It is a classic, Tre. It isn't beat up, and I love it."

"It's old. You need something new, and we only have two parking spaces. I think you'd look good driving one of those Bentleys," he said.

"I don't think—"

"Furthermore, we haven't finished that conversation about your job."

"Tre, are you sure everything is ok?"

"Stop asking me that. I have to deal with a lot. A lot, Katie. Running the office is hard, but I play the hand I'm dealt. We have a great life. I think you're smokin' hot. Everything is fine. Except that it's time, Katie—Oh, good. Our lunch is here."

The waiter set the plates down.

"Time?" she asked.

"Time for you to think about giving your notice," he said.

Katie felt the acid coming up in her throat again. Wine glass in her untrapped hand, she took another sip. "I'm in the middle of a big project right now." Not a lie; more like inaccurate information. She was at the beginning of a project that might be big.

"There is always going to be a project. And then another project." Tre cut his meat into quarters. In one bite, a quarter of his entree disappeared.

"I don't know how long the research might take on this one. I'll talk to Mr. Morrison about part-time, Tre."

Tre twirled *cacio e pepe* around and around on his fork and stabbed another quarter. "I think that's a wise decision. All right. Look. I need to get back to the office. I can't stay gone all afternoon; I have things to do. Big important things on my tray," he said. He scooped a huge portion of the piccata on a pasta spoon and shoved the rest of the entree into his mouth in two more bites. Taking a piece of bread, he sopped up the buttery sauce, leaving the plate as though it had just exited a dishwasher.

Katie looked at her meatballs getting cold. She hadn't even started. "I can get mine to go," she said.

Nodding, still chewing, Tre washed the last of his food down with his third glass of wine, stood, and threw his napkin onto his plate. "Either that, or you can finish, and we can go back separately."

"You go ahead. I'll get a ride back to the apartment."

He started to leave, then stopped. He took two steps back, bent down, and brushed her cheek with his lips. "Call the office. They'll send a car over. I'll see you at home tonight."

She motioned for the server and asked for a takeaway box. Then she paid the check, ordered a car, and washed down her hurt feelings and aggravation with the last of her wine.

## Chapter 11

The driver was waiting outside. In the car, she called her friend Jenny at the McNay Museum to check her availability. Not in the mood for chatting, Katie appreciated the stoic ride back to the Majestic. She hurried into the building, now on a mission, up into her apartment, and secured the painting. Al not at his post, she took her spare keys from a bowl on the big, round table in the middle of the foyer. She placed the painting in the passenger seat and pulled out of the garage. She made her way toward Broadway and retraced the way she had just come, north into Alamo Heights and onto the twenty-some-odd-acre shaded campus, an oasis in an urban space not far from the downtown area.

The McNay Museum, the core of which was once the rambling Spanish-Mediterranean revival home of Marion Koogler McNay, splayed out in front of her. Built in 1927 by Ayres and Ayres, the same renowned firm that designed the Tower Life Building, the stucco mansion's exterior featured arched portals and ornate wrought iron. An enormous central entry hall provided access to wings on either side. In the back, the structure framed a three-sided patio with twin staircases covered with terra cotta Saltillo and colorful hand-painted Talavera Mexican tile on the risers.

The late McNay, at some point referred to as the Gertrude Stein of San Antonio, a self-trained artist with an eye and a passion for art, left specific instructions in her will to establish an endowment for the first modern art museum in Texas. With the father-son team at the helm again, they uprooted chimneys, tore down walls, and installed lighting and cooling systems fit for fine art, transforming the mansion into a museum. The envied venue drew in locals and tourists, not only for art appreciation but as a backdrop for photography and special events. It also attracted talented professionals—some of the most renowned in their field.

Jenny, one such professional, a conservator with a degree in art history from the University of Hawaii at Manoa, she had agreed to a meeting with Katie this afternoon. Mr. Morrison had introduced Katie to Jenny soon after she started her job as curator at the St. Anthony. In Katie's experience, Jenny proved knowledgeable, straightforward, and honest.

At the passenger side of the car door, retrieving the painting, Katie bent at the waist, fending off a wave of nausea. There she paused, a vision of Jenny laughing, pointing at the painting, and stretching out and exaggerating the question, "Did you find this at a rummage sale?"

Recuperating, Katie took the painting and closed the car door. Extreme, yet for her, an effective coping mechanism. "Worst case scenario," she told herself.

At the receptionist desk, Katie asked for Jenny. The volunteer nodded, picked up a phone, and called to a back office hidden behind a reception desk and wall.

"She will meet you here in a few minutes," the volunteer said.

Holding the wrapped painting with both hands, Katie waited in the vast, cool lobby near a group of elementary schoolchildren, holding her breath until she spotted Jenny. Jenny wearing a light-blue silk organza dress that went all the way to the floor, Katie could not see her shoes. With a ruched bodice, a sheer flowing skirt, and hand-painted Nene birds hiding among white hibiscus with bright pink centers, she and the geese seemed to float just above the floor.

"Bonjour! Let's have a look, shall we?" Jenny spoke with a faux French accent.

"Oui, oui!" Katie said.

In her office, Jenny handed Katie a pair of white cotton inspection gloves, and together they removed the protective covering. Jenny laid the painting on a table. Her glasses fastened around her neck by a shimmery gold chain, she placed them on the bridge of her nose. Horn rimmed with rhinestones on the corners, the plastic frames matched her outfit.

Jenny took a handheld magnifying glass with a brass handle from a hidden pocket and looked over the surface of the art, pausing here and there and at the signature. She turned it over and spent a long time on the back, inspecting the stretcher and frame.

"I think that—" Katie started.

Spinning around, Jenny placed a forefinger to her lips. "Shhhh!" she barked. "I'm concentrating!"

"Sorry," Katie whispered.

Jenny placed the painting on an easel in the center of the room and surveyed it from every angle. All the while her arms were flowing, stepping like the prima in a Russian ballet. In tandem with her arms, her hands flowed organically, finishing a long line at the end of her limbs. Lifting her hem, exposing worn brown Jesus sandals, her feet in the fourth position, she spun around, now facing Katie.

"From where did this come?" she asked. Holding her position, she heard Katie's short explanation. "You have nothing," she stated, rather than asked, the French accent dissipating.

"I have nothing," Katie said, shoulders slumped.

"And you checked all the registries? Of course, you did," Jenny said, answering her own question. "Come, sit." She motioned toward two chairs in a corner. She pulled her chair out a few inches beyond the lamp table between them and placed her chin in her hands, elbows resting on her knees. "It's good."

"How good, do you think?" Katie dared.

"Good," Jenny said.

Excitement rising, Katie waited.

"I believe this to be the work of a midcentury artist. The board is Italian. See this? Zecchi. That is a well-known family-owned art supply store in Florence. The oldest one there, I believe. The artist is almost certainly American. The elements are all there, and they harmonize. The piece is unified and well executed. But you already knew that."

"I had a good idea," Katie said. "So?"

"So. We must find Mary Renata Costa," Jenny said. "Or evidence of sale of this piece going back further than the last owner. What do you say we start now? Did you bring a laptop?"

Katie shook her head.

"I will use my work computer, and you can use my personal laptop," Jenny said, pointing to her desk.

The two began searching the internet, with no luck on the exact configuration of the name. Some social media profiles of variations proved unlikely, due to location or age. They found nothing exact and no apparent artist by such a name. With access to various provenance indexes, Jenny searched online for the artist while Katie pored over hard-copy resources, the volumes lining bookshelves in Jenny's office.

"It's possible that Mary Renata Costa doesn't have the same name anymore. Maybe she's married. I have an account for a genealogy search engine. Let me sign in, and we can search birth and marriage records."

"That makes sense," Katie said. "Even if the method seems more like modern-day stalking than forensic archival research."

"Whatever it takes," Jenny said. "If Mary Renata painted this in the late fifties or early sixties, her birthdate would likely range anywhere from the late nineteenth century through the nineteen forties."

Scouring records, they found a handful of possible matches. Narrowing their results down, they discovered a Costa family in Ohio. Italian immigrants, they had brought one of five siblings with them from Europe, then the other four were born in the United States. Opening an Italian restaurant, Mr. Costa, a veteran of the Italian Army, made a home, a living, and raised a family in America. His three sons, Lorenzo, Vincenzo, and Carlo, followed in their father's military footsteps, all joining the US Army. The three boys served in World War II, then returned home to Ohio. Through draft cards, ship manifests, censuses, and newspaper archives, Jenny and Katie gleaned pieces of particulars.

Learning that Lorenzo joined the family restaurant business, that Vincenzo moved to Columbus to work for the Federal Bureau of Investigation until retirement, and that Carlo loved flying planes and beekeeping, deeper they went. The parents, Niccolo and Antonia, also had two daughters, the second-born child, Guila, and the youngest, Mary Renata. Could they have the correct Mary Renata? Was this girl, born on the cusp of the Second World War, the woman who had created the painting?

They found a local newspaper wedding announcement for Guila, listing Mary Renata as maid of honor. But other than that, they discovered little more. All the brothers' memorial services took place at St. Luke Catholic Church, with Guila and Mary Renata entered as survivors. Katie focused on each family member's individual file, entire lifetimes reduced to transactional recordings and condensed to single pages on a computer screen. A one-dimensional reflection, surely there was more left behind than yellowed vital

## Chapter 11

records and phrases on headstones. These histories, having no spaces to enter joyful, passionate, or heartbreaking anecdotes, piqued her curiosity.

Digressing, Katie thought of her mother, retrieving files in her memory to conjure flashes of her contagious laughter and long blond hair, messy and wavy, thrown back across her shoulders. Katie considered her own closeness with the Raeses. There were no stems on the trees to register best friends or favorite pets. Overwhelmed with the desire to preserve the love and loyalty of Mariana, Tacho, and Maria, Katie swallowed. Even Jack and Concho deserved as much. Though not part of her official genealogy, together they had shaped her.

Pressing on, Guila's married last name in hand, Katie shifted her thoughts back to the Costas. People-searching for Guila, they dead-ended with an address in Ohio and a disconnected landline.

"The church," Katie and Jenny stated in unison. Agreeing on the common denominator, they found the phone number.

Dialing the phone, Katie rang St. Luke's in a small town in Ohio. An elderly woman answered the phone and listened with patience.

"How interesting," she said. "Would you mind sending me a photo of the painting? I can give you my cell."

"Of course," Katie told her. "I can send a photo of the back as well."

"Oh my," the woman, who called herself Trudy, said when she received them. "This is beautiful artwork."

"Yes, it is," Katie agreed. "It is why I would like to make contact with Mary Renata."

"I've been here in the church office a long time," the woman said. "The Costas have always been parishioners here. As long as I can remember. I believe Guila is a professor in Columbus."

"Can you tell me about Mary Renata?"

Trudy paused. "Let me think. Yes, I believe Antonia had a younger daughter. I remember something about her. Let me take some notes down. I'll ask Father to access the sacramental records, and I'll call you back."

"I would appreciate that," Katie said. Hanging up the phone, she looked at Jenny.

"Are you hungry?" Jenny asked.

Thinking of her untouched meatballs from lunch, now sad and cold, she said, "Starving."

"Let's go down to Twin Sisters Cafe for a coffee and maybe a piece of cake. We'll take my car."

Jenny did not technically drive a car, but instead an old Dodge cargo van with the last row of seats removed. On the back window was a Save the Bees sticker and another one that said, "What if the Hokey Pokey really *is* all it is about?"

The drive was short. They could've walked. They discussed possibilities over lattes and homemade confections.

"What else is going on with you, Katie?"

"Nothing much. Just working."

"That's a lie. I'm talking about your personal life. No one has nothing going on in their personal life. And even if they do, nothing is something, because nothing means something would be wrong with you personally. I'm talking inner conflicts. Am I correct?"

Katie imagined a crystal ball in front of Jenny's folded hands. "I used my personal funds to purchase this painting, so the provenance matters to me professionally and personally."

Jenny squinted her eyes. "I will accept your response," she said. "For today, anyway."

Afterward, as they pulled back into the McNay, Trudy called back as promised. Katie put the phone on speaker, laying it on the dashboard of Jenny's van.

"I have some information for you," Trudy said.

Katie motioned to Jenny for something to write with. Jenny rummaged through a cavernous console and found a pen and a stray envelope.

"It seems Mary Renata was baptized in nineteen forty. Her first communion took place in nineteen forty-seven. And that bit of information I tried recalling about her earlier. She is married but did not marry here at St. Luke's. Her mother, Antonia, came to us to enter Mary Renata's marriage record because her daughter was abroad. She married in Florence, Italy, to Benjamin Dyer of New York in nineteen sixty-two at the Basilica di Santo Spirito."

## Chapter 12

Armed with a lead and new energy, Katie ran by the grocery store on her way home. Just before six, she chose a baked chicken, a few sides, and salad ingredients. Afterward, hurrying upstairs, she unwrapped the chicken, placed it into a baking dish, and did the same with the side dishes. It was almost time for Tre to arrive home. She shoved the packaging deep into the trash bin and went out onto her balcony to collect some fresh thyme and rosemary from her potted herb garden. She chopped those into small bits to garnish the chicken, spritzed the whole bird with olive oil, and placed it into the oven. In a few minutes, her kitchen smelled like a home-cooked meal. Then she finished the salad and threw the inedible vegetable parts on top of the packaging. All evidence of takeout hidden, she opened a Pinot Noir from Oregon and flopped onto the sofa. Going over her next step and the one after that, she planned until Tre opened the door.

"Something smells good in here," Tre said. Sliding across the edge of the carpet, he went straight to the bar and poured himself a scotch, neat. He swirled the contents of the glass and sipped the golden liquid.

"I opened a bottle of wine," Katie said.

"Nah. I'd rather have this," Tre looked at his reflection in the glass at the back of the bar. He turned slightly, his head elevated, and smoothed his hair, studying his profile. "I'm going to change clothes before dinner."

Carrying her glass, Katie went into the kitchen and removed the baking dish from the oven. Slicing the meat, she arranged two plates with green beans, red potatoes, and the salad. She brought it around to the dining room and placed Tre's at the head of the table on top of an intricate charger that protected the Queen Anne table, with hers to his right. Silverware in place, Tre emerged in casual pants and a T-shirt. He sat down and began eating.

"Is dinner ok?" she asked.

Chewing, he nodded. "It's good. You know I like coq au vin."

"I took my painting to the McNay today to have them look at it. I think I have a good lead." Katie cut her chicken. "It's so good, Tre. I just can't wait to find the artist. I'm already fantasizing about additional works by her."

Tre shrugged. "Listen. I need to set up some client appreciation events. Cocktails. Call my assistant and get the dates."

"Ok," Katie said. "I will."

After dinner, Katie cleaned up the dishes and retreated with Tre to the living room. She reached for his hand, which he exchanged for the remote control and flipped through sports channels. She offered the idea of a movie, but Tre declined, claiming that nothing good was on, and anyway, he was too tired to stay up.

"It's been a long day," he said.

They retired to their bedroom. Katie changed into a cami and got in beside Tre, still in his lounge pants. Moving closer toward him, she pressed herself against his back. He usually fell asleep before her, and though tired, she considered continuing the search where she had left off with Jenny. Closing her eyes, it felt like she'd left the ranch yesterday, or maybe the day before.

"Babe," Tre said, startling her. "Can you move over? You know I can't sleep with anyone touching me."

"Sorry," she whispered, scooting all the way back over onto her own pillow, wondering who else would be touching him while he slept. *Anyone*. Stretching one limb out toward him, she used her arm like a measuring stick for the space between them, reaching her fingertips out a quarter of an inch from his shoulder. Watching the steady rise and fall of his body, sure he was sleeping, she crept, one foot on the floor and then another. She padded around the end of the bed and reached for the antique faceted glass doorknob, careful not to let it squeak when she turned it to release it into its latch.

Back on the sofa, she opened her computer and began searching. *Mary Renata Dyer.* Nothing. *Mary Dyer.* Websites populated for a Quaker martyr; a woman hanged in Boston in the 1600s. "That's definitely not her," Katie mumbled to herself. *Benjamin Dyer*, she typed into the search bar. She discarded a few Benjamins, too old or too young, and then stopped.

*Dyer's. A chain of small specialty grocery stores featuring imported foods and fine wine. Dyer's is a family-owned business headquartered in New York, New York. Founded by Thomas Dyer in 1924. Owned and operated by Adam and Benjamin Dyer*, the internet said.

*If Thomas were alive, he would be ancient*, Katie thought. *Thomas Dyer, Dyer's Grocery store New York*, she typed, finding an obituary.

Thomas Alexander Dyer, 1901–1995
*Thomas Alexander Dyer opened his first grocery store in 1925 in New York City. Joining the Independent Grocers Alliance in 1926, he became a leading pioneer for self-service grocery stores. After the Depression, he opened more locations throughout the city. He and his wife Abigail, both avid art collectors and pillars of their community, were known for their kindness and generosity. A businessman with integrity, he will be most remembered for the love he gave his wife and sons, who were his life's greatest joys. Preceded in death by his wife by 17 days, he is survived by his sons, Adam Dyer and Benjamin*

*Dyer (Mary Renata Dyer), and one grandchild, Alexander Dyer, all of New York, New York. In lieu of flowers, the family requests donations to Xavier High School.*

Sitting up straighter on the sofa, Katie read the obituary two times over again. *Adam Dyer*, she researched. She logged in to Jenny's genealogy account and found what she thought to be the correct Dyer family. With not a lot of activity and most of the people on the Dyer tree listed as private, she could see Thomas and Abigail Dyer, with stems to two sons, Adam and Benjamin, with Adam the eldest, now in his eighties.

Closing out the genealogy site, she continued on the internet. She found a few references connecting Adam and Dyer's Grocery, but nothing solid on Benjamin or Mary Renata. While disappointed in the lack of information, the lack of apparent obituaries kept her searching. Looking for an address to Dyer's Grocery, she found three locations, all in Manhattan. She would call them tomorrow to see if she could find Adam.

Eyes flickering shut, she closed her computer and left it in the living room. Creeping back into the bedroom the same way she had left, she scooted herself under the comforter, her head resting at the base of her pillow.

The sun filtering in and around the buildings created geometry in Katie's room. Chiaroscuro at play, skewed triangles contrasting light and dark threw themselves across the carpet and bed, the rays creating a vertex that reached toward the master bath. Tre's phone on speaker while he brushed his teeth, Katie listened to the voices rising above the running faucet. A conference call, and she discerned at least two other men's angry voices. Tre turned the water off and waited for a pause in the shouting.

"Look. I can understand your concerns, but your portfolio's doing well across the board. Nothing wrong with everybody winning, right? Why don't we discuss it over drinks this week?"

When one of the voices on the other end mumbled an affirmation, Tre disconnected the call. "These guys," he said, continuing his morning routine.

Getting up, Katie thought about joining Tre in the shower. Standing in front of the vanity, she reconsidered and instead brushed her hair. When he stepped out, she turned toward him. "Is everything ok?"

"With what?" he asked.

"I heard yelling on your phone."

"No one was yelling. Animated, perhaps, but not yelling."

"Why?" Katie asked.

"It's nothing, Katie," he told her. "The typical business I have to deal with every day." Brushing past her, he went into his closet and chose a dark suit, white shirt, and tie.

"Ok. I can make you some breakfast."

"No, I don't have time. I'll grab something at the office," he said. With an additional look in the mirror, he ran his hand through his short hair, smoothing it down in the back. "You know, I think I have the hardest job in the world. I'll see you tonight."

Sighing, Katie watched him retreat through the mirror, refocusing on herself. "I have some phone calls to make," she told her reflection.

She gathered her laptop from the sofa and situated herself at the dining table with a pen and yellow legal pad. Starting with the first listing, a Dyer's Grocery near Greenwich village, she dialed.

"Dyer's," a voice answered.

"Hello. My name is Katie Bauer. I'm looking for Adam Dyer. Is he available?" she asked.

"Mr. Dyer? Ummm, hang on," the man said. Hearing clattering, Katie imagined him setting the phone down on a counter or desk. Muffled in the background, she heard the voice continue. "There's some lady looking for Mr. Dyer."

"Who is it?" asked someone from farther away.

"I have no idea," the original voice said, the other response unintelligible. Picking up the phone, they said, "May I ask why you're calling? I can leave him a message at the other store."

"That's ok," Katie said. "I can try back later." Hanging up, she called the second listed location on Hudson near Franklin. "Hello. My name is Katie Bauer. I'm an art curator at the St. Anthony Hotel down in San Antonio, Texas," she added this time, hoping the added explanation would give her more credibility. "I wonder if I might speak to Mr. Dyer."

A girl with a young-sounding voice said, "Mr. Dyer is usually at the other store. It might be better if you leave a message." The girl continued. "Mr. Dyer does not take any calls from solicitors."

"I'm sorry to have bothered you," Katie said. She hung up and dialed the last number. Repeating her introduction, she tried again.

"Mr. Dyer isn't here right now."

"Do you know what time he'll be in?" Katie asked, her heart pounding.

The person on the phone, less wary than the other two, chuckled. "I don't know. He comes in every day except Sundays, but no predictable time."

"Thank you," Katie said. A man in his eighties who came into his store each day on no set schedule. Unlikely he'd take her call, and even if he did, Katie felt embarrassed at herself for her haste. This may or may not be the correct relative of Mary Renata, and Adam

Dyer might be irritated enough at her boldness to refuse her call. Even worse, he could outright refuse to meet with her.

Tapping the pen, she thought about her grandfather and how he might respond in a similar situation. He wouldn't hand out information to a stranger, and there was even less of a chance he'd respond through email. A face-to-face meeting was the only way. She'd have to fly to New York and go to the store on Ludlow, painting in tow. Her only option, she searched and settled on a direct flight from Austin to La Guardia for that afternoon. A one-way, she'd get the return when she got the needed information.

Katie called the hotel and explained her plan to Mr. Morrison. She had plenty of time to pack and stop by Tre's office to tell him she was headed to New York. Next, she called Margaret, as Tre had requested.

"Hi, Mags. It's Katie," she said. "Tre said he had some client dates coming up and to get with you so I can put them on my calendar."

"Sure," Margaret said. "Let me see. The first one, I believe is a week or two from now. Here they are." Clicking through the calendar, she gave Katie exact dates.

"Thank you," Katie said. Then, "Mags, is everything going all right?" she asked.

After a long pause, Margaret responded. "What do you mean?"

"I mean in the office. Business." Katie rolled her eyes at her own use of Tre's words.

"Well. Um," Margaret stuttered, then recovering, she cleared her throat. "Everything is going well, Katie. Thank you for asking."

Margaret's formal tone strange, Katie held her own phone out, looking at it, then shook her head. They exchanged goodbyes, and Katie went into her closet to pack enough for several days. She chose items suitable for layering just in case the weather decided to cool, folded a lightweight black peacoat, tucked her computer inside, and zipped her bag. Changing into travel clothes, Katie slipped a baggy loose-knitted sweater over her head and taking the wrapped painting, she called for her car.

Bags in the boot, she headed to the Tower Life Building and pulled into the parking garage. Leaving the keys for the valet, she promised not to be long. Waving at Arturo, she pushed the elevator button and waited. Once up in Tre's office, she paused at the reception desk. On the phone, the girl covered the receiver and mouthed the words *go on back*. At her desk, Margaret flinched when she saw Katie.

"I didn't know you were coming by," Margaret said.

"I'm sorry I didn't mention. I'm leaving town. A kind of last-minute thing, and I need to tell Tre," Katie explained.

"He's busy today but between clients now." Margaret busied herself opening and closing her desk drawer and rearranging pens.

When she walked into his office, Tre looked up at her. Initial annoyance turned to surprise, and he said, "Katie, if you're here for lunch, I can't today."

"No, I came to tell you I'm flying to New York," she said, excited about her search for Mary Renata. "I'm on the way to the airport now." The look on Tre's face a combination of disbelief and disgust, she suddenly felt like a teenager in trouble. A teenager rationalizing something small, or ridiculous, to a much older, wiser adult. Her face flushed, she felt hot and fanned herself with one hand.

All expression dissipated, his face neutral, Tre asked, "When will you be back?"

"Just a few days. It shouldn't be more than three or four," she said and then added, "I got the dates from Mags like you asked me to. My trip won't conflict."

"Ok, Katie. I have to get ready for my next meeting."

Anxious and scrambling, she went around to his side of the desk. As she hugged him, Tre stood with his arms at his sides. Holding her position, Katie waited until he patted her on the shoulder with one hand. Two times, *tap, tap*. He cleared his throat, and Katie moved away.

"I was thinking maybe we could do a weekend away after I get back," she said.

Already shuffling pages, he picked up a pen.

"I'll text you when I get there?" Katie exited, turning around at the door.

Tre did not answer or look up from his paperwork.

# Chapter 13

Leaving San Antonio with plenty of time, Katie expected at least an hour and a half travel time to the airport. Better to plan for delays, she navigated I-35 to Austin-Bergstrom. In San Marcos, home to Texas State University, the traffic was heavy. Students heading to class or home zipped off and on the freeway. The rest of the drive presented no snags, and before she approached downtown Austin, Katie took the airport exit.

Too jittery to eat, she grabbed a bottle of water and waited for boarding. In the meantime, she picked a hotel below midtown, using her cell for the reservation. All three grocery locations in downtown Manhattan, it made logistic sense. With no checked baggage, the painting, and her carry-on, she asked the flight attendant at the front of the plane if they could be so kind as to store the painting up front.

"It's something special?" asked the woman.

"Yes," Katie said. "The reason for my trip today."

"It'll be safe in here," the flight attendant said, and Katie took her seat. Closing her eyes, she tried to sleep away the four-hour flight. Grateful for the lack of connections, she dozed here and there until the plane touched down.

On trips to the city, Katie liked flying into La Guardia. With an old New York feel, she expected Frank Sinatra to pass through baggage claim in a dark suit with a skinny tie, his fedora angled with attitude. Walking through the terminal, she recalled stories of her mother and how she hated crowds of strangers and the city. Eileen, a homebody, was content to stay on the ranch. But not Lewis. "You'd think we raised him on concrete," Gran said.

As she was growing up, Lewis brought Katie to New York City at least once a year. After the Raeses came, she brought Mariana and sometimes invited a few other friends along. The girls never tired of the MoMA, wandering neighborhoods from Chinatown to Soho, or the evolution of the meatpacking district. From hot dogs with extra mustard from a cart to Michelin star restaurants, up early each day, they never went to bed before midnight. To the top of the Empire State Building, making themselves dizzy on the spiral ramps in the Guggenheim, and drawing circles in Wollman Rink, the blades of their skates carving ice, they soaked in the city.

It is a fallacy to assume the size of a Texan's bank account by his clothing or the age of his pickup truck. Down to earth, and like most Texans not from Dallas, Lewis was frugal. Lewis's genome, spread across generations of ancestors, was steeped in pioneer's grit. The kind who dug wells by hand and protected their families from Comanches, his nucleotides would not allow for waste or ostentation. However, trips to the city were an exception, so whatever Katie and her friends wanted, Lewis made happen. *Let's paint the town and the front porch, girls,* Lewis said before each mini adventure. Out on the streets they'd go, a numbered rare occasion when Lewis traded cowboy boots for dress derbies. At Grand Central Station, arms out ushering Katie and her friends, keeping them all together, Lewis was in his element. Bright eyes reflecting the lights in Times Square, his face relaxed and happy, when Katie was old enough, she realized that Lewis liked bringing her because it didn't remind him of Eileen.

In the taxi, her bag in the back, Katie secured the painting across her lap. She chose to hold it rather than lay it down on the worn, sticky seat covers protecting the cab's worn vinyl upholstery.

She rolled down the passenger window just an inch. A faded green air freshener in a cookie-cutter shape of a Christmas tree dangled on the rearview mirror, its pine fragrance covering types of smells with origins best left unknown. The driver took her through Queens, across the East River, and finally dropped her off at the Gramercy Park Hotel.

The eighteen-story Renaissance Revival was a landmark with a colorful history. Katie appreciated its world-class revolving art collection. With each visit, guests never knew what to expect. From Andy Warhol's avant-garde pop to Jean-Michel Basquiat's frenetic energy to the American masters that comprised the bulk of the collection, visitors were still surprised when Charming Baker or Fernando Botero waited around corners in the lobby.

In her room, she placed the painting down on one bed and turned back the covers on the other. Using both hands, she opened the heavy drapes, peered out, and watched pedestrians hurry along the sidewalks framing the park, at the manicured front yard to the hotel, and at nearby brownstones and surrounding upscale apartments. An hour lost to the time change, Katie didn't think of dinner until seven. Too late to try finding Mr. Dyer tonight, she would do that tomorrow. Deciding against calling ahead, afraid Mr. Dyer would deny her visit, Katie was relieved she hadn't made an appointment for today.

She splashed cold water on her face, touched up her makeup, and went back downstairs to the concierge, who recommended either the hotel's restaurant or a Northern Italian restaurant around the corner. Feeling like a walk, Katie picked the latter. The night brisk and pleasant, the sweater she had worn on the plane was sufficient. She slipped onto the tree-lined street at the front of the hotel and made her way up to busy Park Avenue. At the corner, she paused at a tucked-in historic Episcopal church, admiring its stones and inset red doors. Up a block and around the next corner, she found herself at the restaurant. Shaded sconces lit the Venetian stucco exterior. Inside, the host showed Katie to a cherrywood banquette.

First, she ordered a small plate of melon wrapped in hand-cut prosciutto, the cold honeydew sweet, it balanced the dry ham. Next, she picked a crab cake adorning a mango salad and a glass of pinot grigio recommended by the server. She sipped the crisp wine and thought about green apples. Tilting the glass and swirling, she watched the light from above play in the liquid. Finishing the glass, she asked for another.

"It's special. Uplifting," the waiter said.

"It is very nice. Thank you," Katie said.

Realizing she'd never been to the city alone, she did not feel lonely. A couple in their thirties entered the restaurant. The man took his hand from the middle of the woman's back and pulled out her chair for her. Both seated, the woman reached up and touched the man's cheek. He took her hand and rested his on top of hers. Katie looked into the glass. She stared into the wine looking for her own reflection but found nothing. Once she was back in her room, she climbed into bed and waited for morning.

## Chapter 14

Having left the drapes open the night before on purpose, Katie woke when the sun came up. While errant leaves blew and scattered, she judged through the glass, and considered bending branches and fluttering in the treetops. Not wanting to arrive too early at the grocery, she took her time getting ready. Her waxed canvas tartan lined jacket over her arm, Katie was ready for the city, and went down into the hotel's restaurant and ordered a coffee to go. In the daylight, she paused at the park, a canvas bursting in every hue of gold, crimson, and pumpkin orange. Hundred-year-old elms, dawn redwoods, and honey locusts sheltered rows of boxwood hedges. Texas might have snapshots from seasons, though never with a distinct four—only two were represented. With long, hot summers and unpredictable winters, Katie didn't get this kind of horticulture at home.

After a short walk to the Twenty-Third Street subway station, she skipped down the steps. Watching her feet, she avoided the railing and held tight to the painting. Struggling to secure the painting under one arm, she reached for her debit card down inside her zipped bag. Even though the artwork was covered, she didn't like the idea of resting it on the floor.

A tap on her arm, and a man with his name on his shirt addressed her. "Can I help you with that, miss?" Lenny asked, offering to hold the painting.

"If you could put my card in the machine, I would appreciate it," Katie said. "I need a seven day."

"Sure thing," Lenny said. He completed the transaction and handed her back the two cards.

"Thank you for your help," Katie said.

Without turning around in acknowledgment, Lenny kept walking, one hand raised in the air. More good people in the world than not, still she trusted Lenny more with her debit card than the Mary Renata.

Swiping her MetroCard through the turnstile, she entered the station for the M line. Katie picked a seat on a blue plastic bench. The doors closing, smoky creosote and steel brake dust permeated the car. Later in the morning, commuters in suits read the newspaper. Women in business attire sported running shoes, their designer heels hidden away in leather totes hooked over their shoulders. A teenage boy leaning against a pole, a skateboard in one hand, stared at his phone while two grandmothers buttoned up in dark wool coats and scarves chatted across the way. The train bumping and rolling along, she watched for her stop. Standing, she waited as the train slowed, a shrill screech of metal on metal. The doors opened, and she stepped onto the bumpy yellow platform while others, rushing, jostled her shoulder. In front of her, Delancey Street was labeled on a wall, the letters fashioned out of smaller blue and white tiles, a uniform mosaic. Behind her now, the train continued its journey downtown, like a cadence tapped on a snare drum, the tempo going faster, allegro, as it rolled away.

As she came up out of the subway, the wind of the overcast day whipped at her back. The forecast incorrect, the city decided on its own weather. Watching the street signs and numbers for the address on Ludlow, she walked the remaining blocks. Passing delis and other businesses tucked away under apartments above them, adorned with fire escapes reminiscent of scenes in *West Side Story*, people around her set on focal points in the distance, intent on their destinations. A few more steps, and she looked into plate glass windows framed by glazed wooden frames.

*Grocers* was printed in block letters on a green awning over the entrance, and *Dyer* in the same font above the door. Katie paused. The painting under her right arm, she opened the door with her left, a shopkeeper's bell announcing her arrival. Careful not to bump the painting into the door frame or the woman exiting with groceries in a paper bag, she pushed the door open behind her again. *Dingding, dingding,* the bell rang again, attracting the attention of a young cashier wearing a green apron that matched the awning. She smiled at Katie.

"Welcome to Dyer's. Let us know if we can help you find something," the girl said.

Katie hesitated. Scanning behind her for a manager or someone more senior looking, she saw only shoppers, some looking into cases or roaming down aisles. With no appointment, all of a sudden, unsure and awkward, she approached the girl. "Do you know if Mr. Dyer is here today?"

"I think so," she said. "Let me call up and see." She turned her back to Katie and picked up a phone next to her register.

A man wearing a blue shirt and pleated khaki pants appeared. Too young to be Mr. Dyer, he addressed Katie. "Can I help you?" he asked.

Shifting the painting over to her left side, Katie extended her hand. "Hello. My name is Katie Bauer," she said, trying to keep her words from coming out at once in a jumble. "I am the art curator for the St. Anthony Hotel in San Antonio, Texas. I acquired this painting at an estate gallery that I would like to show Mr. Dyer. I'm here doing provenance research and believe it may have been painted by his sister-in-law, Mary Renata Dyer."

The man squinted. Expecting a complaint or maybe some sort of sales pitch, he looked away, comprehending. Looking past her for a moment, he put a forefinger to his temple, tapping twice. "His sister-in-law?" he finally asked, his eyes widening. "You mean Benjamin's wife?"

"Yes," Katie said, remaining as professional as her excitement allowed. "I believe that Benjamin's wife is the artist."

Looking her over, the man now curious, his demeanor told Katie he believed her credible. "If you could wait just a moment, I'll be right back." After a few minutes, the man returned. "Come upstairs with me. I will take you to Mr. Dyer."

Up a set of stairs on the far side of the store, Katie followed him to a mezzanine, a loft over the front of the establishment. A low wall on the front of the platform, the entire store visible from this level, she surveyed an impressive offering of cheese and meats and sauces surrounded by an array of produce in baskets. Most distinctive, however, were the aisles of floor-to-ceiling wine selections that went on and on.

The man in the khakis introduced her, redirecting her attention to a gentleman sitting in an oak chair with brass rolling wheels behind a simple wooden desk. "Sir," he said. "This is Katie Bauer. She is the curator for a hotel in Texas, did you say?" He looked at Katie, waiting for confirmation. "She is doing some research on this painting that she has here," he said, indicating the package in Katie's arms.

"Hello, Mr. Dyer. You have a lovely store," Katie said.

Mr. Dyer's chair squeaked when he leaned back in it. Looking over the top of his spectacles, he waited.

"Thank you for taking the time to see me." When Katie watched Mr. Dyer's expression change from neutral to a slight smirk, she handed him her card and continued. "I am doing provenance research to find the artist of this painting. I believe that it may have been painted by your sister-in-law, Mary Renata." Still studying her card, he didn't answer. "May I show it to you?" she asked.

Standing, he cleared a space on his desk. Tall and wearing an argyle vest over a white shirt, tie, and dark fine wool pants, he moved neat stacks of paper to a credenza behind him. The man in the khakis came forward and assisted with the task.

"I can take a look." Mr. Dyer waved his hand out over the cleared area.

"All right. This is perfect," Katie said. She took the painting from its cover, unwrapped it, and presented it to Mr. Dyer. The man touched the frame.

Pointing to the signature, she said, "I think this may be M. Costa."

His white, bushy eyebrows flitting on the top edge of his glasses, Mr. Dyer adjusted them.

She gave him time to look over the painting and then said, "There's an inscription on the back I'd also like you to see."

Mr. Dyer gave one nod, taking a step back—Katie's permission to turn the painting over. The man in the khakis inhaled one short breath.

"I can read the Latin, but not the other. I don't do French." His New York City English heavy, he pronounced the word *other* like *otha*.

"Me neither, sir, but it is a French quote that means *more than yesterday, but less than tomorrow*," Katie said.

Crossing his arms, he waited again. "Do you think this is your sister-in-law's work?"

"Arthur," Mr. Dyer asked the man in the khakis, "will you go down and bring us back a cupala cawfees? How do you take yours, miss?"

"Black is fine," Katie said, considering the offer a good sign.

As Arthur retreated, Mr. Dyer invited Katie to take a seat on the other side of his desk. Scooting a metal chair closer, Katie did.

Elbows on the desk, leaning forward, Mr. Dyer asked, "You want to sell?"

"Oh no, sir. No, no, *no*." Katie stressed the final *no*. "Mr. Dyer, sir, I believe that this work is important to the art world." She pointed at the painting. "And not just me. Other professionals in the field who have seen it think so too. I want to display it in my hotel back in Texas for people to see."

"Hmmm," Mr. Dyer said. "Tell me how, again, did you acquire this?"

Katie relayed the information Mr. Pickett had told her about the man who had brought it in from his aunt's estate with no idea how she acquired it.

"Texas," Mr. Dyer puzzled. "And how did you connect this to me?" he asked. Before Katie could answer, he went on. "No privacy with the internet these days."

"Yes sir," Katie said, looking down at her lap.

Back with the steaming cups, Arthur set them down and retreated to the floor of the store. Sighing, Mr. Dyer took a sip from his drink. "A long time ago, a long time ago. My sister-in-law Mary Renata painted."

Pinpricks on the back of her neck, Katie listened.

"But that was a long time ago," Mr. Dyer said.

"Do you know how I could get in touch with her?" The phrase *Mary Renata painted* made Katie's mind buzz.

"You see the gourmet selections and the wine we have here? My brother Benjamin—I guess you could say he's the curator for our stores. He lives abroad with his wife."

Mr. Dyer was guarded, with no more information to give. Crushed with disappointment, Katie's face fell. Seeing the girl's reaction, Mr. Dyer said, "I'll tell you what. My nephew, my brother's grandson, lives not far away from here when he's not traveling for work. Whenever he's in town, he comes to the city, and we have dinner. I have your card. The next time I see him, I will tell him about all of this."

Holding back emotion, Katie wrapped the painting up, thanking the man again. "Please share my contact information," she pleaded without meaning to.

"I said that I would," Mr. Dyer said. "And you said you aren't selling," he said, handing her his card. "If you change your mind, would you be so kind as to let me know first?"

"This painting will not leave my possession without letting you know first," Katie promised, and as they shook hands, an unwritten deal between the two of them was sealed.

Down the stairs and out the front door of the store, on the street Katie's eyes blurred. Back to the Delancey Street station, she rode the subway, getting off at Twenty-Third. She retraced her steps back to Gramercy Park. Phoning Mariana, the call connected before Katie was back in her room.

"Hey, girl. How's New York?" Mariana asked. "And how's the search going?"

Retelling the morning's events, Katie cried into the phone, now lying on the bed on top of the covers. "I'm never finding Mary Renata," she sobbed. "And don't laugh at me, Mari."

"Stop crying, and I'll stop laughing." Mariana laughed more. "Wait. Did you say that the grandson lives not far away?"

"Yes, but I don't know where. He said he comes into the city for dinner." Katie sniffed.

"This shouldn't be difficult. Where would the grandson of a grocery store mogul have a home near New York? Close enough to come into the city? I can do a property search, by county," Mariana said, typing away at her computer. "Nothing that looks right in Westchester."

Katie turned onto her side, closing her eyes, her phone on the pillow beside her, and she let Mariana do what she was doing.

"Nothing plausible in Queens, either. But I may have something in Suffolk. How does this sound, Katie? An address for Benjamin and Adam Dyer. It's in Montauk."

Katie opened her eyes. "A property belonging to the brothers?"

"I bet it's a family home. *Dios mio!* It's right on the ocean, an expensive piece of real estate. Go there! You can be there by this afternoon."

"That would be crazy, Mari. I don't even know if the grandson is there."

"No crazier than visiting the uncle. You're so close! It would be crazy not to go, because what if he is there?"

## Chapter 15

Katie decided Mari was right. What could going up there hurt? She had no return flight yet, so within an hour, the rental car was packed and Katie headed out of the city to Long Island, to the Hamptons. The skies clear, she settled in for the journey. Stop and go, once past Queens, farther out of the city, the traffic cleared for a while. The drive longer than expected, the time still sped along, side by side and single file with European convertibles and fishermen's trucks. With time to think, she replayed the conversation with Adam Dyer over and over again in her head. *He said she painted a long time ago. Does that mean she stopped?* Standoffish an understatement, she reasoned scenarios for his demeanor. She hadn't scheduled an appointment. Of course, he wouldn't be forthcoming with private family information. Her credentials could get her only so far, she was a stranger. Whether Mr. Dyer would share her information with Alex, and possibly even his brother, she couldn't know for sure. She had an address. Worst case, there was always the US mail.

The road narrowed to two lanes in most places the farther she drove, through eclectic communities lined with classic New England or colonial revival homes, farmhouses, and newer modern designs. Iconic churches with prominent steeples, and seafood shacks with colorful awnings and striped umbrellas filled in between the neighborhoods.

Passing East Hampton along the Montauk highway, the road forked, and she diverted to the Old Montauk Highway. Sitting up straighter, both hands on the steering wheel, she slowed the car. Before leaving the hotel in the city, Katie had pulled up the maps at the hotel's business center. The route and address branded in her mind, she looked for the stone driveway she'd memorized from the satellite view.

She rolled past a small wooden sign with the correct address number and pulled the car to the side of the road. Thick foliage obstructed a clear view of the property, and Katie reversed a few feet, then proceeded to the entrance. The wheels on the smooth stone of a narrow drive, wispy beach grasses brushing the side of the car, a 1900s cedar-shake shingle two-story house with dormers on its third level came into view. She parked and sat for a moment, studying the structure's weathered wood cladding and asymmetrical facades. With bright-white trim and an expansive covered porch, it was an East Coast cousin to Gran's house. The property was xeriscaped, with sage and the kind of succulent plants that grow along the sand.

Katie opened her car door. Getting out, she threw her cardigan onto the passenger seat. As she inhaled salt air, rhythmic waves coming in fell onto packed wet sand beyond the dunes. All quiet except for the breeze, she walked up a path that turned into flat stones framed by a manicured green lawn. She approached a set of steps leading up to the porch. A neat hedgerow below, the beds were filled with rock. Simple white columns sat atop pine boards, smooth and grayed. She knocked on the door. No answer, she knocked again.

With a degree of conspicuity, she leaned around to peer in through a big window. There was no movement inside, but she heard lawn equipment noises. Back down the steps, she followed the sound of the engine around the side of the house to a wide, sun-bleached walkway, fashioned out of the same gray boards, leading to a massive rectangular swimming pool.

A man with longish silvered hair wearing a boonie hat, fishing shirt, board shorts, and flip-flops was running a gas-powered leaf blower. He cut the motor. A big, bushy mustache matching his hair hid most of the lower part of his face. The sun warming Katie's shoulders, she moved her sunglasses to the top of her head, keeping windblown hair from her eyes. Waving as she walked over, he spoke first.

"Alex isn't here," he said, taking off his headphones.

"Excuse me?" Katie said.

"If you're lookin' for Alex, he's not here."

"Oh. Alex Dyer." *Alex must be Mr. Dyer's nephew.*

"Yeah. He's not here," he said, wanting to get back to his work.

"Do you know when he's going to be back?" Defying her brain's order to turn around and run back to the car, Katie glued her feet to the wooden walkway.

"Hard to say. Could be tomorrow, next week, or next month."

Looking at her watch, either checking the time or stalling, Katie asked, "Is there a nearby restaurant you recommend?"

"If you're planning on eating and coming back, he won't be home today."

"Oh, no, no. I've driven out from the city and realized I'm hungry."

"Sure," the man said, putting his headphones back into position. "Go up the road into town. You'll see some places along the beach. Get yourself a lobster roll or a piece of fish."

"That sounds great. Thank you."

Back to the car, Katie went the way she had entered, this time taking a right on the highway into Montauk. Choosing a beach restaurant, a combination seafood shack and diner with a hodgepodge of indoor seating and added-on decking, she seated herself in a red wooden folding chair, layers and layers of thick paint making the tabletop like a rubber mat. A waitress dropped off a menu, asking her right away what she wanted to order.

"I'll start with a sweet tea," Katie said, "and a cup of seafood bisque. What else is good?"

"Sweet tea? I know you're not from around here," the waitress said. "But what state are you from? Somewhere down south?"

"Not the south. Texas," Katie said.

"Texas? All the way up here after the season?" the waitress asked, chewing gum.

"I guess you could say I'm here on business," Katie said.

"I suggest this," she said, pointing to a lobster bowl with coleslaw on the menu. "And for that drink, I can bring you water or a soda."

"Then that's what I'll have, with a cup of the bisque. And water is fine," Katie said, handing the menu back.

The bisque was excellent; nothing had ever tasted as good as the lobster bowl. Warm, buttery, mixing with the coleslaw… it was maybe the best seafood Katie had ever tasted, she told the waitress.

Laughing, the waitress said, "We get that all the time. I'm Rhonda, by the way."

"I'm Katie. Nice to meet you," Katie said.

Late in the afternoon after lunch but before supper, Rhonda lingered. Untying her dirty blond colored hair, she pulled back stray pieces creating a new, cleaner bun. "What sort of business brings you all the way out to Montauk?"

"I'm here trying to find the artist for a painting I acquired," Katie said.

"That's funny," Rhonda said. "We have a lot of artists here."

Getting her meaning, Katie imagined summer people invading the Hamptons from the city, dragging canvases, easels, cases of oils and brushes, plein air artists dotting the beaches early in the season until they tired of it, exchanging their art for neighborhood book clubs.

"Not that kind of artist." Katie laughed. "This woman would be older. A trained artist. From a long time ago," she said, repeating Mr. Dyer's words.

Interested, Rhonda looked around. No tables to take care of now, she slid into a chair across from Katie. "I'm from Montauk, and I know everyone here. I can help. Who are you looking for?"

"Mary Renata Dyer," Katie said.

"The Dyers? Yes, the Dyers. What a nice family," Rhonda said. "Mr. and Mrs. Dyer, they've lived overseas for years. I don't even know the last time I've seen them, but Alex, Mrs. Dyer's grandson, we grew up together. In the summers. Same beach bonfires, all of us kids running around together. You know."

Listening to Rhonda, yesterday's frustrations melted. Instead of walls and hurdles, bits of information were emerging and finally getting her closer to Mary Renata.

"I mean, Alex and I are friends. When he's home from work, he comes in here all the time."

"So he travels a lot?" Katie asked.

Nodding, Rhonda switched the chewing gum to the other side. "Oh, for sure. He's a grape whisperer."

"A grape whisperer?" Katie asked.

"I guess I should say a grapevine whisperer. He goes around to vineyards all over the country, helping people grow wine grapes," Rhonda explained.

"Really?" Katie said. "That's different. And interesting."

"Alex is different, all right. Independent and what you'd call solitary. These days anyway."

"What do you mean?"

"During college and after, he had this girlfriend, Cici. Cecilia," Rhonda said, rolling her eyes both pinkies up in the air. "She's not a local. Her family is from Connecticut. You know the type."

"Not really," Katie said.

"Oh, you know. Country clubs, fancy schools, think they're better than New Yorkers. Cici was always here for the season." Then she lowered her voice. "But they rented."

Finishing her lunch, Katie pushed the dishes out of the way. Leaning in, elbow on the table, her chin in one hand, she listened.

"Not long after he was back from Cornell, the talk was that Alex and Cici were engaged. But not according to Alex."

"What do you mean?" Katie asked.

"I remember the day he came in. I told him congratulations. He had no idea what I was congratulating him for." Rhonda looked away, her eyes unfocused. Turning back to Katie after a long pause, she said, "But where was I? Oh right. The engagement."

Katie nodded. "Yes."

"So, what I was saying. Cici had all kinds of designs on Alex—or maybe, rather, she and her mother had them on Alex and the Dyer family. Both made habits of dropping his family name. You know. They own a fancy grocery store chain, and Cici ran around all the time talking about their art and their china. You know what I mean. An embarrassment for Mr. and Mrs. Dyer. Such nice people. And theeennnn"—Rhonda drew out the word for dramatics—"it all came to a head. Cici's mother planned a huge party. Had it planned all summer for the end of season, apparently. Invited everyone in Montauk. All the Dyers went." Rhonda drifted. "Was that the last time Mr. and Mrs. Dyer were in town? I'm not sure." Her attention back on Katie, she continued. "Anyway. Unbeknownst to Alex, it was supposed to be their engagement party. It was Cici's job to get him to propose at some point over the summer. In the meantime, she was measuring for curtains in that beach house. But he never did. In the end she hoped he'd propose at the party. It didn't work out that way either."

"Wow," said Katie.

"Exactly," Rhonda agreed. "And much later, when Alex finally came back…you won't believe this. He told me that without his knowledge, Cici and her mother spent the summer designing wedding invitations!"

"What do you mean 'when he finally came back?'" Katie asked.

"Sorry, I got ahead of myself," Rhonda apologized. "The night of Cici's big party, Alex arrived with the Dyers."

"Benjamin and Mary Renata?" Katie asked.

"Yes," Rhonda said. "The Dyers. As soon as they arrived, friends and neighbors started slapping Alex on the back congratulating him. He took Cici up to her room and asked her what was going on. She danced around the subject, but when he saw boxes of those invitations, complete with thank-you cards and return labels with Alexander and Cecilia Dyer printed on them, he was out."

"Out?" Katie asked.

"Yes. He left. Went straight down the stairs and out the front door. Without saying a word to anyone. He left and didn't come back for at least a year. No one knew where he'd gone."

"Not even the Dyers?" Katie asked.

Rhonda touched her on the shoulder. "Believe me, I asked the same thing the next time I saw him. I asked him, 'Alex, did you let your grandmother know where you were?' He did, though. He never would've left without letting his grandmother know. She kept his secret, however. Got on the plane to go back overseas without saying a word."

"So, Rhonda," Katie said.

"Yes?"

"You said overseas. Where do the Dyers live?"

"I'm not sure," Rhonda said. "Somewhere in Europe, I think."

"Do you know how I could get in touch with Alex?"

"Not really. Like I said before, I see Alex when he comes back here." Dinnertime, patrons were arriving at the restaurant. "Listen," Rhonda said, "it was nice talking to you, but I have to get back to work."

"Yes, nice meeting you." Calculating the time to get back to the city with the rental car, Katie asked, "I don't have a reservation for tonight. Do you recommend a place I could stay?"

"Sure," Rhonda said. "There are a few places on Emerson right on the beach. Can't beat the view."

"Thank you again for everything," Katie said, paying her bill. On Emerson Drive, she found low-key beachfront hotels, condos, and a bait and fishing tackle shop. The signs in front of them were classic, the kind you'd expect to see on an old highway before they built the interstate to route traffic away from population centers. Katie imagined looking at a black-and-white postcard, windblown sand piled up along the road, blurring the boundaries. She parked the car, took the painting and her roller bag from the trunk, and wheeled the bag into the office. At a small check-in counter, a tan boy with sun-streaked hair falling across one eye gave Katie a key. Following his directions, she found her room. The inside decor modern, bright, and cheerful, with a balcony overlooking the ocean, Katie opened a large set of sliding doors, letting the sound of the waves and the beach air in. Stepping outside, almost time for sunset, she kicked off her sandals and stepped into the sand.

A few beachgoers took advantage of the last bit of sunlight; a mother encouraged her little girl to gather her pail and shovel; a young couple walked along the edge of the water holding hands.

## Chapter 15

At the shoreline, Katie let the waves come just up to her ankles, hopped back, then shuffled forward as the water retreated. A tiny crab, its body translucent, skirted around, following the tide, and buried itself over and over in the wave wash. She backed up farther, safe from the spray; knees up, both arms wrapped around them, she sat, wondering what the sunset might offer this evening. Its fiery orb over her right shoulder, the real show was out front over the water. Pinks and oranges took over the blue in the sky, trading places, their hues deeper and more vibrant as evening took over the day.

Standing, Katie brushed sand from her legs, gathered her sandals, and went back to her room. Leaving the door ajar, she showered. Afterward, in just a towel, shivering from the drop in dusk temperatures, she pulled the door and secured the latch. She brushed her wet hair and sat on the bed, resting her head on the layers of propped-up pillows. Then she took out her computer, connected to the hotel Wi-Fi, and began a new search.

*Alex Dyer Montauk wine*, she typed, pulling up a substantial list of articles, some from several years back. *Cornell Top Viticulture and Enology Student, The Real Heroes of Winemaking—A Discussion with Viticulturist Alex Dyer, Meet the Expert, Alex Dyer.* Keeping tabs open to read the articles, she typed a new search, *viticulture.*

"Viticulture, the science and study of grapevine cultivation especially for the purpose of making wine," Katie read aloud. "While it has evolved with scientific and agricultural advances, it is an art that requires the appreciation of wine-making techniques." Processing, she continued. "So Alex, the grandson of Benjamin, curator of wines for the Dyer family business, and Mary Renata, artist, is a viticulturist."

Another search. She typed *Alex Dyer viticulturist.* More articles populated. *Up-and-Coming Wine Region Brings in the Big Guns—Alex Dyer, Alex Dyer—Transforming a Vineyard on the High Plains.* Looking at the dates, she saw the latter had been published two weeks prior. Closing her eyes, she put her hands down on the bed on either side. Shaking her head slowly, she picked up her phone to call Mari.

Mariana answered on half a ring, starting the conversation after she picked up without saying hello. "Where are you? Did you find the house? Did you find Mary Renata? When are you coming back? And what are you doing about Tre?"

"I'm at a quaint beach hotel in Montauk. You would love it. But listen. You just are not going to believe all of this," Katie said, and she retold the events of the day, ending with the story of Alex and the crazed nonfiancée. She added, "And I found information about Alex online. No social media that I can find. Articles about his profession. He's a viticulturist."

"A viti-what?" Mariana asked.

Laughing, Katie explained. "I wasn't so sure either. But among other articles about him, listen to the most recent publication, from just two weeks ago," Katie said, and she read the article to Mari.

"You are telling me the grandson of your artist is a vineyard consultant. An expert on growing grapes for wine. He is the best lead you have to the artist. You have traversed cross-country to New York City and are now at the most eastern tip of Long Island only to discover that Alex is on the High Plains of Texas."

"That's right."

Mari's laughter infectious, Katie joined in.

Regaining themselves, Katie added, "Maybe. If he's still there. Let me let you go. I need to book a flight for tomorrow. And then call Tre."

"*Buenos suerte*," Mari said. "Keep me informed."

"I will," Katie said. "Good night." She hung up and then searched flights departing the city the next day. Wanting to give herself plenty of time to drive back and return the rental car, she selected an evening departure. Once booked for ten East Coast time, she dialed Tre.

"Hello," he said.

"Hi."

"How's the city," Tre said, a statement rather than a question.

"Actually, I left there this morning. I'm in Montauk."

"Montauk. As in the Hamptons?" Tre said. "Well, isn't that nice."

"I'm not on vacation. I'm working, Tre."

"Yeah, work. You have no idea the kind of day I've had. The kind of week I've had and what I've been dealing with. I honestly think I have the hardest job in the world. And you're off in the Hamptons? I don't even know what you're thinking," Tre said. "Look. I've got big, important deals on my tray. I don't have time for this. I just need to know when you're coming back."

"I'm coming back when I told you I would. A few days," she said.

Tre grit his teeth. "What day?"

"I promise I will come home as soon as I finish running down my lead."

"Your lead? Listen, Katie. I have had it with you and your research. We already agreed that you were quitting your job, and here you are, in the Hamptons 'working,'" he said.

Hearing the ice cubes clinking inside of his glass, she sensed the call on speaker. She imagined Tre in the kitchen of their apartment in San Antonio, fists clenched at his sides, veins bulging at his temples, leaning over the phone on the countertop, hands free, yelling at her. She still hadn't brought up the subject of the Taylore and what Tre planned to do with it.

"Hello. Hello? Are you there, Tre?" Katie asked.

"Yes, I'm here. God O' mighty! I'm here!"

"I can't hear you," Katie said.

"Katie! I can hear you. I'm here!" he said.

"I don't know what happened. I must have lost you." Then *click*, Katie disconnected the call. Her heart racing, she looked at her phone. Recent calls displaying on her screen, Mariana number two on the list, shaking, she dialed her friend again.

"Hello?"

"Mari."

"What's wrong?" Mariana asked.

"I just hung up on Tre. He was screaming at me and drinking and angry, and I hung up on him."

"Good for you. It's about time you stopped putting up with that behavior from him," Mariana said.

"I didn't exactly. I pretended the connection was bad. Like I couldn't hear him. I did the 'hello, hello, are you there?' thing, and then I just hung up," Katie explained. "I'm a little sick to my stomach."

"You didn't really do that," Mariana said.

"I did. I really did," Katie said.

"Katie, this might be funny. But *manana*. He was angry because why? Don't answer that. He's always angry about something. Isn't that right? *Impredecible*."

A long silence on the line, then Katie answered, "Yes. And, unpredictable."

"What are you going to do? Tell me. This argument is about you resigning from your job?"

"Yes," Katie said again.

"Katie. Have you indicated to Tre you are quitting? Are you letting him assume you are? Because you want to avoid the conflict?"

"That's accurate," Katie said.

"You can't keep allowing him to think this if it isn't your plan. You have to decide and tell him. This artist you are seeking. Why are you doing this?"

"Because. Mary Renata's work is important. I have a piece of something that the world needs to see. And there's more. I know there's more. If there is, I want to find it." *Beep, Beep.* Tre's number flashed on her screen.

"What are you going to do, Katie? Are you going to forget about this important art you as a curator have discovered? Will you fly back to San Antonio tomorrow and let Tre hide you away in the penthouse except when he brings you out for special occasions?"

*Beep. Beep.*

The attorney in Mariana had forced her bold personality out, making Katie feel like the defendant in a cross examination. Exhausted from the day, impressed by Mariana's passion yet unoffended, Katie answered, "No. I'm not flying back to San Antonio tomorrow. But Mari…"

"But what?" frustrated, her friend interrupted.

"I just want to get along. I don't want to anger Tre further. I don't want conflict. I want us to be happy."

"I know that. But you have to tell him, Katie."

"I know. I will. But also, I'm not quitting. I'm not stopping until I find Mary Renata," Katie said.

"That is what I want to hear," Mariana said.

She placed her phone under the unused pillow in the empty space beside her, and as it buzzed away, Katie fell asleep. No alarm set, she woke up late the next morning. Bundled in the covers, she pulled them from around her face and peered outside. She had fallen asleep last night without thinking to close the heavy window coverings; still, no sun flooded into her room. A jogger ran by under the blustery sky, followed by a woman walking two identical black-and-tan dachshunds. Digging her phone out from under the disheveled bedding from the night, she found six missed calls from Tre. An hour earlier on central time, he might be on his way to the office. Clenching her teeth as he answered her call, she heard fumbling.

"Katie. Sorry, I dropped the phone."

"Good morning. I thought I might catch you before you got to work."

"Yes, you did. I just got coffee; I'm on the way there now."

"I wanted to let you know, I'm on the way to the airport. I have an evening flight. When I get back, I want us to sit down and talk about some things."

"Sure, sure. That's fine. I have to run. Pulling into the garage now."

"Goodbye. I love you," she said. The words squeezed fast onto the end of the sentence; he was already gone.

## Chapter 16

Relieved that last night's argument was forgotten, Katie didn't rush to rise. She brushed her hair, swept it back, and put on a pair of leggings and a heavy cable-knit sweater. On foot, out of the hotel parking lot, she went away from the beach and came upon an old-fashioned diner. Planning on just a coffee to go, she changed her mind. A counter ran along one side, with chrome barstools and dark-red covered vinyl seats. Katie couldn't resist. In the kitchen, bacon sputtered and sizzled on a large flat griddle, its smoky fragrance coiling upward and settling on the ceiling before dissipating. A man wearing all white flipped it with a spatula, perfect and crispy, and rang a bell as he plated.

She seated herself at the bar and ordered coffee, which came in a classic Victor porcelain mug free of any ornamentation. None needed; the coffee-flavored coffee inside tasted superb. To suit the ambience, Katie ordered bacon, eggs, and toast. The chilly day no deterrent to her mood this morning, the sounds in the diner were the low voices of people talking between bites over breakfast and the muffled clanking of dishes back in the kitchen. A brisk walk back to the hotel, and charged for the day, she sat back on the bed and opened her computer.

Enjoying herself before checkout time, she reviewed the other articles on the open tabs, rereading some and saving the rest into a file. Planning for after her flight landed back in Texas tonight, she reserved a hotel and a rental car and mapped the route to Mary Renata's grandson.

The drive back to LaGuardia was uneventful. Katie put picturesque towns, villages, and hamlets behind her, only their zip codes and histories differentiating them. Leaving Suffolk County, she passed into Nassau, the island here more populated than the one before it, and then into Queens. On the Long Island Expressway, the Manhattan skyline in view, she wouldn't go back into the city. Patient, she crept along a sea of vehicles and taxis, returned her rental car, and went to the departures counter.

"Where are you headed today?" the lady at the check-in counter asked.

"Lubbock," Katie replied, handing the woman her driver's license.

"Lubbock or leave it." The woman winked.

"That's what they say," Katie said.

"I've printed out your tickets. You have a short layover at DFW. Have a good flight."

"Thank you," Katie said, passing through security, then waited at her gate. At boarding, the agent scanned her tickets and pointed at her bag.

"Too big for the overhead bin on this plane," she said. "We'll check it through, and you can pick it up in Lubbock."

Katie removed her wallet from her bag, and the agent handed her a baggage claim ticket. Turning around, Katie slipped a thin elastic information tag onto the handle of her carry-on and left it behind. At the door, an attendant turned her around. Pointing to the painting, she said, "That won't fit above or under the seat."

"Would you mind placing it in the captain's closet?" Katie asked. "It's a valuable painting."

The woman, a tenured air hostess wearing a polyester uniform; opaque, skin-toned pantyhose that made a swish swish sound as the woman squeezed through the aisles to her undersized jump seat;

orthotic shoes; and hot-pink lipstick, shook her head. Defeated, Katie knew continued protest would be an exercise in futility. Not going all the way back to the counter, she approached the loader on the jet bridge instead, summoning her sweetest voice.

"Will you please put this somewhere safe and secure?" she asked. "It's a sentimental gift. From my grandmother."

"Will do," he said, taking the painting from her.

The disappearing canvas, combined with fuel fumes and stagnant air, convinced Katie to get to her seat. She thought she might vomit right there in front of God and everyone else on the jet bridge. Taking a deep breath, she didn't vomit, but sat down and buckled up instead. As a precaution, however, she searched through the back pocket of the seat in front of her for one of those little white biohazard bags. The unsympathetic flight attendant took up temporary residence near Katie's aisle seat, her hand resting on the empty luggage bins overhead. The woman's perfume overwhelming, Katie turned her head, staring out at the tarmac. When the plane took off, closing her eyes, imagining *Exordium* flying around during turbulence, bouncing over toppled bags and crates, its frame twisted like a bread tie, Katie decided to hold a grudge against the woman for at least the rest of the flight. Changing her mind, she decided instead to hold one forever.

When the flight touched down in Dallas, the pilot announced that everyone should remain seated as they waited for a gate. Severe thunderstorms showing on the radar, many flights were grounded. Focused on getting the painting back in her hands, Katie argued with herself about worrying, but gave in twenty minutes later.

"Still waiting for that gate, folks," the pilot said. "Looks like they're sending us over to another terminal."

"Perfect," Katie said, the delays cutting into her short layover. Deplaning, Katie tripped on the edge of the exit door. Waiting for her package on the jet bridge, she looked down at her right shoe, which was pulling apart between the insole and its bottom. Retrieving the painting, which appeared intact, she planned on taking a closer look at her gate. She checked the board; most flights flashing delayed, she took the Skylink back to concourse A. The gate crowded, flight not yet boarding, she sat on the carpeted floor and leaned against the wall to survey the package.

The outer fabric cover dingy on the corners, a dark streak on one side, nothing torn, she looked inside. All the wrapping intact, confident the painting was unscathed, she retied the duck cloth and rested it in her lap. A thirty-minute delay turned into over an hour, the time after ten p.m. This time, a kinder, less jaded version of the former flight attendant allowed the painting on board, stowing it in the front closet. When the plane touched down in Lubbock, Katie reviewed the next steps. Rental car, hotel, shower. The last flight in, she and the other passengers made their way to baggage claim in the sleepy terminal. Her right shoe flopping, she slid it along to keep her foot inside. One by one, the passengers collected their luggage until Katie was the only one left. She watched the metal belt go around in circles until she accepted the truth that her bag had not arrived. With the airline baggage office and rental car counters closed, she'd have to call tonight and return tomorrow for the rental car. She took a cab to a hotel in town and called the airline.

"You can stay on the line or leave a message. We can call you back when it's your turn in about seven hours," the recording said. She left a message and hurried to shower and sleep.

The next morning, she examined her stale clothes, worn for too many hours yesterday. The weather muggy and still raining, the sweater was too bulky and all wrong for the day's conditions. Her hotel was just a block from Texas Tech University. *There must be a store within walking distance.* She inquired at the front desk, which was manned by university interns. A clerk wrote down the names of two shops for Katie, one full of collegiate sports apparel and officially licensed everything, the other a small boutique featuring "game day" outfits.

Deciding against a college T-shirt paired with yesterday's leggings, she chose the boutique. A plethora of dresses, tops, and pants in university colors abounded.

"How can I help *ewe* today, darlin'?" A middle-aged woman wearing jeans and an embroidered top approached Katie. Platinum hair just long enough to tuck behind her ears revealed gemstone-inspired stamped fashion jewelry with other matching accessories, necklace, bracelets, and rings.

"I hope so," Katie said. "The airline lost my bag."

"Oh, good heavens. Don't you worry. We're gonna fix you right up," the saleslady said. "Are you alumni, honey?"

"No, I'm not. I'm just here on business."

"Most of our apparel is game day and spirit wear. But that doesn't mean you can't wear red or black any ol' time."

"Something neutral would work best," Katie said.

"We can figure this all out right quick. How about you go on into the dressing room, and I'll bring you a few things to try."

The woman brought Katie several items from the racks: a jumpsuit, a few pairs of jeans, and two dresses. All some form of denim, each piece denim trimmed, denim enhanced with rhinestones, or fringed denim. Among them was a pair of jeggings, stretch jean leggings. Katie refused to even try those on.

"Cain't get more neutral than denim," the woman said, giving her time to try the outfits. "How'd those work out?"

From the other side of the dressing room door, Katie said, "I think one of the dresses might work."

"How's the size in those jeans, dear?"

"They fit, but they have a little too much bling for me."

"Honey, I don't think you can ever have too much bling but suit yourself."

Katie stepped out of the dressing room in a denim shirt dress with pearlized snaps all the way down the front, the least obtrusive item in the pile.

"Don't you look cute as all git out!" the woman said. "You gotta try one of these wide belts to go with it. We just got these in. All the red ones are gone, but we still have black and brown. The rhinestones on the buckle make those snaps stand out!"

"I think I'll skip the belt today, but I'd like to get a pair of shoes to go with this. Maybe a pair of sandals?"

The woman hurried away and brought back three large boot boxes in her requested size.

"We have a limited stock from the summer, but it's fall, and that means boot season. Any of these will look just precious with that dress," she said.

Leaving the store wearing her new outfit, denim dress, and plain black cowboy boots, Katie surveyed her reflection in the boutique window. She looked like an online advertisement for a cowgirl costume, minus a buckskin trimmed vest. Her airplane clothes and half-broken shoes in an oversized boutique tote, the rain coming again, she ran the rest of the way back to the hotel with the plastic shopping bag over her head.

## Chapter 17

Katie took a taxi back to the airport. Her original car reservation canceled due to her late arrival, they found another vehicle for her out in the rental car lot.

"You're sure you have nothing midsize?" Katie asked.

"Nope. All we got is this here subcompact foreign job," the man from the rental car place said.

"At least it's a nice color," Katie said. "Lime green."

The man chuckled. "Well, you won't be sneakin' up on anybody, that's for sure." The agent handed her the keys. A wad of tobacco in between his gum and lip, he rearranged it with his tongue, then spit a stringy wet strand of the stuff out on the ground. The rain sprinkling around them turned into heavier drops, a crack of lightning flashed, and thunder boomed in the distance.

"That's too close for me." The tobacco chewer whistled. "I got to get back inside anyway. Y'all be careful out there," he said. "There's more weather movin' in."

The rain pelted the windshield of the tiny car. Katie could reach the passenger side window, her palm flat, without extending her arm. She started the engine and found the lights and windshield wiper controls before placing the car into gear. Water building in the parking lot, the car low to the ground, the water splashed up on the bottoms of the doors. Leaving the airport, Katie navigated south, toward Terry County. Even with the weather conditions, she should arrive at the vineyard in under an hour.

Lubbock behind her, the road less populated, Katie rolled across the Llano Estacado. The high-mesa, flat, featureless grasslands stretched as far as she could see. Miles between properties, an occasional farmhouse was surrounded by nonindigenous trees planted for breaks from never-ending winds that howled across the plains. She slowed the car as the weather worsened, the rain turning torrential. Katie turned the wiper blades to the highest speed. Water rushing across the highway, pooling in places on the roadside, eyes straining, she focused on taillights in the distance ahead of her. Turning onto a farm-to-market road, no vehicles in sight, she considered pulling over. The shoulder too narrow, Katie decided against it. Only ten or twelve miles to go, she slowed the car to twenty miles per hour. Her view through the front and side windshield a wash of white and gray, the road ahead of her invisible, she inched along.

All at once, every light on the dash of the little car lit up. The wipers frozen, made slash marks suspended on the glass, and the car slowed on its own. Pressing the accelerator, nothing happened. The road was straight and flat, but with the steering wheel and brakes locked, Katie had no control of the vehicle. When the tires stopped rolling, the display still bright as the Fort Worth skyline, she struggled, turning the locked ignition to the off position. *Ding, ding, ding, ding, ding.* Wriggling as hard as she could, she shut the engine down. Electronics dark, the chiming stopped, and Katie took a deep breath. Holding her mouth as right as she could, she turned the key to the on position. *Click, click.* Nothing happened except for a lone, glowing lightning bolt icon. Lime green, the warning light matched its paint job. Spurts of heavy rain coming in waves, the engine refused cooperation.

Katie squeezed the steering wheel. On the left-hand side of the road, running parallel to a fence, she made out rows of grapevines in the blurry, distorted landscape. Wishing the rain to stop ineffective, she had a decision to make. Out here, in the literal middle of nowhere, someone might not drive by for hours. She could call the rental car company, but closer to her destination than the airport, that seemed futile. With one last look at the painting on the passenger side, then another out the driver's side window through the storm, Katie took the keys and got out of the car. She crossed the asphalt, and just off the left-hand shoulder, she slopped down the road, bootheels deep in mushy grass and red mud.

Coming from behind her, an older-model Ford pickup approached. Head down, her arms swinging by her side, she kept going. The truck slowing, she moved off the pavement into the grass. A man in a felt cowboy hat pulled next to her. Window down, he yelled out over the storm. "Hello, ma'am! Are you the one who left that roller skate back there on the side of the road?"

Katie turned toward him, one hand shielding her eyes from the rain. "Yes. My rental car broke down," she said.

"Where you headed?" he asked, his words drawn out slow and careful, as if they were two neighbors chatting over a backyard gate.

"To this vineyard. This vineyard right here," Katie pointed, her forefinger emphasizing each word.

"You don't say? My name is Webb. This here is my vineyard. Get in. I'll give you a ride the rest of the way."

Not a time to consider taking rides from strangers, Katie ran around the front of the Ford and got in. The man grabbed a Mexican saddle blanket from the back seat and handed it to Katie.

"Get this around yourself," he said. "You're drenched to the bone."

"Thank you," Katie said, teeth chattering.

Before moving the truck, the man asked, "What're you doing out here coming to my farm in the middle of a thunderstorm?"

"It's a long story. Such a long story." Katie leaned back on the headrest.

"Well. We got time for the *Reader's Digest* version."

"My name is Katie Bauer. I'm looking for Alex Dyer. I read in an article you'd hired him as a viticulturist for your vineyard."

"I sure did." Mr. Webb put the truck back into drive. "Is there some kind of trouble?"

"No, no trouble," Katie said. "I found a piece of art that I believe his grandmother painted. I'm trying to verify it."

"Being that it looks to me you're charging hell with a bucket of ice water, it must be something important."

"It is," Katie said. "And it's back there in that roller skate I left on the side of the road."

"I can take you to Alex. He's set up on my place. But I reckon we should get that important item out of the rental first."

She nodded her head, and he put the truck in reverse straight back about half a mile. Using a tarp for an umbrella, Mr. Webb held it over her head while Katie got back into the broken-down car on the driver's side and dumped her clothes out of the big plastic bag. She wrapped the painting in another layer, and they hurried back to the truck. Through an open gate, the man turned down a long gravel road. Vineyards on both sides, Katie looked forward. A long, low brick ranch on the right, he rolled toward an Airstream trailer tucked in beside a barn on the left side of the house and parked the truck in front of an awning extended out over a square of green artificial turf.

"Hop on out." Mr. Webb handed her the painting. "This is where Alex is."

The colorful sarape still around her shoulders, a disheveled caricature of a rodeo queen, Katie got out of the truck and under the awning. Holding the wrapped painting, she stood steps behind the man while he knocked at the door. A rain jacket lay over the back of a chair, and a muddy pair of work boots rested at the bottom of a small set of steps.

"Alex!" he called. "There's someone here to see you."

The door opened from inside, and a yellow Labrador retriever poked her nose out, wrinkling and sniffing.

"Hello, Daisy." Mr. Webb adjusted his cowboy hat and scratched the dog under her chin.

"Please tell them I'm not doing any more interviews, Mr. Webb," a man said from inside the trailer.

"She ain't a journalist," Mr. Webb said. "She says it's about your grandmother."

Footsteps across the floor, the door opened. Taking a step back, Daisy sat. Interested in the situation unfolding, her ears perked up. Just out of the shower, in a pair of shorts and a polo, Alex appeared, a wet mop of dark hair still dripping.

"This here is Katie," Mr. Webb said into the trailer.

Katie took two steps to the door of the Airstream to finish introductions. Alex surveyed her for a moment, disappeared, and returned with a towel.

"Can I help you?" he asked, extending the towel.

Holding the painting in both arms, frozen, she had no hands to accept his offer.

"Let me get this for you," Mr. Webb said, taking the painting.

"All right," Katie said. "Thank you."

While Mr. Webb secured her cargo, Katie toweled off the plastic.

"Can you turn it around now?" Katie motioned with the towel. Mr. Webb did, and Katie dried the other side.

"That was for you, but…" Alex said.

Katie finished the task near the top of the bag, ensuring no water leaked inside.

Clearing his throat, Alex repeated, "Can I help you?"

"I'm Katie Bauer, art curator at the St. Anthony Hotel in San Antonio. I have a painting that I believe to be a work of Mary Renata Dyer."

Crossing his arms, he stared at her. The rain still poured, gusts of wind forcing intermittent sprays of water under the awning.

"Take this and put it inside, Alex." Mr. Webb handed the painting over. "I'll let you two figure this out. I'm going back up to the house to hunker down, looks like for the rest of the afternoon," he said.

"Come inside," Alex said.

"I should take these off." Balancing, Katie tugged, pulling off the one boot, then the next. She peeled off her socks and laid them over the top of her wet, mud-covered red boots. She removed the damp blanket from her shoulders, folded it into quarters, and laid it on the back of a chair next to the rain jacket.

Stepping up into the RV, Daisy swished her tail across the floor.

"Hello, there."

Standing, her front end going the opposite direction of the back end, the dog wagged her whole body. Katie knelt to eye level with the Lab. She rubbed the dog's soft muzzle with one finger.

"Don't get too excited, Daisy," Alex said. "Have a seat," he told Katie, directing her to a sofa bench along one wall. "I was about to make a cup of coffee. Would you like one?"

"Yes, thank you," Katie said.

Alex poured water into the carafe of a French press and heated it in a microwave. Beans into a burr grinder, he used a teaspoon, adding the ground coffee into the vessel, and stirred. Giving it time to steep,

## Chapter 17

he tapped the spoon on the side of the glass and transferred it to the sink to rinse. Katie used the towel to dry her hair.

"My rental car broke down on the way here. Mr. Webb found me out on the road." She tried redeeming herself. "I was on the way here to find you."

Alex pushed the plunger and poured the beverage into two unmatched cups. He handed one to Katie and took a seat across from her in a booth at a table that now held the Mary Renata. At her feet, Daisy stared up at her. Each time they made eye contact, Daisy swished her tail, then laid her nose on the sofa alongside Katie's leg.

"Daisy," Alex warned.

"She's not bothering me."

His composure intimidating, Katie sipped her coffee.

With no mercy, the rain pelted down, plinking and clicking on the roof and the sides of the structure.

"I've only been through a few of these." Alex looked up at the ceiling.

"They're something, aren't they?" Katie agreed, then, "Thank you for the coffee. I hope I haven't imposed on you. Well. I'm sorry that I have imposed on you."

He was intrigued, more amused than annoyed. "My only plans this afternoon include listening to the storm and breathing in the petrichor," Alex said, brushing back his hair with one hand. His legs crossed, mannerisms and vocabulary of a businessman, rough calluses and dark crevices in the creases of his skin, his hands strong like Tacho and Grandad's, distracted Katie from what she wanted to say.

"You said you came here to find me?" Alex said.

"Yes. Well, no. Not exactly. I've been looking for Mary Renata Dyer. You are her grandson?"

"I am," Alex said.

"Good. I'm so glad," Katie said. "Because this would all be even stranger if you weren't."

"I agree, though I can't quite decide what this might have to do with me. Or my grandmother," Alex said. Then, looking at the package on the table, he read, "Blossoms and Britches."

Nothing to do with the coffee, Katie felt her face warming. Standing, she removed the protective layer. "It's just a bag someone gave me. Because of the rain, I wanted to keep the painting dry." Leaning back, coffee in one hand, Alex gave her space to continue.

She folded the plastic, placed it on the vacant side of the booth, removed the canvas cover, and peeled the inside wrapping. Alex put his cup down and sat up straighter.

"Let me turn this around so that you can get a good look. Maybe you will be able to decide if it is your grandmother's work."

Alex stood and took half a step back. Grasping the frame, he studied the painting. After a minute or more, his body tense, he asked, "Where did you get this?"

"From a gallery in San Antonio," she answered. "Is something wrong?"

"I would like to know who had this before you. Do you know?" he asked, his eyes focused on the art, his words a metronome.

"It came from an estate in New Braunfels, Texas," Katie said.

"It's been gone for a long time." Still resting her head on the bench, Daisy stood and yawned. "May I purchase this from you?"

His jaw and forearms flexed, muscular thick fingers clenched, Katie's next fear was that she wondered whether Alex would let her have it back. Rather than responding to his last statement, she asked, "So you do recognize it?"

Alex cleared his throat. "I do. Will you take a check? Or if you'd prefer, I can do a transfer."

Avoiding his questions, Katie pressed. "Can you tell me more about this piece?"

"I can tell you that it has been gone for a long time. It belongs to my family, and I'd like to buy it from you. Your goal is to sell it, correct? Name your price, and I will pay you."

The situation precarious, Katie paused. "Please." To slow her imminent exit, she sat down again. "Can we talk?"

"We can talk about how much you want for this painting. As a curator, you buy art to sell it for your employer. Is that right?" Arms crossed again, Alex towered over Katie in the small space.

"I suppose in certain cases, I do. But I wasn't looking for you to sell this piece. I'm searching for the artist because I want to bring it to the public." Reaching out her hand to touch the frame, Katie gestured, a light touch on the corner, her voice low and even. "Beyond the obvious elements and skill of the artist, her work is unflinching. There is nothing common here. Not to be reduced to a mere commodity," she said.

Weighing her words, Alex scrutinized Katie's tone and expression. Daisy looked up at him. Reaching out, Katie patted the dog.

"If that is the case, then what do you need from my grandmother—or me, for that matter?" he asked. "It's your painting to display as you wish."

Taking a deep breath, Katie chose blatant honesty. "I don't want to simply display this painting. I want to introduce Mary Renata and her work. Not just this one. If others exist, I'd like to display those as well. Of course, if your grandmother is willing."

Their opening ended, his king castled, Alex calculated his middle game. Deciding to break open the center, he said, "There is more."

Katie swallowed hard and asked, "Is there any way you could arrange for me to meet her?"

Pausing, he picked up his coffee and tapped the side of his cup.

Her phone rang, startling both of them. "I'm so sorry, I have to take this. I hope it's the airline calling about my lost bag," she said.

It seemed her bag had never been loaded on the plane. "Would you like for us to deliver that to Lubbock? We can have it to you this afternoon," a hopeful voice said.

"I am not in the best spot right now. My rental car broke down. I am sort of stranded and don't know when I can be back at my hotel. I do need my luggage today, however," Katie said.

Putting the conversation together, Alex said, "I can give you a ride. Or have them deliver it here."

"Are you sure?" Katie asked, covering the phone with her hand.

"I'm sure. Tell them to deliver it here. Give them the address."

Katie gave the address of the winery. Hanging up, she said, "I need to call the rental car company to tell them to pick up their roller skate."

"What?" Alex asked.

"The rental—Mr. Webb called it a roller skate." Katie laughed.

"That sounds like Mr. Webb," Alex said. "I'll give you a ride back after you get your luggage. With this weather, it's unlikely that you'll get another car today."

"What about my bag? I wonder if they'll get it to me like they promised."

"They will. You wouldn't believe the remote places I've had delayed luggage delivered. The airlines are professionals at misplacing luggage, but also pros at delivery. Is it coming from San Antonio?"

"No. It's in Dallas right now," Katie said.

"I apologize. I thought you said you curated for a hotel in San Antonio?"

"I do. It's just that…well, I connected through Dallas from the East Coast. I came here from New York, my initial lead to the Dyers,"

Katie pointed to the signature on the painting. "M. Costa led me to your family."

"How was that?" Alex asked.

Katie stood and turned the painting over. "In a genealogy search, I found a Mary Renata Costa related to Benjamin Dyer."

Alex translated the back, tracing the words with his finger, "The beginning. More than yesterday less than tomorrow." Aware of the inscription, he'd never seen it before, though he had heard his grandfather say it a hundred times through the course of their searching. He recognized the handwriting. The curves and ligatures unmistakable from a hundred notes in his lunch box, to birthday cards, and shopping lists on the refrigerator door, the flourishes on the *y*'s as familiar as the smell of homemade biscotti baking in his grandmother's kitchen.

"I found your family grocery store. And your uncle." Alex's silence prompted her. "And then I went to Long Island." Eyes widened, he raised his brow. "I went to the Dyer home." Katie turned her arm over, palm up. "Your house on the beach. It really is a beautiful place, by the way. I met your gardener. He told me you weren't home and didn't know when you'd be back. I stayed in Montauk for a night, and to be candid, I used my time there discovering articles about you online, the most recent about the work you're doing here in Texas. Taking a chance you might still be at this vineyard, I booked a flight to Lubbock and came straight here." Without taking a breath, she went on. "In conclusion, I've stalked you. But not in a creepy way. Only to attach the artist to the painting. I hope you don't think I'm somehow unstable. I know all this must sound crazy."

Alex didn't speak, so Katie kept going. "I should have been more professional about this. It's just that I was so torn between waiting or writing you a letter at your address. I couldn't find any contact information for you online."

"I appreciate your honesty," Alex said. "So far you don't seem creepy. I would be more inclined to say tenacious. Would you like to have a glass of wine? I was just about to open a bottle and make some dinner."

# Part II

# Chapter 1

"I think we've done a fine job. A fine job, just the two of us," Antonia said, adjusting her pillbox hat, just a shade darker than her blue suit. Smoothing her pencil skirt, she pushed up three-quarter sleeves.

The last weeks had blurred past—graduation from Vassar, moving out of her dorm, collecting friends' addresses. Her whole life had been packed into double-locking vinyl suitcases and a large trunk, and then Mary Renata and her mother were riding the train from Poughkeepsie to the city. After a few days of recuperation and shopping, the two enjoyed brunch before Mary Renata's embarkation.

"Thank you for everything, Mamma. The Plaza has been such a treat, and I appreciate all my new clothes."

"You deserve the splurge. You've worked so hard over the last four years at school refining your art. After summer with *Zietta*, you will be back at it in the fall."

"I know school abroad is a lot of money. I feel guilty."

"No, you don't," Antonia said. "How many girls can study in Italy at the Accademia? You must let your light shine. Your Pappa and I will make sure that you do."

"I know you are right and want the best for me. I've had such a wonderful time with you. I only wish Pappa could've been here."

"You know your father. He thinks he can't leave the restaurant."

"You're sure everything is okay back home?" Mary Renata asked for the hundredth time.

"I am sure," Antonia assured her daughter, patting her on the shoulder. "I need to find the ladies' room. If the waiter comes, please tell him I'd like the salmon."

In the washroom mirror, Antonia blinked, dabbing the corners of her eye with a tissue. She took out a silver compact and powdered her cheeks, blending the areas absent of makeup. She clicked it shut and rubbed her thumb across its floral engraving. It had been a parting gift to her from her own mother, when as a young girl she immigrated to the United States. She carried it with her always. With a few extra bobby pins, she secured strands of dark hair streaked with gray back under her hat. Sniffing, she pressed the tissue to her nose before going back out to the dining room. Keeping a promise to her husband, she would not reveal Niccolo's condition to any of their children.

Back at their table, menus removed, Mary Renata smiled up at her mother.

"You look just lovely in that yellow cashmere, dear. I do believe your hair is prettier than ever."

Long dark hair flowing, Mary Renata, using both hands, pushed it all to the back. "Barbara tried to convince me for a year to cut it into a flip-up like the other girls."

"I'm glad you didn't," Antonia said.

"Me too, though I might wish I had. Aunt Luciana's last letter said all of Tuscany has been stricken by a terrible heat wave. *Lo Scirocco.*"

"Don't you worry," Antonia said. "When you get to Luci's house, you'll be too busy enjoying the wine to notice the temperatures. And before you know it, you'll be walking around Florence all bundled up in your peacoat and scarf."

"Oh! I ordered a scone for each of us. I picked cucumber for me and blueberry for you, and here they are!" Mary Renata clapped her hands once. They tasted each other's delicacies, declaring everything both delicious and tied for flavor.

"We should finish and get over to the pier." Antonio checked the time. "We don't want to be rushed."

They collected their pocketbooks and Mary Renata's train case and waited in the lobby while the valet hailed a taxi. No other cumbersome baggage—the hotel concierge had sent Mary Renata's trunk and suitcases ahead of her arrival. After a short drive through the city, south through Times Square and past the Empire State Building, they arrived at the crowded docks on the edge of the meatpacking district. Holding gloved hands, shoulder to shoulder, they pushed forward.

"I don't have to board yet. I still have some time," Mary Renata said.

"I'll stand right here in this spot until you're out of sight." Antonia squeezed her daughter's shoulders and gave her a quick kiss on her cheek.

Together the two stared up at the superliner. The length of five city blocks, she waited high up in the water, sleek, and majestic. From stem to stern, the mighty ship, full of activity in preparation for departure, deckhands heaved huge mooring ropes, waiting to release them from their giant cleats. Groups of passengers making their way up an elevated gangway dwindled, a burst of steam from the stacks accompanied the ship's mighty roar, and Mary Renata turned and hugged Antonia.

"You best go now," Antonia said. "One last thing." She pinned a small gardenia to her daughter's Peter Pan collar.

Not wanting to let go just yet, Mary Renata held on a little longer. "I love you. Tell Pappa and my brothers and my sister the same!"

"Have a wonderful trip, darling. Keep in touch, and please let me know when you arrive."

"I will, Mamma," she said, and up she went, bright as the lemon pattern on her circular skirt.

Holding her position, Antonia watched Mary Renata disappear up into the ship. Shielding her eyes from the sun, she waited until she spotted the girl in yellow along the railing on the upper deck. A little jump, excited, her daughter found her mother in the crowd below and waved. The waters beneath the hull churning, the captain pushed back into the river and up the Hudson. Clearing the pier with loyal tugs at her side, the big ship, slow ahead, was underway.

Her mother moving farther away, Mary Renata ran back to the stern along the rail, in and among other passengers, laughing and waving all the while. White handkerchief in the air, Antonia watched until her daughter and the giant vessel became a tiny speck far down the river.

## Chapter 2

The pier out of sight, passengers dispersed and drifted away from the deck. Down sets of exterior stairs and back up again, Mary Renata navigated to the afterdeck on the port side. At the taffrail, she admired the Manhattan skyline, considering its form, a silhouette of overlapping rectangles, prisms, cubes, and angles. Philosophy and architecture in motion, she marveled at its art from her perspective.

Lost in the lines of the cityscape, she was startled by a nearby voice. "It's quite a view." A young man dressed in a gray suit addressed her, the wind blowing his trilby off and up over Mary Renata's head. Grabbing at its brim, she caught the hat before it flew overboard. Gasping together, both surprised at the wind and her quick reaction, they broke into laughter.

"You've the reflexes of a sapper!" he told her as she handed the hat back.

"I don't know about that," Mary Renata said, her dark hair blowing around her shoulders.

"Thank you for saving my hat. My name is Benjamin Dyer," he said, extending one hand.

"Pleased to make your acquaintance. I'm Mary Renata Costa."

"So nice to meet you too, Mary Renata Costa," Benjamin said, her small, gloved hand in his, taking note of her eyes, a soft brown that reminded him of butterscotch. "I'd better hold on to this." He was referring to his felt. "I was about to go inside and explore. Care to join me?"

"Our rooms won't be ready until later. I think that's a splendid idea," she said, and like a gentleman, he extended his right arm, bent at the elbow. She looped hers through, and they wandered into the ship's interior. Benjamin wore horn-rimmed glasses and a sack suit with cuffed, flat-front pants. A New Yorker, he wasn't a Princeton boy. Maybe a Harvard, but more likely a Yalie.

Strolling up onto the main deck of the floating city, they explored shops and salons. On the promenade deck they found the main hall, and the sun deck containing squash racket courts, gyms, and outdoor lounging. Down the levels they went, discovering swimming pools, Turkish baths, theaters, restaurants, a post office, an infirmary, and administrative offices. After checking with the purser, with still some time before their rooms were available and luggage delivered, Benjamin suggested they try the sun deck.

"What about the library instead?" Mary Renata suggested. "It's warm outside and so crowded out there."

Inside the cool recesses, walls lined with intricate marquetry panels, they perused an impressive book collection. Mary Renata lingered in fiction. Taking a new volume by Harper Lee from a table, she whispered, "I've been so consumed with my studies, I haven't had time to read as much as I'd like. This title is popular." Running one hand along the bindings, she stopped on the *M*'s. "Somerset Maugham," she said, pulling two more from the shelf. Bending her knees, she chose one more. "And a book of short stories by Maupassant."

"Quite a well-rounded selection," Benjamin said.

The library empty but for the two of them, Mary Renata checked the books out for the duration of the journey. Benjamin suggested a pair of velvet tufted barrel chairs in a corner.

Mary Renata flipped through her selections. "I've a penchant for irony. Did you know Maupassant died in an asylum?" she asked, and quieter, "Of syphilis?"

"I did not," Benjamin admitted.

"Tragic," they both said at once, causing Mary Renata to giggle.

"I'm sorry; that isn't funny," she said.

"You are correct," he agreed. "Nothing funny about syphilis," to which he too laughed, she louder this time, covering her mouth as not to gather the attention of the librarian. Surrounded by stories, no longer strangers, they spoke in hushed voices.

"So," she asked, "if you don't mind my asking, what is the purpose of your travel? Are you going to France?"

"I'm on business," Benjamin said. "My family owns a handful of neighborhood grocery stores in New York. My father and my brother run them in the city. Over the years, with the coming of the big supermarkets, we've specialized."

"How so?" Mary Renata asked.

"Specialty imports, cheeses and meats, and wines from Europe. Spain, France, and Italy."

"I see. So, you make trips to Europe and tour around seeking the finest for your store?"

"That's exactly right. Several times a year. I've a flat in Italy that I use as a home base when I'm abroad."

"What about your travels?" Benjamin started to ask, his words interrupted by a public address system, the loudspeaker broadcasting a long list of names for whom rooms were ready.

"That's me!" Mary Renata exclaimed when she heard her name. Excited to get into her stateroom, she collected the stack of books and jumped up. "I'd better get going," she said.

Standing, Benjamin offered to walk her to her cabin.

"You don't have to do that. Nice meeting you, again," she said, turning to go into the hall.

"Nice meeting you too," Benjamin said. He wanted to say something else but was unable to find words, not wanting to be rude or appear too forward. Still, he should've made plans with her for dinner, or maybe coffee in the morning. *There's nothing funny about syphilis.* Placing a palm against his forehead, he couldn't believe he'd said that rather than something cleverer. Sighing, he sat down again, his head back against the chair. He had to know more about the dark-haired girl with the caramel eyes wearing such happy yellow.

Into the elevator and down another hallway, a steward waited by Mary Renata's door. "Good afternoon, miss." He unlocked the door and handed her a key. "Please look around to ensure all of your luggage has arrived and that the room is to your standards."

Gazing about, Mary Renata noted sateen drapes tied back over two portholes. A full-sized bed with stacks of pillows awaited. She couldn't wait to get in with her books. "Everything looks perfect, and all my luggage is here. Thank you," she told the steward, who reminded her that he was at her service if there was anything else she needed or thought of later. After he closed the door, she fell back on the bed, feet dangling over the edge. Had she been rude before? Well-mannered and well dressed, if a little nervous, Benjamin seemed like a nice man. She could have let him walk her to her cabin. Rolling over on her side, she picked up the thick volume of short stories. Adjectives and irony dancing in her mind, she closed her eyes, falling asleep on top of the covers.

Composing himself, Benjamin rose from the library chair. His room not yet ready, with an idea, he took the stairs down to the restaurant. Waiters and busboys buzzed about, setting pristine white tablecloths, while managers inspected silverware and place settings. The dining room was set in round tables of eight, each held a large bouquet of fresh peonies, baby's breath, and other greenery. A little bald man in a black suit and bow tie approached Benjamin. Front of the house, the maître d', Benjamin bent his tall frame. Intent on his words, the shorter man listened. Hands in pockets, hopeful, Benjamin waited for his response.

"I am happy to accommodate your request, sir. We can put you here, at table nine. I will see to it that Miss Dyer's place card is to your right."

With a boyish grin, he adjusted his glasses and prepared for dinner.

Waking just before six in the evening, Mary Renata yawned. She hadn't eaten since brunch with her mother, and was starving. Smoothing out the duvet, she stacked her books on the nightstand. Not unpacked, leaving the trunk intact, she rested her robin's-egg-blue suitcase on its side, clicked open both latches, and opened it on the floor. One by one, she removed the formal dresses Antonia had folded and tucked inside, and she placed them on hangers. She shut the closet door but didn't latch it and hooked one and then another hanger on the top edge of the door, displaying for herself two of three. In a corner of the room, she hooked another hanger on a lamp shade, then two more on a built-in set of shelves. Draping the last on the headboard, down over the pillows, and a few more askew on the bed, she stood in the center of the cabin. Taffeta, satin, silk, and brocade left Mary Renata surrounded with choices. She reached for an emerald green and lake blue, the bodice belted out of the same fabric. Then she slipped out of her clothes, wrinkled from her nap, and laid the dress across the foot of the bed. After her shower, Mary Renata brushed her long hair, fastened large rollers, and took a smaller case from her blue one. She unzipped its lid and removed a pink hair dryer with a matching stand. They'd purchased it at Bergdorf's, along with the peacock-colored dress she'd wear tonight. Her hair dry, she left it in the rollers while she did her makeup. With precision, she drew perfect cat eyes and finished with a pale lipstick. Removing the rollers, she let her hair fall in waves. She picked up pieces from both sides and fastened them at the back and up high.

She pulled the dress over her head and slid the other laden hangers to one side of the mirrored doors on the closet. Surveying her reflection, she smoothed hidden netting under the skirt. Working a clasp on a string of pearls, she checked herself from the side and the back, looking over her shoulder at the girl on the other side of the glass. "Why put all the effort into dressing for dinner?" she asked. The girl did not respond but stared back, the slightest smile at the corner of her lips. Choosing gold kitten heels and a matching evening clutch, embellished with tiny sewn in pearls, Mary Renata skipped out the door and to the main dining hall.

As she approached the entrance, voices from the crowded room grew louder. Somewhat out of place, she looked for the host. Mary Renata turned at a tap on her shoulder.

Clearing his throat, Benjamin spoke. "Nice to see you again."

"Oh. Hello," she said. He looked taller than before in a slim-cut tuxedo, and his hair appeared darker than out on the ship's deck earlier in the day.

The bald maître d' from earlier appeared. "How are you this evening?" he asked, shaking Benjamin's hand. Before they could answer, he called a host over. "Please escort Mr. Dyer and Miss Costa to table nine."

Two others seated so far, Benjamin nodded at a couple across the table. The host held a chair out for Mary Renata, and she placed her pocketbook near her place setting.

"You look lovely," Benjamin said, adjusting his glasses.

"Thank you," Mary Renata said. Wiggling her feet inside her gold shoes, she fidgeted with the menu.

After they ordered, Benjamin picked up the conversation where they had left off.

"Are you on holiday?" he asked.

"Of sorts. My parents are sending me to my aunt as a culminating gift for my graduation. She lives in a family villa. A one-way trip. After the summer I plan to study art in Florence." Intent on her words, Benjamin watched her eyes and mannerisms. He liked the way she talked. "I've never been overseas before, so I'm excited."

"Where did you graduate?"

"Vassar. Just a few weeks ago."

"Congratulations." Benjamin nodded his head, urging her to continue.

"Now I'm off to the next adventure! What about your alma mater?"

"I don't have one," he explained. "My brother and I always worked in the stores with our father as children. After Xavier, I went straight into the family business."

Seeing a puzzled look on her face, Benjamin lowered his voice. "You didn't think Princeton?"

She shook her head. "No, but I considered Yale."

Throwing his head back, Benjamin laughed. "I'll try to overcome that."

Cutting his steak, he asked if she'd like more wine. Feeling all grown up, Mary Renata said she would. "It's good," she said, "but I expect you'd know better than me."

"You can never stop learning about wine. The industry encompasses so many areas of study. Science, chemistry, geography, and farming."

"I imagine the business side of things includes economics and marketing too."

"That's right." Benjamin raised his glass. "And the best teacher is experience."

Mary Renata touched her glass to his and took another drink.

"Close your eyes and tell me what you taste," he said.

"Berries, but just at first. Then something like vanilla." She opened her eyes.

"How perceptive." Benjamin raised his eyebrows. "See? You know more than you thought."

The table now full, a lot of talking around them, a woman next to Mary Renata broke in. "Excuse me. I don't mean to eavesdrop, but are you discussing the wine over there?"

Cupping one hand to his ear, Benjamin said, "Sorry. I didn't hear what you said."

There were too many voices, distracting and noisy. The man asked, "Would you like to meet us for a drink after dinner?"

Benjamin looked at Mary Renata. With a why-not shrug, she nodded.

"Sure," he told the man.

After dinner the two couples made their way to the lounge. Positioning themselves on two settees facing each other, they waited to order, the men agreeing on dry martinis, while the two women settled on wine.

"So," said the woman. Overstuffed, billowing out of the top of a scoop neckline on her fitted blue-and-gold brocade, she bent her elbows. Both hands up, she pressed her forefingers to her thumbs, pale cleavage overwhelming her ensemble. "We are on our annual holiday. We stay in Paris every year, don't we, darling?" The man nodded. "In our fabulous penthouse overlooking the Seine, with a view of Notre Dame. Simply fabulous," she said, this time drawing out the latter word in a tone that reminded Mary Renata of a talking doll with a pull string. "My husband will take me to Fred's in Paris first thing, won't you, darling?" In the affirmative, he nodded his head again. Grabbing both earlobes decorated with substantial emeralds, she chatted on. "We got these there last year. Isn't that right, dear?" Without waiting for her husband's answer, she eyed Mary Renata's simple strand of pearls. "I prefer precious gems. Only the best for me!"

Clearing her throat, Mary Renata commented, "It must be lovely having a view of Notre Dame."

"Yes and no," the woman said, smoothing her coiffed hair. "You know, Notre Dame is very historic, so there is that. It's close to our expansive Parisian apartment, however, and I abhor the hideous carved creatures on the structure. It is just so old. Frankly, I don't know what people see in such old buildings."

"I wonder if Victor Hugo would agree," Mary Renata said, and Benjamin chuckled.

"Victor? Who is Victor?" the woman said.

Benjamin steered the conversation. "If your apartment is near the Seine, it must be historic?" he asked.

Benjamin and Mary Renata stared at the woman, blinking, while she continued chatting.

"Mostly everything in Paris is old, so of course our apartment is too," the woman answered. "But you wouldn't know it. We renovated in the most modern style. Painted right over worn and peeling paintings on the ceilings, didn't we, dear? I couldn't stand the fading paint—all those exposed beams and layers of brick. Now it is perfectly smooth, white, and clean. My husband is in advertising."

The woman tapped the top of Mary Renata's hand. "He's on Madison Avenue." She winked. "You know. Absolutely fabulous bonuses."

Grateful for the waiter's arrival, Mary Renata closed her eyes for a moment. Sighing, she rolled them up beneath her lids. The husband ordered two martinis for himself.

"May I?" Benjamin asked Mary Renata, gesturing toward the wine list in her hand.

"Choose carefully. I am a bit of a wine snob, aren't I, darling?" The woman addressed both Benjamin and her husband.

"Of course, you may." Mary Renata touched Benjamin's sleeve. "You are the wine expert, aren't you?"

Catching her eye, Benjamin grinned. "Let's go with this Portuguese Malvasia. If that is fine with you?" he asked the woman, who waved her hand.

"Is your husband a wine expert?" she asked Mary Renata. "A sommelier, I dare ask?" Pursing her lips, she smirked, looking at the pair from the corner of her eye.

"Well, you know. As a member of the royals of Liechtenstein, he picked up oenology, initially as a hobby. He now selects wine for the monarchy, don't you, Your Highness?"

Intent on the olive in his glass, Benjamin said, "Yes, you know. Royal duties."

The woman's mouth gaped open. "Royalty?"

"Why, yes. And this lovely lady"—he put his arm around Mary Renata's shoulder— "happens to be a princess of Luxembourg, aren't you, Your Highness?"

"Our families have been friendly for centuries." Mary Renata leaned into Benjamin's shoulder. "But for now, we are traveling to our country villa in Italy."

"And from our vineyard and winery there, we will ship back some carefully chosen vintages," Benjamin finished.

"You live in Liechtenstein?" asked the woman, mental wheels turning.

"No. Oh, no. His castle is far too drafty," Mary Renata said.

"Your castle isn't what I'd call warm and cozy, dear, what with stone floors and all that marble."

"You are so right," Mary Renata agreed. "Don't you find castles ever so dreadfully drafty?" she asked the woman.

Meanwhile, the husband, on his third martini, ordered another. Unable to chatter or find common ground, the woman grabbed her husband's sleeve. "I'm terribly tired. We're ready to go, aren't we, dear?"

The husband's drink arriving just in time, the men stood, shaking hands. Mary Renata encouraged the woman to visit her if ever they were in Luxembourg. "Just send a calling card in advance. Address it to the Grand Ducal Palace, Luxembourg. Attention Princess Mary. I will receive it straightaway," Mary Renata said, unflinching.

The woman started to offer her hand, but thinking otherwise, turned to exit. Changing her mind, she turned back toward the two, performing an awkward curtsy. Her knees too far apart, she teetered all the way up. Her face flushed; she recovered while her husband finished his drink.

The couple out of earshot, Benjamin and Mary Renata burst into laughter.

"How did you come up with Liechtenstein?" he asked.

"I like to read," she said through more laughter. "And what about Luxembourg?"

"Same number of syllables?"

"That makes sense," Mary Renata said.

A fun secret between them, she accepted Benjamin's escort to her cabin. Lingering at the door, they made plans for dinner the next evening, and the next, their plans and the ship floating along the waves of the Atlantic.

In the afternoons, Mary Renata posted letters, read, and napped. She attended events with Benjamin like the fancy headdress parade, where passengers wore feathers, tiaras, and box hats decorated with playing cards or flowers, and they ended each evening dancing. The trip drawing shorter, Benjamin held her closer on the second-to-last evening. Mary Renata teased her hair up high, adorning it in the front with a large rhinestone barrette given to her by her brother, Carlo, for graduation. Floating out of the main hall on Benjamin's arm each night, hand up, she pageant-queen waved to the woman from the first night's dinner. Fingers poised, her wrist turned a lightbulb. For more dramatic effect, she even emulated washing the windows. *Wash, wash, wash*, with no less than a royal smile. By the last evening, drawing attention from the woman's newly acquired covey, they all whispered and pointed at the princess of Luxembourg.

The mighty ship plowed through restless currents, bulging and meandering through wayward bankless rivers. Out on the open sea, powerful winds pulled at the water's surface, causing a great rotation. Nonetheless, the vessel stayed true to her course, pushing forward to the coast of France and the port of Cherbourg.

Before dawn, they crossed the Celtic Sea and entered the English Channel. After breakfast, Mary Renata, in a mood of melancholy, strolled with Benjamin around the upper deck, the air cool and the sunshine warm. It seemed a blur since Antonia had left her at the port in New York. She hadn't yet processed the enormity of her journey. This huge step taken, her feet soon on European ground, Mary Renata realized it might be a long time before she'd see her family again. Staring into the distance, she took two breaths in.

"Everything ok?" Benjamin asked, taking her hand, his fingers touching hers.

Mary Renata looked up at Benjamin, squinting into the sun not far above the horizon. She was not sure when she'd decided she liked him. His presence grounding, he was nothing like other boys from school. He was stable but not serious, strong but not overbearing, and confident without arrogance. Pointing starboard, littoral land in the distance, she asked, "Can you see France?"

"I can," he said.

"I feel far from home," she said, answering his original question. She did not admit apprehension and anticipation of loneliness with their impending embarkation.

He reached for her other hand with his free one, and she faced him. "Don't," he said. "Look at this expanse of ocean. It can take you right back home anytime you want."

"I suppose you're right," she said, blinking, a single tear finding its way down her cheek.

Reaching up to brush it away, he kept one hand on her face. "Would you like to travel together to Florence?" he asked.

Confused for a moment, she said, "I thought you had plans in Paris and the French countryside."

"I did. I planned on working my way across France, over to Spain, and ending up in Florence, but there's no reason I can't start at the far side. Call your aunt and tell her I'll deliver you. Without being too forward, I'd very much like to see your family vineyard."

Mary Renata liked the way Benjamin looked at her, unwavering. She peered back into his eyes, like the plains of the sea, his gaze deeper than the Atlantic.

Leaning closer in, he said, "And I'd like to spend more time with you." His hand still on her face, he leaned down and kissed her on the mouth, gentle at first, then deeper. Nothing but the wind around them, yesterday and tomorrow were of no concern. Benjamin was nothing like any other boy. Not even close.

A bit dizzy, she regained herself. "I'd like that." Her heart racing, she placed her hand over his. "I have to pack my room."

"I do as well. Would you like to meet in the lobby after? We can wait there while we dock and collect our luggage."

Mary Renata agreed and went back to her room. All the dresses still hanging about her cabin, she folded them. With less precision than Antonia, she finished in no time. The room all packed, she changed into a long-sleeved boucle, plaid shirtdress with four large buttons, and a pair of low block heels with silver buckles, comfortable for the next day's travel. Her hair tied back with a silk scarf, she chose a black leather pocketbook with a long enough strap for cross body and wrist-length natural-colored leather gloves. She gave the room a once-over, sat on the edge of the bed and placed a call to her mother as promised.

"Hello, Mamma."

Sometime after midnight in Ohio, Antonia answered. "Hello, dear. We've been waiting to hear from you! How are you? How is the voyage going?"

"Mamma, is it late there? I'm not sure of the time difference."

"It's late, but don't worry. We're glad to hear from you," Antonia said.

"I can't talk long, but it's perfect. More perfect than I ever could have imagined. I'm having the time of my life, Mamma," Mary Renata stopped herself. Thinking again, she decided against too much detail. "We're almost to port. I met a wonderful friend on the ship! We're riding the train together to Florence."

"How nice you have a traveling companion!" she said. "Please let me know when you're safe at Luci's. I will telephone her to let her know your ship is in France. When should I tell her to meet you?"

"I won't have an exact schedule until I get to the train station. Will you tell her not to worry, that I will call her when I arrive in Florence? My friend and I may stop over in Paris."

"Paris? You are having a wonderful time! Oh, I can't wait to hear all about it. I'll call Luci and tell her you may be a few days delayed. Before you go, your Pappa is right here. Say hello."

Niccolo stirring, a light touch, his wife shook him. "Mary Renata is on the phone," she said, one hand cupped over the receiver.

As he cleared his throat, coughing, Antonia supported his shoulder, her pillow behind his back.

"Hello, *Piccola*," her father said. "We miss you."

"I miss you too, Pappa. Thank you for my trip. I'm having such a wonderful time."

"That is good to hear. Make me proud at the Accademia. And call your mother," he said.

Mary Renata smiled. "I will, and I will. I promise," she said. "I love you."

"We love you too. Be safe," he said, and replaced the phone in its cradle.

Three thousand, eight hundred and five miles away from their daughter, the two parents settled back into bed. Niccolo handed his wife her pillow and rested on his back. Helping her husband get comfortable again, she arranged the covers, pulling them up to his chin. Laying her hand on his chest, she watched its rise and fall, feeling the steady breathing of sleep until she could keep her eyes open no longer.

Mary Renata did not disconnect the call until she was sure her mother had replaced the phone into its cradle. She couldn't decide why she had told her mother she might stop in Paris. She and Benjamin had never discussed any such plans. Sitting on the edge of the bed a little longer, she shook her head. Was she buying time? Privacy? *Maybe both*, she decided. Tucking that thought away, she placed her luggage by the door and went down to the lobby to meet Benjamin.

The next few hours were hectic as they piled their bags into a cab and arrived at Cherbourg Station. Checking the schedule, they chose the next train to take them through Paris and on to Florence. Almost a day's travel through France, rolling across the country, they'd view the sloping landscapes, old villages, and fields of sunflowers. After dinner, they'd spend the night on the train and wake up in the Medici's ancient city on the banks of the Arno River.

# Chapter 3

The rain steady, Alex stowed Katie's luggage in the exterior storage at the back of the Airstream and removed a small folding table. Dry under the canopy, he set it up and placed two chairs on either side. After some time for consideration, he felt he'd been defensive, if not harsh, toward Katie. She seemed genuine, and if impulsive, though she didn't seem to be looking for anything other than answers and his grandmother. As admitted, she was interested in more art. Alex didn't know how he felt about that, and furthermore, what his grandparents would think about the "more" part. One thing he was certain of, however, was that his grandfather would be interested in the story about this girl who had brought this painting and placed it in his hands, all the way out here in Lubbock, Texas.

"Can I help?" Katie asked.

"Sure," Alex said. Back inside the Airstream, they chopped tomatoes, onions, carrots, garlic, and pancetta and sauteed the mixture in olive oil. "I'm going to cheat this a little," Alex said, adding a can of crushed tomatoes. He opened a bottle of wine and poured a generous dash into the sauce, along with cooked ground veal.

"I think the noodles are done," Katie said.

"Let me get that heavy pot," Alex said. He took the pasta off the gas flame, poured the boiling water into a strainer in the sink, and rinsed it with cool water. He turned the Bolognese down, and then, with the open bottle of wine in one hand and two glasses in another, he said, "Let's let that simmer while we drink this outside. Would you like a sweatshirt?"

Katie started to decline, but the strong winds whistled across the plains, and the RV swayed. Holding on to the counter with one hand, she thought otherwise.

"Open that closet." Alex gestured toward a small door. "Look on the top shelf, and take your pick," he said.

Katie took the one on top and unfolded it. "Nice. Classic and well-worn." Cornell was splayed in big block letters across the front. Frayed on every edge, there was a small hole in the sleeve that Daisy had chewed as a puppy. The weight of it reminded Katie of one of Gran's quilts.

"You might want these too." Alex handed her a pair of socks.

"Thank you." Katie looked down at her bare feet. "Dry is good."

Back out under the awning, Alex poured the red blend. "The Llano Estacado is quite a place." He pronounced Llano like Yah-no. "Not to be confused with the town of Llano of course." The next time he said it like Lan-oh.

"I'm impressed," Katie said, "with your correct mispronunciations. And your geography."

"Just when I think I have all of them figured out," Alex said. "Sometimes you go with the correct Spanish, and sometimes you don't."

Katie laughed. "Don't even try. There are no phonetic rules. No logic."

Alex let out an exaggerated breath. "I just try my best to follow the locals."

"Smart thinkin'," Katie said.

Enjoying the wine and the company despite the weather, the sleeves too long, Katie pulled her hands inside, bundling herself into the sweatshirt. "Tell me about your grandmother." She tucked her feet up into her chair.

"My grandmother. What about her?"

"When did she become an artist?"

Leaning back, Alex swirled his glass. Careful, he gave Katie a little. "After she graduated from Vassar, she went to study art in Florence, where she crossed paths with my grandfather."

"Your grandfather who travels for the store! Your uncle told me about him," Katie said.

"He doesn't travel so much anymore. My grandfather spent his entire career cultivating relationships with vintners all over Europe. He's getting up there in age, but Dyer's employs a few people who do what my grandfather used to do by himself. Now he manages them."

"So, they live in Europe?" Katie asked.

"They do."

"Where in Europe?"

"Italy."

"But back to her painting."

"Yes, of course. You know, she never talked much about her work when I was growing up. She finished her training and stayed in Florence for a few years. She had a gallery for a time not far from the Pitti Palace."

"That's quite a feat for a young artist."

"I believe she received a small inheritance from her father," Alex explained. "After she went abroad, she never saw him again."

"Why didn't she? What happened."

"I believe he had some kind of heart condition," Alex said.

"How sad."

"I suppose. They were my great-grandparents. I never knew them." Alex said.

"What do you know about the gallery?"

"Like I said, I don't know much beyond its location. It was on the other side of the Arno. I don't know how long she had it. Only for a few years after she and my grandfather married, and after my father was born."

"The other side?"

"Florentines refer to the south side of the river as *Oltrarno*. Have you been to Florence, Katie?" Alex shifted.

"Rome, but not Florence," Katie said.

A few years ago, she'd gone on a Mediterranean cruise with Tre and his parents. Once in the port at Civitavecchia, they had piled into a shuttle bus and took the guided tour with as many other cruisers as could squeeze in. Shoulder to shoulder, they'd rattled along for over an hour, wandering the city for less than half a day. In a rush, they had snapped photos of the Coliseum, a famous cathedral she couldn't remember the name of, and more of Trevi Fountain, surrounded by a permanent crowd. Marching them through the streets holding his colored sign on a stick, the tour guide directed their group to a small gelato shop. Peering down a small street, Katie spotted a tucked-away coffee shop, but before she could venture off, Tre pulled her back to the tourist-infested piazza, where they ended up dining at a restaurant with pictures on the menu. Unable to at least linger over a carafe of more-than-decent table wine, Harriet dragged them through what seemed like every retail tourist store between there and the harbor. Back on the ship, Harriet weighed down with as much *limoncello* as she and Harry could carry, she'd decided she was now an expert on the city. Raving about Italy for months to their friends in Dallas, she added *grazie*, *prego*, and *ciao* to her lexicon.

After their vacation, Harriet insisted on a garish Tuscan kitchen remodel, hiring a local artist to paint a mural of a vineyard. In the foreground were rows of vines laden with oversized bright-purple fruit, and in the distance, a structure that looked more like Westminster Abbey than a typical Italian villa. Walking among the vines, a woman dressed in a long white dressing gown tossed back her hair, a red ribbon in one hand, the other carrying a basket full of grapes. Giant Degas prints occupied another wall, the others all plastered gold, while every inch of countertop space was embellished with hopeless bowls of painted papier-mache produce. The new cabinetry, all wrong, was Victorian carved mahogany. The remodel complete, she and Tre attended Harriet's next party, which was intended to draw compliments, if not envy, from scads of neighbors and couples from their golf club.

Embarrassed, Katie was thankful Alex did not ask about any of the details of her Roman holiday. Before he could, she asked about the river.

"The Arno River runs through the city. On one side are most of the major attractions to the city, like the Duomo, museums, and the Via de'Tornabuoni, where people come from all over to shop."

"And Michelangelo's David?" Katie asked.

"Yes, that too," Alex said. "But the *Oltrarno* has more of a neighborhood feel, even today. My grandparents still own an apartment there, one they bought together when they were young."

"Did they get married in Italy?"

"They did."

"Where? In Florence?"

"Yes. At Santo Spirito Basilica in Oltrarno, just a block from their apartment. My grandmother walked past there each day on the way to her gallery."

"Oh," said Katie. "Have you been?"

"To the church?"

She nodded.

"Many times. It's quite an interesting work of engineering, in fact, the last by Brunelleschi. He died two years into the construction.

While the inside is elaborate, with geometric columns and marble and artwork, the outside facade was never finished and is unexpectedly plain," Alex explained.

"An unexpected surprise inside," Katie said.

"Yes," Alex said, studying the girl in his sweatshirt.

"So Mary Renata painted and ran a gallery, while Benjamin traveled Europe procuring the best wines to export to New York. They married in a famous basilica in the Oltrarno. What an incredible, romantic story."

"I think so," Alex said.

"Was your father born when they lived in Florence?"

"He was," said Alex.

"How many children did they have?"

"Just one. My father." Alex's answers growing curt, Katie pushed a bit more. Without all the answers of Mary Renata's history, she brought her question back to the art.

"You said she kept the gallery for a few years?"

Alex nodded. "Even after my father was born. Some days my grandmother took my father with her, and some days she left him with a friend of hers, a sister at Santo Spirito church I told you about. There is a garden within the walls where he played while my grandmother painted."

"What happened to it?"

"The gallery?" Katie watched Alex, taking in every bit of history. "She never reopened after a catastrophic flood in the sixties. The water rose out of the banks of the Arno and rushed through the town, flooding everything on both sides."

"How high did the water go?"

"High enough to cover bridges and at least the ground floor of every building."

"What happened to her paintings? Were they destroyed?" Katie asked.

"Some could have been. Art and books and monuments all over Florence were damaged and destroyed. It took weeks for the Florentines to clean up the mess."

"That must have been terrifying. Did she stop painting after the flood?"

"I'm not too sure," Daylight fading, Alex stared out into the soggy landscape, considering Katie's questions. After a moment he said, "We don't think of our grandparents as actual people."

"I know what you mean," Katie agreed. "By the time we came around, they just were."

## Chapter 4

The padre zipped his rain jacket. A worn, gray-handled hoe in hand, its blade sharp, smooth on the spaces where he held it, he stepped out of the rectory. Once outside the ancient stone cottage, he looked up at the sun peeking through low, dark-purple thunderheads and sending scarce rays over the hill. Weathered hands pulling up his hood, he looked across the valley in the direction of the mountains, wondering about their snowcapped peaks. An endless wet autumn, he'd been hoping for time to weed the vegetables. He strode a few yards to the garden out back. After a few rows, the clouds overtook the small bit of light. Gray enveloping the sky, the wind blew, and sprinkles turned into larger, steady drops again. He pushed the flat edge of the implement into the saturated ground, gauging the amount of water in the soil. He surveyed the valley and went straight back inside to make phone calls to his friends in the city.

## Chapter 5

Just after lunchtime, Mary Renata was working on a commissioned piece in the loft of her gallery. Surrounded by canvases, paints, and drop cloths, up here she was free to create without worry of spatters or overturned paints. No interruptions today, heavy rain keeping locals and tourists indoors, intent on her work, she jumped at the ringing of her phone. Holding the paintbrush in her teeth, she used two hands to climb down the ladder. On the entry level, she removed her apron, draped it over a rung, and inspected her shoes for any paint transferred onto the shiny brick floor.

Arriving before the ringing stopped, she grabbed at the receiver. "Pronto?"

"Thank goodness you've answered!"

"*Sorella*. Is everything ok?"

"Yes, Mary Renata, for now. It seems as if all the heavy rain upriver is causing flooding. You should come get Thomas and go straight home!" "Thank you for calling, Sister. I'll clean up, and then I'll be right there."

Mary Renata tidied up the loft and washed her brushes and then her hands, scrubbing off paint from elbows to fingers. She traded walking shoes for tall rubber boots and gathered her things. Then she turned off the lights and locked the door. Taking an extra moment, she peered in through the windows at the canvases on the walls, as if she were a passerby. Popping up her umbrella, she stepped onto the sidewalk, the Pitti Palace just steps behind her. A five-minute walk to Santo Spirito, she stopped at a favorite *salumeria* on a *vicolo*, a narrow alley, along her way. Ordering three porchetta paninis, she waited while a boy sliced thick slabs of seasoned pork, then laid each on open slices of fresh bread. Wrapping them in parchment paper, he asked, "Can I get you anything else?"

A few more days away, Benjamin wouldn't be home until the weekend. Mary Renata decided on a few items just for her and Thomas. She took a quarter kilo of soppressata and olives suitable for a tapenade. She could go to the market on Friday or Saturday morning for groceries and prepare a nice dinner for Benjamin's return. And maybe his favorite dessert. In her mind, she created a shopping list while the boy sliced the meat.

Mary Renata sighed. She and Benjamin had argued before he left for business the previous week, and they hadn't spoken since. Thinking back, she couldn't remember the reason for their quarrel. But the harsh words, both his and hers, and the loud slam of the door when he left reverberated through her mind. She didn't like thinking of it, but angry incidents between them were becoming all too common.

The boy held up a scoop of brown *leccino* olives. On the other side of the counter, Mary Renata nodded, and the boy put them into a container.

Benjamin traveled for work every week. Sometimes, he was gone for longer. Was she beginning to grow used to their time apart? Or did she resent it? If she admitted it to herself, she didn't see Benjamin the way she used to. These days, his imperfections glared at her. He possessed a human range of emotions, some of which she did not admire. Short patience with Thomas and her, his annoyance was apparent. Did he feel the same about her? She placed an involuntary hand to her neck, pressing on the small V-shaped bone below her neck. Dropping her head, she blinked hard and took a deeper breath. Benjamin hadn't phoned the entire week.

"A liter of *ricotta di pecora* too, *per favore*," Mary Renata requested.

"Si, Signorina," he said. Scooping the cheese into a container, he wrapped up her order. "You're the last customer today. The weather is getting worse, no?"

"Maybe," Mary Renata said.

Out the door and onto the sidewalk she went, hugging the buildings. Piazza Santo Spirito quiet and deserted, unusual this time of day, Mary Renata pulled her umbrella down around her shoulders, keeping her groceries in the brown paper bag close. Looking up, she saw Sister Gianna at a side entry to the cloister of the basilica, in an open doorway with Thomas. Squinting through the rain, he held up his hand, waving at Mary Renata. His frame small in a yellow rain jacket and boots, she hurried the rest of the way across the piazza to her son.

"Come inside, out of the rain" Sister Gianna said. "I'm glad you're here."

A man in a formal cassock stood beside Sister Gianna.

"Hello, Father," Mary Renata said. "I hope he wasn't any trouble. Were you good today for *Sorella*?"

"Of course he was." Sister Gianna bent down and kissed the boy on the top of his head. She brushed her check against Thomas's light hair, her skin as smooth and unblemished as the stiff white coif framing her face.

"You should get home quickly," Father Ivan said. "There is word that the Arno may come out of its banks. Fill your bathtub with water as soon as you get home. Take this bread with you as well," he said, handing her two fresh loaves.

"Thank you, but we have plenty. I've brought you porchetta for lunch," Mary Renata said, pulling the paninis from her bag.

"Take the bread. Sleep on the top floor of your flat tonight. It is best to take precaution," Father said, placing his hands on Thomas's shoulders. "You go home now and take care of Mamma."

Serious, the boy nodded.

"You'll go straight home, won't you?" Sister Gianna asked, hugging her friend. "Call us when you get there."

Pulling away from the girl's embrace, Mary Renata looked at her. Her typical demeanor quiet and calm, Sister Gianna seemed anxious and even demanding. Confused, Mary Renata tried to discern her demeanor. Her first friend in Florence, she'd never seen this side of the other girl.

---

Benjamin's flat too small for the two of them, Mary Renata and Benjamin had chosen their own on the left bank of the Arno, near the Piazza Santo Spirito. With a rooftop large enough for a garden and four levels, the space was surrounded by good neighbors and full of light. Walking distance to Mary Renata's gallery, the basilica they attended on Sundays, and the markets where they shopped, the logistics made sense.

Midweek, Benjamin on a work trip in France, Mary Renata stopped at a market where farmers and vendors from outside the city displayed their wares. She perused a colorful table of produce and selected vine-ripened tomatoes for a marinara. For a tart she'd make on the weekend, she bought citrus fruit and a few apricots. Next, she purchased two types of cheese and paused at a selection of silks. Considering a piece in deep blue with a pattern of water lilies, she juggled her bag. A piece of fruit rolled away, the bottom step of the church stopping its motion. A young woman dressed in a habit, her bright face and happy eyes an irony to her somber tunic, stopped and picked up Mary Renata's lemon.

I think this belongs to you," the nun said. "Can I help?"

"Thank you." Mary Renata took it from her and restored its position inside her grocery tote.

"You're welcome. You look familiar. Aren't you one of our parishioners?"

"My husband, Benjamin, and I are. I pass by here most days, on the way to do my art. I've a small gallery this side of the Pitti Palace."

"That's wonderful. I would love to see your work sometime."

"I will give you the address! What do you do at the basilica?"

"Whatever the sisters and Father Ivan need, but in the mornings, I mostly work in the garden. In the afternoons I bake for the market." The woman revealed a large basketful of homemade buns and pastries. "I am Sister Gianna."

That day, and on many after, the two women shared coffee and stories. Not much older than Mary Renata, the sister told of her life and how she came to the place where she was. She was the youngest of three children; her family was from Northern Italy. Her father, a banker, and her mother enjoyed fine things—furniture and jewelry, servants and nannies to help with the children, and a driver who took them to private schools.

Their lifestyle a fortunate backdrop, the forties arrived, bringing with it both economic and political chaos. As the months and years passed, Mussolini, Italy's fascist prime minister, seethed with bellicosity, his narcissism wounded with the notion he might be second in the Axis alliance. His agenda imperialistic, he enforced antisemitic laws and deportations on Jewish Italian families. The Italian government began confiscating assets, evicting Jews from their homes, and sending them to internment camps.

Gianna's father adjusted, moving and hiding assets, but the dictatorship squeezed harder. Mussolini underestimated the cohesive nature of the Italian people and their will. With the help of resistance networks, Catholic friends, and Franciscan nuns, Gianna's parents smuggled their children into a convent to keep them safe. They purchased forged identification documents. The church created baptism records for the children and took them south to Florence, where the children were first disguised, then assimilated into Catholic schools. Gianna and her siblings were taken in by families and given Christian names and new lives.

Mary Renata, a transplanted girl from small-town Ohio, considered the circumstances that set her in the life she'd made for herself in Italy, and those of her friend, Sister Gianna. How strange and at the same time beautiful it was that they sat together, having a *cappuccio.*

"The world is full of beauty and sorrow," Mary Renata said, their position overlooking the Boboli Gardens behind the palace.

"Sorrow brings out beauty in people and in the world. It gives us the ability to see things we never noticed before. It propelled us together and laid out a path for solidarity." Sister Gianna said. "The people who saved me did it out of kindness. Together we found strength in unity."

"And in friendship," Mary Renata said.

After Mary Renata rearranged the groceries and umbrella and took Thomas by the hand, they traversed the few blocks to their apartment. Laughing all the way, they weaved back and forth across the empty street, sloshing in the puddles.

"Can you hold the umbrella?" Mary Renata placed her hand on Thomas's back. To the right of wooden double garage doors, she unlocked a heavy exterior door. Once inside, she pulled it closed behind them. The space was a large private garage, in years gone by a carriage and horse storage. It was empty today; Benjamin had their car this week, his business meetings in and around Bologna. "Let's take our boots off," she said.

"Yes," Thomas said. "I'm wet!" He stomped on the bricks and stone, shivered, and kicked off his rain boots. He shrugged out of his jacket, shook it off, and carried it to the bottom of the flight of stairs. The little boy leaned the umbrella against the wall, and up just two steps, he reached over and hung the slicker on an ancient iron hook once meant for bridles or other tack. Mary Renata did the same with hers. The paper bag soggy, she held it tight against her body, hand on the bottom.

"Do you want me to carry that?" Thomas asked.

"No, thank you, sir," Mary Renata smiled down at her boy. "But I'll let you help me put these groceries away. Then we can change clothes and have a nice cup of coffee."

"That sounds good, Mamma," Thomas said. Up the inside flight of stairs they went. He pulled himself up on a forged iron banister. At the top landing, they entered the apartment through a carved olivewood door. Mary Renata used to joke with Benjamin that she fell in love with this apartment before him. On the level above the ground was a kitchen, living space, two bedrooms, and a bath. The next encompassed a large bedroom with an en suite reserved for guests. Above that floor was another living space with a balcony that overlooked an internal gated and shared courtyard. On the other side of the living space was a door to the *terraza sul tetto*, a rooftop patio covered in vegetables and herbs and healthy decorative greenery spilling over their pots. Along one side was a clothesline and a metal settee where Mary Renata enjoyed Chianti in the evenings after Thomas went to bed.

Forgetting all about the groceries, Thomas ran to the kitchen and scooted a stool around the counter. "I can make the coffees, Mamma!"

"You do that while I put this food away," Mary Renata said. Leaving out the panini she'd share with Thomas, she remembered Father Ivan's instructions. "Be careful, Thomas. I'll be right back," she said, heading up to the guest bathroom.

Using the step stool, Thomas pulled an espresso cup and a larger mug from the cabinet. Taking a scoop from a canister, he emptied beans into a grinder and turned the crank on top. Using a spoon, he filled the portafilter, tapped it on the counter, then placed it into the coffee machine in a locked position. He switched it on and waited.

"I'm ready!" he called, just as Mary Renata appeared on the staircase.

"Go ahead; I'm here," she said.

Thomas pulled down on the lever three times. "I'm making a big one for you," he said, handing the cup to his mother.

"Excellent," Mary Renata said, and took a sip.

"Now for mine." He jumped off the stool, went to the refrigerator for milk, and poured it into the mug over his own.

"You're quite the barista," Mary Renata said.

"I know, Mamma," Thomas said.

Outside, the wind blew, thunder shook the shutters, and the rain poured without relenting. Going to the window across from the kitchen, Mary Renata peered out. Looking up and down the street, she saw no one except a bedraggled wet dog hurrying home to its family.

"Meow, meow."

"Is that you, Leonardo?" Above her, a big tabby crept down the roof tiles. "There you are!" she said. Reaching up, she lifted the cat, brought him in through the window, and latched it. "I have a fun idea, Thomas."

"What is it?"

"Let's have a picnic in the upper den. We'll take pillows, blankets, some books to read, and panini for supper."

"Can Leo come too?" he asked.

"Of course, he can."

## Chapter 6

Early Thursday evening, on his last appointment of the day, Benjamin arrived late at a winery south of Bologna. In heavy, unabated rain, exhausted from his wet business clothes and navigating through limited vision in the windshield, Benjamin sighed. Glad the week was almost over, he considered the way he'd left things with Mary Renata. Angry at the time, he'd slammed the door without telling her goodbye. He intended to call, but the week passed by and he hadn't. Deciding to ask Mr. Villafranca to use his telephone after this meeting, he pulled his four-door Alfa Romeo Giulia onto a dirt lane leading to the villa and winery. In Benjamin's opinion, Mr. Villafranca grew the best Sangiovese grapes in all of Italy.

Parking near the door, he looked up. Mr. Villafranca jogged through the downpour carrying a large black umbrella. Benjamin opened the door and greeted the older man. "*Grazie*, Lorenzo. It's good to see you."

"Let's get inside!" Mr. Villafranca yelled through the downpour.

The two men hurried up the steps of a sprawling stucco home through an arched doorway. In the foyer, Benjamin removed his shoes. Lorenzo's wife, Annamaria, offered him a towel.

"How are you, Mr. Dyer? I'm surprised you came today."

"I apologize for being so late. But I'd never cancel on my favorite vineyard."

"I thought as much. Do you plan on going back into Florence tonight, Benjamin?" Lorenzo asked.

"I did. Or in the morning."

"No, no, no! Not the morning," Annamaria said.

"There is time to talk about wine, but later. Come. Sit." Lorenzo led Benjamin over to his dining table. He disappeared for a moment and returned with a glass of red wine and a map.

"What is this?" Benjamin asked.

Looking over the top of his spectacles, Lorenzo put his hand on Benjamin's shoulders. "Have you spoken with your wife? She is in Florence?"

"Yes. With our son. I haven't spoken with her in a few days." Benjamin felt the warmth on the back of his neck. His heart rate quickening, he asked, "Why?"

"There is too much water," Lorenzo said.

"But it always rains in the fall," Benjamin said.

"Not like this. Listen," Lorenzo said. "It is raining, but too much. The snow has melted up on the mountains. The river valley is soggy, and all the water is headed to Florence." Pointing at the map, Lorenzo drew a line with his finger. "If you are leaving, you must go soon. Otherwise, you'll never make it into the city."

"No," Benjamin said. "That can't be."

"Yes. It is already flooding in parts of the valley south of the mountain. Let me show you the route to take."

Lorenzo traced the map with his finger. "Look here. You can stay on high ground over the mountain by taking the road to Cavallina. Go east there. Then the road turns south. Continue until you reach Fiesole. From there, continue to Maiano. I think you can make it that close to the city."

"What do you mean, 'that close'?"

"Florence is going to flood. The water is rushing to the city like a funnel. Basements are filling. Sewers are backing up."

Annamaria went to the kitchen. Back with a thermos of hot soup, another full of water, and a loaf of fresh bread, she said, "I would try to convince you to wait until this storm passes, but I know that you will not. Take these too," she said, handing him a pair of tall rubber boots.

"I will not." Benjamin stood. "Grazie. To both of you. May I use your telephone before I go?"

"*Si*," Annamaria said.

He dialed his apartment in the city, but the phone would not connect. There was a fast-buzzing tone on the other end of the line.

"I can't make a connection," Benjamin said.

"The phone lines may be down," Annamaria said.

"Dio venga con te," Lorenzo said, embracing his friend.

"I hope I won't require any divine assistance," Benjamin said.

"But in case you do," Annamarie said, "Dio venga con te."

"You better get going. Let us know you got through safely as soon as you can," Lorenzo said.

Without another word, Benjamin looked at Lorenzo hard, started the car, and headed south. Night upon him now, he drove up and across the Apennines with wipers on high speed. Determined, he put one kilometer after another behind him. Around ten p.m., the rain pelted down so hard he could not see. He pulled the shiny blue car off the roadside and waited. He dozed off and awakened again at a loud boom of thunder. Still raining hard, the water poured across the road. *It had to let up.* Another hour passed, and then another, and Benjamin eased the car back on the highway toward Florence. In the town of Fiesole, he checked his watch. Early morning, the sun would be up soon. On winding roads, he crept toward Maiano. In the middle of the road, a policeman slowed him to a stop and tapped on his window.

"You cannot pass here, *signore*," he said.

"Why not?"

"It is too dangerous," the policeman told him. "The Arno River is out of its banks. The entire city is flooded."

"I need to get to my wife and son," Benjamin said, his voice cracking.

"Not by car. It is impossible to go any farther."

Conceding, Benjamin pulled over and parked at a small restaurant. He took the thermos of water, pulled on the rubber boats, and set off on foot. In about an hour, the sun peeked through a hole in the gray sky over his left shoulder. He reached the fringes of the city and picked his way closer to the river. He needed to go south and to the west to get to the Oltrarno. Through neighborhoods he went, the water deepening, until the city of Florence, a horrific caricature of Atlantis, loomed in front of him. From rooftops, people yelled at him to turn back. He placed his hands on his knees and stopped. With nowhere to go, he looked down into the dirty, oily water rushing by. More shouting drawing his attention, they signaled down the street to a man in a boat. Shouting louder and louder, they pointed at Benjamin. He turned around and saw a man approaching in a wide, low, and sturdy *vecchi barchetti*.

"Do you need help?" he asked. "Are you ok?"

Disoriented, Benjamin stared at him. Was the man in the boat a mirage? He looked at this sea of cars, metal, splintered wood, and other out-of-place items.

"Signore! What are you doing out here?"

"My wife. My son. I must get to them," Benjamin said.

"Where are they?" the man asked.

"The Oltrarno. Just beyond Piazza Santo Spirito," Benjamin told him. "I have to get there."

Using a long wooden pole, the Barcaiolo steered closer to the bedraggled American knee deep in the muddy water.

"The river is strong near the middle. Very strong, *Signore*. The Ponte Vecchio has been damaged."

"I have to get there," Benjamin repeated, steadying himself on the side of the *barchetti*.

"Get in." The boatman reached out his hand.

With the man's help, Benjamin hoisted himself into the boat. Still holding the thermos of water, he took a long drink and offered some to the man.

"Grazie. I have more if you need some," the man said. "First, we go west, then south toward the Duomo."

The morning grew late, and the rain kept falling. The man pushed the boat through the eerie, quiet streets turned canals. Seeing something splashing in the water ahead of them, Benjamin pointed. "Look there! What is that?"

Squinting, the boatman pulled the boat alongside a struggling, drenched sheepdog. Grabbing it by the scruff of its neck, Benjamin pulled the dog inside. With little strength, the exhausted animal's claws scratched the top of the low vessel. It shook itself off and collapsed on the floor of the boat.

"What is all over him?"

The boatman threw a rag over to Benjamin. "Try this," he said. "It is oil."

"Oil? Something else too. You smell terrible, ol' boy," Benjamin said, rubbing the dog's back and sides.

"The water ruptured heating tanks. Sewers collapsed as well." The farther they went, the deeper the water, obvious by levels on surrounding buildings. "Your apartment, Signore? Is it?"

Benjamin understood. "My wife is fine. She's well beyond Santo Spirito. Down Via del Serragli. She has access to a rooftop terrace," he said, refusing any alternative.

Pushing along, they passed apartments with people huddled on rooftops. "Everybody ok?" the boatman called. Most of them waved or shrugged. They passed a few other boats with families or single riders curious to see the effects of the rising waters. The big dog was an observer like his shipmates. Benjamin rubbed its rough fur and matted ears.

On the Via Ricasoli, they paused at the Accademia Gallery. Beyond the Gallery of the Prisons, at the back of an expansive hall, stood David on his pedestal. Looking out across the floors, the mighty shepherd boy was as helpless to stop the flood as the rest of the Florentines. Splashing through the water, the boat rocked as they approached the Duomo.

Benjamin tensed. "The water's getting deeper."

"Yes," the boatman said. The water swirling around the baptistry nearly covered doorways.

They traveled parallel to the river. Nothing to do but wait and paddle. At some point, when the boat began rocking beyond their zone of comfort, they went north a few blocks for a while, then ventured back to the channel. Benjamin watched the level of the water, moving faster here, making the boat harder to control.

"I don't think we can cross this afternoon, *amico*." The boatman looked out over the flooded city. "*Mi dispiace*."

"Per favore, do not apologize. You've tried. I don't think so either. It would be foolish to try to cross."

"Si. *Suicidio*. Let's get out of here. Come with me to my house. Is it true you have nowhere else to go?"

"That is true," Benjamin said. "I have nowhere else to go."

## Chapter 6

Back to the boatman's apartment in the *poggio gherardo*, not far from where he found Benjamin, they pushed the vessel as far as they could, then sloshed along the rest of the way in mud. Up to a second-floor apartment, they made a fire to heat coffee and shared bread, the sheepdog at their feet. After dark, Benjamin fell asleep on a sofa.

The next day, the sun shone through mammatus clouds, their bulges and pouches emerging from a large and flatter base. "Good morning," said the boatman. "The water receded over the night. My boat is certainly aground now."

"Grazie for your help. I must go to the Oltrarno now," Benjamin said.

## Chapter 7

That night, Thomas fell asleep on Mary Renata's lap. Looking down at him, she considered his transition from baby to child. He possessed a sense of maturity and gravity beyond his years, including an unusual degree of empathy. He played with other children but spent his days mostly with adults. Was this a mistake? No, it couldn't be. Thomas was surrounded by people who loved him.

Smoothing his hair from his face, something like guilt mixed with regret crept near her. She knew she hadn't been as patient and understanding as she should have with Benjamin. She promised herself to make efforts to express gratitude, to be a better partner. They shouldn't have argued with Thomas in earshot. Mary Renata felt terrible that their little son had heard their angry words. Tears filled the corners of her eyes; it was unacceptable. Vowing to close the gap between herself and her husband, she also knew she must keep Thomas distracted through this storm, to keep him from worrying.

Sometime after midnight, she'd fallen asleep with the lights on, leaning against the sofa, sitting up on the floor. Waking before dawn, she rubbed her eyes, stretching against her sleeping position. Gaining coherence, she struggled to comprehend a loud roaring noise. Moving Thomas's head to a pillow, she listened. *What was that? Was it wind? Was it beyond the river, or closer?* She walked over to the French doors, opened one side, and stepped out onto the balcony. Gasping, she covered her mouth with one hand. The courtyard beneath her gone, it was now a deep gray pond. She picked up the sleepy little boy and placed him on the sofa. Leonardo followed, jumped up, and rearranged himself at Thomas's feet.

Mary Renata hurried down the stairs into the kitchen and ran to the window. The day was beginning, and the sun lit the backdrop of a monochrome sky. Down below in the street, a rushing river, debris of every sort with metal, glass, light poles, and pieces of vehicles swept by. Clenching her teeth, she closed the window and paused at the door to the exterior staircase leading down to the garage. Shoulders back, a deep breath, she pulled it open fast. Another dark and murky pond, like in the courtyard, the water all the way up to the landing on the stairs, she slammed the door closed. Why was the water so black? How high would it rise? Inside the apartment, she pressed her back against the door, deciding what to do next.

"Sister Gianna!" she said, running across the room to the telephone. She picked up the receiver. No service on the line, she pressed the metal switch hook again and again, to no avail. Taking a deep breath, she closed her eyes and lowered her head.

As if it were a typical morning, she layered two pieces of bread with Nutella for Thomas. She gathered more supplies from the kitchen, some cups for water, and extra bread and headed back up the stairs. She filled the cups for drinking from the tub and stared down into the water. For the two of them, this water would last a long time. More than a week if they needed it to. Just as she reached the den, the lights went out. Now approaching eight in the morning, she slid back down on the floor, reclaiming her position from last night. She chose a novel from the coffee table, opened it, and began reading while Thomas slept.

Today was Friday. Benjamin should have been home last night, or at the latest, this morning. There was no way he could've made it into the city. *Surely, he wouldn't try.* Her thoughts making her chest tight, throughout the morning the roar of the water grew louder. Each time she checked at the window downstairs, the one she'd brought Leonardo through yesterday, she monitored the level of the water. Inch by inch, higher it rose. Across the street she saw a neighbor peering out.

"*Caio*! *Caio*, Mrs. Bianchi. Are you all ok over there?"

"Si, si." Mrs. Bianchi waved back. "And you?"

A gesture, something to say, Mary Renata thought, *what would either of us do if we weren't?* She opened the entry door. The water hiding the landing now, it was growing closer to the level where she stood.

"Mamma! Mamma!" Thomas called.

Mary Renata closed the door and hurried back up the stairs to the upper den. There Thomas stood looking out over the balcony.

"Where is Papa?" he asked. "Is he out there?"

"No, he isn't. Come over here with me, and let's play a game."

"I don't want a game. I want Papa."

"He will be here soon. As soon as the water goes down. There's been a lot of rain, but see? It's stopping. Let's go down to the kitchen and make some lunch." Attempting normalcy, she picked him up and carried him down the stairs. They spent the afternoon and evening reading books, playing with the cat, and making tents out of the sheets in the upstairs den. Mary Renata slept off and on through the night, watching the water turn to mud in the streets and wondering where Benjamin might be.

## Chapter 8

He pulled on the rubber boots and stood. The sheepdog followed him to the door, which he closed behind him, the dog's whimpers turning to loud howls before Benjamin reached street level. With an audible exhale, he paused for a moment, then went back up the stairs and opened the door. The big dog wagging his tail, the boatman said, "He must belong to you now."

"I think he must," Benjamin said. "C'mon, boy." Almost in a jog, he hurried back the way they'd come the day before. The water was gone, the streets now covered in slick mud. The dog's head never more than a few inches from Benjamin's right, they traversed the city together. South toward the river, Benjamin turned west to pass north of the Santa Croce. Without considering obstacles or destruction, he crossed the Ponte Vecchio, the Arno flooded with a thousand colors. Still intact, the bridge covered in logs and other debris, on he went. People now out and about, some wandered in circles, unsure what to do, while others shoveled, scooping mud into buckets. Now at Piazza Santo Spirito, he broke into a run, the dog still at his side. Just before nine o'clock Saturday morning, at the apartment, not stopping to remove his mud-caked boots, he took the stairs two and three at a time and crashed through the door.

"Mary Renata! Mary Renata!" he called, his heart pounding, pulse racing.

"Papa!" Thomas cried, running down the steps ahead of his mother.

Catching the boy in his arms, he looked to the top of the stairs at Mary Renata and did not take his eyes from her over the next weeks as they cleaned, retrieved the car, packed, and relocated to the family villa in the countryside, raising Thomas and generations of Maremma sheepdogs.

## Chapter 9

"Are you hungry?" Alex asked. "The Bolognese can cook for hours, but it's edible now."

"Sure," Katie answered, following him into the Airstream. "How can I help?"

"Take this bottle of wine out, with these utensils," Alex said, opening another. "Let me plate the food, and I'll be right out."

Katie took the wine and poured each of them a glass. Inside, Alex prepared the plates of pappardelle, grating fresh parmesan on top. While she waited, she thought of checking her phone, but on second thought, didn't dare. Best to leave it switched off until later.

"This is good. Thank you for dinner," Katie said, twirling the thick noodles on her fork.

"You're welcome," Alex said.

"We were talking about grandparents." Katie steered the conversation again. "Your grandmother closed the gallery after the flood?"

"Yes. After the flood they moved to the country," Benjamin explained.

"Oh," Katie said. "Did you grow up there too?"

"I did," Alex said.

"Where in the country? On a farm?"

"There was a house and land there that originally belonged to my grandmother's family. Her aunt lived there. My grandfather learned about growing grapes in their vineyard."

"So are your parents still in Italy?" she prodded.

"No," Alex said. "Both of my parents are gone."

Katie watched his expression. "Oh. I'm sorry."

"It's ok." Alex looked across the table at her. "I was only two years old when…" He trailed off. "I don't remember them. Sometimes I think I do, but what I perceive to be my own memories are likely stories my grandparents told or photos of them I've seen many times. I don't know if that makes sense."

"It does. I lost my mother when I was four. An accident at the ranch. I was there with her and have no recollection of any of it. I want to remember more than I do. But I only have these flashes of her, fleeting short clips."

"What sort of clips?" Alex asked.

"Little things. Random ones. I remember her hair. I remember certain patterns from her clothes; riding a horse with her. More than any of that, I remember after she was gone."

"What do you mean?"

"I mean, I remember her not being there. I remember wondering where she was and my grandmother being there instead."

Alex nodded.

"My grandparents helped raise me on our ranch. I guess your grandparents must've done the same?" Katie asked.

"They did. I grew up in Italy. They gave me a wonderful childhood. My grandparents were great. They still are."

"I feel the same about Gran and Grandad," Katie said. "And my dad. I can't imagine losing both parents." She folded her hands, looking at Alex. In a lower voice, she asked, "What happened?"

Focused on the wine in his glass, Alex considered her question. Inquisitive, Katie's questions bordered on invasive. What did she want? It was possible that she wanted information about his grandmother, that she wanted it for background on the art and artist, but he didn't know this girl. Considering his words, he decided public information from the past was harmless enough. As much as Alex wanted to shut the conversation down, the painting inside the Airstream gave him motivation to continue.

"I was around two years old, so I never knew anything except what my grandmother told me. She wanted to protect me. I understand that now."

"I can understand that too," Katie said.

## Chapter 10

In the kitchen, Mary Renata hugged Thomas and then her daughter-in-law, who was carrying her young son.

"You look beautiful, dear," Mary Renata told her.

"Grazie. I got this dress for the trip," Gabriella said. She put the baby down in the highchair, he with a handful of her long, dark waves.

"Ow! Alessandro!" Gabriella said. "Let go! And then you have fun with Nonna."

"We are going to have a wonderful time," Mary Renata said. "Maybe Nonno will fly the kite for us this afternoon."

The baby chewed on biscotti, his hands and face sticky with the brown-sugar biscuits.

"Good idea," Thomas said. Tall with light-colored hair, he looked like Benjamin. He rubbed the top of his little son's head. "See you in a few days," he said.

"Not too much work," Mary Renata said.

"No, no. Just one meeting, then I'm all hers," he said, squeezing Gabriella's shoulders.

"The Musee d'Orsay?" she asked, smiling up at him.

"As long as you'd like," Thomas said. He kissed his mother on the cheek. "Love you, Mamma. Where's Papa?"

The grapes soon ready for harvest, Benjamin spent most days out in the vineyard, pruning and picking. He insisted everything be done by hand like the old days, a culture without heavy machinery. Before the pickers came, over and over, Benjamin walked the rows, observing the comfort of the vines and the color of the stems and the seeds.

He checked their plumpness, the taste of the fruit, and the health of the leaves. Benjamin spent a lifetime learning, first from Mary Renata's people, from locals, and study and tentation; still, he discovered new things.

"He's out with the vines. You know your father. He will be out there all afternoon."

"You're right. Tell him we love him too," Thomas said.

"I will, I will," Mary Renata said. Turning away, not watching them go, she took the baby from his chair and washed his hands and face.

For the next three days, she and her little grandson flew the kite with Benjamin, made animal figures with clay, and took long naps. They spent afternoons in her studio above the garage, he finger painting on an easel while she worked on projects of her own.

Thomas and Gabriella lived in the city in the family apartment where Mary Renata and Benjamin had started out. Close to the train station, it made sense for business, and besides, the two preferred the activity of Florence over the vineyard. Sometimes on weekends, the young couple came to the country to visit, but Mary Renata loved these special occasions when it was just her and Alex.

On the night before Thomas and Gabriella's return, after supper, the three of them would take a walk in the olive grove. At dusk, Mary Renata put a light jacket on Alex, handed Benjamin a cardigan, and took a shawl for herself. Quiet except for the crunching grass beneath them, the last of the light from the day filtered among the branches. Down into the orchard they went, Alex between them, each holding one of his hands. Patient, they walked along at Alex's pace. Eyes on his feet, he took big, lumbering steps, stomping the ground. The shaggy white dog came between Mary Renata and Alex, herding the boy. At the country villa, the sun set, crickets chirped, and Mary Renata knelt beside Alex.

"Look," she pointed upward. "Do you see?"

Big brown eyes looking into hers, he followed her finger up into the trees.

---

Thomas and Gabriella ran through the train station and boarded their delayed train. Out of breath, laughing, they found seats at the back of the first car, and he stowed their luggage. Gabriella scooted into the seat closest to the window, leaving room for Thomas on the aisle.

Outside Paris, a young woman on an inbound train from the suburbs to the south panicked when her train passed her usual stop. Unaware of a seasonal schedule change, jumping up, she pulled the emergency stop, afraid she'd be late picking her children up from school.

To get the train moving again, the engineer exited his cab. He went to the back of the lead car and reset the brake system. The lever sticking, he grabbed another for leverage, budging the handle just enough in the process. Half an hour late, as instructed by dispatch, the driver skipped the last stop. Passing it by, the train rolled along. Approaching the station, he passed a caution sign. Anticipating the downhill track into the station, he applied the brakes.

---

Alex looked at Mary Renata, then back to the tiny insects. Down beside the boy, Benjamin caught one of the bugs and released it; the creature crawled on Alex's hand. With wonder, caution, and one chubby finger, Alex touched it before it flew away.

---

The train refusing to slow, the brakes barely worked. Frantic, the driver notified the control station. Alarms sounded in all the compartments, and Gabriella grabbed her husband's arm. Thomas checked his watch. He placed his arm around her shoulders, and she leaned into him, covering her exposed ear with her hand.

Leaving his post, the driver of the inbound surrendered, relinquishing his train to fate. Storming to the back of the train, passing through one car and the next, he ushered passengers with him.

---

Alex shrieked with glee, and Mary Renata and Benjamin laughed in unison. The big dog, his head level with Alex, joined in, wagging his tail, he licked the boy in his face. Benjamin rubbed the dog's ears, and Alex wiped his cheeks with his hands.

"He likes you, doesn't he?"

Alex bobbed his head while Mary Renata used her own sleeve, helping him dry his face.

---

At the controls of the delayed train resting on the platform, the driver stayed, giving the order, "*Evacuer! Evacuer immediatement!*"

Arm in arm, Thomas and Gabriella stood, but in the back seat, the mass of other passengers hindered their movement.

Gravity winning over the faulty brakes, wheels sticking and slipping across the top of the track, the rails squealing, the train hurtled into the station toward Thomas and Gabriella's platform. Without brakes or a driver, the out-of-control train flew, the high-pitched screaming of metal wheels against metal rails resonating.

---

Delighted, Alex clapped his baby hands and reached at the blips of light twinkling through the leaves, among the trunks and branches silhouetted against the darkening sky. Alex grabbed at the glowing beetles while they slipped through his fingers. Fascinated by its synchronous bioluminescent flashing, Alex studied a firefly that landed on his sleeve. Benjamin hoisted Alex up on his shoulders, the little boy's head back, his arms in the air waved through the tiny ripples of light.

———

The driver of the delayed train, refusing to leave his post, continued to shout warnings over the intercom. The moving train hurled itself on its horrible path. Relentless and unfettered, Thomas and Gabriella, still at the rear of the first car, it smashed into the delayed train. On impact, the traumatic force peeled back and crumpled steel like newspaper, a sickening noise splitting the car in two, the car of the runaway train encased inside the car on the platform. In Paris, on Platform One at the Gare de Lyon, a black cloud settled, concealing the wreckage.

## Chapter 11

Over the next few weeks, time stretched without end, the sun reluctant to rise or set. Normal routines taking great effort, her arms heavy, Mary Renata willed herself to take milk from the refrigerator. Buttering a piece of toast or making a jelly sandwich a formidable task, she forced smiles for Alex. Several times per day, taking him outside a merciful distraction, he ran around and played with the dog, or she pushed him on a swing. The oddest juxtaposition—she felt like a spectator in an audience watching herself as the lead in a terrible, tragic play, with Benjamin in a supporting role.

Following the news, she and Benjamin packed a bag and drove to Florence. Inside the car, time paused while the outside world passed. Rude and insensitive, not waiting, the hillsides rolled by while tall and stately cypress trees mocked her with virtual immortality. On the outskirts of the city, Mary Renata stared through homes and shops while Benjamin navigated alone. An errant tear found its way down the side of her face, falling onto her collarbone, then was absorbed by the sleeve of her blouse.

Once inside the apartment, Mary Renata wandered from room to room. Carrying a basket of toys for Alex, she set them in the living area, and picked up the phone.

"Sister Gianna," Mary Renata said, settling into the couch. "Benjamin and I are here in Florence. Can we come over?"

Sister Gianna paused for an extra moment. Something foreign in her old friend's voice, she was unsure of what it could be. A knot forming in her stomach, acridity rising in her throat, she asked, "Mary Renata. What is it? What is wrong?"

Clearing her throat, Mary Renata said, "I need to see you right away."

"Please come now, then," the sister said, hurrying to the entrance of the cloister. Watching the far side of the piazza, she waited until she saw Mary Renata and Benjamin with the little boy in tow round the corner at the Via Mazzetta. Using a smooth stone to keep the door from shutting behind her, the *sorella* hastened to greet them, maneuvering around vendors packing up the day's unsold vegetables. Her steps quick and short, the habit flowing behind, annoyed pigeons fluttered out of her path. Reaching them just before the fountain in the square, Sister Gianna gazed into Mary Renata's ashen face and clouded eyes, then took her elbow. Carrying Alex under one arm, no words, Benjamin looked at Sister Gianna. Placing one arm around Mary Renata's shoulder, holding her tight, she led the little group back to the open door.

Lifting one leg, placing it down, the same motion on the other side, Mary Renata concentrated on completing each step, her finish line the opening to the basilica. Once inside, protected in the shade of the arcade, Mary Renata's footing gave way. Her burden pulling Sister Gianna down along with her in the hallowed hall, she fell to her knees, collapsing into the arms of her dearest friend. The folds of Sister Gianna's tunic cascading across the concrete walk, Mary Renata grasped handfuls of the fabric. Her wails echoing beneath the arches, Sister Gianna held on to her friend until her racking body subsided.

Sister Gianna helped Mary Renata up and went toward Benjamin, her arms outreached. In kind, Alex reached out too. Instead of embracing Benjamin, she took the child. Swaying back and forth, she patted his back, her hand soothing. In a minute, he rested his head on her shoulder.

For the better part of the week, Mary Renata and Benjamin in Paris, Alex stayed with Sister Gianna at Santo Spirito. They spent the days on errands to market, sharing cups of gelato, and playing in the gardens shielded by heavy columns. Alex splashed in the fountain, just like his father so many years before him. Sister Gianna watched the boy laughing at fish peeking from under the lily pads, the sun on his face, golden. Beneath the cold recesses enveloping her came the tiniest bit of warmth from within. Placing one hand on her chest, she felt for it, willing it to grow. Bending over in the plant bed surrounding the pool, Alex took a miniature daisy from a patch of bellium. Toddling over, he handed it to Sister Gianna.

"*Dum spiro spero.* While I hope, I breathe," she whispered. With two hands, she brought the boy's face to hers and kissed his cheeks over and over, causing them both fits of uncontrollable laughter.

## Chapter 12

"I got most of the information from the internet when I was older," Alex said. "My grandmother answered my questions when I asked, but I could tell it caused her pain. So I stopped." He cleared his throat, hoping he hadn't divulged too much.

"It's the same way with my dad. We don't talk about my mother. My grandmother told me bits and pieces about her and put together a photo album, but that's about it," Katie said. Both finished with the pasta, Katie offered, "Let me help with these dishes."

"No, no. I'll put them in the sink and take care of it later," he said, clearing the plates and taking them inside. He left the door to the Airstream open and came back. "There are two more glasses of wine. Would you like to share them with me?"

"Sure. I appreciate all your hospitality."

Alex stepped out of the Airstream, the wine in hand. "I enjoyed it."

"Me too," Katie said, her face flushed.

Over the rest of the bottle, he talked about the layers and the flavors brought about by the limestone laden Texas terroir.

"You know, the way wine tastes is more about place than anything else. The weather, the soil, and the topography all determine what kind of grapes we get." Alex swirled his glass.

"The more I learn about wine, the more I realize how little I know."

Alex pointed at her. "Intuitive. My grandfather always says you can never stop learning about wine. He claims he still learns new things."

"I understand. I feel the same way about art." They clinked their glasses together.

Alex indicated the bottle on the table. "These tempranillo grapes were grown here on this land."

"I appreciate that. My grandfather says the same thing about his cattle when we barbeque at the ranch." She grinned and took a sip. "Cattle and wine—they both come from the land."

"And a lot of hard work."

"And knowing how to raise them."

"I don't believe that this area of Texas has even hit its stride when it comes to growing, though it's come a long way since the seventies."

"You must be referring to the story about the Texas Tech professors making wine in the basement of the chemistry building," Katie said.

"I am. Those men figured out that grapes could be grown here just as well as grain and cotton."

"Texas has a lot of land. And here we sit. On the largest, flattest expanse of it on the planet," she said.

"God bless Texas," Alex said.

"Indeed." Stretching, Katie stifled a yawn.

"Are you ready to go back into town?"

"I should. And I shouldn't keep you any later," Katie said.

"This evening was both unexpected and nothing less than pleasant. I would've been up late anyway." Alex shifted his eyes up at the plinking on the metal roof. He picked up the empty wine glasses and put them inside. Then he took a roll of packing tape from a drawer and secured the wrap and plastic back around the painting. "That should get you back to San Antonio." Alex handed the package to Katie. "Wait here for a minute. I'll get your luggage." Back out of the rain, he came inside, opening an umbrella. He motioned for her to get under. Together they went to the truck. He helped her inside and stowed the painting on the back seat.

Passing her broken rental car, Alex laughed.

"Terrible car. Terrible little car," Katie said. "I still have to call them to pick it up."

"I can't believe that anything was ever made in that color," Alex agreed.

Relieved to not be driving back in the rain, Katie relaxed, and they chatted about things that neither of them would remember the next day, or at all, but only the ease of their banter. Katie directed Alex to her hotel, and he pulled under its awning. He ran around to her side and opened her door.

"Let me help you get this up to your room." Alex pulled the handle on her luggage and handed her the painting. "Here, let me have that back. I can rest it on top."

At the elevator lobby, viewing her blurred reflection in the doors, an internal shriek escaped Katie. Her eyes glued to the steel, Alex said, "Are you all right?"

Unable to look away, the too-large sweatshirt hung down to midthigh over the new denim dress, her hair air dried and wavy, she squished her toes inside the wet boots. "I shocked myself." Raising both hands, a pair of wet socks in one, she motioned at herself, head to toe. *Ding.* The elevator door opening, they stepped inside with her baggage.

Looking down at her, Alex chuckled. "Let's just say you look well-traveled."

Her face warmed as the elevator opened on her floor. Down a patterned carpeted corridor to her room, she unlocked it with her card. Alex stayed in the hall, propping the door open with his hand and arm while she took her things inside one at a time. Smoothing her hair back, she turned back around.

"Your sweatshirt." Katie touched her shoulders.

"It's ok. I'll get it back from you another time." Alex pushed his hair back from his forehead.

"Well. Thank you again for everything. I'm thrilled that I sort of found Mary Renata."

"Let me get your contact information before I go. I'll be in touch after I talk with my grandmother." Alex handed her his phone. While Katie typed, Alex looked at the wrapped painting leaning against a desk. He pulled his eyes away when Katie handed his phone back.

"I'm looking forward to it," Katie said.

"I'll talk to you soon." Nodding his head, Alex moved his arm from the door, and Katie closed it behind him. Pressing her back against it on her side, she took a deep breath, her eyes focused on the ceiling. Midway to the elevators, Alex stopped, resisting an overwhelming urge to go back for the painting. If he'd have liked Katie the slightest bit less, he would have.

# Part III

## Chapter 1

Based on emotion or logic, calculated, or without any rationale at all, Mary Renata considered the curiosity of choices. Life cartographers, they afforded roads, bridges, steep mountains, and every other topographic feature. All encompassing, she knew they had brought her to the place she was, right at that very moment.

Making choices from the time she was young, some of those, she believed at the time, took careful thought and focused attention. In other instances, in retrospect, when she was old enough to have any of that, it seemed as if she had been picked up from one spot and moved to another by a force great, and yet so subtle, she was unaware. Like one of those moving walkways in airports it took her to a finite point without regard or permission.

Now that she was not young, Mary Renata thought of it often. How she had arrived at this place. About how will wrapped up with providence somehow set her down with ease, onto this familiar chair, drinking a perfect glass of wine, under this ivy-covered pergola, next to this dear man.

Their routine each day sometimes consisted of a stroll through the olive grove. The ancient trees told their own stories. Each twisting trunk grew upward, exposing emerald leaves, their undersides silvery in the light breeze. Other times, they chose the vineyards, winding down this row or that, inspecting for any inconsistencies on the vines. As the days grew cooler, they might choose just the gardens near the house. And after, sitting together with minimal remarks, they viewed rolling hills far in the distance.

For many years, they settled into this contentment, for so long she thought hard to remember anything before it. Yet here they were. Here she sat beside him. She reached over to touch his hands. Not those of a businessman, but instead, a farmer or carpenter. He had worked with them his whole life; they sometimes ached at night. Touching his fingertips, she traced the knuckles and valleys back toward his wrist.

He turned and faced her, and when he smiled, the lines on his face showed the patina of a well-used map, long traveled together. His features were classic and sculptural, with a straight nose and symmetrical chin—even with age, a handsome man. His dark eyes, still full of youth, lingered on her for an extra moment. Behind them, the farmhouse stood, unrelenting and unaware of time, weather, or shifting landscapes. Now they lived here in a rambling two stories of bisque-colored stone and tile. Like them, the ancient house had seen wars, generations, world leaders, and even children come and go.

"Let me pour you another, my bella." He loved the nuances of the Romance language that so many years ago, they had learned together—its rhythm and musicality. Brushing her cheek with the back of his hand, he motioned toward the bottle of wine on the small table between them.

She nodded, then, "In just a minute. Let me go inside to get some bread. And cheese."

She stood, turning toward gray-green shutters attached to the masonry on either side of each window. Late in the year, the sheers fluttered, an invitation for the October winds. Inside, whitewashed plaster flanked terra cotta floors, and overhead, massive wooden beams supported the over-five-hundred-year-old structure. Archways gave way to reveal brick and frescos underneath the ages. Her sandals clicked on the tile, and they slid across colorful hand-knotted carpets. The temperature dropping, she pulled her cardigan a little tighter.

## Chapter 1

From the cupboard, she collected bread, and from underneath the island, a board. From a fallen branch, Benjamin had planed the wood, sealing it with beeswax and oil. Slicing the baguette, she arranged it with fruit, his favorite calabrese, some pecorino, and a Spanish Manchego. In the loggia, the protected columned patio that ran along the east side of the house, she carried the tray and a blanket swept from atop a trunk, her floral-patterned silk shift brushing against her legs and the sofa. Returning, she placed the blanket around his shoulders and tucked it in between his back and the chair. Making a tiny *panino* from the board just for him, her cell rang. Brushing a strand of hair away from her temple, he reached up to rest one hand on the back of her neck.

Accepting the call, right away, she placed it on speaker. "Hello, my darling," she said, waiting for the voice on the other side.

"Hello, Nonna." Trading bits of information with Mary Renata, Alex asked if his grandfather was there.

"He's here, dear. You're on speaker."

"Oh, good. Hello, Nonno. I have something I'd like to talk to you about."

Benjamin looked at Mary Renata. She cocked her head, placing both palms upward.

"Your grandfather and I have finished our wine. I was just about to go inside for more." Shrugging, a slight half smile, Mary Renata went back inside.

From start to finish, Alex told Benjamin the tale of the wet, bedraggled girl appearing at his doorstep in the middle of a Texas Panhandle rainstorm carrying the painting lost long ago. Uttering the words, Alex barely believed them himself and expressed as much to his grandfather.

"I left the painting with her. I wanted to turn around and go back for it, but I didn't." Driving back to the East Coast, Alex questioned his decision over and over. To put a stop to the replay of scenarios, he'd called his grandparents.

"The important thing is that you've found it," Benjamin said. "You feel certain that it will stay in her possession?"

"Yes. Like I explained, she is interested in more. For an exhibition."

"There are more." Benjamin adjusted the phone on his lap.

"There are." Amarillo in Alex's rearview mirror, Daisy's front feet on the console, his arm resting across the dog's shoulders, they stared at the vast horizon beyond the end of the road. In the panhandle, the southernmost end of the Great Plains, horizontality stretched on and on. Straw-colored grasses sprouted from tawny earth, and the blooms on the yucca gave credence to the town's namesake. The drive on Highway 40 now familiar, the sameness here was something he had learned to come to terms with.

"Do you believe she would be willing to make a trade?"

"That is exactly the reason I'm calling you, Nonno." Alex sipped his coffee.

"Unless you hear otherwise from me or your grandmother, proceed in that direction." Mary Renata returning, Benjamin smiled up at her.

"Are you telling Nonna?"

"Telling me what?" Mary Renata took her seat next to Benjamin again. He covered her hand with his.

"Of course I'm telling her," Benjamin said.

"What is this all about?" Mary Renata sat up straighter. "Now I'm curious."

"Alex. You should get back to driving. Please be safe."

"I will, Nonno. Love you, Nonna."

"I love you too. Please let us know when you get back to Montauk." Mary Renata leaned over closer to the phone in Benjamin's hand.

When they disconnected, Benjamin looked over at his wife. "You are not going to believe what Alex just told me."

Never blinking, Mary Renata listened to the story.

"It's found. It isn't lost anymore. After all these years. After all this time," Benjamin repeated.

Mary Renata stood, walked over to the edge of the terrace, steadied herself, and took a deep breath. Sipping her wine, from this vantage point she stared out over the orchard. The news, like an enormous charge of electricity in a single burst, a whoosh of old sadness and hope churning all at once, mixed up with relief not for herself but for Benjamin.

Joining her, Benjamin wrapped his arms around his wife. "We are going to get it back," he whispered, pressing his cheek against hers.

They stayed just like that in silence until the current sheepdog came and forced her head between the two, letting them know the sun was down and it was time to go inside.

That night in bed, Benjamin stared up at the ceiling. Reaching for Mary Renata, his hand on her shoulder, he could tell by her breathing she wasn't asleep. "I want to hang it where it was before."

Mary Renata shifted. Turning her body, she placed her hand on her husband's head and stroked his hair at the temple. Benjamin pulled her closer and, his head on her shoulder, drifted off before Mary Renata. In the moments between wakefulness and sleep, her lucid dreams were of colors and paint pots and mixing oils on a palette, her hand, grasping a large bristle brush, flowing across a canvas.

## Chapter 2

Back from the St. Anthony early this afternoon, Katie stretched all the way out on the sofa, her arms straight above her head, one flopping over the edge. Light spilling into the apartment, she hadn't been this relaxed in weeks. Relaying the good news about finding the artist had left her boss pleased, and she felt herself skipping on the walk home today. After her travels, however, she felt tired. As she considered a nap, feeling herself drift, her phone buzzed on the coffee table. Reaching for it, she turned it over. A quick inhaled breath, she sat straight up. Paralyzed for an instant, she answered.

"Hello?"

Almost to St. Louis, Alex wondered whether she would answer. "Katie? It's Alex."

"Oh. Hello. What are you up to?"

"Daisy and I are driving back to the East Coast," Hearing her name, Daisy's tail thumped the back seat. "I wanted to let you know I spoke to my grandparents."

"Really?" Katie cleared her throat. Using her free hand, she felt for her carotid pulse. Without any effort, her index finger found it right away, the vein thumping strong and fast.

"Yes. They said it is fine with them if you'd like to choose some of my grandmother's other paintings for your exhibit."

Covering her mouth with her hand, Katie leaped from the sofa. She jumped up three times, landing on her living room carpet, soft thuds Alex couldn't hear.

"Hello?" Alex wondered if the call dropped.

"I'm here. I'm still here. That is great news." Katie sat back down, breathless.

"I thought you might be glad to hear that. But the other reason I'm calling is to ask if you'd like to come out to Long Island to look at my grandmother's other art. I thought you could make selections for your exhibit."

Before speaking this time, Katie did a lap around the perimeter of the rug. "I am. Glad. Happy. And yes. Yes, I would like to come take a look."

"Ok. Not this coming weekend, but the next, I have a benefit to attend. My family is one of the sponsors. I go to represent them. As you know, my grandparents are in Italy, and my uncle isn't social, so it's all on me. I'd like for you to be my plus one. If you are interested." Alex waited for Katie's answer, and after a long pause, he said, "But only if you want to. Please, don't feel obligated. You can come and look at the art for your exhibit either way."

A mental configuration forming, Katie drew lines between points. An approximate number of days to package and receive art. How long to unpack and prepare for exhibition? Devising a theorem of, *if this then that* she went through a mental list.

"I would love to come look at the art and attend the event with you." Katie wondered whether she was too enthusiastic. Without even looking at her calendar, it didn't matter. She'd clear anything and everything for this.

"Great. It's a plan, then."

"It's a plan," Katie repeated.

"The benefit is on Saturday, but if you'd like to travel say, on Thursday, we'd have the day Friday to go through the art."

"I can make that work." Katie took a breath.

"Ok. Let me know your arrival details, and I'd be glad to pick you up at the airport," Alex said.

"You don't have to do that. I can rent a car."

"No need to rent a car. I don't mind picking you up," Alex said. "By the way. It's black tie. So that you know how to pack."

"All right, then. Thank you. And thank you for letting me know. I'll look at flight options and get back to you," Katie said.

"I'm looking forward to it." Alex patted the front passenger seat.

"I am too," Katie said, and disconnected the call.

Daisy jumped up next to Alex, wiggling from nose to tail, the yellow dog licked his hand. "Did you hear that, Daisy? She said she's flying to Montauk. You never can tell about people, though she seems like a nice girl. I guess she did find us through the painting. She wants more of that art, doesn't she?" Daisy grunted. "If she got the painting as she said she did, do you think we should feel bad for dangling more of it in front of her?" Ears perked up, Daisy cocked her head to one side. "No. We aren't unscrupulous people. We need our painting back, and there are other paintings she can choose from to exhibit. Wouldn't you say that's a win-win for everyone?"

―――

Katie stood up, then sat down and picked up her computer. She stood again. She could get the ticket later. In independent celebration, she danced around the living room, spinning into the kitchen and into her bedroom. She jumped up and down on her bed and collapsed onto the pillows. What time was it? Almost five. She called downstairs to a bistro on Market Street, ordering two specials and a salad for sharing. Twenty minutes later, back upstairs, she plated pork chops and garlic-roasted grits. Tre loved grits.

"What's for dinner?" Tre came around into the kitchen just as Katie finished arranging salad on the side. Leaning down, he brushed her cheek. "That looks good, but," he said, flicking the container from the restaurant. "I guess cheating every now and then is acceptable."

Her humming subsided. She kept her smile, only real from the outside now, taking the plates to the table.

At the bar, Tre made himself a double bourbon, neat. A lone sound in the apartment, the leather bottoms of his oxfords clicked on the shiny plank flooring. Katie's back to Tre, they came closer. *Click, click, click.* In no particular rhythm, her body stiffened at their lack of timing or destination.

"Are you hungry?" She turned around.

Shrugging, Tre pulled out his chair, sat, and Katie followed.

"It's good, don't you think?" Katie asked.

Tre nodded, chewing, and then, "Did I interrupt something? What were you doing when I got here?"

"Nothing. I just came home a bit early, and—"

"And you didn't have time to make dinner?" Tre interrupted, shaking his head.

"No. I was going to say… I mean… I got busy. Some work things came up."

Tre stared at Katie, his fork up. Under his gaze, she played with her hair with one hand. She dropped her knife and reached for it where it had fallen under the table.

"You were gone longer than you said." Tre pushed his grits around, making a new pile.

Katie came up from under the table. "No. I said…I think I said three or four days? That is what I said. Right?"

"Uh huh." Tre worked his tongue around his mouth. "That's what you said. You were gone for four nights."

Flushed and hot on her neck, Katie took a drink of water. The crystal felt as cold on her lips as the water running down the back of her throat. Closing her eyes, she drank longer, gulping. Surprised at the empty glass, she studied its dry bottom. Tre tapped the fork on the edge of the china.

"Oh. Right. Four nights." Katie set the glass down. Her mouth was still dry. "I'm thirsty." She rose from the table and went into the kitchen. The tap water running between her and Tre, Katie refilled the glass. "Tre. I found the artist for the painting I got permission from to exhibit. I'm going back up to New York next week to collect pieces." Without correct articles or punctuation, she went back to her seat. Both hands clenching the edge of the table, her eyes on Tre, she readied herself for…*what?* And her next thought was, *whatever comes next.*

"I guess that means you forgot about my client appreciation happy hours and dinner." He tapped again.

Katie looked down. The misophonic sound reverberated in an echo. The tines of the fork scraping the plate, inflated and unbearable, she resisted an urge to take it from him.

"You don't have to attend the Wednesday social at the office. But next Friday and Saturday night, I expect you to be there. With me."

"I'm supposed to leave on Thursday." As if holding it down, Katie held the table tighter. Relieved of the tapping, she didn't flinch when the fork flew, somersaulting down the runner, an animated tumbling pass. His chair screeching across the floor, Tre stood and stormed into the bedroom. Opening and slamming doors in the master closet, now half undressed, in an undershirt and boxers, he stomped back into the dining room.

"What in the hell is this?" In one hand, Tre held the wadded Cornell sweatshirt that Katie had left in the laundry hamper. The bulging veins on the side of his head matched the ones in his neck.

Katie stood, reaching for it. "I got that in Lubbock."

"Cornell has a campus in Lubbock?" His voice was loud, just a notch below yelling. He threw it on the floor.

Midstep, Katie stopped. "The airline lost my luggage. I picked it up at a thrift store."

"I don't believe you. As a matter of fact, I think you're a damn liar, Katie."

Three feet away from the table, in open space trapped in no man's land, she stood there. Not daring to speak or go around him, she waited. He stormed back into the bedroom and returned wearing a collared shirt, a pair of shorts, and running shoes. He grabbed his keys and went out, slamming the heavy entry door behind him.

Certain he was gone, free to move, Katie stacked the plates. She scraped the leftovers into the trash, washed the dishes by hand, and left them to dry beside the sink. Then she retrieved her computer from the sofa, closed the door to her bedroom, and laid it on her bed. Making the shower hot as tolerable, she let the water pour over her. When it ran cool, she stepped out and brushed, then blow dried, her hair.

Back in bed, pillows propped behind her back, she glanced over at the closed door. She turned off her lamp and slid down under the covers.

Sometime after two in the morning, Katie startled awake at the front door slamming. Tre stumbled in, groaning when he bumped into a credenza, then a group of barstools situated around the counter, a mechanical effect like pushing a row of standing dominoes. The bar on the other side of the bedroom wall, she heard ice clinking into a tumbler. Then the sound of Tre tripping over his feet, followed by expletives strung together, a grammatically correct sentence full of flavored adjectives, he ended it with a noun combined with a familiar prepositional phrase. Gritting her teeth, she closed her eyes in a state of feigned sleep.

Flipping the lights on, he threw the sweatshirt at her. Diving onto the bed, he shoved it into her face, her breathing muffled. Forgetting to pick it up after the dishes, she remembered she'd left it out on the floor.

"Liar, liar, liar," he said, again and again. Holding her head so that she couldn't move away, he pressed harder, covering her mouth and nose with the garment.

Katie knew that rabbits played dead if threatened. *Fluffle*, Katie thought. *A group of young rabbits is called a fluffle.* In tonic immobility, she took slow breaths into the heavy cotton, waiting until Tre tired, rolled over, and passed out. Still dressed, on his back snoring, his smell reminded Katie of an unshaven man wearing flannel drinking at a run-down pub in an urban shanty town in long-ago New York City.

She got up and collected her computer and cell phone. Into the closet, she pulled on leggings and tied her running shoes. She packed a bag with work and casual clothes and collected her toiletries, taking necessities for at least a week. As if in a tranquil vacuum, ticking off a list in her head, she tucked away toothpaste and toothbrush and secured her shampoo and conditioner in zip bags, along with her makeup. The surly, drunken bum still in the same position, she left the bedroom. She turned around halfway to the foyer, went back, and collected the sweatshirt from near her pillow.

Down on the still street, she debated walking to Mari's. Deciding against carrying her things all the way there, she found a cab in a block and in a few minutes found herself knocking at Mariana's door.

---

"I am a liar." Katie took the cup of tea offered by her friend.

"What were you supposed to say?" Mari curled her feet up underneath herself, tying her long hair into a knot. "The sweatshirt is on loan from a sexy grape farmer I stalked in Lubbock?"

"No. But I could've been more truthful." Katie sipped the hot drink.

"I disagree. He's dangerous, Katie."

"I shouldn't have lied. And he was drunk."

"You couldn't have told the truth. Who knows how he would've reacted. Listen to yourself, Katie. Tre's always drinking. It is not an excuse. But here you go again." Mariana waved her arms. "Blaming yourself for his terrible behaviors. What happened next?"

Katie retold everything from the flying utensil to Tre blacking out.

"Did you look through his phone while he was passed out?" Mari asked.

"No. I didn't."

"I'm telling you. He's dirty. Why were you holding on to the table like that?" Mariana didn't wait for Katie's answer. "Why were you wondering and ready for what he was going to do next? Why were you pretending to be a dead rabbit, Katie?"

"I wasn't pretending to be a rabbit."

"Fine. But how do you feel when you're around him? Like a partner or a servant? Ok. You can answer me now," Mari finished. "I'm getting another cup of tea."

"I wouldn't say subservient. But maybe a subordinate. Sometimes. And nervous all the time. That part is my own fault because I haven't been honest."

"Do you think that nervous is the best descriptor?" Mari kept prodding.

Katie looked down into her teacup. She took the wedge of lemon and swirled it inside. "Intimidated. I often feel like a teenager in trouble with a parent."

"When do you feel that way, Katie?"

"Not all the time," Katie admitted. She looked up from her cup. "It hasn't always been like this between us. We used to have the best times together. When we were in school everything was just… *easier.*

"You two were kids then."

"We were. I've been going over and over it all in my mind. I've tried to pinpoint the shifts that brought us here. But I can't. I only know that they have been gradual. But now, here we are."

"And here you are," Mari said. When do you feel like a partner or at least an adult in his presence?"

"When everything is going exactly as Tre wants things to go. When I'm where he thinks I should be. When I am doing something for him." Her voice crescendoed, and she rose and paced across Mari's living room. "When I am doing what he wants me to do!" In front of Mari, she bent her knees, bringing her face closer to her friend's. "Things are great as long as I'm doing whatever it is to, to tell him what he wants to hear." Katie stopped, considering her own words, their meaning resonating. "Mari. When I'm with him, I'm not connected to him. I'm just. There. Like an object."

"What do you mean?"

"I think. I think he sees me in relation to himself. An object that completes his image. An image of how he believes he's perceived by others. And he punishes me if I don't comply. As an example, the more I immerse myself in work, the more I think that he would get pleasure taking it away from me."

"Like pushing you to quit?"

"Yes," Katie said.

"Do you think he knows how much you love work? Or maybe it doesn't matter to him?"

Katie placed one hand on her chin. "I don't know."

"Why did you lie to Tre?"

"Because I wanted to avoid conflict with him."

"The kind of conflict that ends with him suffocating you? Do you think you would lie to someone to whom you were connected? In a two-sided relationship? To me? To your dad?"

Considering her family, Katie shook her head. "No. I wouldn't lie to any of you."

"Do you think you are a liar? Or are you a scared rabbit, trying to survive? I want to know. I want to know why you are tolerating his behaviors."

"Like I said, Mari. These things that are happening have been gradual. I suppose it's because I want to get along. And I suppose I love him."

"What does that mean?"

"What?"

"What does that mean? That you 'love him'—or each other, for that matter?"

"I mean. I guess it's a feeling. Of caring and compassion."

"But what else, Katie? Love is a partnership. Where two people celebrate each other's victories. Where they watch out for each other above anyone else and push each other toward higher goals. All the time. You are supposed to be evolving together for the better."

"And this is coming from the one who juggles how many men?"

"This conversation is not about me, but because you mentioned it, I have standards." Mari yawned. "And I think you have some things to think about. Feelings are not facts, Katie. It is important that you separate the two. I have to get up in a few hours. Are you going to work?"

"Yes. I have so much to do to get ready for the exhibit. And I have to get ready to go back to New York."

"Do you need some clothes? What did you bring?" Mari picked up Katie's bag.

"I have things for several days." Katie took the bag from Mariana.

"When do you think you'll go back for the rest?"

"I can't even think about that right now, Mari."

"Of course. I understand, and you know you can borrow anything of mine that you need."

"Will you go dress shopping with me? Maybe this weekend?"

"I will. That is another conversation we need to have. And Katie, everything is going to be ok, but maybe just not today," Mari said.

Giving Mari a final squeeze, Katie retreated into the guest bedroom. She fell asleep and didn't open her eyes until the city woke up, the morning light spilling over her.

## Chapter 3

The next few days were uneventful. Still, Katie had a visceral response each time her phone buzzed with a text or email. She booked a flight to La Guardia and sent Alex the details. Her trip set, she spent long days at the hotel filling the calendar with events, writing press releases, and marketing.

In the evenings, when Katie wasn't looking, Mariana studied her friend. She gauged her mood from the way she moved to her expressions.

"How does your day look tomorrow afternoon?" Katie asked.

"I don't think I'm too busy. Why?" Mariana arranged fruit on a plate. The microwave dinged, and she took out a bag of popcorn to share.

"I need to get a dress for that event up in New York." Quieter than usual, Katie looked tired.

"Tomorrow? I can get off work early if you can." Mariana paused. "Maybe we can go for drinks after? This popcorn is ready." Mariana reached for two bowls and carried a platter into the living room.

"I'm not hungry," Katie said.

Under the bright light in her kitchen, Mariana stopped. "Katie, what is that on your face?" Katie reached up. "No. The other side. It's a yellow mark."

"Is it makeup?" Katie asked.

Mariana took a closer look. "No. It is not. If you are not eating, at least sit with me. It's too soon for bed." Mariana set the bowls and fruit on the coffee table.

Katie slumped down on the other end of the sofa. "I feel tired. I haven't been sleeping well."

"I understand." Mariana ate popcorn while Katie stared up at the ceiling.

Each night since she'd left the apartment, Katie lay in bed, waiting for sleep. Placing one hand beneath her sternum, Katie pressed down; she went over it again and again with two fingers, quelling the acridity she felt there. Replaying the scene again and again, she pictured Tre's red face before he left that night and then after he returned. She remembered the way he had cut his eyes at her and the way he'd glared and pointed. She took a deep breath and held it in. Rolling onto her side, she balled her hands into fists, recalling her grip on the table, as if applying more pressure might soften him or make him look at her. Then afterward, his eyes glassy and face slack, his hand covering the back of her head, the other holding the sweatshirt over her face strong, the muscles in his hand and forearm flexing. Katie pressed the tender spot on her cheek. Tossing to the other side, she distracted her thoughts with the upcoming exhibition and drifted off into another fitful sleep, the kind full of strung-together dreams she wouldn't remember.

The next morning, Katie and Mariana decided to meet back at Mari's before lunch. They changed out of their work clothes and took Mariana's car. Happy to see Katie smiling and hungry, Mari suggested lunch at Cappy's in uptown, one of their favorites. Choosing an outdoor table under the trees, the girls shared a bottle of pinot grigio on a tucked-away-from-the-city patio that bordered an established neighborhood, the kind where people raked their own yards, snipped their hedges between gardener visits, and waved at each other when they went out walking in the evenings. Leaves fell, floating onto the colored umbrellas and sliding off and onto the wood decking, while pigeons pecked at errant crumbs.

"The scallops are good." Katie said, cutting into one buttery stack. Still watching her friend, Mariana ate her Milanese.

"I haven't heard from Tre at all. And thank you for not asking about him."

"Are you surprised?" Mariana cut the meat and mixed it in with arugula.

"I am and I'm not. You can never tell about Tre. He gets angry, and then he gets busy with something else. And then it's like nothing ever happened. Or he's seething under the surface, and you don't know when the next explosion might happen."

Mariana didn't know what else to say, so she didn't. She let Katie marinate on her own words. They finished the wine and decided to start their venture at Saks Fifth Avenue. Midweek, the store was uncrowded, and they perused dresses, discussed fabrics and lengths, and considered possibilities. The salesclerk took their choices to the dressing room, where they hung, waiting for the girls.

Mariana and the saleslady helped Katie into the first dress. Out from behind a curtain and up onto a fitting platform, Katie turned, viewing herself from all angles in the mirrors while the other two women surveyed, analyzed, and critiqued.

"What do you think?" Katie liked the dark bodice and lighter skirt.

"It is pretty, but it looks a little too much like prom." Mariana smoothed the organza skirt.

"I agree," said the saleslady. "The bow makes it immature. Let's move on."

Going through the dresses, one by one, contemplating silk and satin, Katie stepped out and up in a form-fitting, black modern silhouette. One sleeve long and one off the shoulder, tucked in at the waist, it flared at the bottom. Katie placed one hand on her hip.

The clerk hurried out of the fitting room and returned with a pair of high stilettos.

Katie slid into them and picked up her hair, tangling it up high. Holding it there, she decided, "This is the one."

"That is definitely the one!" Mariana turned around. At the doorway to the fitting room was a crowd of two, one applauding with enthusiasm.

"Beautiful, Katie. Just perfect!" Both laden with shopping bags, there stood Hilary Edwards and another woman.

Hilary put her purchases down near Mariana and came over, extending her hand to Katie. Katie stepped down from the platform, and Hilary embraced her. "You must be dress shopping for the cocktail party your husband is throwing this weekend! We're doing the same." Hilary pulled on the sleeve of the dress. "I love this on you. We have to run. Picking up kids at school!" Hilary gave Katie another quick hug and waved on her way out of the fitting room. "See you in a few days! We're looking forward to it!"

Mariana stopped at the pallor in Katie's face. Turning her head, Katie took a few breaths. "Let's pay and get out of here," she told Mariana.

Garment bag in hand, the girls exited the store. Mariana pushed the liftgate button on her key fob and laid the dress flat in the trunk of the car.

"There's a new martini bar not far from my office. Want to try it?" Mariana buckled her seat belt.

"I guess we can," Katie said.

Mariana took them through neighborhoods, weaving her way on the surface streets to Broadway, all the way into downtown. Parking the car a few blocks away was easier than circling or vying for a random spot, so they strolled, enjoying the early evening. The streets were filled with people on their way home, or meeting for drinks or dinner, the overtone of a day accomplished. Katie soaked in the low hum. Urban dusk upon them now, vertical shadows' sprawl cast angles down onto pedestrians on sidewalks and crossways.

A man in a suit stepped off the sidewalk around them and nodded. "I'm on my way. I'll see you in a few minutes," he said into his cell.

Two young women stepped out of an office. Heads together, they gossiped about their day and their colleagues.

"Here we are." Mariana stopped at a set of steps. Skipping up and seated right away, they sipped on their drinks.

"Ok. This other conversation we need to have." Mariana set down her drink. Crossing her arms, elbows on the table, she waited.

Katie knew what Mari wanted to talk about. "Will you take me to the airport tomorrow? Around eleven?" Mariana held her position. "I'm flying up there to collect the other Mary Renatas for the exhibit."

"And?"

"And that's it." Katie finished her drink. Turning her head, she looked for the server, signaling for another martini.

"Katie. He asked you to be his plus one for an event. That is a date. Another for me too," Mariana told the waiter.

Katie shrugged.

"You could have gone up there for the art without going along to a black-tie event."

"Maybe."

"Have you talked to him since you made your flight arrangements to New York?"

"Just texting. I gave him the details. My arrival time," Two new drinks arriving, they arranged them on the table and sent the used glasses back. "I said I'd rent a car. He insisted on picking me up."

"That is what I thought," Mariana smiled into her new concoction.

"I admit that he doesn't not like me. He's polite. Polished."

Mariana laughed and turned her cell face up. "Is that your phone or mine?"

"It's mine. It's Tre," Katie scrolled through the incoming messages. "Here we go. Hilary is a fast worker."

"What is he saying?" Mariana leaned in closer.

"He says that Hilary ran into me shopping. That I must've come to my senses. That he knew I'd show for his party like I should," Katie took her wallet from her handbag. "We should get going. I still need to pack, and I have a long travel day tomorrow."

## Chapter 4

Suitcase ready to go with new dresses and borrowed shoes, ready for whatever the weather brought, Katie pulled her bag from the back seat of the car while Mariana pulled the handle on the luggage up and over the curb at the San Antonio International Airport.

"I'll pick you up Sunday night." Mariana handed the roller bag over and draped a trench coat over Katie's arm. Katie adjusted her ponytail and smoothed the front of her tucked-in button-up. Impatient vehicles dropping off passengers behind them, Mari closed the liftgate, ran around to the driver's side, and waved. "You look beautiful. And professional. Have a wonderful time."

Only carry-on today. All checked in, Katie sped through security and arrived at her gate in minutes. A full flight, the gate attendants started boarding early, and after accounting for everyone on the manifest, they took off. Midway through the flight to Charlotte, the pilot came on the intercom. "Good afternoon, ladies and gentlemen. We were able to get off the ground early in San Antonio. With the help of favorable tailwinds, we should have you at the gate about thirty minutes ahead of schedule today. We've turned off the Fasten Seat Belt lights, so feel free to move about the cabin now, but expect some bumps the closer we get to Charlotte. We're keepin' our eyes on that disturbance out there in the Atlantic. On behalf of our Dallas crew, thanks for flying with us today. Sit back, relax and enjoy the remainder of your flight."

Texas well behind them, somewhere over Mississippi, Katie stared down at the clouds. After the turbulent days leading up to her flight, filled with lost sleep and fitful dreams, the bumps promised by the captain's welcome lulled Katie to sleep. She awoke when the landing gear touched down on the runway in North Carolina. As they taxied, she turned on her phone and found messages from Alex.

*Hope your travels are going well today. I hope the storm isn't causing delays. Let me know if you get a chance during your connection.*

Katie read the messages again, waiting for the Seat Belt light. She deplaned and checked the board in the airport. A string of other flights showing delayed and with no need to change terminals, she located her next flight and headed over. A large crowd with groups of people polluted the gate. She rechecked the flight numbers. She had been wrong. This was an earlier flight to New York getting ready to board. Without hesitation, she headed straight to the counter and addressed the attendant.

"Excuse me. I'm scheduled for the later flight to La Guardia, but if you have any empty seats, I'd appreciate one." Katie slid her ticket and ID across the bar.

With zero eye contact, the ticket agent clicked away on her keyboard. *Clickety click click. Click. Click.* Hair pulled back into a tight bun, peach blush and matching matte lipstick, the woman stared at the screen. After one more bout of furious clicking, a whirring under the counter made Katie smile.

"Here's your new boarding pass. Next!"

A man in a wrinkled business suit waiting behind her threw his attaché up on the counter. Katie grabbed her paperwork and got in the back of the boarding line. A slight rush of adrenaline, the new flight topped off with an aisle seat, Katie replied to Alex.

*It's not causing any delays so far. The weather says it might be on its way to a tropical depression, though. I was fortunate enough to grab a seat on a flight that gets me in two hours earlier. I know this is last minute, so please don't rush. I can rent a car or wait at the airport.*

Seconds after pushing Send, her phone rang. "Hello?" Katie answered, the noise of the intercoms loud in her other ear.

"Katie, don't rent a car. Picking you up is the only thing I planned for today. I can leave right now and be there in time."

"Are you sure? I don't want to inconvenience you."

"I am not the slightest inconvenienced."

"All right, then. See you in a few hours."

"I will be there," Alex said.

Katie stared down at her cell. She turned it off, put it into her pocket, and waited for boarding. She traveled down the crowded jet bridge, buckled into her seat, and settled in for the flight. In a long queue for takeoff, Katie considered her own excitement for this trip. The thought of getting her hands on additional Mary Renata pieces a personal and professional win, she also wondered about entanglements.

In Montauk, Alex felt for his wallet in his pants pocket and grabbed a set of keys from a kitchen drawer.

"Ok, Daisy." Alex took the dog's chin in one hand. "I'm off to the airport to pick up Katie. You remember her from Lubbock, right?" Daisy gave Alex her full attention. "I'll be back in a few hours. You stay here."

In the detached garage, he removed a cover from the car stored inside. He revved the engine, reliable as always. Alex closed the door behind him and checked the time. With traffic light, he arrived at the airport in under three hours. Parking the car, he decided to meet Katie inside. He texted her. *I'll be at the arrival's hall in under ten minutes.*

*Taxiing now, waiting on a gate.*

*All right. I'll be here.*

Once in the terminal, Katie passed a restroom. Turning around, she went inside and checked herself in the mirror. A few stray strands of hair fell around her face, and she chose one to tuck away. Thinking of the cool air back on the jet bridge, she pulled on her light-colored coat, leaving the double row of buttons undone. She caught the airport train and followed the route to passenger pickup, where Alex was waiting. He saw her first and took casual yet measured steps.

"Hello. There you are." Katie stopped a few feet in front of Alex.

"How was your flight?" Alex reached out, taking her bag from her. "Here. Let me get that for you."

Katie released the handle. "It's not heavy," she said, and then, "Quick and bumpy."

"I've got it," Alex confirmed. "Is this it?" He realized he had expected to see the painting again. But why would she bring it back here? There was no reason she would have.

"Yes, I didn't check a bag." Shoulder to shoulder, Katie walked beside Alex, rolling her bag out of the airport toward short-term parking.

"Thank you for picking me up," she said. "You didn't have to come inside."

"It's no problem, Katie." Out in the sunlight, he thought she looked pretty, her hair light around her face but darker underneath near the nape of her neck. "Here we are." Alex looked away as he used a key to open the trunk of the big black car.

"Wow, an eighties model M5." Katie took her tote from her shoulder.

"I love this car. My grandparents keep it stored at the beach house. I take it out and drive it when I'm home." A few errant drops of cold rain fell from puffy clouds shaded dark on their edges, as if by a thick graphite pencil, giving them dimension and light. The roller bag stowed in the trunk, Alex slammed it closed, then opened the passenger door for Katie. She shrugged out of her coat, got inside, and laid her tote in the back. She watched him around the front of the car, dark hair just touching the collar on his starched button-up shirt, his skin tan against the white.

"Are you a car enthusiast?" Alex maneuvered out of the lot.

"I wouldn't go that far, yet I do have an appreciation for these classics. How was the traffic coming out?"

"Not too bad. I took the highway. We'll go back that way too."

"It's nice being a passenger this time," Recognizing certain landmarks, others seemed new.

Not running out of things to talk about, the two chatted, Alex pointing out this beach, that lodge, or a road to a certain lighthouse. "If we get time, I'll show you the one in Montauk. It's my favorite." Alex pulled into the parking lot of a familiar restaurant. "Are you hungry? I made dinner reservations for tonight, but maybe you'd like something before then?"

"I'm not starving, but I'd love a cup of coffee."

"Perfect. And to go with that, this place has the best pie around."

Before Katie had the chance to tell Alex she'd patronized the restaurant before, they were inside and accosted by an exuberant and animated Rhonda.

"Alex! And it's you! You found him!" Rhonda hugged Alex, pointing at Katie. Unable to control her emotions, Rhonda hugged Katie too. "Sit down! Here in this booth! Alex, I have to tell you all about my friend here!"

Alex looked at Katie with amusement, yet no surprise. "She will tell you," Katie assured him.

"I believe she will." Alex sat at the booth across from Katie. Over coffees, apple crisp, and coconut cream pie, Rhonda slid into the seat beside Alex and filled him in on her encounter with Katie. Finishing, Rhonda stacked their plates. "You'll have to try the chocolate next time." She touched Katie's shoulder. "I'm so happy the way this all turned out. How long are you stayin'?" She looked at Katie.

"Until Sunday," Katie said.

Rhonda raised one eyebrow, holding it there until Alex spoke.

"Tell me. What is new with you, Rhonda?"

"You know things never change here much. Except I have one big thing to share."

Alex and Katie waited.

"Mr. Stewart. He's retiring soon. You know he's had me running this place for a while now."

Alex nodded. "For a few years. Isn't that right?"

"More or less. But that isn't the news. You know, Montauk will always be home. I don't drive a new car or shop at fancy stores. Over the years, I saved up quite a nest egg for myself. Mr. Stewart would never sell to any of the big corporations or developers who fly around here like vultures. Anyway"—Rhonda lowered her voice, but not much—"he's selling it to me. I'm buying the diner."

Alex put his fork down and rose from the booth. Standing, he embraced Rhonda. "That is wonderful news." Relinquishing his squeeze, both hands still on her shoulders, he stood back, looking at her. "Good for you," he said.

"Thank you. I won't let Mr. Stewart down. I'll always keep it like he intended."

"Of course you will."

Katie finished her dessert, surveying the interaction.

"Until Sunday?" Rhonda repeated.

"She's come up to look at more of my grandmother's art," Alex explained. "For an exhibit at the hotel where she works."

"You don't say." Rhonda drank each word in. "In Texas?"

"Yes, in San Antonio," Katie said.

"I've never been. But San Antonio is a place I always wanted to go," Rhonda said.

"You'll have to visit sometime, then."

"Are you going to the benefit on Saturday at the club?"

Drinking the last of her coffee, Katie nodded.

"Yes. She's coming with me." Alex stood up, laying bills on the Formica table.

A smile spread across Rhonda's face. "You two are too cute." She touched the tip of Katie's nose. Katie decided she did not find this annoying. "If you have time on your way out, please stop by Sunday and tell me all about it," Rhonda said.

Assuring her they would, they buckled back into the BMW and drove into Montauk.

Katie didn't remember whether she'd mentioned her accommodation plans. "I made a reservation," she told Alex. "The same place I stayed last time."

"You did? You're more than welcome to stay at my place."

"I wouldn't impose on you," she said.

"You wouldn't be. But I can take you to the hotel if you'd rather," Alex said, going through town.

"I can unpack, change, and meet you for dinner?"

"I'll pick you up at six thirty."

At the hotel, Alex took Katie's bag from the trunk. A faded wooden Vacancy sign on hooks clacked against its post. Wheeling her bag inside a déjà vu, the same surfer kid sat behind the counter. "What's up?"

"I have a reservation for Katie Bauer. Checking out Sunday."

"Cool." The kid handed her a key. "You know the way, right?"

"Right."

Up a short set of exterior wooden steps leading to a long deck, Alex carried her bag. "Are you sure you want to stay here? There are four empty bedrooms at my house."

"I can stay here. I wouldn't want to take advantage of you," Katie said.

Alex held the door like he had in Lubbock. With a look indicating they'd already breached the subject of what was and wasn't an imposition, he handed Katie her luggage. "I'll see you at six thirty, then."

"Six thirty."

Alex stopped and turned, looking back at Katie's closed door. He took his keys from his pocket, tossed them into the air, and caught them with the other hand.

Wondering whether Alex thought her socially inept or moronic, she had no idea why she'd said *take advantage*. What was wrong with her? Maybe she could stay at the big house on the beach. There was plenty of room there, but she didn't know whether she should.

Katie placed her luggage on a folding rack. Her room muggy, she clicked on the wall air conditioner at the knee level, an old, clunky unit. She pulled the sliding door curtain windows open and flopped across the bed, limbs out like a starfish. It felt great being horizontal. With time for a nap, she drifted in and out, then sat up to focus on the beach and the gray-green Atlantic.

## Chapter 5

Humming, Rhonda gathered plates and glasses and took them to the dishwasher.

"What's with you?" he asked, wiping wet hands on his permanently gray apron.

"I like my job and my customers." Rhonda kept humming.

"Hmmph," said the dishwasher, dunking his hands deep into a sink full of soapy water. "It looks like another group of them just walked in."

Rhonda came out from the kitchen to find a multitude of patrons, a sea of bright floral prints and cardigan sweaters. A woman with white hair, pixie cut, approached her. She reminded Rhonda of Joan Rivers. The teeth and hair anyway. Rhonda knew this woman, and the woman knew Rhonda and had, for the better part of two decades. Now, however, the woman did not acknowledge this, but that mattered zero to Rhonda.

"We need a table for eight. Can you seat us?" Like a French bulldog, the woman's bottom teeth protruded with an underbite.

Her thumb on her chin, Rhonda tapped her lips with her forefinger, looking around the near-empty dining room. "Do you have a reservation?"

"No. No, we do not." Prepared for disappointment, the woman sighed.

"Let me see what I can do," Rhonda took a stack of menus from behind a counter. "Will this do? We can put you by the window, a nice highway view."

"Yes. This is acceptable."

Rhonda shook her head, stifled a laugh, and pulled out a chair for the woman's daughter. "Hello, Cici. How've you been?"

"Oh my! I didn't recognize you, Rhonda! So good to see you! We must catch up!" Cici said.

"Yes, we must. I have so much to catch you up on." The slightest smile on Rhonda's face, she took a pen from behind her ear and began taking orders on a small yellow notepad. Cici, her friends, and her family were not locals and never would be. Fixing her lips into a straight line, Rhonda's loyalties lay with Alex Dyer and his family. They were old Montauk.

# Chapter 6

After her shower, glad she'd brought extra dresses along, Katie chose the shorter one and a pair of flats for dinner. Leaving her hair down and straight, she took a little longer than usual with her eye makeup.

Right at six thirty, her phone rang. "I'm here. Walking up now."

"Ok. I'm ready." Katie picked up a small handbag with her phone. Sitting on the edge of the bed, she jumped at two quick knocks at her door.

"Hello," Katie said.

"You look great. I like your dress," Alex said.

"Thanks. Did you notice that I'm also dry?"

"I did. That makes twice today."

They both laughed, and Alex got her door again.

"You look nice too." She noticed Alex had changed— he looked tall; a shirt tucked into black trousers, he wore calf-leather oxfords. Katie thought about a delicate gold chain she had once left unlatched on her dresser. Weeks later, she'd picked it up again, finding it with an unwearable knot. Getting it undone took a safety pin, patience, and the better part of an hour.

"The club is a few minutes away. It isn't crowded this time of year. Mainly locals. It's also the venue for the benefit on Saturday."

"Ok."

"And tomorrow, when we go through the art, maybe you'd like to help choose a piece to donate."

"I'm so excited to see all of your grandmother's work."

"I know you are. It is why you're here." Alex looked over at Katie, nodding in agreement. "Here we are," he said. In front of them loomed a rambling structure, the roof with many steep gables, and rows of rectangular windows. In the center was a large brick turret flanked by horizontal matching dormers. Alex pulled under a covered entrance, and the valet came over to the driver's side. Another opened Katie's door, and she waited for Alex to escort her inside. They entered through a lounge framed in dark mahogany paneling, with cabinetry fit for a formal library. Large panels of wood shone in symmetrical squares held together with thick moldings. A long bar ran along the length of the room. Alex stopped near the counter flap and greeted a short, round man wearing a classic speakeasy uniform, a white tuxedo shirt, bow tie, and suspenders.

"Hello, George. How are you this evening?"

"I'm doing well, Mr. Alex."

"How's that boy of yours? He must be fourteen or fifteen now."

"That's right. Going into high school next year."

"He's still playing ball?"

"He sure is. He made the team for next year." George stood a little taller.

"I'm glad to hear that, George." Alex reached across the bar, cupping the other man on the shoulder.

"Could I get you two something to drink?"

"I think so. Would you like to drink wine tonight, Katie?"

"I would." Katie looked from Alex, then to George.

With no further questions, George went into a room behind the bar and reappeared in moments with a bottle. He opened it and poured a small amount for Alex to taste.

"Oh, that's the one." Alex pointed at George, his cue to pour a full glass for each of them.

## Chapter 6

Taking two stools, they sipped the wine. The bar was already crowded, yet more people arrived for drinks and dinner. Soon, everyone was surrounded with lively talking—the hum and comfort of the neighbors they knew. An attractive older woman asked Alex about Mary Renata, wondering when his grandparents might come stateside. A few other men her dad's age, Katie noticed, arrived from the golf course, asking Alex where he'd last been on business. And on it went, but not in a tedious way. To each, Alex addressed their questions, answering with genuine thought, first introducing Katie as a friend of his, a professional art curator from San Antonio, Texas. They all regarded her with polite interest, and then a girl caught Alex by the arm.

"Well, if it isn't the long-lost, elusive Alex," she said.

Turning, Alex shifted his body toward the bar, closer to Katie.

"Hello, Cecilia," he said.

"And who do we have here?" Cici extended a pale, limp hand with tiny, manicured nail beds and a gold ring embellished by a large mabe pearl.

"Cecilia, this is Katie Bauer. Katie, Cecilia."

Katie extended her hand; Cici barely touched it but left it there too long. "Cici," she said through her nose, her voice reminding Katie of a type of waterfowl. At the ranch in Texas were stock tanks on each cross section of grazing land. Man-made with a backhoe, a muddy reservoir created by digging a dish-shaped crater with a dam of earth on one side sustained cattle, provided makeshift swimming holes for summertime, and created habitats for year-round and migrating ducks and geese heading to or from south Texas and as far as Mexico. Not a duck, but Cici's high-pitched honk rang more reminiscent of a snow goose.

"Did I say something funny?" Cici honked again, studying Katie's face.

"No, you didn't. It's just that it is such a pleasant evening. Nice to meet you, Cici." Katie withdrew her hand and used it to pick up her wine.

"Indeed, it is." *Honk. Honk honk.*

Turning his shoulder to Cecilia, one elbow on the bar, Alex addressed Katie. "Are you ready for another glass?"

"Yes, please." Katie put down her empty glass, and Alex motioned for George. *A group of snow geese is called an avalanche. Even though snow geese mate for life, there is no name for a pair of them. If one dies, the other mourns for up to two years.*

Ignoring all cues, Cici inserted herself halfway between the two stools. "Are you visiting from out of town?"

"I am," Katie answered.

"How long are you staying?" Cici pressed.

"Here's our wine. Thank you, George." Alex took the two new glasses.

"Aren't you from Texas?" Cici put her hand on the back of Katie's stool.

"I sure am." Katie smiled at her.

"Weren't you recently in Texas, Alex? Did you bring her back with you?" Pointing at him with her ring hand, Cici laughed a little too loud, attracting the attention of her mother. Standing nearby, she ended her conversation with the men from the golf course.

"I can't believe my eyes!" A petite woman dressed in a lightweight wool suit stood on her toes and, wrapping both of her arms around Alex's neck, caused him to lean down. He shifted a foot on the barstool.

"Hello, Diedre." Alex took a deep breath, then exhaled.

"How long has it been?" Diedre asked.

"Years! Ah ha-ha!"

Her expression incongruent with forced laughter, Cici's face fell flat and joyless.

"Diedre, this is Katie Bauer. She is a friend of mine. An art curator from Texas."

"Oh my. Do you work at a museum or something?" Diedre asked.

"No, I work at a hotel," Katie said.

Cici and Diedre exchanged glances.

"Do you mean you buy art for the rooms?" Cici giggled. "Factory prints with plastic gold frames?"

Diedre laughed too.

Katie refused to break eye contact. "Not at all. I curate art."

"Katie creates a world-class impression with art in the public spaces of her hotel. She chooses and arranges their installations and organizes their rotating collections. She also has a master's degree in art history. What are you doing these days, Cici?" Alex asked.

Cici stopped laughing, and Alex and Katie waited for her reply. "I still work in the little store back home." Now her voice sounded small, like a sparrow.

"Good. That is good." Alex took a drink of his wine.

"Alex, can you tell me where the restroom is?" Katie asked.

"I can. At the end of this room, go around to the left."

"If y'all will please excuse me." Off the stool, Katie exited, following Alex's directions.

As soon as Katie's back was toward them, Cici took the other girl's seat, Diedre drifting away into the crowd. "'Y'all.' How cute."

"What are you doing, Cecilia?" Alex leaned back.

"Don't worry, I'll return the seat to her. When did you get back in town?"

Before he could answer, their attention was diverted to Katie's phone, lying face up beside her bag. *Bzzz, bzzz, bzzz.*

"Uh oh. Looks like someone's being paged." Cici looked over at the phone. Like her recent handshake with Katie, her eyes lingered too long.

Standing, Alex shook his head. "I'm sure our table is ready." Back again, Katie approached the bar. Reaching across Cici, Alex retrieved Katie's phone and purse, handed them to her, and then picked up their wine. "I've got these, Katie. Let's go have dinner."

"It was nice meeting you," Katie said.

"Likewise," Cici said, and settling into the stool, she watched Alex and Katie's backs until they disappeared into the dining room. "Make me a martini, George." Behind the bar, George poured the liquor into a shaker cup, stirred, and strained it into an ice-cold cone-shaped glass.

"Stirred." Cecilia sighed.

"No bubbles." George set the sage-colored transparent drink in front of Cici. "You're welcome," he said.

She took the olive skewer and ate the first of four. Then she picked up her phone and typed in the name of Alex's new friend. Scrolling through the hits, she found a few articles, then social media options.

---

Katie's phone buzzing again, she glanced at it and turned it off. "What a pretty spot." Overlooking the marina, all the boats were put to bed. Except for the dark silhouettes of a few mainsails, Montauk lake lay quiet. Early evening, the sun, low in the sky, cast an amber glow across the water. "I don't want to look away." Katie laughed.

Alex reached across the table, redirecting Katie's attention. "It was awkward back there. I'm sorry about that."

Katie waved her hand at him. "Don't apologize," she said. "Really, it's fine."

"I'd like to explain. May I tell you a bit more about it?"

"If you want to."

"Cecilia is an old friend. We dated when we were kids. At the end, I didn't leave it the best I could have. Not my best moment. Not a graceful exit."

"I understand. I'd like to think the current version of ourselves is better than past ones. I would hope so, anyway."

"I would agree with that. The way Cici and I used to be way back when was fine for then. When we were kids," Alex said.

"Until you got a little older, and then it wasn't?"

"Exactly. We were this couple that everyone expected together. We were playing a role. Our best smile for every event in every photo. Out front for everybody to see. And when I realized how young I was, I knew the direction we were going was all wrong, too soon," Alex said.

"Why?"

"Because I knew that real life extended beyond the next party, the next wedding, the next event, and I knew it went way beyond Montauk."

"Until you're older, you don't realize how young you were."

"Touché." Alex raised his glass to Katie, and she touched hers to his. "I moved ahead. My jobs took me farther and farther from here. It's a strange thing but coming home feels like going back in time. The people who never leave never change. No matter how many years pass."

"I guess there is something to be said for consistency."

Raising his forehead, Alex nodded. "There is also something to be said for complacency."

"Either way, wine makes for great philosophy," she admitted.

"And so it does," Alex agreed.

She had fish, and he the lamb. All the light fading from the sky, they bantered about the past, what they might do tomorrow, and the weather. Their plates long cleared away; they lingered over the wine. Sounds from the bar, clinking glasses, running water from a tap all subsiding, the hum of tired servers finishing up their shifts in the recesses of the room, Katie asked what time they closed.

"After we leave," Alex said.

"Oh, I don't want to be rude." Katie looked around.

"We aren't," Alex assured her.

When the wine was gone, and after two espressos, they decided on a plan for the morning.

That night, Katie stared at herself in the bathroom mirror, studying her face. She felt somehow different, trying to decide how, considering whether it was this unfamiliar environment or something else.

*Life's about choices*, she heard Grandad's voice in her ear. Was she making choices, or was she floating along, like a lone and broken cypress branch, letting the river take her where it would? She wasn't sure. Katie got into bed and sank into the covers, the sheets up around her face. She was tired but excited about getting into Mary Renata's art. She knew she should close her eyes. Focusing on long and even breathing, she willed shapes, colors, and lines out of her head.

## Chapter 7

The next day, early as promised, Alex picked Katie up at the hotel. He'd stopped on the way for coffee and handed Katie a hot cup. She wrapped her hands around the thick sleeve. Clouds hanging low in the overcast sky, the wind whistled, and sand whipped across the road. Minutes later, Alex parked in the garage, and then they followed a covered breezeway to the porch. A large and slow-moving storm, taking its time, meandered up and toward the coast. Organized in intervals, whitecaps, long and predictable, came in a rhythm. The swell pushing the waves up from their floor, curls breaking, the sea spray blew across their crests just before closing out.

Watching from windows, Daisy ran along the inside of the house, guessing which door they'd choose. Pausing, Katie pulled her tote up higher on her shoulder. Planning to work, she'd brought her laptop and notebooks.

"Let me take that bag for you." Entering closest to the kitchen, Alex placed her things on the seat of a barstool. "Come around to the front. Let's watch the waves." Katie followed Alex to the beach side of the house. Leaning on a wooden railing, they looked out at the sea. "The surf is coming up." Two boys in full wetsuits stood on the shoreline, deciding where to paddle out.

"I think that's the kid from the hotel." Katie pointed.

"It is. He surfs all the breaks around."

"Do you?"

"Surf? Some. But I didn't learn until I was a teenager. Those kids"—Alex pointed to the boys on the beach—"started as soon as they could walk."

"Maybe even before?"

"Possibly." Gauging Katie like the boys on the beach gauged the sets coming in, Alex asked, "Are you ready to take a look at those paintings?"

Katie looked away from the ocean, then to Alex, and did a little jump, clapping her hands together. "So ready."

Alex considered her enthusiasm. "Let's go look right now, then." As they proceeded up a formal staircase, arriving at the second floor, he added to his thought. *Genuine. Passionate.* Shaking away his next thought, up they went on another flight of more rudimentary stairs—plain pine treads painted a glossy white. He took her into a finished attic. Katie, quietly humming no tune in particular, skipped up the steps behind him. The ceiling in a peak reflecting the roofline, long boards stained gray ran the length of the room. Going around to each dormer, Alex opened interior shutters, allowing for extra light. Wooden crates and boxes were stacked on one end of the big room next to brittle brown paper and piles of twine. Painted canvases, all shapes and sizes, some framed, some not, leaned against various wall spaces.

"I opened most of these to make it easier for you to go through." Alex shifted some boxes out of the way. "They aren't organized except by size. We can rearrange them however you'd like."

Standing back, Katie surveyed the paintings. "There are so many."

"There are. It is the bulk of my grandmother's work."

Choosing a stack of large pieces on the far-left side of the room, she decided to work her way across.

"Do you want to hold the opposite corners while I look through them?"

"Sure." Alex positioned himself on the other side of Katie.

Moving half a dozen pieces, she said, "Let's lay these out. Starting here." Together they arranged the paintings, leaving several feet between them. Katie stood over each, moving back, then closer again. Stack by stack, they laid the paintings until they covered the entire floor, a patchwork museum. She paced the room again, and again. Standing back, she crossed her arms, studying the pieces.

"What a progression of volumes," Katie said. "I see some definite themes. Themes are often indicative of time periods," she stated aloud, talking to herself or maybe to no one. Then she looked at Alex. "Do you want to help me rearrange? I'd like to try to categorize them."

"Of course. Where do you want to start?"

"Let's take these first and put them over here." Katie pointed. "They're all city scenes."

"Yes. I think most of them are set in Florence. This is the Ponte Vecchio. A view looking up the Arno. This…" Alex held a framed piece in his hands, about the width of his shoulders. Looking into the canvas, past the paint and the brushstrokes, he focused on the lines. "This is our apartment in Florence."

Looking over Alex's shoulder, she saw the cobblestones, the textured, worn facades, colored plaster walls, and eclectic entry doors delineating each apartment. A rooftop terrace with potted trees and plants, and on the second level, on a balcony with a small table and two chairs, sat two men wearing suits and ties. Drinking coffee, they observed neighbors strolling by and the weather.

"Who are they?" Katie pointed to the men.

"This is my grandfather and his brother."

"They're young men."

Alex agreed. "About my age now."

"Look at the conversation they're having. You can hear them talking over the other noise in the painting. Down the street here, there is a store and people moving along the sidewalk. Look and listen. The neighborhood is quieter than the voice of your grandfather." Katie picked up another piece. "In this one, the noise of the crowd at this market is louder than the people sitting together at the café." She pointed to the right side of the canvas. "And what do you hear in this one?" she asked Alex, gesturing to a woman hanging laundry on a small line on a rooftop, a tabby cat watching from a ledge.

Intent, Alex considered for a moment. "I hear the wind blowing the linen."

"Yes! And the big cat purring. Look at this!" She pointed at two sparrows, one with a twig in its beak, the other wide open.

"I didn't notice them." Alex looked at the birds on clay tile rooftops in the background.

"All right. I think these landscapes vary somewhat." She pointed to other paintings. "This one, this one, and here."

"I'd say so too. I'm also certain most of these represent our property outside the city."

Katie was drawn to an impressionistic piece. "A vineyard," she said. Her eyes gravitated to leafy shades of green and dark bunches of fruit, the trunks on the rows smaller in the distance. She pointed at a structure on the horizon.

"That is our villa." Alex picked up another piece. "I don't remember seeing most of these." He sat down on an ottoman, holding a canvas depicting a retreating man, a hat covering most of his face and a long-sleeved work shirt, by his feet a basket of grapes. One hand held a bunch of dark berries and the other a pair of shears, snipping it from the vine. Two patient sheepdogs waited alongside him. "Here is another one of my grandfather."

"He looks like the other harvest workers in the field." Katie pointed at other men working the rows.

"My grandfather wouldn't have it any other way." Alex turned the painting over. "*My Vigneron,*" he read. "My grandmother's handwriting."

Alex watched Katie's eyes move across the canvas, taking in colors and perspective. "Unless you'd like to keep this one here, I'd like to put it in the exhibit."

"Whatever you want." Alex placed *My Vigneron* aside and picked up another. In this one, a portrait, an olive-skinned woman held a baby, a handful of dark hair in one plump hand.

"A self-portrait?" Face flushed, Katie's pulse quickened, and she held on to one corner of the unframed canvas.

"No. This is my mother and me."

"Oh," she whispered. The two of them studied tiny lines near the angle of the woman's outer canthus, the edges of her mouth turned upward, but only just. Her hand rested on the baby's shoulder, strong and gentle, cradling and supportive all at once. "Look at her. Oh, Alex."

"I just noticed that." Alex stared into the painting at the stranger, into the reflection of his mother's eye painted by his grandmother. In the background of her iris, an unseen window and the curve of the baby's forehead, his silhouette more defined in her pupil.

Sunshine spilling through the dormers illuminated Katie and Alex for a few moments until the clouds disrupted the light. The attic was a set, and with their heads together, the two made a pretty picture on their makeshift stage. Alex cleared his throat. "Did you know that it's already three o'clock?"

"I didn't."

"What do you think about taking a break? We could go get a bite to eat."

"Sure," Katie said, giving Alex space to put the painting in its group.

Back the way they had entered under the covered walk, Alex said, "Daisy can go with us. We can take the truck this time." He clicked the leash on the happy dog, opened Katie's door, then let Daisy into the back, where she made herself comfortable.

"The sky is getting dark over there." Katie pointed in the direction of the beach.

"It is. We should check the weather when we get back." Into town they went, past Katie's hotel a few blocks, and arrived at a lunch counter on South Edison.

"This is an interesting place. Should we sit outside?" Katie ran one hand across a table.

"Hey, man, what's up?" A kid from the surfer crowd looked up from his sandwich.

Smiling, Alex slapped him on the back, and head down, the boy went back to chewing while they approached the lunch counter.

"Hello, Alex." A pretty, middle-aged woman with long brown hair pulled back greeted them. "Back in town for a while?"

"A while. How are you doing today, Joan?"

"Just great. Keeping an eye on that storm." The woman nodded, motioning with a nod toward the outside.

"We are too. This is my friend Katie," Alex said.

"Hello, Katie." The woman picked up a pencil. "What can I get you today?"

"I don't think I'll be able to resist the fish burrito."

"Good choice," the woman said. "How about you, Alex?"

"Make it two."

"Excuse me for a minute," Joan said. Pencil up, she raised her chin, tilting her head. "Shhh! Listen!" Kitchen workers behind her stopped, all of them listening to a radio somewhere in the back. "Did you hear that? Looks like they expect a hurricane, making landfall just to the south of us tomorrow evening. Sorry about that, you two. Could I get you anything else?"

"I think that's it, and thanks for the weather report."

"My pleasure. We'll have this out to you in a few minutes."

Daisy at their feet, they sat opposite each other at an outdoor table. The wind blowing, Katie tucked her hair back. Over the burritos, they talked about storms, the pile of paintings in the attic, and how to spend the rest of the afternoon.

"I thought we could stop by the market and pick up a few things before heading back."

"Okay," Katie said. *Thump, thump, thump.* The yellow dog approved their plan.

"It's up to you, but you might want to reconsider your accommodations for tonight. There's no generator at your hotel, and it's been there awhile, but it's not as stormproof as the beach house. It's up to you, though."

About to speak before thinking it over, Katie stopped. Those sliding doors in her room. An all-glass wall facing the water. She looked across the picnic table.

"We can go by and pick up your things, or some of them, before the market."

"We could at least pick up my clothes for tomorrow."

They drove back to Alex's, loaded with purchases of local jellies, cheese, olives, chicken salad, and other morsels. Along the road, trees bent away from the water. "I think the outer bands are getting closer," Alex said.

Back at the beach, a man jogged down the driveway toward them.

Alex opened the rear door of his truck and collected the groceries. Katie helped, reaching from her seat in the front.

The man approached the truck. "Let me help," he said. Stepping back, he stopped.

"Yes, Katie. Let Nick get those. Nick, this is my friend Katie."

Daisy jumped out on Alex's side.

"I see you found Alex." Nick cocked his head, raising one eyebrow. "Let me take those from you," Nick said.

"I did and thank you." Katie recognized the man from before. "Nice to see you again."

"Thank you, Nick. What's it looking like out there?" Alex led the way around the big porch.

"Just upgraded to a tropical storm. They're saying it'll likely be a hurricane by the time it makes landfall. Probably tomorrow afternoon or evening," Nick said. The three walked toward the porch. "I've got most of the storm shutters secured, except for upstairs."

"Let me put this stuff away, and I'll get up there and help."

"No need for that. I'll put these bags here. You two take care of this, and I'll finish up outside. Nice meeting you again, Katie," he said before going back out.

Katie took the food items out of the bags while Alex filed them away in the refrigerator and pantry.

"Nick was here the first time I came looking for you," she said.

Alex emerged from the pantry. "Oh, no. Did he chase you out of here?"

"Pretty much," Katie said.

"Nick lives in the caretaker's cottage. He was working for us even before I came here for high school." Alex lowered his voice. "He gets territorial, especially when we aren't home."

"It's ok. I was intruding."

## Chapter 7

"You weren't," Alex assured her. "Would you like to go walk out on the beach? We can get back to the paintings after he's done banging around up there."

"Sure," Katie said.

Whitecaps on the water, the wind blew and whistled. Katie tied her hair up into a knot. While they walked down the path between the yard and the beach, Alex caught himself staring at her profile and then at her hand laid across the yellow dog's head. Without intention, she moved it down on the side of Daisy's face, and the dog leaned into her knee, both watching the waves coming in closer and closer. They walked down the beach a few yards, and Katie removed her shoes, digging her toes into the sea foam gathering at the water's edge.

"That is freezing," her voice high pitched, and she jumped back, laughing. "But I have to do it one more time." Katie tried again, this time in water up to her ankles. Her feet now covered with sand, she held her shoes, and Alex took them from her.

"We get our share of storms on the Texas coast, so this feels familiar," Katie said. "I kind of like them."

"You do?"

"Yes. They're distracting in the best kind of way." She wrapped her arms around herself. "Their chaos overtakes chaos." Katie looked out at the horizon. "That storm out there is coming. It'll come, then leave with the quietest calm. And when it's gone, then we'll know that we made it to the other side of it."

Like the outgoing tides ebbing toward the sea, Alex felt something pulling him. He took a step backward, but he couldn't stop it any more than he could stop the hurricane in the Atlantic. The wind kept blowing, the swells rose, and he looked at the girl, her hair coming undone. He didn't know her, and yet he'd known her forever. Wondering about that, he asked if she was cold.

"A little. Do you think it's getting choppier out there?"

"Yes, let's turn back." Alex reached out, his hand on her shoulder, lingering on the back of her arm, for eight more steps up the beach. Katie counted. Two steps turning around, and then six more, her skin prickling from the sea spray and his fingertips. As they looked back toward the houses, the rooftops disappeared, blending into the opaque mist with the sky.

"I hope Nick's done up there." Alex squinted.

Inside the yard, the ladders put away, Alex turned on a water hose for their sandy feet. Splashing around, Daisy joined in the game. Katie coaxed the dog up onto the porch and held her still, her hand grasping fur and a fold of skin on the scruff while Alex hosed the sand from her.

Turning her head, Daisy licked Katie's hand. "You're welcome." With her other hand, Katie caressed the dog's ear. *Thump, thump, thump.* Eyes lifted, with a wrinkled forehead, Daisy looked from Katie back to Alex.

"How does a towel and glass of wine sound?" Alex asked.

"That sounds perfect." The three went into the house, a gust slamming the back door behind them. Shutters secured over the windows, the house was darker inside but not gloomy. Alex flipped on the kitchen lights and retrieved two towels from a half bath tucked under the stairway.

"Thank you." Hair down now, it fell in waves around Katie's shoulders. Bringing it all to one side, she blotted it with the towel.

"Try this." Alex pushed a glass of wine across the kitchen island. "Should we get back to our task?"

Sipping the wine, Katie nodded.

"Let's take the rest of this with us," Alex said. He corked the wine, and the two headed back up the stairs. Turning over a crate, a makeshift end table, he set the bottle down and seated himself back on the ottoman.

"I think we left off with this one." Katie moved her thumb from the edge of the canvas, noticing numbers scrawled on its edge. "What is this?" Heads together, they deciphered them. Jumping up, Katie went to the group of city paintings, looking for more dates. "Look! May 1963. Another one, same year."

"These are all from the nineteen sixties," Alex said.

"And these of the villa are from the seventies." Katie gasped.

"What is it?"

"I didn't notice a date on the painting I have back in Texas," Katie said, "but I wasn't looking. Wait here! I'm going to go get my phone!"

"I won't move," Alex promised. He could hear Katie laughing all the way down the stairs. Smiling, he heard her bumping around in her kitchen, imagining her throwing her bag onto the counter, golden pieces of hair falling forward while she searched for her phone. Daisy on her heels, the two bounded back up the treads. Sitting down on the floor, the screen black, Katie pressed the power button. As soon as it came to life, off all day, messages populated. No, it had been off since the night before. Since before dinner at the club. Sinking down onto the floor, Katie waited for the dings to stop.

"I forgot I had this off."

"It's ok. Do you need to take care of some things? I can go downstairs," Alex offered.

"No, no," Katie told him. "Some of these messages are from my friend Mariana. The painting is over at her house. I mean, I've been staying over with her, I guess I have." Katie stumbled over her words.

Elbows on his knees, hands clasped, Alex leaned forward.

"I'd like to explain." Katie recalled Alex's words from the night before.

"You don't need to."

"I want to," she said.

His chin in one hand, Alex listened while Katie told him her story, minus the details she would only tell a best friend. When she got to the end, Alex remained on the ottoman.

"It seems this trip may have been well timed," Alex said.

"Or not timed well at all," they said together, then laughed. Not because it was funny, but rather because it was a thing they shared—knowledge of exits, graceful or not—timing, or lack thereof, resulting in some wisdom gained whether they wanted it or not.

"I should make a phone call."

"Why don't you go back down to the second-level hallway? After you go down the stairs, take the first door on your left. There's a sitting area in that bedroom where you can have some privacy. I'll stay up here and keep going through the stacks."

On the edge of a small, upholstered sofa, Katie dialed Tre.

"Hello, Katie. I knew I'd hear from you." Tre leaned back in his office chair. Turning toward the windows, he looked toward the skyline and loosened his tie.

"Tre."

"Where are you? Are you on the way to my happy hour?"

"No, Tre."

"Look, Katie. I'm sorry."

"Sorry for what?"

"For whatever you need me to be sorry for."

"Ok, Tre."

"What is that supposed to mean 'Ok, Tre?'"

Closing her eyes, Katie shook her head.

"Hello? Are you there?"

"I'm here." Now she was the one who sounded like a sparrow. *A group of sparrows is called a quarrel.* Distracting herself with the irony, she imagined herself a baby sparrow, beak open wide, translucent skin, and vulnerable. Her mind drifted to a sparrow about to be eaten by a cat, or alone in a nest that fell out of a tree, or about to be run over by a tractor.

"…because Katie, you can't do this. We are soulmates. You can't get along without me. So you just get into that new dress you bought at Saks and get on over here tonight. Wait. I'm willing to give you a free pass for tonight. Come be by my side, where you belong, by tomorrow at the dinner. No later than that."

"I don't think I can make it." *Sparrows are neutral-colored, social birds.*

"The least you can do is meet me halfway, Katie. I'm *trying* here."

"I'm working, Tre. I told you that." *House sparrows can live for a decade or more, and they mate for life.*

"I'm busy. I don't know what you told me. Use that credit card you have in your wallet and do what you need to do to get back here." *The male sparrow builds a nest, attracting a female, and they stay loyal to one another, rearing baby sparrows.*

"I'm sorry, Tre." Standing for the sake of her own clarity, Katie steadied herself.

Encouraged, Tre pushed forward. "Get yourself back here. We can forget all this ever happened."

"Please don't be mad. I have to finish what I'm doing here. But threatening me is not helpful. Please don't threaten me." *Sparrows can fly and fend for themselves at a young age, only a few weeks old.*

"Katie," he warned, "don't you dare. Don't go there. Think about what your behavior would do to Mother. She treats you like her own daughter. You know. You should be ashamed of yourself."

"Ashamed?"

"Yes. You of all people. You should be grateful to her. Especially since you don't even have a mother." His words were absorbed by the plate glass behind him.

A bitter wave, cold as the Atlantic, washed over Katie. "I do have a mother. And I have to go," she said, ending the call.

Tre looked down at his cell and tossed it. He took his feet off the desk and stomped on the floor. He picked up his coffee cup and threw it across the room, smashing it against the wall. The dark-colored water ran down the side of a particle-board bookcase, making streaks on the wall beside it, then pooled on the carpet next to shards of porcelain.

Hearing the crash, Margaret got up from her desk. She paused and then knocked once before opening the door to Tre's office. Looking out the big windows again, Tre sat there, rubbing his palms on his pants, from his upper thigh down to his knees and back up again. Like eyes traveling around a painting, Margaret started with Tre, the main action. Next, the dark liquid against the white wall drew her eyes there, down to what used to be a cup, now a mass of obtuse angled shapes, to the fractal cityscape in the background beyond the glass, and then back to Tre. "Everything ok?"

Sighing, he put his hands up. "Yep. Never been better. Margaret, you need to make arrangements to attend the dinner with me Saturday night."

"I might have trouble finding a sitter late notice."

"I'm sure you'll figure it out. Why don't you take the rest of the afternoon off? Organize that babysitter. Maybe do a little shopping," He tugged on his tie, pulling it over his head, and threw it on the desk. Tre cleared his throat. "I meant to tell you earlier, that's a nice skirt you've got on today." He crunched one side of his face, a bad attempt at a wink; Margaret hoped he had something in his eye.

She turned around and went back to her own desk. Sitting there for a long moment, she opened a drawer and retrieved her handbag and a file. Thumbing through it in the elevator, she knew she had to make some hard decisions. Not that she hadn't realized this for a long time; it was just one of those things pushed away with justifications for the sake of avoidance until ignoring became impossible. Margaret was no idiot. She saw and understood what Tre was doing. She realized that the company compensated her well, but there were ethics, morals, and of course, her own license at stake. Margaret was going to take the rest of the afternoon off, but first, she needed to call Mr. Haman.

Katie looked down at her phone. Exhausted, over, and done, she wished she could change the dynamic between them as easily as ending their call. For so long, she had been hoping things would change. *A wish is not a plan, and hope is not a method.* Grandad and Lewis both said that.

Back up to the attic, Alex looked up from a stack of paintings, noting Katie's flushed cheeks. No more natural light coming through the shutters, he had dragged a few lamps closer to the crates and ottomans to better light their workspace.

"Everything good?" Alex touched the top of her hand. The one holding the phone.

Embarrassed, Katie knew her face was red. "I'm fine. Everything is fine. Let's call Mari now."

"Ok."

Mari answered on the first ring. "What is happening there, Katie? I have been waiting and waiting to hear from you."

"It's going well," Katie said.

"Well? What does that mean?"

"I'm here with Alex looking at Mary Renata's art. Are you home? I was wondering if you could do me a favor."

"Am I on speaker?" Mari asked.

Katie had no idea what Mari might blurt unfettered. "Yes. I'm just putting you on now." Katie felt her forehead perspiring.

"I'm home, and I would be glad to do you a favor." Mari said, reverting to a more professional voice.

"The painting that I got from Mr. Pickett. It's in my room, in the closet. Will you take it out and unwrap it?" Shuffling noises on the line, Mari located the package.

Mari laid her phone down beside the art. "Katie. I've got you on speaker now. I have the painting here on my dining room table."

"All right. Remove the paper. Look on the edge of the canvas and see if you can locate any writing. Numbers, or a date."

Mari turned the painting over. "There's a handwritten note on the back. Exordium. The beginning. And something else in French. But no date."

"Nothing on the edges?"

"The canvas is folded over on one side. Should I take out a tack and unfold it from the frame where it is attached?"

"Yes, do that."

"Wait! I do see something here, Katie."

"What does it say?"

"It says, 'Summer nineteen eight-eight.'"

"Nineteen eight-eight?"

"Yes. That is correct. Summer nineteen eight-eight."

"Ok. Can you take a picture and send it to me?"

"Yes. I am doing it right now."

"Thank you, Mari. That's what we needed. I'll call you later tonight." Katie hung up the phone.

Frozen, his face with a sudden and noticeable pallor, Alex pointed to a pile of paintings. "Those are all from the sixties. And these here are seventies."

"Yes, and these are from the eighties. Early eighties." Katie looked at the dates to verify. "What about *My Vigneron*?"

Alex stepped across the room and picked up the painting from Katie's exhibit pile. "Nineteen eighty-seven. Do you see any dated later than nineteen eighty-eight?"

"I'm not sure. Let's look and see." The two set about the room, turning canvases over, finding dates along the edges. "I don't think so, Alex." Katie stopped. "You don't think I have the most recent piece?"

Placing both of his hands on Katie's shoulders, Alex looked down at her. "Nineteen eighty-eight is when the accident happened."

"Your parents' accident?"

"There isn't anything here past nineteen eighty-eight."

"Oh," Katie repeated. "Oh."

Alex put his hand through his hair and rested it for a moment on his forehead. He paced back and forth across the room, then back to where Katie stood. He sat back down on an ottoman.

Katie took a seat on the one next to him, the crate with the wine between them.

"When my grandparents and I moved to the States so I could go to high school here, we moved our personal things to the city. Movers came to the villa. Because my grandfather still traveled back and forth for work, and because we spent holidays in Italy, there was less space in our brownstone, and most of the larger furniture items stayed. The movers packed our household goods, some art from the collection inside this house, some of my grandmother's art. The paintings we brought were individually wrapped and crated, then placed into larger crates, all cataloged and numbered. My grandparents and I watched it all go into the trucks, and then the trucks took the crates to the docks, where they were put on ships and sent to New York. Have you ever seen movers pack for an international move?"

Sitting crisscross, one elbow on her knee, chin in one hand, Katie leaned toward Alex and shook her head.

"Things aren't necessarily packed in by room or category. They fit the pieces in like a version of 3-D Tetris. They fill the crates in with boxes of dishes, cushions, however need be, to keep things from shifting or moving around. When we took delivery, there were some things missing."

"What things?"

"Personal items, a box of kid stuff from my room, kitchen items of my grandmother's."

"How do boxes disappear from crates?"

"A hundred ways. Maybe the crates open by accident, or maybe dock workers rifle through them. Maybe customs. But also. What was also missing in the shipment was the painting you brought to me in Lubbock."

Drawing in a quick breath, Katie sat up straight. One hand over her mouth, eyes wide. she could not take her eyes away from Alex. He matched her gaze, and reaching across the makeshift little table, Katie grasped his wrist. They stayed like that for a whole minute, until Alex spoke again. "My grandfather filed claims with the moving company to recover the lost items. When they couldn't locate them, he retraced the journey as best he could. That summer we moved, we spent many hours in warehouses and searching on docks. But we never found any of it."

"What about your grandmother? Was she upset? Did she help you and your grandfather?"

"No. She never came along with us. My grandfather was so determined to get that painting back. I feel comfortable saying he was like a man obsessed. After months of searching, my grandmother begged him to stop. He wouldn't hear of it. After school started, he traveled back to Europe for work and searched there too, but nothing."

Katie imagined herself examining the painting for the first time, at Mr. Pickett's shop, and then again with Alex, Mary Renata's handwritten words on the back. *The beginning. More than yesterday, but less than tomorrow.* "That painting somehow made its way from Italy to Mr. Pickett's shop. And to me and back to you. Do you think she painted it before or after the accident?"

"There aren't any pieces here dated after nineteen eighty-eight."

"Do you think that's why it was so important to your grandfather?"

"Maybe."

"Maybe because she gave it to him? Maybe because…" Katie couldn't finish the sentence.

"It can't be."

"It might be."

"Alex! Alex! Are you up there?" Nick called from below.

Alex stuck his head in the stairwell. "Hey, Nick. Come on up."

Nick appeared at the second-floor landing. "I've got it all secured. Looks like that storm is headed straight for us now."

"Really?"

"Yep. Sure is. It's slowed down some and will probably be here sometime tomorrow night. The morning after that at the latest."

"Thank you for taking care of it."

"No problem. I'm heading in for the night. Give me a shout if you need anything."

"This is getting exciting," Katie said.

Alex turned, searching her face for any sarcasm. "You think so?"

"I do. I'm looking forward to it."

"You mentioned your fondness for errant weather this afternoon."

"I did."

"Yes, you did."

Alex cleared his throat. Without breaking her gaze, Katie reached out an arm's length to the side of her, picking up a small oil, an abstract landscape of a field of poppies in a wide, gilded frame. "It isn't your grandmother's." She turned it over. "I believe it is European. About thirty years old."

"Mmhmm," Alex maintained eye contact.

"I think it would be nice for your donation."

"I agree."

Katie pressed her empty hand flat on the floor to keep her torso straight.

## Chapter 8

Down the road from the Dyers, in their vacation rental, the one they always rented, Cecilia, her mother, and friends huddled around a laptop in the kitchen.

"Do you think they're together?"

"What was she wearing?"

"How were her shoes?"

"Where is she staying?"

"What is she doing here?"

"Blonde. Southern-ish. But not exactly," Cici made a face, clicking on photos and friends, going from one page to the next. "More like westernish."

"Western? What does that mean? Like a cowgirl?"

All the girls giggled.

"Giddy up!"

"Not dressed like that, but something about her accent. Something about her demeanor."

"Was she rude?"

"Not rude." Cici focused on a faraway corner of the ceiling. "But it was like she was too relaxed. For the club. And the people at the club. She didn't seem to have the least interest in revealing anything good about herself, and without a care about who anyone else, or even who I was. Or what they thought!"

"Aloof? Was she well put together? Or not?"

"Will you all stop talking? I'm trying to figure all of this out. Besides her professional postings, most of her profiles are locked down."

"Who is this?" Someone pointed at a tall man in a photo with Katie. "He's here in another photo."

"I don't know. Let's go look at that article." *Click. click. click.* "Harold Haman III, senior financial advisor." Cici typed the name in the search bar. "Let's see who Harold Hamon II is."

"His father! You're so smart, Cici!"

"They own a financial firm. Here is his mother, Harriet." *Click, click click.* "It seems she is involved with charities. Here she is again, part of women's clubs and a theater foundation. Well, what do you know? Girls! Come here and look at this photo! Do you see what I see?"

All the girls crowded around Cici's computer. There was Katie, in a photo with Tre, his parents, and her father. Her right hand was on Tre's shoulder, her left holding a glass of champagne, its liquid color matching a golden hue in her form-fitting dress.

"She isn't ugly."

A sizable diamond was prominent on her hand holding the flute. "Harold Haman III is Katie Bauer's fiancé."

"Girls, look at this." A little sloshing from a martini glass, one of the friends pointed at a television. The drapes wide open, facing the beach, they looked out at the surf.

"Mother. Shouldn't we prepare?"

"I don't know what we could do, Cecilia. We have plenty of water and food."

"And alcohol." Someone giggled.

"The shutters, the windows, I meant."

"I'm not getting out there and doing it. Are you?"

"No, of course not."

"I can try and call the owner."

"Wait!" Cecilia slammed the laptop cover, both hands in the air. "Alex has a caretaker. He stays in their cottage. What's his name—Steve or something?"

"Great idea, Cici!"

"It's genius! I wanna go too!"

"I have to change." One of the gigglers ran up the stairs.

"It's getting late, why don't you wait until morning?" Diedre asked.

Determination crossed Cici's face. Not the sort of determination that comes from success after pursuing a long-sought-after goal, but rather the entitled sort, summoned from the overindulged and spoiled. Intent on having her way no matter the consequence, Diedre knew the futility of argument. After all, Diedre was the engineer of the stunted adult baby standing before her in the kitchen of the vacation house they always rented.

Diedre put a hand toward Cici's face but didn't touch her. "My beautiful girl."

"I know, Mommy. Wish me luck."

"Luck." Diedre made a kissy face.

Before the group went out the door, Diedre called to Cici. "Always a winner, dear."

"I am."

Minutes later, Cecilia and her entourage pulled into Alex's drive. Piling out of their rented minivan, they went around to the side door closest to the kitchen. Both behind the island, Alex and Katie opened jars and packages of crackers and cheese bought earlier at the market. Before knocking, Cici watched them under the light of a pendant lamp hanging over the kitchen island. Facing each other, there they were, laughing. Something was funny. What was it? Cici wondered. Katie dropped a cracker on the floor, and they both went down to pick it up, bumping heads on the way up, laughing more. Katie now had the cracker in her hand. She gestured toward Alex's mouth, he opened it, and she fed it to him.

The entire entourage gasped. "Did you see that?"

"Yes! I'm not blind." *Bam, bam, bam*! Cici whacked the door with an open palm. Alex and Katie finished what they were doing before looking toward the noise. Slipping onto a barstool, Katie stayed put. Still chewing, Alex went to the door.

"Alex. Thank God you're home!"

Blinking, Alex looked down into his hand at a small assortment of wafers. Choosing one with the other hand, he ate it, waiting.

"Alex, I know it is late, but…" Cici said.

"You are correct. It is late."

Cici shuffled her feet, the rest of the girls silent. "Aren't you going to invite us in?"

"Cecilia. I thought you had better manners than this. I am surprised you came unannounced. As you said yourself, the hour is late, and as I'm sure you've noticed, I am occupied." Intent on his hand, Alex chose, then ate, another cracker.

"I was wondering if you could possibly lend, ummm, Steve to us for a little while."

"Who?"

"Steve. Your caretaker."

"We don't have a caretaker named Steve."

"Alex, stop. Whatever his name is. We need help at the beach house. Nothing is boarded up, and this storm is coming." Cici's voice escalated, growing with equal parts of panic and demand. Willing herself to keep her right foot planted, she crossed her arms.

Alex finished his cracker. "Good night, Cecilia. I hope all of you have a good evening. Be safe out there."

Standing tall, Cici stared at the door.

"Close your mouth, Cici."

"Let me drive, Cici. You sit on the passenger side."

An invisible second hand sweeping across an invisible dial, the girls waited for their stunned friend, who wasn't budging from the veranda. Again, someone touched Cici's shoulder.

"Cici. Cici. Cecilia! Come on! Go get into the car." In a near catatonic state, Cecilia turned around.

Back in the van, the dark was quiet except for the night beach sounds, the elevated surf, and the tall grasses brushing together in the pauses between the waves. Focused on Cecilia, waiting for what might come next, they all held their breath.

"What are we waiting for? Let's go! Ugh!" Cici crossed her arms the way she had up on the porch.

The rest of them exhaled. The driver backed out, gravel crunching beneath the tires. "He was so smug."

"Rude, really."

Cici sat silent, staring out the window.

"They certainly were cozy. Looked like she's there for the night."

"You don't know that!" Cici broke in. "What was he supposed to do? I mean, she's here for business. What exactly did that dumb waitress say? Something about a painting?"

"Yes. She said she was looking for Alex. She had a painting of his grandmother's. She went all over the place and then found him in Texas."

"If she found him in Texas, then why is she here?"

"Maybe he invited her."

"What if he invited her for tomorrow night?"

"She's engaged. To Harold something."

"I wonder how much Alex knows about her?"

Cici had already thought of all this. Shuffling her cards, she considered orders in which she might play them.

"What time are the hair and makeup people coming tomorrow?"

"Yes! I'm so excited." A tiny applause erupted from the back of the van.

"Ask Mother," Cici said. "She arranged it."

The girls rode back in silence. Back at the rental, Cici disappeared up the stairs with her laptop without a word, leaving the others drinking and discussing clothes, hair, and tomorrow night's impending party. With the lights off, Cici stared at the ceiling, the girls' voices muffled down below, then in the room next to hers.

After the house grew quiet, Cici lay awake. *Maybe I'm in shock.* She thought she was done playing it over and over in her head, that terrible day so long ago that ended the summer. Since the club the night before last, she couldn't believe the time that had passed since the last time she had seen Alex.

She spent that entire season attending parties and dates just as she should, to Diedre's exact specifications. She'd calculated the correct percentages of alone time and social time, making sure the right people saw them as a couple. Each planned, impromptu beach bonfire meant long beach walks home, just the two of them. Diedre invited Alex over for dinners, and his grandparents for drinks, though Mary Renata and Benjamin never accepted. Cecilia gave Alex every opportunity to do what he was supposed to do. In the summer between their junior and senior year, and after that fall, over Christmas break, when she didn't get a ring, Diedre let Cecilia know she needed to step things up.

## Chapter 9

The middle child of three, Diedre grew up poor. Her family was not lower middle class, but Packington peasant poor. Her parents both worked at a soup factory in Camden, New Jersey, where she grew up. Her family was too proud to accept social services. Before paydays, when all the leftovers in the refrigerator had gone into a baked crust and the leftover pie was eaten, she and her brother and sister sometimes went hungry. Hungry enough to learn that drinking a cup of warm water at night helped one fall asleep. Diedre's parents were never *not* working double shifts to pay the rent, to keep the lights on, and to buy groceries. After she and her siblings graduated from high school, her mother took in laundry, and her father worked on the side as a handyman to help pay for the kids' higher education. During Diedre's first semester at community college, an initiation to education through literature, she imagined her family like Upton Sinclair's characters. The cycles in their own jungle familiar, they awaited the next unseen setback. As they watched the weeks and months pass, they never got ahead. Diedre vowed to cross and move far beyond the river.

She earned a certification as a nursing assistant, and by the time she landed her first job at a hospital in Camden, she'd smoothed out her accent, removing red flags from her vernacular. With her first paycheck, she went to a salon and lightened her hair to a soft beige, and then bought her first brand-new outfit and two proper pairs of shoes from a department store. At the hospital, she met Cecilia's father, an intern hailing from Fishtown, an Irish Catholic working neighborhood across the river from Jersey. He liked Diedre's style and attitude, and after passing his boards, he moved her to the northern part of the state. Diedre stopped working after that, and before their two children were in school, their father got on as a medical director at a hospital in Connecticut. He was a good fit, but before long, their marriage suffered a tragic yet stale denouement. They had grown apart, and though it was time to end things for good, both wanted to do what was best for everyone. That worked out all right for Diedre in the financial settlement section of the decree. Always savvy, she used a portion of her divorce proceeds to secure a 1930s-built, bank-owned Cape Cod in Westport. She gave it new paint on the inside and out and some fresh landscaping, then moved herself and the children in, legitimately enrolling them in the best public schools an address on the county tax rolls could buy. By the time they were in high school, it was time for Diedre to get out of the house.

Students of linguistics know the etymology of the French word *cliche*. Derived from the process of stereotyping, a cliche is a form of printing developed in the eighteenth century to create multiple copies from a mold. For newspapers or other high-speed press runs, the sound of the machine, the mold against metal, made a clicking sound, hence the origin of the word. An onomatopoeia. The redundant, predictable noise is synonymous with overused words, an idea, or a stereotype indicative of an individual. While one such cliche was applicable to Diedre's divorce, the other was so to Diedre herself.

By the time the doctor and Diedre's division was legal, the kids had driver's licenses, giving her the freedom to commute to New Haven for a job at a lighting store. It was a high-end store, the kind where rich people from nearby mansions came to procure interesting fixtures, find vintage chandeliers, or have modern pieces custom made. Diedre liked working there. She made commissions, and at the very least, it wasn't real estate. At her post, in Chanel pulled from the back of her closet and a Rolex on her wrist, she looked as expected.

It was a stretch being able to afford Montauk summers, but even when the kids graduated college, Diedre kept prioritizing and managing so they could keep going. Over the years, with vacations and other things, she strove to set both children up for the lifestyle she was determined that they'd have. It was hard to find a balance between wanting them to have everything she hadn't and spoiling them. She accomplished the latter and knew she'd overdone it. While it worked out fine for Cici's brother, Diedre wondered about her daughter. With a degree in liberal arts from one of the little Ivies, it wasn't likely that Cici would ever be sitting in a corner office of a financial organization like her brother. As for now, Cecilia still worked in a local women's clothing boutique, waiting on the other former high school classmates who had never left. Given her daughter's pretty face, the lack of prospects not only astounded Diedre, but it also kept her up at night.

Cecilia knew she'd disappointed her mother that summer. Diedre made it clear that Cici had better close the deal, because there was no way she would tolerate her kids turning out poor. Cici also knew she should've listened to Diedre, ensuring a backup plan, but she hadn't. And now here she was.

Alex had been so angry with Cici, especially after he saw the wedding invitation prototype in her room. He'd picked it up, realization set in, and without a word he'd walked out, down the stairs, and out of the house, leaving Montauk that night without speaking to her. Later that evening, after Diedre had shut the celebration down and gotten the guests out of the house, Cecilia went to Alex's grandparents. He wasn't there. They hadn't heard from him and had no more idea than Cecilia where he'd gone.

Too mortified to show their faces, the next few summers, Diedre and Cecilia skipped their trip to Montauk. When they went back, they were never there when Alex was. And now that they were, that Texas girl was in the way. The Dyers were private enough that Cecilia could not believe Katie was inside the beach house with Alex. Couldn't believe he would allow her to go through Mary Renata's art. Why would he allow it? All this speculation a waste of energy, Cici knew she did not have enough information to figure out the answers. There was only one way to get them.

# Chapter 10

Alex's palm on the doorframe, he pressed against it until he heard the latch click into place, and he met Katie back at the kitchen island.

"Some people's kids."

"Yes. Some people's kids."

"Where were we?"

"In between the strawberry jam and fig preserves."

"The figs are good."

"Mmhmm." Katie thought so too. She thought of the queen fig wasp, finding her way into a small opening to pollinate, her wings and antennae snapping off as the tiny insect dove in, relentless on her path. *A group of wasps is called a swarm. Everyone knows that.*

A few glasses of wine later, they sat on the big porch facing the water, wind blowing around them. Katie in a corner on a wicker patio sofa, Alex handed her a heavy cotton throw, and she pulled it up around her shoulders. Not too far from her curled-up form, Alex leaned back, his feet on a coffee table. The clouds overcast, no lights up at the house, the beach dark, the waves boomed at the shore.

"It might be raining in the morning, but I'd like to show you our lighthouse."

"If you'll lend me a rain jacket, I'm game."

"I can do that."

Katie stifled a yawn. "I'm sorry about that."

"I can take your things to a guest room if you'd like. Ground floor. I have a feeling you'll sleep better there." Standing up, stretching, they folded the blankets and pushed the pillows back into place. Alex brought Katie's bag to a room with a big canopy bed and showed her the door to the bathroom. "I'll see you in the morning."

"Good night," Katie said. She shut off the light in the bedroom, placed her bag on the bed and took out something to wear the next day. She removed all her clothes and stood for a moment in the dim light from the bathroom spilling across her and the duvet. She listened to the wind and the waves, their voices muffled by the sturdy old house. After a quick shower, she found a robe on a hook on the back of the bathroom door and slipped it over her naked body. Then she pulled back the layers one by one and climbed into the bed. Pillows around her, still in the robe, she lay on her side, pressing her face into the down. She thought about calling Mari but didn't, deciding to keep the evening, the fluffy robe cocoon, and the feel of the crisp sheets all to herself.

## Chapter 11

Turning over again, Cici fought with the sheet kicked down under the comforter. Sitting up, she reached down between all that to pull it up where it belonged, squinting her eyes at the light pouring in from out in the hallway.

"Oh, good. You're still awake." Diedre sat on the side of the bed.

Propped up against the headboard, Cici, buttoned up in white silk pajamas, stared at her mother.

"I'm here to help."

"Ok, Mommy." Cici blinked, her forehead wrinkled.

"What happened earlier? When you went over with the girls?"

Cici's eyes filled with tears, and she shook her head. "He didn't care at all to see me. He slammed the door in my face."

Diedre turned her head, legs crossed, and placed her chin in her hand. A closed fist over her mouth, she fixated on the floor. "Cecilia." She paused. "We must be very, very careful. You know how the Dyers are. Very private."

"Mother, I know! Don't you think I know that?"

"No more impulsive moves." Diedre squeezed Cici's arm.

Cici drew back, lowering her voice. "Ok. I know."

"I saw you on your computer earlier. Tell me what you know."

Cici did, including the information from Rhonda, the photos she'd found online, the fiancé, his background, and the small bits of information about his family.

"I can't believe she's there. In that house." Cici found herself stuck on that thought.

"He must want something from her."

"We know what that something must be, Mother."

"Don't underestimate Alex. He isn't common. What did that waitress tell you again?"

"Rhonda? Oh, I don't know. Mother, she's nothing. A nobody. Who knows if she's even telling the truth."

"What did she say?"

"Something about some painting. That Texas girl had a painting done by Alex's grandmother."

"Then that's it, dear."

"That's what, Mother?"

"The painting. Alex wants the painting."

## Chapter 12

Waking to a light knock at her door, Katie found herself in the exact position in which she had fallen asleep. "Alex?"

Alex opened the door, just an inch or two. "Are you hungry? I made breakfast." Daisy's nose at knee level, her tail thumped against the door.

"I'll be out in a few minutes." Katie sat up and stretched. Feeling rested, she put on leggings and a tank top and brushed her hair and teeth. Daisy was waiting right outside her door, and together they found Alex in the kitchen.

"How did you sleep?" He pushed a small tray toward the barstool she chose.

"So good. There are some serious luxury hotel things going on in that guest room." Katie picked up a strawberry.

"What do you mean?" Alex took a baking sheet from the oven and placed it on top of the stove.

"The pillows, the sheets, the comforter. And don't even get me started on the robe."

"Ah. That's all my grandmother. She tells a story about my grandfather taking her to The Plaza for an anniversary. She loved the hotel so much, she got rid of every linen in the apartment in the city and the house here. She replaced them all with 'those fancy hotel sheets,' as my grandfather called them." Alex started to say something else, then stopped.

"Well. I thank her. I haven't slept that well in a long time. What are you making?"

"My specialty. *Sfogliatelle ricce.* Try one." Alex placed one of the warm pastries on a plate and passed it over to Katie and then took one for himself.

"What's inside?" Katie took another bite of the sweet, flaky confection.

"Ricotta. My grandmother learned to make this from her sister. When I was a kid, my favorite filling was Nutella. I lived on that stuff the first half of my life."

Katie ate her pastry, one leg tucked up on a stool under her, the other dangling.

"Espresso or Americano?"

"Espresso, please."

"If you're still up to it, and if it's not raining too much, we could go out and see the lighthouse this morning."

"Yes, let's do that."

They finished breakfast, loaded up into his truck, and, armed with an umbrella and slickers, drove to the eastern tip of Long Island. The weather keeping visitors away, they had the museum and grounds to themselves.

Up 137 steps they went, Katie in front, alternately holding the rope railing or pressing her hand against the roughness of the brick walls. Stopping at a porthole, she peered out at the gray Atlantic. Once in the top of the glassed-in tower, they stood, as the waves hurled themselves against the rocky shore below.

"'A speechless wrath that rises and subsides,'" Katie looked down.

She felt Alex coming up behind her, inches away. "'The storm smites it with all the scourges of the rain…'"

"'…against its solid form press the great shoulder of the hurricane…'" Katie finished the stanza. "I'm trying to remember how I know that."

"I'd guess it could have something to do with middle school."

"Likely," Katie agreed. "Thank you for bringing me. It's beautiful up here, in spite of and because of the impending storm.

"Despite this lighthouse, there have still been shipwrecks out here."

"Really?"

"Yes. See how big the swells are now?"

"Mmmhmm."

"They'll get even bigger with a storm surge. From a sailor's viewpoint, the rocks and sandbars might be hidden. Can you imagine how hurricane-force gusts would push ships toward the land and smash their hulls onto the coastline?"

"Isn't it strange how predictable hurricanes are?" Katie watched the waves crash against the rocky shore and bluff faces down below them. "How many there will be in a season. Their pattern, their path. But not their intensity. You never know about that."

"I suppose you don't. Let me go in front this time." Alex led the way down. "In case you stumble."

She wrapped her head around history and analogies, and without incident on the stairs, they went for a seafood lunch on the lake, both the company and the bechamel just right.

After lunch, Katie glanced at the time displayed in the car. "What is the schedule for tonight?"

"We should get there around six. Do you need anything from the hotel?" Alex asked. "We could go by if you need to. If you get ready at my house, we'd save one trip in this rain."

Katie considered the guest space at Alex's. Agreeing with the plan, she got her things together, taking her dress in its dust cover.

"Give me your bag," he said, popping the handle up. "Do you have everything now?"

"I think so." Katie looked around the neat room. The maids had come since she'd been gone, making her bed and replacing the towels.

"Ok, let's go. I bet Daisy is getting hungry."

"Yes. Let's go feed Daisy." Katie went to the passenger side of Alex's truck.

"Wait," he said. "Let me get your door."

Once at the beach house, Alex carried her things to her room and hung the dress in the closet. "I'm looking forward to this evening," he said.

"Me too."

After he left the room, Katie fell back onto the bed, images of hurricanes, spiral staircases, rocky cliffs, and Longfellow's words swirling in her head.

Securing most of her hair with a few bobby pins, stray strands and pieces falling around her shoulders, Katie chose simple stud earrings and a pearl necklace. She slipped on Mari's black pumps under the long evening gown. One shoulder bare, she found a wrap Mari had included with the shoes. Last, she untucked her small black clutch from the zippered pocket of her suitcase. She checked her phone before placing it inside—no messages—and took a deep breath.

In the living area, she found Alex in a black tuxedo with Daisy at his feet. Taking Katie's image all in, Alex tried not to do anything impolite with his eyes. Her hair up, stray strands and pieces falling around her shoulders, dress hugging her body all the way down, she stood one foot forward, with the ease that only those beautiful enough can achieve. Alex's pause lasting seconds as he went through the list of adjectives in his head, he considered which were appropriate, complimentary, but not crossing any lines.

"Stunning."

Katie examined the toe of Mari's shoe.

"You look stunning."

She looked up at him, her green eyes striking. She lifted her head a little higher. "Thank you. Are we ready?"

"Mmhmm." Grateful for the task of finding keys and for the actions of closing the door and getting into the car, Alex had no words for the greater part of the next five minutes.

Alex valeted the car as before at the club and went around to Katie's side while one of the attendants assisted with her door. He gave her his arm and they went in, she holding the little painting they'd chosen to donate in her other hand. Not quite passing the long bar, they entered a banquet room on their right. Long tables were set up along one wall, displaying all sorts of items on which to bid, including baskets of wine, weekend getaways, ski trips, unique dining experiences, and other art. A man with white hair, pointed features, and wire-rimmed spectacles approached Alex with a quick step. Shaking his hand, he grasped the younger man's shoulder with his free one. Coming together, they met in a brief hug.

"It's good to see you, Mr. Gideon." Alex could not remember not knowing Mr. Gideon.

"You look well. How are the grandparents?"

"They're fine. Thank you for asking. Please, meet my friend, Katie Bauer."

"Nice to meet you, Miss Bauer. Could I take this and set it with the others?" He motioned toward the painting in her hand.

"Yes, please. Nice to meet you also."

"Alex, would you mind saying a few words to get the auction going after dinner?"

"I'd be glad to."

Mr. Gideon handed the small painting to two women coordinating the items and left. Alex and Katie browsed the room, admiring the formal table settings, neutral local blooms, light-colored dahlias, and greenery. A server with a tray of champagne offered flutes, which Katie declined.

"Me neither. Let's go see George."

"Hello again, George," Katie said. "I wonder if you could make me a ranch water?"

George and Alex raised their eyebrows.

"Tell me what's in one, and I'll be glad to."

"It is made with tequila, club soda, and lime juice. I would prefer an anejo, or a reposado, if you have that."

George nodded. "We do. I have an extra anejo imported from Jalisco."

"Perfect. It isn't tequila if it isn't from Jalisco, is it?"

"Not at all." George brought the bottle down from the shelf behind the bar. "Would you like to taste it first? This is a nice one. Aged in French oak barrels."

"That's ok. I trust you."

"I appreciate that." George poured the dark-amber-colored liquid.

"I'll have the same," Alex said.

George nodded.

"You know. The state of Jalisco happens to be blessed with a dark, loamy volcanic soil, in which agave plants so happen to thrive. Down in the valleys there, the days are hot, and the nights are warm, producing peppery, even spicy tequila. Up higher, there is more rain and cooler weather, so you get more floral notes. With the more aged, you might get cinnamon, chocolate, or fruits. You might detect certain barrels."

"You are full of surprises."

"I'm from Texas."

"You may have mentioned that."

"My grandfather is a rancher and farmer. Not to discount those tequila tours from long-ago spring breaks counted for something."

"Well, then. Here's to the terroir of tequila. And to Texas." Alex tipped his glass.

"To Texas and tequila." *Clink.* Their glasses touched, and they drank.

Choosing the same seats as the night before, Katie sat on Alex's right. Her legs crossed, the high slit on her dress revealed skin on her upper thigh, its deep olive tone matching that of her shoulder. Alex resisted touching her there again, as he had on the beach. He slid Katie's drink closer to her and picked up his own with his left hand, dropping the right to the top of her knee. Not looking down but tracing the bone with one finger, finding the right spot, he left his palm there, cupped on her patella.

Hands make humans human. One of the most powerful parts of the body, they can bring adversarial nations to peace. They can prove honor and allegiance or hold another's in solidarity or kindness. With a single, impulsive strike, they can destroy an entire family. They can crush things or cradle them. They can nurture and cultivate. Containing over one hundred thousand nerves, delicate and complex, they can give and elicit the most intimate forms of affection. Katie did not flinch or move away from the one touching her now, thinking that this must be some type of poetry.

As she sipped her drink, the alcohol warmed the back of her throat and then her chest cavity. In a moment, she shifted, but first placed her hand over his because she didn't want him to move it.

"French oak barrels."

"I was thinking about grapes now," she said.

"What about them?" Alex hunched his shoulders, now at her eye level.

Katie smelled the sweetness on his breath and noticed a tiny white scar on the curve of his lip. For a few seconds she heard a rush, like crashing waves from earlier—or was it the rain? "The intricacies of growing them, and choosing, and aging, and blending them. How those grapes are made into wine that is layered and perfect, or not."

"It's a lot to think about."

"It is."

"And you know. If you make something into wine, it doesn't make it good just because it's wine."

"That's true. And good wine can go bad."

"In that case, it is still wine, but it is also still bad," Katie said.

Something in his peripheral vision made the corner of Alex's eye twitch, a grating noise distracting him.

"...so maybe we'll see you at dinner?"

Reluctant, Alex and Katie turned toward the talking.

"...all the tables are set for eight."

"No, Cecilia."

"We can save seats..."

"No, thank you."

"I hope I'm not interrupting anything." Cici's gaze centered on Alex's right hand and Katie's left one. Not knowing what to do with her own, she flailed them.

Cecilia *was* interrupting something. This perfect, comfortable meter, the rhythm now broken, Katie inhaled. Removing her hand from Alex's, Katie stood. "Excuse me; I'll be back in a minute." Escaping, she headed to the restroom. Feeling herself hurrying, an uncontrollable urge to break into a run, she paused, then restarted her steps, slowing them.

Retaining his composure, Alex stared hard at Cecilia.

## Chapter 12

"What? What is it, Alex?" Cici chirped. Blinking, her eyelashes matted, they appeared tangled in a too-white area below her eyes.

*Sparkly,* Alex thought. Why was Cici covered in so much glitter? And why were her features so accentuated? Her hair up high, pulled tight and frizzy on the ends, she looked a lot like Diedre. Squeezing his eyes shut, he shook his head, then folded his hands together on the bar.

"If you don't mind"—his words directed at the covey flocked around her—"I'd like a word with Cecilia."

"They're my friends, Alex. They can stay."

"Enough."

"Why, Alex, I don't know," Cici said.

"You do know," he said. "I said enough. And I mean it."

"You all can go now go now now go!" Cici's words ran together.

Alex did not pause, and the other girls, gaping, did not go. Mustering any empathy he could, he softened his tone. "I'm sorry if I hurt your feelings. I'm sorry that we ended like we did. It's my fault." He placed one hand on his chest. "I should have been forthcoming. But the point is that. It. Ended. And it ended a long time ago."

"But why are we talking about any of that? Don't you think we could just—"

"I'm telling you everything that I think, Cecilia," Alex said. "I don't want to chat casually or in private. Either here, at the beach house, or anywhere. I don't want to do that now, tomorrow, or ever, for that matter. Now please. Please go with your friends and your mother. I hope all of you have a nice evening. Enjoy yourselves." Alex stood, dismissing Cecilia. "There you are, Katie. Let's go find a seat for dinner. I think they are ready to serve."

Navigating through the room, Alex brought her to a table with two empty chairs. "May we sit here?" A man, already standing, pulled chairs for them both.

"We could not be more pleased if you would. Hello." An attractive woman, hair pulled back in an old-fashioned tortoise comb, extended her hand to Katie. "I'm Emma Anderson, Alex's next-door neighbor. We've known him his whole life." Mrs. Anderson looked around Katie as Alex sat. "My, you look so handsome."

"Yes, he does," Katie said.

Through the double doors at the front of the room, open to the bar where they'd left Cecilia, she stood watching them. Her face sweating, red cheeks flushing through behind a ghostly wall of cosmetic powder, her heart racing, she placed a thin hand over her mouth, stifling an involuntary screech.

Following her friends to a table, Cecilia situated herself so she could see Alex. "Alex Dyer will not dismiss me," she whispered. "I. Will not be dismissed."

In college, Diedre had practiced smiling in the mirror. In a psychology class, she learned that real versus fake smiles were detectable. She practiced the fake ones using the muscles used in real smiles. Over the years, she had sold a lot of lamps and fooled a lot of people. Beaming in her daughter's direction, she shook her head. "Mm, mm, mmm," she smiled.

Cecilia did not hear her mother. Refusing to eat her food, she pushed it around on the plate.

"Cecilia, dear. Would you like to go to the ladies' room with me?"

Cecilia shook her head.

"Everyone is finished eating. Come with me." Standing, Diedre placed her napkin on the table. Near her daughter's chair now, she placed a hand on the back of it. Taking Cecilia's napkin from her lap, she did the same with hers. "Let's go."

Left without a choice, Cecilia went with her mother. Diedre ducked into the women's locker room, right next to the restroom.

No one would enter here in the evening, but Diedre locked it just in case. "Cecilia. When we spoke earlier about Alex, I wasn't aware of the extent of the situation."

"What does that mean? Extent of the situation?" Arms crossed, Cici leaned against the vanity, studying her nails.

"Cecilia. You can see how enamored he is with this girl."

"Mother. You don't know."

"Cecilia, do not make a fool of yourself in front of these people. Of all people. Not these." Diedre threw one arm out, swinging it overhead.

Erratic, uneven breathing accompanied by loud sniffling escaped Cici.

"Cecilia, not now. Get a hold of yourself."

The overdone girl balled her hands into fists. Lips pressed together, the bottom one protruding, feet together, she bent her knees, and a loud piercing screeched from her vocal folds. Chaotic and inconsistent, it escalated into a roar, an evolutionary scream meant to rouse the primal brain of anyone within hearing distance. Not Diedre's brain, however, which was conditioned to everything Cecilia. Thankful for the walls between them, the kitchen and the dining room, Deidre waited for the tantrum to run down. Tears inevitable, Diedre patted Cecilia's head, rolling her eyes over the top of Cecilia's unfortunate updo.

"Mommy! I'm so mad. So, so, so mad!"

"There, there. Clean yourself up, Cecilia." Nothing resolved except for smeared mascara, Cici and Diedre took their places again. It was not the place for addressing it now, Diedre reminded herself. She would call Cici's father next week. He could deal with her for a while.

John Gideon was making another announcement, and Alex asked Katie if she'd like another drink.

"Yes, but let me go get them. He might call you up there."

"You're right. If you're sure you don't mind."

"I don't. I'll hurry." Alex stood and helped Katie with her chair. At the bar, Katie ordered.

Behind her, Cecilia cleared her throat. Trapped between the girl and the bar, Katie could not escape.

"Hello, Katie."

"Hello."

"You look beautiful. I like your dress," Cecilia said.

"Thank you. I like yours too." It felt like George was taking forever.

Cici smoothed her silvery sequins. "Are you having a nice time tonight?"

Hearing Alex's name announced, both girls looked back through the doorway.

"I'm having a wonderful time. Even with the weather." Katie motioned toward the outside with her hand.

"Hmmm. Yes. Just look at him." Cecilia turned her attention to Alex, now up in front of the room. "Alex is always so confident and put together. So polite too."

*Where is she going with this?* Katie wondered.

"He's also very private. The Dyer family is very private." Cecilia studied Katie. "But I can tell you, from my own personal experience"—George delivered the drinks—"that he is a man. Like any other, regular man. Men do certain things to get what they want. You know what I mean."

Katie took a drink.

Leaning in like they were friends, Cici giggled, swirling the olive on the pick in her glass. "Let me tell you a little secret. A confession, if you will. Just between us girls."

"What's that?" Katie asked.

"I looked at your social media, Katie. It seems you are quite private as well."

Katie fought a familiar urge. The one from her last night in the apartment. The one from yesterday at the club, and the one from earlier when she forced her feet to stop moving. She hated it. Hated that this sad, pale, strange little girl positioned between the bar and her seat made her feel like bolting. Using the drink in her hand as an anchor and a barrier, she sipped.

"But I did see that you're engaged."

Katie gripped the glass tighter.

"To a Harold Haman. Isn't that right?" A half smile. Half a head taller than Katie, Cici looked down on the other girl. Katie stared at Cici without blinking, the second time in a period of days considering a fluffle. Only the reference to Harold, rather than Tre, kept Katie from flinching. And then Katie considered Cecilia's hair. Pulled back, but not in a sleek way, the updo altogether too poofy, the word that came to mind, made Cici's head appear large in proportion to the rest of her. *Maybe her head is large.* Katie imagined the hair billowing out like a balloon, her body floating up and bumping on the ceiling.

Cecilia was unsure of what reaction she sought; this wasn't it. Katie seemed unaffected. Serene, even. Something about the way she stood against the bar, where Cecilia intended her own body as a barrier to the dining room—Katie did not appear trapped but instead stared through her and into the big room.

"What were we talking about?"

"Assumptions, I believe," Katie said. "They are a waste of time and often inaccurate."

"What? We weren't talking about anything like that. Oh. Right. Men. We were talking about men. That's where we were. And how they all want something." Shifting her position, Cecilia turned toward the seated crowd, a handful of people clapping as Alex continued speaking. She got herself back on track. "Alex wants the painting you have. That's why he invited you up here. To get the painting back." Pleased with herself, Cici completed the rest of her smile.

Not surprise, but something inside her shook Katie from the inside out. Her mind drifted to her favorite Rudyard Kipling stories as a child. The laws and hierarchy of the jungle, she understood. Living on a ranch, rules ensured survival. There were dangers to contend with, care taken to protect one another, and unbreakable alliances. Quarrels came about now and then, and differences got sorted out. Anybody across the fence treated with good manners, each was trusted only when you knew they could be.

Katie turned to George and ordered a second drink for both of them.

Most mongoose species, like Katie's favorite Kipling storybook animal, live solitary lives. *Indian gray mongooses have no group or family categorization. Baby mongooses are helpless and blind when born but leave their mothers as young as four months old. After that, they need no companionship or help to survive on their own.*

"I—I'm not finished with this one."

"Are you ok? Is your hand shaking?" Katie asked. Cici's nails, with a recent manicure, appeared to have lima beans glued on top.

The ice cubes clinked against the inside of Cici's glass.

Katie finished her drink and moved it away. "That's all right. I'll drink this one too."

*A mongoose is wary, quick, and though small, vicious if need be.*

"I should go back to my friends."

Katie shifted her position, placing Cici between herself and the bar. "Oh, that would be too bad. We were having such a wonderful conversation." *Mongooses are known to kill poisonous snakes with speed and agility.* Through a set of glass side entrance doors, Katie looked out into the storm, using the pause in conversation to ponder Cecilia's words. The things she said about men wanting something and that Alex wanted the painting. It could be true. The reality of that stung. Stung in the way that might have made Katie fly out into the rain and wind like a stray gazelle evading a lion. But not now. For a few reasons. One. While Katie would normally choose to avoid conflict, this girl had come clear over the fence without cause or permission, and Katie wasn't having it. Alex might want the painting, but Katie also wanted more Mary Renata art. Two. Cecilia had the kind of eyes that never changed expression, and Katie didn't trust her farther than she could throw her. And three. Three was standing right in front of them now, touching Katie's elbow, and the way Alex looked at Katie negated all reservations in reason number one and confirmed her instincts in reason number two.

Dismissed for the third time in two days, Cecilia balled her fists again.

Extending her right arm, Cici pointed at Katie. "Alex! She's engaged!" Like a weathervane in the wind, a sudden change of direction, she pointed at Alex. "I told her that you! All you want from her is that painting! I know! I know because that stupid waitress told me everything!" Taking large huffs of air in through her nose, one after the other, Cecilia's nostrils flared. Arms locked, she puffed, practically on her tiptoes, she took a step toward Alex.

"You do know everything, don't you? Good for you," Alex said.

Behind the bar, George cleared his throat. And then again, more exaggerated this time, he slid a drink across the bar to Alex, two shots of bourbon, neat. "Thank you, George," Alex said. He took a drink and examined the amber liquid. "You know, Cecilia. Your omniscience must be beneficial in your work. An important aspect for waiting on people. Hanging and folding things."

Cecilia opened her mouth, and air escaped, a shrill note at the end, her astonishment lingered.

"I'll tell you something else, Cecilia. That waitress is an integral part of this community. That waitress runs a business. That waitress provides a valuable service. She employs people. It isn't a good idea to call people who are three steps above you 'stupid.' After all, what does that say about you?" Alex finished the rest of his drink, dismissing Cici for the fourth time in two days.

She didn't go. Frozen, she stood there, her mouth hanging open.

Alex offered Katie his arm, and she linked hers through his. "Are you interested in getting out of here?"

"I was thinking the same thing."

"George, can you please call for the valet?"

"Glad to."

Without giving Cecilia any more thought, consideration, or glance, Alex and Katie left.

A boy from earlier pulled the car around. "Be careful out there, Mr. Dyer."

"You too. I don't think we've seen the worst of it yet."

Doors to the vehicle closed, Alex asked, "Are you ok?"

"Yes, I am. I'm fine. Are you sure it's ok that we left early?"

Keys in the ignition, Alex cleared his throat. "It was time to go. I performed my expected part. The company inside was not conducive to a relaxing evening. And the weather is deteriorating."

"Ok, then."

"We are going to take it nice and slow back to the house."

"It's hard to see." Straining, Katie bent forward in her seat.

"I've got it. No worries. It's just rain and wind. There doesn't seem to be any flooding on the road."

Water splashed up in the wheel wells and onto the doors, creating a small bow wave behind them. Alex turned on the hazard lights and moved the car toward the center of the road. Smooth and intentional, taking twice as long to return as it did to arrive, Alex pulled into the driveway. Slowing, he took the garage opener from the visor, and the door lifted.

During the ride home, he almost did, then didn't. But now, it seemed, an unconscious debate decided, he asked, "Katie. What did Cecilia do? Or say, or both? I hope she didn't overstep, though chances are, that is probable."

The rain pelted down on the old car, and for a moment Katie concentrated on the way she liked its smell, a combination of clean leather and wax, like melted crayons.

Foot on the brake, Alex waited.

"She said what you heard her say. The reason you invited me here was to get your grandmother's painting back." There it was. All laid out.

Sighing, Alex pressed his lips together. The car in park, he turned in the seat toward her. "That is true, but only in part. I invited you up here, Katie, because I liked your tenacity. I liked the idea of showing my grandmother's art. I was drawn to your excitement about all of it, and that is why I asked you to the gala."

Katie considered his words. "I am excited about your grandmother's art. I want to do the exhibit."

Alex pushed his hand over the top of his head and pulled the car into the dark garage.

"That was a nice thing you did," Katie said.

"What? Nice?" Alex asked.

"You stood up for Rhonda."

"I've known her for years. She's a hard worker. She's self-made. I respect that."

"I do too. Alex. There's something else. I want to give the painting that I got in San Antonio back to you. I want to send it when I get back to Texas."

---

Alex almost protested. But then a familiar feeling overcame him. One that he recognized so well but could not label. Did he have this because his grandparents had raised him? Was it because he'd lost his parents, yet didn't remember them? Sometimes he wondered, though did not know.

He remembered standing on the edge of a playground with his grandmother. She was kneeling, encouraging him to go play with the other children. He wanted to, he did. But something inside kept him from charging out right away. After a few minutes, though, Alex chose to join in on the monkey bars, the swings, or a game of chase. Not at all awkward, he'd run and play until Mary Renata called for him, and he often begged her for five more minutes.

When he picked Daisy out of her litter, it was the same. He went back to the breeder three times. The first, standing back, he watched the puppies.

"She was the first one out of the pool. I swear her eyes were barely open. I call her Sassy," the woman said.

Alex didn't choose that day. The next time he went back, two weeks later, the furry bundles tumbling over each other, one of them ventured out on her own, up and over the edge of the blue plastic kiddie pool, toddling toward him. He picked her up, and she pulled her head back. Tail wagging, she licked his face before nuzzling and wiggling, finding the perfect spot on his neck and shoulder. The third time, he picked her up and took her home for good.

After the breakup with Cecilia, at first, he wondered about his reaction, whether it was impulsive, leaving the party like he had. Alex knew what Cecilia was after. Everyone did. But when he saw those invitations, he decided. Much later, he realized the demise of that relationship, or rather its inevitable termination, was a process that could have been much less slow and painful.

Gauging Katie's tone, Alex considered her level of determination.

---

Halfway expecting some response, a nod of agreement, or protest, Katie gave him a minute. She didn't know what to make of his silence. Was it apathy? Was something keeping him from saying "Yes! Please send the painting back!" Or "No! You keep it!"

The storm dictating their actions, it forced them inside before any resolution. The rain blew in sideways sheets. They hurried down the breezeway, an umbrella in all four hands bumbling, and Katie shrieked. Relentless, fat raindrops, intense and freezing, drenched them. Inside, it was dark.

"First, let me get us some towels and check and see if the generator is on."

Katie took a few steps toward the windows facing the ocean. She couldn't see the surf from inside, but only the rain hurling itself against the windows, the wind roaring. Alex came back with the towels, and they dried themselves well enough to stop the water from dripping onto the floor. Daisy sat in front of them, her head hanging. "It's pretty scary out there, isn't it?" Katie rubbed her ears.

"The generator is taking care of the necessities," Alex switched on a small dim light in the kitchen. "How do you feel about changing and meeting me back out here?" Alex watched for any expression or tone, a hint of whether Katie might be upset. Or angry. Or uninterested.

Looking down at her wet clothes, Katie removed her heels. "Yes," she said. "Ok."

Returning in joggers and a thermal crew pushed up to his elbows, Alex decanted a bottle of burgundy. "Here's hoping that any volatiles expel quickly." He gripped the edge of the counter with both hands. Shoulders hunched, eye level with the center of the vessel, Alex said, "Please feel free to express yourself, your true aromas and flavors," he said. Satisfied with his request, the wine, clearing and full of promise, waited for pouring.

"Did you say something?"

Alex looked up from the decanter. Katie's hair was smooth and pulled back from her face. Her eyes vibrant in the dim light, she looked like an actress in a set, a movie he couldn't remember the name of—something in black-and-white. "No. Yes. Rather, just thinking aloud. About this wine and dispelling any astringencies." Alex took two glasses from a cabinet behind him. "I thought about moving those two chairs away from the window and positioning the sofa over this way, so we can watch the storm."

As they rearranged the furniture together, Alex pulled a coffee table closer for their drinks.

"I like this." Katie sipped hers.

"Do you? This comes from a vineyard my family has done business with for a long time. It's in the Cote de Nuits region. They make one of my grandfather's favorite wines. Mine too."

"Thank you for sharing."

The distraction of the Burgundy wearing off, Alex set his glass down. "Katie."

"Yes?"

"I want to apologize for subjecting you to Cecilia. I'm embarrassed about it, and I feel bad."

"It isn't your fault."

"I disagree. It is. I hope you won't hold it against me."

"I won't. You can't control the actions of other people."

"Here's to avoiding the actions of other people."

"And to storms."

"And to storms." Katie couldn't agree more with the first part of their salute.

The wine velvety and intense, they sampled more than one bottle. The winds blew throughout the night. The house, no stranger to another disciplined tempest, only lost a cedar shake or two. The eye passing over before daybreak, its silent shout caused Katie to shift, waking up on the couch next to Alex. Closing her eyes, she listened to the rain in the distance. When it arrived, it was soft at first, then pelted down harder. She fell asleep again.

No planes the next day or the next, Katie and Alex spent Sunday and Monday going through and titling pieces and taking photos of them. She called the hotel for assistance, initiating the processes for website marketing and brochures and sending emails to regular collectors. Mary Renata's permission a gift, she wasn't interested in attending the exhibit.

"It took a lot of convincing from me and my grandfather for her to allow us to do this show. She said, 'What a lot of nonsense. No one could be interested in those old paintings of mine.' And my grandparents travel, but only when they want and where they want to go."

Katie broached the subject of Alex's presence, but not in an overt way. *Maybe he doesn't want to go either*, she thought, and kept at the task of the paintings, a little afraid the Dyers might change their minds. Alex wrapped the art in brown paper, and Katie marked each one in preparation for the packers. They drank more wine and discussed attributes.

## Chapter 13

On Monday night, Katie checked in for her flight, sending Mari the new itinerary. Arriving at San Antonio International, Mari parked in short term and waited just past baggage claim at the bottom of the escalators. When Katie rounded the corner, appearing at the top, she saw her friend and lifted one hand. Mari stepped backward, not just to allow other travelers to pass, but to study Katie.

"You don't look like you have been through a hurricane." She hugged her. "I'm glad you're home safe."

"I feel good. Me too."

In the car, Katie told Mari about her trip. When they arrived back at the apartment, they sat in the parking garage while Katie finished. Then, curled up on Mari's sofa, Mari had questions.

"She yelled at you? She pointed at you? She stalked you online? What did you say?"

"After the pointing? Nothing. Alex didn't respond to anything about 'Harold' or the painting. He defended Rhonda. He left her speechless," Katie said.

"He put her in her place?" Mari asked.

"No, Mari. From what I can tell, Cici isn't the kind of person who can be put in her place."

"What are you going to do?"

"About what?"

"About Alex."

"Nothing. I don't know."

"Katie! There are too many I don't knows!"

"Maybe I need to be alone for a while. To figure things out."

"What does that mean? Living alone? By yourself? Why would you do that? You have me. You have the ranch."

"I could stay here a little while longer," Katie said.

"I do not need to tell you, but of course, as long as you want. Move in with me."

"Maybe."

Mari grabbed Katie's hand. "Yes, do!"

"And one more thing. Will you help me get my things out of Tre's apartment?"

"Yes. On a condition."

"What condition?"

"I'm calling our fathers."

Katie started to disagree, but Mari wouldn't allow her to.

"No, Katie. Trust me. It's better if they are there."

---

Tre's week was not going his way. He threw the new set of house keys on his desk. He hadn't heard from Katie in days, though Margaret had reminded him of the East Coast storm, asking whether he'd tried to contact her.

"I have no idea what she's up there doing. A storm doesn't keep her from calling or texting. Or coming back when she said she would. You know what, Mags? I have other, more important things on my tray. I clearly don't have time for this." But where was Margaret today? After ten, he hadn't heard from her either, and it didn't look like she'd been at her desk this morning. Taking big steps, Tre marched up to the reception desk.

"Where's Mags?"

The girl behind the desk dropped her pen.

"Well? Where is she?"

"I—I'm not sure." Her pallor unnoticed, he stomped back to his desk, slamming the door behind him. Fumbling for the pen, she didn't need it, and dropping it again, she dialed the senior Mr. Haman.

"Hello."

"Mr. Haman. I'm calling as you asked. Tre's asking for Mags."

"All right. I didn't mean to run so late. That East Coast storm made a mess of things. We drove."

"How far out are you?"

"We are on New Braunfels Avenue."

Exhaling, the receptionist watched the door. The elder Mr. Haman could not arrive soon enough.

---

The driver looked up into the rearview mirror. "I'm doing my best to avoid this traffic."

"I appreciate it." Mr. Haman looked at his watch and then glanced at the man across the seat of the big black car. "It's just a couple of miles, Luke."

Luke, a young executive accompanying Mr. Haman, nodded. A fist resting on his chin, he tapped his foot on the floor mat.

Exiting the freeway, the driver chose the surface streets, winding through a historic neighborhood. The mid-nineteenth-century homes in Lavaca, developed for working-class families, were as eclectic in nature as the families who first lived in them. Original residents consisted of mostly Germanic heritage but were also Polish, Hispanic, and African American. Vernacular structures with independent styles included adobe with tile roofing, saltbox, and bungalow. A residential grid, the streets emptied onto South Presa and into downtown.

## Chapter 13

Without his assistant, and out of sorts, Tre threw the keys and a string of expletives against the wall. Fuming, he could not focus on anything work-related. The dinner with Margaret had not gone as he'd intended. Certain his clients were happy, that wasn't the issue. It was Margaret's demeanor. She referred to him as Mr. Haman the entire evening, ran back and forth with the wait staff to check on—well, whatever she was checking on, and did not drink. At least twice he'd put a drink in her hand, and both times, she managed to set it down. He'd made the effort. He'd given her a half day off to get herself ready. Not at all happy with her choice in attire, her appearance more businesslike than festive, he wished she would have run her clothing choice by him first. The dress short enough, Margaret paired it with opaque tights. Though fitted, she'd worn a black turtleneck underneath and sat across from him at dinner rather than next to him. Her shoes nondescript, he couldn't recall their brand; they were too clunky for his taste. He hated the costume jewelry she'd worn. It looked cheap. Was it something religious? A cross? Maybe it was a sea animal or a flower. Who knew? Who cared? Tre sighed, the keys glaring at him from across the room.

"Oh, well." He shrugged. Not all that attracted to her anyway. "No big loss," he said aloud to himself. "She's got that kid. And she could use a few more curves for my taste." Tapping the fingers of his left hand on the desk, he considered moving her to the front reception and interviewing someone new. He had to admit, however, she had done a great job bringing him drinks the other evening. The last thing he remembered was leaning up against her on the way to the elevator at his apartment. Had she stayed over? Unsure, he woke the next day still dressed, not in his jacket but in his suit pants. Where was that jacket? Standing, he adjusted his gaze around the glare in the window to see his profile reflected in the floor-to-ceiling glass overlooking the city. Projecting his jaw, he smoothed underneath his chin with the tops of his fingers. His hand on his chest, it traveled down across his trim abdomen. He thought about scheduling an appointment with his personal tailor this week. Speaking of tailor, he had a few good lines on the Taylore. Chuckling at his own wit, that was where he would start his day—unloading that art he never intended to keep.

---

Eager to get started, Katie went in to work early to update on the Mary Renata art collection and exhibit timelines. She also scheduled shipping arrangements and contacted the hotel's attorney's office for the documents that needed to go out. Already midmorning, Mari waited at a coffee shop down the street from the Majestic. Her phone ringing, she answered the incoming call from Roberto.

"We just pulled off the freeway," he said. Lewis had driven his truck into town today, toting plastic bins and other supplies he thought Katie might need.

"I'll meet you there." Mari grabbed her pocketbook and keys. Heading out onto the sidewalk along Houston Street in heels and a pencil skirt, she called Katie.

"Leaving the hotel now. I'll see you in a few minutes." Her face flushed in the two-block walk, Katie half ran there. Her heart pounding, she couldn't wait to get her things out of the apartment. With everyone's help, they could be in and out within an hour. Arms crossed, Mari stood between Roberto and Lewis. Her black hair looked pretty. Pulled across one shoulder, it was shiny in the sunlight.

"I see you're dressed for moving day," Katie said.

"No jokes right now, Katie. You know these are my clothes!" She pushed a pair of big sunglasses up on her head.

"Hey, Dad. *Tio.* Thank you both for coming."

Lewis squeezed her shoulders. "Of course. Let's get busy."

"Yes. And let's hurry."

"Gran sent a load of bins and packing materials."

"You know, Dad, I haven't thought about how much of that I'd need."

"Well, honey, you don't need to. Roberto and I will bring it up. Go on, now. We're right behind you."

Inside the cool and quiet building, Katie pressed the up arrow. Arms still crossed, watching the elevator come down, Mari willed the door to open. Once on the floor, they paused at the big door to the apartment. Katie retrieved the house key out of her bag. In the lock, it refused to turn. She wiggled it both ways, taking it out and putting it back in again. She and Mari stared at each other.

"What a piece of work," Mari said.

---

The driver pulled into the parking garage at the Tower Life Building and made a three-point turnaround in the tight space. Mr. Haman said, "Thank you for waiting. I won't be long. There you are, Margaret." Margaret had stationed herself on a bench at the side entrance of the building where Mr. Haman had instructed her to wait. He placed his hand on her shoulder as they went inside. "Margaret. This is Luke Weaver, from our Dallas office."

Margaret extended her hand. "Hello, Mr. Weaver."

"Let's go up," Mr. Haman said. At their suite, he hit the doors, Luke and Margaret half a step behind him. Not pausing at the reception, they went straight around to Tre's office, barging in without knocking.

Just stirring cream into his third cup of coffee, Tre stood up. "Dad? Dad. What are you doing here?" Splashing the liquid, he muttered, wiping the mulberry silk Italian cotton cuff with his hand.

"And Mags? Mags! Where have you been?" Looking from one person to the next, the coffee stain unresolved, Tre struggled to find context.

"Tre, Mr. Weaver will be taking over this office. Starting today. Don't take anything with you. You're leaving. And you're coming with me."

"What in the hell are you talking about?" Tre scoffed. "I'm not going anywhere. And Mags, you can get back in your chair out there. I'll deal with you in a minute."

Margaret looked at Mr. Haman. "Margaret can stay put. After the stunts you pulled, we are all waiting on the phone call from our friends at the SEC. Get yourself down to the lobby. And put yourself in the car. You are coming back to Dallas today. With me. Close your gaping mouth and move."

Tre turned around to his—rather, Mr. Weaver's—desk and collected his cell phone. Mr. Haman steps ahead, Tre followed his father. Nothing to do except stare at the spectacle, Margaret and Luke watched Tre bend down and pick up a set of two keys on a ring in the middle of the floor.

Without speaking, Mr. Haman ushered Tre through the downstairs lobby and into the waiting vehicle. "Please stop by the apartment on Houston Street," Mr. Haman requested.

"Of course," the driver said.

"Get your clothes. Your toothbrush, whatever else you need."

"I had it under control." Tre muttered under his breath.

"The days of you controlling anything are behind us. You won't be out of my sight." The driver took North Saint Mary's Street, clicking on his turn signal as he passed the Empire Theatre.

Tre rubbed the cuff on his pants, digging through his door pocket.

"What are you doing?"

"Looking for a wet wipe or something."

"Enough with the coffee stain. Enough. You have no idea what this firm is about to go through. It's going to be a miracle if either one of us has a shirt to wear when this is over. Much less seven fifty for a mocha latte. We'll need to make it quick. Pull up here. Behind that Ford." Mr. Haman recognized that truck. It belonged to Lewis Bauer. Tre recognized it too.

Bringing the bins, Roberto and Lewis collided with Katie and Mari on the sidewalk. Before the big black car rolled to a safe stop, Tre threw his passenger door open on the street side and hurled himself toward the group of four. Katie's arms now crossed, Mari's hands and elbows in the air assisted her with a full and dramatic explanation of the situation with the dysfunctional key. Taking a deep breath, Mr. Haman stepped out too. By the time he reached the group, he caught Tre's arm, which was tugging at one of the bins Lewis held.

"What is going on here, Katie? What are all these people doing?" Tre's fine cotton shirt with the coffee stain on the cuff now half untucked, his hair tousled and covering one eye, one of his black Berluti oxfords was untied.

"I don't like your tone." Mari stepped into the center of the irregular circle littered with packing materials.

"Whoa there, boy. Nope. No. Easy, now." Lewis held the bin tight. Roberto placed his on the sidewalk.

"Tre! Keep your hands to yourself." Mr. Haman held his son by both arms now.

"I need to know what exactly is going on!" Wrenching one arm from his father, Tre pulled away.

"Katie. Is there something I can help with?" Mr. Haman asked.

A small gray bird flitted above them, gliding up under the eaves on the covered walk, to a nest hidden from passersby. *A quarrel of sparrows*, Katie thought. *Though small, sparrows are persistent and even competitive.*

"I'm here to gather my things, Mr. Haman."

"You're not taking anything out of there!" Tre pointed up.

"Tre. Did you just stomp your foot? Did you really just do that?" Not erratic, but in concert with her words, Mari's arms flew again.

"But I can't," Katie continued.

"You can, Katie. Go on up. Take as long as you need. I'll wait down here with Tre. I'm sorry, Lewis. Where are my manners?" Mr. Haman extended his hand, now free. "Roberto," he said, shaking the other man's hand.

"My key doesn't work." *If threatened, house sparrows are defensive.* "But I live here. I live here, and I want to get inside." Not on purpose, Katie elbowed Mari, stepping closer to Tre in the odd-shaped circle.

"I am her lawyer. She lives here! She absolutely can collect her things." *If another bird attempts to nest in their territory, sparrows will destroy eggs and even kill the other's young nestlings.*

"Oh, please, Mariana. Why don't you just stay out of this. All of you! This is none of your business!" Tre stepped forward, then so did Mr. Haman. And Lewis.

Mari tried squeezing between them. "You'd better be glad I'm here on professional business, Tre Haman." Just in case, Roberto placed one arm around his daughter's shoulder.

Now Mr. Haman directed his attention to Tre. They all did. Without words, Mr. Haman and Lewis shouted the same message. Despite their differences, their faces mirroring hard-earned knowing, both dared Tre to defy either one of them. Mr. Haman extended his hand, palm upward, toward his son. Tre stared at it. Mr. Haman shook his head at the daftness of this overgrown boy. "The keys, Tre."

Tre complied but took a step toward Katie. He reached out for her arm.

"Nossir," Lewis said.

Mr. Haman handed them to Katie. Holding Tre's gaze, her hand a fist around the keys, she said, "I'm going to get my things. And I'm taking that painting." *House sparrows are aggressive and even ruthless and have been known to kill other nesting mother birds.*

"That painting is mine." Veins bulged on Tre's temples. His volume increased. "It's mine!"

"Katie. Go gather your things. You take that painting." Mr. Haman pointed at Tre, then at the car. "You. Get in the car."

Katie did not turn her back until Tre did as he was told. As the car door slammed, people walking on Houston Street stopped and stared at the guttural noises emanating from the shaking, parked car.

Lewis and Mr. Haman waited in the elevator lobby for the girls while Roberto assisted them inside. He stacked bins of clothing near the door. Closet and bathroom cleaned out, Mari asked if they should start in the kitchen.

"No. That's everything. Nothing in there belongs to me." Katie stood between the dining table and the bar. The table where she sat with Tre only days before; she recalled the flying fork and the fluffle. She walked back into the bedroom for one last look, went over to the bookcase, and pulled a handful of copies. One with a familiar yellow binding, and a few more. Reaching up, she took another from high up on the shelf.

"Is that all?" Mari hugged Katie, and she nodded. Their cheeks touching, Mari pulled her closer.

The apartment appeared as it always had. One could never tell she'd been there and gone, the small pile of bins holding her things the only evidence. Before Roberto picked them up, Katie dug in her bag. "Tío," she said, handing him the Simon Bolivar gold-edged coin.

"Not just yet, Katie. You hold on to it. Solo un poco mas," he said.

"Yes. Listen to Papi. I think you should keep it a little longer too," Mariana said.

One arm full of books, the Taylore in the other, Katie took the elevator down one last time with the others.

"Good luck to you, Katie. You have quite a future ahead of you." Another way he and Lewis were alike, Mr. Haman did not say things he didn't mean.

The bins and the girls tucked inside, Mr. Haman watched Lewis drive away, back to the ranch outside town. Mr. Haman was sure they had a pretty nice place out there in the hill country. When Lewis turned the corner at the end of the street, Mr. Haman pulled his hands from his pockets and opened the door to the big black car. He had quite a mess to clean up.

## Chapter 14

Alex closed the door behind the courier and dropped the large package inside, then carried a thick envelope to the kitchen island. The paperwork from the hotel's legal team spread out on the counter, he'd need to sign, initial, and Express Mail it back in time for the exhibit. As expected, everything was the way Katie had explained. But now, the days and conversations spent with the girl from Texas lay before him, reduced to a sum of transactional legal documents. He hadn't expected that. Going over them again, Alex signed his own name and filled in the spaces for Mary Renata. He would not open the package. He knew what was inside.

Days after the hurricane, when travel turned back into a semblance of normal, he'd driven Katie to Queens. That feeling inside every passenger, whether arriving or departing an airport that propels them along, making sure all luggage and personal items are intact, along with the unknowns of airport security lines—Katie and Alex decided it best to drop her off in the departures lane rather than park and walk inside. Rushing around to the trunk of the car, Alex lifted her luggage and placed it up on the sidewalk. He delayed for a moment, and extending the handle on her bag, he didn't let go just yet. The air still clean from the storm, with blustery promises of fall, he leaned toward her. He brushed her cheek, and her hair smelled like it was still summer. Katie leaned in too, her bag toppled over, and they both went to catch it. Her tote resting on top went sideways, items spilling out in all directions.

"Oh, no!"

"I'm sorry, Katie. I've got it!"

A man from the check-in valet brought over a lip gloss, while Katie and Alex picked up the rest. Once everything was back together, organized again, Katie said, "I'd better get in there."

"Yes. It's time."

The trunk of the car agape, Alex still on the sidewalk, he watched Katie go. Into a revolving glass door, she didn't exit inside but came all the way back around. Struggling with her bag, sunglasses falling, and tote sliding off her arm, she called to him.

"The exhibit!" she said. "We never talked about it. Can you come?" Katie took two steps forward.

A shrill, vibrating pea distracted them both. A security guard, her attention on Alex, whistled again. *Preep! Preep!* Solid and rectangular shaped in an official uniform and fluorescent vest, the woman did not look like one to be trifled with. "Close your trunk, sir. You got to get movin."

Waving at the guard, Alex closed the open trunk but kept his eyes on Katie.

"Come if you can!" she said again, and when he nodded, she went back inside. When she disappeared into the building, Alex pulled away from the curb. The nod he'd given her was not a commitment but, rather, an acknowledgment. He didn't know how comfortable he felt or what situation he might walk into in Texas, and he had no desire to put Katie in one, either. *Does she really want me to go?* Driving her to the airport, he had wondered why she hadn't come right out and asked in the days before. A decision today unwarranted, he could think about it more.

As he drove back from Lubbock, the excitement he'd had about the art Katie had brought was now gone, like a house he had lived in a long time ago or a car he used to drive; these things were relegated to mere memories. The handwriting on the box leaning near the door matched that on the packages wrapped in brown paper that were packed and loaded onto a truck days earlier. All his own doing, there he sat, the architect of this hostage, ransom situation. The trade made to his terms not the triumph he had envisioned, Alex thought of a Greek king. *What was his name?* He thought for another moment. *That's right. King Pyrrhus. The Greek king who fought the Romans and won the war but lost his best troops, most loyal commanders, and friends. The lost canvas, a war won, but at what cost? A Pyrrhic victory.*

Without careful thought, vacillation, or gambit, Alex unlocked his cell. He did not wait, weigh, or consider. Dialing the airline, he would not express the documents. All propriety and proper RSVPs aside, he'd fly into San Antonio the afternoon before the event, check into a room at the St. Anthony, and deliver them himself.

## Chapter 15

When Mary Renata's art arrived in San Antonio, Katie composed the show from blank walls. She unwrapped paintings and laid them out, trying various groupings and orders. During the design phase, she liked using an experimental approach, both exciting and terrifying. Considering colors, shapes, patterns, and the way the public would move through the space, she settled on displaying them in chronological order. She liked the way she and Alex had discovered the dates on the canvases and thought that a chronology both honored and told the story of Mary Renata's work. With help from the hotel staff, she spent days working long hours positioning moveable walls. Together they marked, measured, leveled, and perfected the lighting. The afternoon before the exhibit, the staff gone, Katie stood in the center of the room alone. She walked the space and turned in a circle.

"Hello!" Mari and Mr. Morrison came around the reception table set for the event.

"Another successful installation. Once again, you've brought the art and the space together," Mr. Morrison said. "I wanted to come and check on you before I left." He stepped closer to Katie. "You've done an outstanding job with this, but Katie. We have not received the paperwork. You know we must have it before the exhibit."

"Yes, sir. I do know. I will check into it and make sure it is all in order."

"Good enough, then. I'll leave you girls to it. And I'll see you tomorrow night."

"Wow," Mari said, picking up a brochure on the table. On the cover was a black-and-white photo of Mary Renata from her younger days in Florence, and underneath, a simple biography crafted by Alex. Inside were thumbnails of the art included in the exhibit and information about each piece. On an easel, next to the reception table, a larger poster also featured a photo of the artist, chosen by her grandson. "Katie, I am no expert, but this is beautiful." Mari browsed the room. "These paintings seem special. Look at the neighborhoods, cafes, churches, and people dancing. And this one I love. Do you think it is religious?" The girls studied bright colors and shapes. "It's a stained-glass window, don't you think?"

"I think so. And these figures here—they are nuns kneeling, I believe."

"Oh, yes. I see that now," Mari said.

"It's a lifetime of stories, isn't it?"

"Don't they make you wish you knew more?"

Katie laughed. "Yes. The more I know, the more I want. It's the reason one painting led me to the rest of these."

"What else do you need to do?" Mari asked.

"What do you mean?"

"What paperwork was Mr. Morrison talking about? What do you need before the show?"

"The contract, Mari. The permission from the Dyers."

"Where is it?"

"I sent it to New York. For Alex to sign and express back."

"What has he said about it? Did he send it yet?"

"I haven't spoken to him, but I don't know why he wouldn't."

"Are you telling me that since you've been back, since you received all of this art"—she waved her hands—"you haven't spoken on the phone or texted?"

"No."

"Why not?"

"I don't know!"

"What is all of this 'I don't know?' Katie! You do know! So, why?"

"I guess because of the storm, and we were busy packing all the art, and Tre. All of that. And then I felt like a complete moron when he dropped me off at the airport." Katie told Mari about the chaotic departure, how she shouted a verbal invitation between the revolving door and the parked car. "I couriered the paperwork and the painting back to Montauk like I told him I would."

"Dios mio, Katie. What if he does not send the documents back?"

"I didn't just throw those things in the mail hoping he'd get them. He will."

"You don't know this person. He might not."

"I know enough to know he will."

"Call him when we get in the car."

Katie called. The call went straight to voice mail. She left a message.

## Chapter 16

Alex relaxed in the taxi from San Antonio International Airport to the St. Anthony Hotel. Unworried about delays, he knew he'd make it sometime that evening. The exhibit the next day, there was no need to stress.

The cab pulled up at the curb across the street from Travis Park. The valet helped him with his bag and pulled on the big brass handle, opening the heavy door to let him inside. Later in the evening, a few people lingered about, finishing dinner, or wandered to the bar. At the desk, Alex pulled out the documents and explained that Katie Bauer needed them for the exhibit.

"We can take those from you now, sir."

Alex handed them across the counter and asked if laundry services could press his clothes. He also got a recommendation and directions for a local men's store. He needed a few items.

"They'll take care of anything you need, Mr. Dyer," the clerk said, handing him an address.

In the historic lobby, Alex noted the green-hued decor. It matched Katie. This was where she worked. Waiting for the elevator, he imagined her in the space.

The next morning after coffee, he set out the few blocks to Penner's, the men's store recommended by the clerk. A perfect seventy degrees and clear skies, he enjoyed the walk and getting out in the city.

The sidewalks in the area less crowded, he wandered past an eighteenth-century cathedral and historic government buildings.

Finding his destination on the corners of West Commerce and Cameron, he stepped inside. Browsing for only a moment, he was greeted by a salesman.

"Welcome in. Have you shopped here before?"

"No, I haven't. I got into town late last night and realized I left without a full suitcase."

"What can we help you with, then?"

"I need a few essentials," Alex said.

The man brought Alex several options, shirts in basic colors and sleeve lengths, ties, dress socks, and some casual pants, a tape draped around his neck. "What brings you into town?"

"I came for an art exhibit."

The man stopped measuring. "At the St. Anthony?"

"Yes," Alex said.

"Fabulous. Just fabulous. It's going to be a wonderful event. My wife works at a university here in town. She's been talking about the exhibit all week. The paintings were done by a mysterious Italian artist."

"That is interesting."

"Isn't it? I'm Mario, by the way. And you are?"

"Alex Dyer." The two men shook hands.

Measurements completed, Alex chose a few accessories along with a white and a blue long-sleeved shirt and two short-sleeved ones. The salesman urged him not to trust the cool temperatures outside for long.

"I will make sure our tailor finishes this by this afternoon. We will deliver them to your hotel."

"That would be great. Thank you," Alex said.

"It's what we do. Did you hear that?" the man asked the cashier. "He's here for the exhibit at the St. Anthony."

"How nice!" the woman said. "Have a wonderful time on your visit."

"I will. Would you have a recommendation for a place to get lunch?"

"Hmmm. Between here and the hotel. Why don't you try Saveurs Two Oh Nine? It's a lovely French bakery and bistro on Broadway," she said.

"Thank you again," Alex said. He appreciated the standards, high quality, and personalized service that the family-owned business offered. Taking the cashier's suggestion, he lunched on the most perfect crepes paysanne and pistachio macarons this side of the Atlantic. He even took a half dozen of the colorful pastries *aller*. Nothing in his hand except the sturdy little box, he remembered the dead battery on his phone, back on the nightstand. He had to stop and buy a charger.

Errands completed, Alex found his tuxedo pressed and hanging in his room. He showered, dressed, and sat in an easy chair, overlooking Travis Park. He stood up and pulled on his collar. He checked his bow tie in the mirror. Sat down again. Stood again. Four o'clock. *I'll go down and have a few drinks.* His phone still charging, he left it. On the way out, he took the brown-paper-wrapped package with him.

The lobby was quiet as he stepped into the St. Anthony Club. Pub style, dark paneling, with gilded framed art faced the bar, there was only one other couple seated close together on a leather sofa. Choosing a barstool, he picked up a menu from the marble countertop.

"What can I get you?"

Considering an old-fashioned, Alex closed the menu. "I'll have a ranch water," he said. *When in Rome.*

"Sure thing. Do you have a tequila preference?"

"Bartender's choice. I trust your recommendation," Alex said.

"Here you go. This is the reposado I like to drink." The bartender placed a napkin down, then the drink. "You must be here for the exhibit tonight," he said.

"I am," Alex said.

"Everyone is talking about it."

"Who? What are they saying?"

"People who work here, but people who come in too. Locals. They say the art is a large body of work, dating back to the sixties. Nothing too recent, but the artist is still alive. European, I think. An unknown, discovered."

"I can't wait to see it," Alex said.

# Chapter 17

Katie and Mari arrived an hour and a half early. Tonight, Mari was dressed in a flowy bohemian sheath, not her usual style. The dress was low cut and layered with gold embroidery in and among its pintucks. Pairing it with gold penny knot mules, Mari thought the outfit made her look arty. Hair down and smooth, Katie went with a short, black, crepe cocktail dress. Mari insisted she add yellow gold chandelier earrings.

"Just the right amount of fun," Mari said.

Some of the office staff attending the event chatted near the front desk. "Katie. We got the paperwork. We're good to go," one of them said.

A hand on her chest, Katie breathed out. "Thank you," she said. "Mari, let's go around and check on the catering."

"I thought you weren't worried," Mari said.

"I wasn't."

"Hmmm. Ok. You go check on the food. I'm ready for a drink. Would you like one?" Mari asked.

"I would love one," Katie said, a small laugh and another sigh escaping her.

Mari joined her, giving her a brief hug.

In opposite directions, Mari headed to the St. Anthony Club and Katie to the kitchen.

On his second drink, Alex checked his watch. A striking girl in an ivory dress and high gold heels stepped in. She glanced at him with a quick, polite smile, then rested both arms on the bar, elbows out. "Two ranch waters, please," she said.

Alex chuckled, catching Mari's real attention.

"Is there something funny about ranch waters?" she asked.

"No, no, forgive me. I wasn't laughing at you."

Mari studied the man in the tuxedo. His knees tucked up high, he looked tall sitting down. Placing one hand on her hip, she shifted, her toe brushing against something between his stool and the bar. Reaching down, Alex turned the package, moving it over so that it leaned against the legs of his seat rather than protruded.

"Oh, I'm sorry."

"Not your fault. It was in the way," Alex said.

Mari looked down at the rectangular package wrapped in brown paper. On the outside, she noticed a familiar script in large black letters. Beneath a name and address, at the bottom, was the phrase *Exordium belongs with you*. A succession of blinks, her black eyes knowing, Mari pointed at the package. *Blink. Blink, blink.* Then she pointed back up at Alex. "The papers. You didn't send them. You brought them." She pointed down at the package again. "And you… You brought the painting."

Wondering who this might be, Alex turned his head to one side.

"Excuse me"—both of her palms forward, Mari placed them in the air on either side of her head—"for being presumptuous, but you"—she pointed at him again—"you must be Alex. I'm Mariana. Katie's friend."

Alex's face slid into a smile. Standing, he offered his hand. "It's nice to meet you, Mariana," he said.

"Welcome to San Antonio. Nice to meet you too." Looking up, Mari mustered all her skills, silent query, and intuition, and surveyed the stranger in front of her. "Let me take you to Katie," she said.

The painting secure in his arms, Mari led Alex to Katie in the exhibit hall. Stepping into the brightness from the carpeted hall, Mari called for her friend. Katie came around one of the walls and halted midstride.

Silhouetted within the room's white walls and art, the three stood, a still frame, the paintings displayed and well lit, the echoes of their steps silent.

"Look who I found." Mari's words restored Katie's motion but not Alex's.

There she was. The girl with soggy socks drenched in a High Plains rain, in a sleek formal gown at a country club gala, and huddled up in a chair under an awning, her sleeves pushed up in his tattered old sweatshirt.

A ranch water in each hand, Mari handed one to Katie, but she didn't take it. "You came," Katie said. "But I don't need that." She looked down at the package.

There she was again, hair pulled back, sitting cross-legged, frames and canvases piled around her. She sat on a high stool, one leg dangling, sampling a homemade pastry.

Taking his eyes from Katie, Alex saw the room. Starting on one wall, the paintings they'd chosen drinking wine in the attic, were more formal now and uniform. He looked at another wall and around a corner, a storyboard from a new perspective—they'd always been there. Frames from a lifetime, scenes he recognized and others, only speculated about.

"Look what you've done," Alex said. This was the girl asleep on his shoulder, one hand resting on his yellow dog at their feet, waiting for a hurricane to pass. "Thank you, Katie. Thank you for my grandmother."

Katie raised her head. Alex reached for the corner of his eye. Then, taking the package in both hands, he handed it to Mari.

She turned around, placed the ranch waters on the floor, and took the painting from him. His hands free, Alex placed them on Katie's shoulders. "You didn't need it. But I thought you'd like to include it. And I came here because I have something to ask you." Not knowing his own question until that moment, he decided.

"What is it?" She asked.

"Would you like to accompany me to Italy? Come with me. Let's take *Exordium* back together."

Alex standing there, offering to take her to meet Mary Renata—Katie reached out, joy spilling over as she wrapped both arms tight around Alex's neck. "I don't want to be a mongoose!" she said. "I admire them. But I don't want to be one!" *Though fierce and independent, solitary mongooses have no companion, only coming together with another mongoose to mate once a year. They live and sleep alone in burrows.*

"Did you just say mongoose? I think she just said she doesn't want to be a mongoose. Is that what I heard?" The painting out front, Mari stared at Alex.

"I have no idea. But I feel certain she's coming with me to Italy," Alex said.

After cleaning up the ranch waters and unwrapping the painting, they decided to place it on an easel at the entrance to the exhibit that, in the end, brought Mary Renata's art to an impressed and very pleased public.

# Epilogue

They'd traveled too many hours to count, though it didn't feel that way. Sleeping some on the long flight, they'd arrived in the morning. Too little rest, here in the Birthplace of the Renaissance, Alex was running on Katie's excitement and she on chiming bells, cobblestones, and something ancient and remarkable around every corner. Once in the city, they stopped to organize their luggage. He took the suitcases and she a backpack and the painting. Both starving, he took her to a tiny delicatessen. Only room for standing and one high-top table for two, they shared a porchetta sandwich with savory herbs and flaky bread. Without asking, the man at the counter delivered a *caffè* for him and a *cappuccio* for her. Lingering over their drinks, Katie checked the time.

"If we miss the train, we can take the next one," Alex said. "Let's walk that direction and have a glass of wine. Or two."

They did, stopping along the way here and there. The sights of the Duomo and cathedrals, the piazzas and galleries all marvels, the bricks under their feet held secrets of the centuries. Katie's intrigue was more focused on carvings on ancient doors in the *viuzze* throughout the city. It didn't matter where the winding alleyways led; the light and the dark, a tapestry in the narrow labyrinth, still led them to another intimate café with a table in the window made just for them.

"We aren't far from the station," Alex said. "Should we catch a train?"

"I might not ever be ready to leave here," she said.

"When we come back, I want to take you to the Oltrarno," he said.

"There's so much more I'd like to see, but David's been here for quite a while. I suspect he will be here next time."

"We have time," Alex said.

They did. After harvest season for Alex, Mr. Morrison was happy to give Katie the time off to go and meet with her artist.

They caught the next train, or maybe the one after that. The regional made stop after stop in each commune, village, and borgo, the Tuscan countryside rolling by. "The next one is us," Alex said.

Seated next to the window, Katie gathered her things. "How far is it from the station to your grandparents?" she asked.

"Just a few kilometers."

"Will we rent a car?"

"No."

"A taxi?"

"Don't worry. We won't have to walk the whole way."

The station was a small block structure. Alex and Katie, the only two off at the stop, pulled their luggage from the train.

A ten-minute walk into the village, up a slope on a rock path, they passed stone buildings adorned with bright geraniums on windowsills and balconies. A woman hanging laundry on a rooftop waved, and then they arrived in a tiny piazza with a fountain. There were no tourists like in Florence. At a corner, a patio surrounded a building protruding into the street.

"Let's go inside here," Alex said.

A barefooted boy sweeping around tables and chairs stopped his chore and threw his broom away. "Allesandro?!" he said, running inside, shouting Alex's Italian name. Katie and Alex stepped into the trattoria. The boy ran back into the kitchen, then back to Alex again. Alex grabbed him around his middle with a half spin and set him down, messing his hair.

"Ciao, Paolo," Alex said, the boy grabbing Alex around his waist this time.

A man came out of the kitchen. Wearing an apron tight around his broad torso, he wiped his hands on it. His steps quicker, arms open, he embraced Alex. "Alessandro! Benvenuto a casa."

"It is good to be home as always. Please meet my friend Katie."

"Ciao, Katie," he said. He gave her a light kiss on each cheek, then stood back. "Bellissima." He threw one arm around Alex's shoulder. "No one told me! I didn't know you were coming home!"

Alex leaned in closer. "No one knows," he said.

"Oh! Santo Cielo! Wait here!" The man ran back to the kitchen, returning with a bag of bread and pastries. "Take this. For Nonna."

"Grazie, Emilio," Alex said.

"Prego, prego. You'll be back for supper tonight? No, No, of course not. You've traveled. But tomorrow? We will see you all tomorrow?"

"Tomorrow," Alex said.

"Paolo! Take them out back. Take the car and get them out to the villa! Help signorina with her baggage."

The boy took Katie's things, and the three of them went out through the kitchen to a narrow alley, to a Fiat 500 parked tight against a wall. The boy tossed what luggage he could into the back.

"Alessandro, you get in here," the boy said, indicating that Alex crawl past the driver's seat into the front passenger side. "Signorina. You go in the back," he said, their backpacks and the painting stacked beside Katie. "Pronto!" the boy said. He pulled the driver's seat up as far as it would go, and with the car in gear, still in bare feet, he pushed in the clutch with his toes. Up on the edge of his seat, his chin lifted past the top of the steering wheel, they bumped along the alley and onto the proper street. "Here we go!"

Leaning up into the front, Katie put her hand on Alex's shoulder, and he turned toward her. "How old is he?" She mouthed the words.

Alex shrugged. "Paolo, you've grown so tall. How old are you this year?"

"Fourteen! Almost fourteen this summer!" Without slowing, he swerved, just missing a few chickens in the road. Her left hand on the back of Paolo's seat, her right on Alex's, Katie held on, imagining the little car operating on two wheels, one front and one back, both on the driver's side. Out of the town the way she and Alex had come from the train station, just a mile or two, Paolo turned onto an unpaved, packed roadbed. White dust billowing behind them, Paolo made an abrupt stop and turned onto a narrow lane, and Katie lurched forward.

Lined with Italian cypresses framing rows and rows of grapevines, the little road curved up and around. At the vanishing point, a tower grew larger, revealing the cornerstone of the villa. Once a piece of an ancient town wall, the rest of the house was built around it and because of it. A group of men gathered among the vines near the house, Paolo honked the horn again and again, he and Alex waving at them. Two enormous sheepdogs out with the men bounded toward the car. Tails wagging and happily barking, they ran alongside the Fiat. Katie took her left hand from the seat, and grasping the painting, she crinkled its wrapping. *Beep! Beep beep!* Paolo skidded through an open iron gate on a pebbled drive. He threw the car into park, jumped from the car, and hurried around to the trunk. Alex got out too and opened the back door. Taking the painting into her lap, Katie held on. A rock wall framed by a neat hedge row wrapped around a courtyard. The structure rose, green shutters on its open windows, and billowy sheers inside blew around window boxes full of greenery and blossoms. Alex gave Katie a minute. She looked like she needed one.

"Do you want to take that?" he asked.

Katie nodded, crinkling both corners. Near the main entrance to the villa, coming down a set of steps and through an archway, a woman appeared. Standing taller than her petite stature, she shaded her eyes from the sun. Her once-dark hair, now streaked with silver, was long and tied back. When she recognized Alex in the drive, she stopped on the second-to-last step. A light breeze blew the hem of her skirt up around her shins. The afternoon sunny, hands on her hips, she waited, one foot crossed in front, the toe of her gold sandal resting on the tread behind her.

"Ciao! Ciao, Signora!" Paolo brought the bags up the steps. A big grin on his face, he matched the woman's stance.

"Grazie, Paolo. Grazie for bringing Alessandro." She placed a hand on the top of the boy's head.

"Prego, Signora! Bye-bye, Alessandro. Bye-bye, pretty lady!" Paolo said.

"Grazie! We will see you later!" Alex waved at Paolo, the boy already back in the driver's seat, a new cloud billowed behind the car back the way it had come.

Mary Renata held her grandson. "Surprise," he said.

She placed one hand on Alex's cheek. "Somehow the unexpected is always expected. And you must be Katie. Welcome, dear. You're just as Alex described."

Announcing Alex's arrival, the dogs ran back to the men approaching the driveway.

Still mute, Katie stood holding the painting. Alex turned, waiting for his grandfather. "He's coming. Let's get you both and your things inside," Mary Renata said.

"Yes, ma'am," Katie said. "I can't believe we're here," she whispered.

Alex shook his head and laughed. "I've got this, Katie," he said. He took the package from her, and they followed Mary Renata into the kitchen.

Benjamin, just behind them, bounded into the house with the dogs. "My boy!" Tall like his grandson, he held on to Alex, unembarrassed by the tears on his cheeks. Taking away one arm, he used it to pull Katie in too. "I'm so glad you're here," he said. "Both of you! Hello, Katie." Benjamin hugged the two of them.

Mary Renata took the package that Emilio sent and set it aside. Too early to eat, she laid prosciutto and cheeses out on the butcher board counter. Pouring wine, they celebrated.

Alex told them about how they'd hand carried the painting. Seated next to Mary Renata on the living room sofa, Benjamin asked questions, and Katie told her story, relaying the adventures that had led her to Alex. Alex jumped in, telling again how Katie had found him at the vineyard in the rainstorm and placed the painting into his hands. They all laughed at the broken rental car and the soaked cowboy boots. Katie told how she'd traveled to Montauk, met their neighbors, and after, how she'd sent the painting back, and then of Alex bringing it to the exhibit in San Antonio.

"And we all know how that turned out," Alex said.

Tears again, Benjamin wiped them away. "I can't wait any longer. Let's take a look at it."

"Such a sentimental." Mary Renata brushed Benjamin's temple.

Katie took the painting and removed the paper with Alex's name and address, turning it over and over until all the layers were gone. She held it up for everyone to see.

"May I?" Benjamin took it. They had it back. Here it was, after all this time. Right here on the sofa between him and Mary Renata. "Katie, I have to ask you. What was it about *this* painting that made you go through all you did to find us?" Benjamin asked.

"Because it made my heart beat one tick faster." Katie's eyes moved from the canvas to Alex's grandfather.

Benjamin nodded, and Mary Renata looked at him. "The choices we make are often the ones that make our hearts beat one tick faster, aren't they?"

Unable to speak, her husband nodded again.

"Nonna?" Alex asked.

"Yes, dear?"

"There's something I have to ask you."

"Ask," she said, her arm around Benjamin's shoulder.

Mary Renata watched her husband. He studied the painting like it was the first time he'd seen it, he imagined it, remembered it for all these years. The lines were still there. But after all this time of remembering, there were ancillary elements that he thought he noticed, maybe for the first time. The way the fireflies twinkled in the evening sky, the shadowy lines of the trees, like soldiers in rows, and the color of sunset were not the same. A warm, comfortable feeling came over him, like stepping into a place from long ago—a childhood bedroom perhaps. There were things so familiar but also things that were new. They couldn't have been. The painting was static. Yet here he was, seeing them for the first time.

But for Mary Renata, nothing was new. She knew every brushstroke. Every line and every color. A collage of pain, the blood of a lost son, and the promise of raising a grandson were there, just as she placed them on the canvas.

"When Katie and I were in the attic in Montauk, we went through all the paintings. We found your dates, Nonna, on the edges of the canvases."

Sipping her wine, Mary Renata nodded.

"But this painting." Alex went to the sofa beside his grandfather. "This one was dated the year of the train crash."

"That is right." Mary Renata said.

"But we found nothing else dated after it. So my question…" Alex leaned over, reaching for his grandmother. "Did you stop painting because my parents died, and you had to take care of me?"

Mary Renata set her glass down. "Come with me. All of you," she said.

Katie, Alex, and Benjamin followed her up the stairs in the tower of the old house. At the top, she opened a door. Linseed oil and turpentine permeated the space, canvases leaned against the walls, and palette knives were scattered on tables. Mary Renata pulled a drop cloth from a well-worn easel. She took her seat on a wooden stool and pulled out a palette and tubes of paint. The brush an extension of her limbs, she worked the color across the frame. "Do you see? I can do this anytime I want to." The paint splashed. It flowed and played, going where it belonged and sometimes where it didn't, bleeding into art.

Holding her breath, Katie watched this artist. The paintings at the exhibit somehow encompassed in a time capsule, she had thought they were all done. That there were no more paintings. But now, Mary Renata sat before her. Like the book of Genesis, Katie was witness to a new creation.

"My passion for art brought me to Italy. On the way, it introduced me to your grandfather. While art was central to bringing me here, when I lost your father, I realized art was not the only thing providing me life. I had your grandfather." She paused, reaching for Benjamin, and then Alex. "I had you. And the things you bring to my life. Like Katie. Alex. The art taught me what was important. It didn't stop. Life shifted. My ability to express myself through art transformed into the food I made for you and the books I read to you, the music we played, and the stories we invented. You are not a tragedy of a son who lost his parents. You, your grandfather, and I are not victims. Every step of the way, I did what I wanted to do. Raising you into the man you are, and the life I have with your grandfather is everything that I wanted. I didn't stop anything because of you." She put down her paintbrush. "I am who I am because of you."

"And I am who I am because of you," Alex said.

"The life I have is the one I created. It is one of beginnings. We always chose new beginnings," Mary Renata said.

Katie looked around the quiet room, the art supplies, and the woman who had created an immortal body of work. She gazed out an open window framing the backside of the villa. The sun low in the sky, angles of light pervaded branches in an olive grove. The rows of trees uniform, their stately twisted trunks dappled in shadows. In the background of the orchard, on the lowest part of the horizon, were bright embers. Warm with energy, they blended into a big sky above rolling farmlands. The tops of trees twinkled with light that faded up into the blue, not dark enough yet for stars. "Alex," Katie said, motioning for him. "This is it."

Alex looked out with her. "What is it, Katie?"

"The painting. It's *this* olive grove." Minus the silhouettes of two adults and a small child, the entire scene lay before her, the painting she'd carried thousands of miles, like a rendered photograph. "This is the real-life canvas."

Mary Renata came over to the window. "Why don't we go enjoy the sunset from the terrace," she said.

Before twilight, Alex took Katie for a walk down in the olive grove. He offered his arm, and she took it, her fingers laced through his. Mary Renata and Benjamin watched the two of them from their vantage point, where they sat most evenings. Fireflies out, dusk would be there soon. Benjamin took Mary Renata's hand in both of his.

"What do you make of them?" he asked.

Reaching across, she covered his hand with hers, the curves of their skin completing a circle. "Exordium," she said.

# *About the Author*

Photo by Karen Lloyd Photography

Julie D. Simmons grew up in South Texas where books were her passport to destinations she could only imagine. When she was old enough, she traveled to those same places. Never taking the guided tour, she went to get the smell on her skin and the dirt on her shoes. She now lives in Seguin, Texas with her dogs, her family, and her bees. She enjoys reading, traveling, growing things, art and wine. She aspires to write good stories that people remember.

Printed in the USA
CPSIA information can be obtained
at www.ICGtesting.com
JSHW021959070224
56895JS00001B/1